I0645962

SAVE IN DEFENSE

The Chancellorsville Chronicles

Volume Three

C. L. Gray

The Stainless Banner Publishing Company

www.thestainlessbanner.com

For Elaine
W.B.

"Save in defense of my native State, I have no desire ever again to draw my sword."

General Robert E. Lee
April 20, 1861

Chapter One

Washington Arsenal
Washington City
August 21, 1865
7:00 a.m.

Lieutenant General Thomas Jackson stepped out of the prison's dark hallway and into the bright sunshine. The morning air was cool. He breathed deeply – to the bottom of his lungs. The first true breath he had taken since his arrest. He glanced up, past the prison walls, to the cloudless sky. It was a picture perfect summer morning.

That is until he looked to his right and saw the large gallows in the shadowed corner of the prison yard. Four ropes dangled from a sturdy crossbeam. Nooses swayed above a long platform. Under each noose waited all the bits and pieces necessary to carry out the ghastly deed: a hood and smaller pieces of rope to bind the prisoners' hands and feet. Four executioners stood at the ready, waiting to play their part in this infamous moment in history.

Seeing the nooses sent a surprising sense of relief dashing through Jackson. The Yankees planned to hang the prisoners at the same time. At least this small mercy would spare him the agony of watching his fellow cellmates murdered before his eyes.

A happy, excited chattering echoed through the yard. Jackson looked past the guards flanking him and was flummoxed to see that the Yankees had allowed spectators into the yard to witness the execution. Milling about in the shadows of the wall opposite the gallows were men in stiff collars and women in bright colored frocks. In horror, Jackson's breath rushed from him. There were even children present!

General James Longstreet led the prisoners past the bystanders. Their chattering ceased, leaving the yard quiet and unsettled. When he passed, they erupted into a high-pitched buzzing that reminded Jackson of a swarm of locusts.

The fat corporal turned and faced the prisoners. "Keep moving!" He commanded sharply.

The order was unnecessary. The prisoners had not stopped since they had emerged from the prison.

Robert E. Lee walked beside Jackson, his hand resting lightly on Jackson's arm. He nudged Jackson lightly in the ribs with his elbow and with his eyes gestured for Jackson to look up.

Jackson did as directed and observed sunlight reflecting off the sentries' rifles. His heart fluttered wildly. The guards were facing inward, watching the drama as it unfolded in the yard. From this clear dereliction of duty, it was obvious the Yankees weren't expecting any threat from the streets below. Had Stuart been captured? Jackson forced the thought from his mind. The guards' position could just as easily mean that they had no idea Stuart was coming.

Jackson saw that the prison gates were flung open. Another crowd, unruly and demanding entry, had gathered in the street at the arsenal's entrance. Soldiers kept them out with bayonets.

"Halt!"

The four men came to a stop at the bottom of the gallows. A steep wooden staircase led up to the platform.

Longstreet turned and faced Lee. "General Lee..."

The fat corporal swung his rifle through the air and slammed the butt down on Longstreet's left shoulder. Longstreet's knees buckled and he staggered in pain. "No talking!" The corporal barked. "Next one who talks gets my bayonet in his heart. General Sheridan can hang your dead body for all I care."

Longstreet rubbed his shoulder and glowered at the corporal.

A drum began to roll. Time was up. Jackson's hope that Stuart would rescue them evaporated. It was too late.

"Let's go," the corporal ordered. He gestured up the stairs.

Lee released Jackson's arm and squared his shoulders. "I'll go first." He climbed two stairs then turned back and smiled at each prisoner. "It has been my privilege to serve with you." His voice was strong.

Longstreet snapped to attention and drew his right hand to his brow in a crisp salute. General Joseph Johnston and Jackson quickly did the same. Tears sparkled in Lee's eyes. He returned the salute, turned away from them for the last time, and climbed the rest of the steps. A waiting guard grabbed him by the elbow and yanked him toward the far end of the platform.

Johnston climbed the stairs. At the top, a Union soldier grasped his arm, but Johnston wrenched free. He turned back and looked down at Jackson and Longstreet. Both men saluted. Johnston returned the salute. The guard seized Johnston's arm and dragged him down the platform after Lee.

Longstreet smiled at Jackson. "We made a formidable pair, didn't we?"

Jackson returned the smile. "Yes, we did. We made the Yankees pay in blood."

"I should have said this sooner, but it's been an honor to serve alongside you." He took a deep breath and climbed the steps.

Jackson gazed up into the sky and closed his eyes. "Father, into Your hands I commend my spirit." A slap on the back of his head caught him unaware.

"Move!" The fat corporal shouted in his ear.

Jackson slowly climbed the stairs. A guard shoved him toward the last noose then pushed him out onto the trap door. His arms were jerked behind his back and his hands tightly secured. The rope burned the skin on his wrists. The guard bound his ankles. He felt the hood slipping over his head.

"I don't need that," he said quickly.

"Orders."

The hood was jerked down over his face.

Jackson closed his eyes. Instead of black burlap, Jackson beheld Anna and Julia, laughing and smiling in the foyer of Reverend Hoge's house. "Lord, please take care of my family," he whispered.

The drumming ceased. Was he going to be the first or the last to hang? He never got an answer. Gunfire filled the air.

★ ★ ★

Jeb Stuart and the column trailing behind him galloped over the Long Bridge and into the quiet streets of the Federal capital unobserved. There wasn't a soldier in sight. Stuart made a sharp right turn and headed down the long straightaway that led to the prison. Up ahead, the arsenal's walls loomed over the surrounding buildings. He threw up his hand and brought Centurion to a quick halt. He could see the faint figures of sentries posted on the walls. He fished his fieldglasses from their case and focused. He smiled. The guards were facing into the prison.

He lowered the glasses. "Mosby," he called to Colonel John Mosby, who was riding on his left. "Tell the sharpshooters to take out those sentries."

Stuart raised his glasses again. A large crowd thronged the arsenal's gate and blocked the entrance into the prison. He grimaced. There were children in the crowd.

He pulled his repeater from his saddle boot, wheeled Centurion around, and addressed the fifty men riding with him. "Don't hesitate to kill anyone who stands in our way. If you do, we may lose General Lee and General Jackson. Understood?"

The men murmured their acquiescence and withdrew their rifles from saddle boots and pistols from holsters.

"Are the sharpshooters in place?" Stuart questioned.

Mosby replied in the affirmative.

Stuart started down the street at a trot.

Up ahead, six gun shots reverberated through the quiet street. Sentries tumbled off the arsenal's wall.

"Let's go, boy." Stuart pressed his heels into the stallion's side.

At a dead run, Centurion crashed into the crowd. Instead of dispersing, the people jammed together, forbidding Stuart entrance into the prison. He urged Centurion forward – a 1200 pound battering ram. There was some movement but not enough to get through. He fired his repeater in the air. The rest of the column hit the crowd at full speed; the men firing their guns. Fearing for their lives, the crowd scattered. The way into the arsenal opened.

But not for long if Stuart didn't act quickly. Even now guards were swinging the large gates shut. Stuart fired and dropped one guard as he strained against the gate. From behind came gunshots. Two more guards fell dead. The rest gave up and fled into the fort.

Stuart rode into the prison yard. He glanced about for new threats and saw Sheridan running toward the safety of the prison. He fired three shots over the little man's head. The bullets struck the fort's wall, spraying brick dust onto Sheridan's uniform. Sheridan slid to a stop, whirled about, and glared at Stuart. Four sentries slammed to the ground. They were dead.

The rest of Stuart's men raced into the yard. They leveled their rifles, searching for any sign of danger. The audience gave a surprised whoop before falling silent. Fitz Lee quickly ordered ten soldiers to round up the spectators and keep them out of the way.

Stuart thrust his repeater into the saddle boot. He jumped off Centurion and sprinted toward the gallows.

A fat corporal barred the way to the steps. He lowered his rifle and fired.

Stuart dove to the ground. The bullet hit the ground inches from his ear. He somersaulted to his feet, pulled his LeMat from its holster, aimed quickly, and fired. The corporal spat up blood before crumpling to the ground.

Stuart stepped over the body and hauled himself up the stairs. He raced down the scaffold's platform until he reached the man standing at the far end. None of the prisoners had nooses around their neck, though all were bound and hooded. Stuart ripped the hood off the prisoner's head and revealed Lee. He holstered his LeMat and drew a knife from a sheath on his belt. The ropes were no match for the sharp blade. They fell to the platform in a heap.

"Papa," Stuart said quickly, "Fitz is waiting with Traveller. Can you make it by yourself?"

Lee nodded with a smile. He started down the platform. Fitz dismounted and ran toward the gallows. He met his uncle at the bottom of the steps.

Stuart freed Johnston and Longstreet. Once they were clear of the scaffold, Stuart pulled the hood from Jackson's head.

★ ★ ★

Jackson's world slowly turned from black to a wonderful panorama that overwhelmed and delighted him. The prison yard was filled with Confederate soldiers, rifles leveled at any blue uniformed soldier still alive. The prison wall had been stripped of its sentries; over a dozen of them lay dead on the ground. The rest were nowhere in sight. The crowd, now silent, cowered against the prison's wall.

Jackson smiled grimly. Mosby had his pistol trained on Sheridan, who was holding his hands high in the air.

In front of the gallows, Fitz Lee helped Lee into Traveller's saddle. Colonel McClellan, Stuart's adjutant, directed Johnston and Longstreet to their mounts. Jackson gave a small laugh. Joe Morrison held Little Sorrel's reins.

Jackson's hands were freed. He rubbed his wrists, forcing the blood back into his hands. A knife sawed at the ropes binding his ankles. Jackson didn't need to see Centurion's empty saddle to know it was Stuart. The scent of horses, leather, and cologne filled his nose.

The ropes fell away. Jackson turned and saw Stuart sheath his knife.

"Let's go home," Stuart said with a smile.

Jackson practically jumped down the stairs. Little Sorrel spied him and capered about like a joyful retriever. Jackson grabbed the bridle's cheekpiece and rubbed the Morgan's nose to quiet him. "Captain, I'll take the reins now."

Morrison tossed them over. Jackson swung up in the saddle.

"Go! Go!" Stuart hollered from the platform, gesturing toward the fort's gate.

"Let's go, General." Morrison turned his mare.

Jackson gave Little Sorrel the signal. With a relieved sigh, he watched Lee ride out of the prison. Johnston and Longstreet followed. He urged Little Sorrel to pick up the pace. He passed through the arsenal's gate and into the street.

Stuart sprinted to Centurion and threw himself into the saddle. He wheeled the thoroughbred around in a tight circle and fired his LeMat in the air. "When we surrendered at Covesville and Jeffersonville," he shouted to the stunned crowd and glowering soldiers, "we believed our paroles would allow us to return to our homes in peace. But that wasn't the case. We weren't the ones who broke the surrender terms." He pointed the pistol at Sheridan. "You did. Our men were innocent of the charges against them. What's worse, you knew it. All we ask is to be allowed to honor the surrenders we signed and rebuild our shattered country. If you permit us to do so, we'll surrender our arms and disband. But the men we rescued here will never fall into your hands again. That point is non-negotiable. We'll fight to keep them."

He gave Centurion his head. The thoroughbred streaked from the arsenal.

Chapter Two

As Stuart's column receded from view, Nathan Bedford Forrest stood on the Long Bridge and prayed for a sea of blue uniformed soldiers to come crashing down the street toward his position. He peered through his fieldglasses, but the streets were surprisingly empty for a weekday morning. He lowered the glasses and cursed in disappointment.

His men were stationed on the older bridge, the one the Yankees had designated for humans, horses, wagons, and carriages. Down river, almost within arm's reach, was the new bridge that carried only rail traffic.

"Colonel Kelley!" Forrest called to his adjutant. "Let's set up a barricade at the end of the block just in case the Yankees whip up the courage to attack. Use whatever you can lay your hands on."

Kelley rounded up a dozen men and led them down the bridge.

Forrest heard the report of gunfire from the south. He rubbed his hands in anticipation. The fight was on at the arsenal. Any minute now the streets would be filled with Yankees!

But the gunfire didn't bring any Yankees. However, it did bring a small audience from the houses near the bridge. Men and women stood on their porches and searched for the source of the gunfire.

"Get 'em back in their houses," Forrest directed the soldiers milling about him. "If any of 'em threaten you, shoot 'em."

The soldiers trotted down the bridge.

"General Forrest!"

The voice came from behind him. Forrest saw about two dozen men approaching from the direction of Alexandria. He tapped King Philip and met them. "What can I do for you?" He questioned the officer in charge.

"I'm Major Whiting," the officer introduced himself, "General Rodes' adjutant. The general sends word that the city is ours."

Forrest gasped in surprise. "That was quick."

Whiting smiled. "We caught most of the Yankees in the chow line or in bed. General Rodes sent us in case you need help."

Forrest gestured down the bridge toward the quiet street. "I don't need no help, but thank General Rodes for his offer."

"Yes, sir." Whiting gave a salute and headed back toward the city.

Forrest sighed in frustration. He had only signed on to this rescue to fight, and so far he hadn't fired one shot in anger. Where were the Yankees?

"General Forrest!" Kelley shouted, waving his hat in the air. The hat now waved in the direction Stuart and his men had disappeared almost twenty minutes ago. "They're returning!"

Forrest gave King Philip the signal, and the war horse ignited in a burst of speed. Forrest reached the barricade and reined up. He raised his glasses and peered down the street. The rescue column was moving swiftly. They didn't look to be pursued but that might change at any moment. "Colonel, let's clear a path."

Kelley barked the order and the soldiers hurriedly made a large hole in the half-erected barricade.

The ground shook as the column drew near. The troopers flowed through the gap. Forrest watched them go by, searching for Stuart and Longstreet. In the middle of the pack, he caught sight of a gray haired man riding a large gray. A thrill danced down Forrest's spine. He recognized Robert E. Lee from the pictures he had seen of the great general in the papers. He smiled as Longstreet galloped past him.

McClellan pulled up. "We got them all."

Forrest hadn't seen Stuart yet. "Where's General Stuart?"

McClellan's face revealed his alarm. "I thought he was right behind us." He wheeled his horse about. "Should I go back..." A smile cut off the sentence. "Here he comes now." There was relief in the adjutant's voice.

9

"Go on, Colonel," Forrest directed. "I'll wait for General Stuart."

McClellan nodded and hurried after the column.

Stuart reined Centurion up. "What's the situation?"

"General Rodes has control of the city," Forrest reported.

Stuart smiled. "Excellent. Let's get out of here."

Forrest nodded. "Colonel Kelley, have your men rebuild the barricade. Once done, mount up and meet us at the rendezvous point." He chased after Stuart.

★ ★ ★

The rendezvous point was a burned out, abandoned house on the outskirts of Alexandria. Weeds overgrew the lawn, and the white picket fence that had surrounded the home in happier times was now faded from rain and snow. Stuart rode through one of the large holes in the fence, followed by Forrest. From the backyard came the shouts of happy voices. Stuart continued around the blackened foundation to the garden. Beneath a giant oak, a group of men huddled together exchanging handshakes and greetings. To the left of the oak, a covered wagon waited. The mules brayed as they stamped impatiently in their harnesses and flicked flies away with their tails.

Stuart flung himself from Centurion and pushed his way into the group. The four prisoners stood in the middle thanking the men who had just rescued them.

"Gentlemen." Stuart shouted to be heard. "We're going to split up here and go our several ways. General Johnston, you're going with Mosby."

Johnston stiffened. Stuart knew the man well enough to know that he disapproved of the plan.

"Why are we separating?" Johnston questioned.

"I assure you, it's only temporary. As soon as it's safe, y'all be together again."

The answer satisfied Johnston.

"General, if you're ready," Mosby said.

Johnston swung up in the saddle. He smiled at Stuart. "Thank you for my life."

Stuart returned the smile. "You're welcome. Be careful, Mosby."

"I will." Mosby rode away, followed by Johnston and fifteen men.

"General Longstreet, you'll be going with General Forrest."

Longstreet whirled about in surprise. He spied Forrest standing by King Philip. "Forrest!" He laughed in joy. "What are you doing in Virginia?"

"I'm lookin' for a fight, but I ain't found one yet," Forrest said, walking over to the group.

"General Lee, General Jackson." Longstreet gestured toward the generals. "I want you to meet my cavalry commander, General Nathan Bedford Forrest."

Lee extended his hand. "General Forrest, your reputation has preceded you. Thank you for your help in this matter."

Forrest flushed. He shook Lee's hand. "My pleasure," he stammered. He turned to Jackson. "General Jackson, it's an honor to meet you, sir."

"The honor is mine," Jackson responded graciously.

Stuart clapped his hands impatiently. "General Forrest, do you know where you're going?"

"Not exactly, but your adjutant does," Forrest said. He hurried over to King Philip and vaulted into the saddle.

Stuart turned his attention to McClellan. "Any questions?" McClellan shook his head. "Then get going."

Longstreet gave a small wave to Lee and Jackson and hurried after McClellan. Forrest had already disappeared around the side of the house.

Stuart gestured impatiently and the wagon driver slapped the reins. The mules pulled and the wagon rolled near, scattering the group that remained.

"General Lee, you're going to go with Fitz," Stuart said.

"Why am I going in that?" Lee pointed at the wagon and backed away.

Stuart gave him a puzzled look. "I heard you were sick. I thought it would be easier for you."

Jackson burst into laughter. "Just how you did you come to learn that General Lee was ill?"

Stuart's smile was mischievous. "How many times do I have to remind you that I'm the eyes and ears of this army?"

"Uh-huh," Jackson laughed again.

Stuart beheld the hurt expression on Lee's face. "Doctor McGuire's waiting for you at the safe house," he said gently. "He'll take good care of you."

With a sigh, Lee surrendered. He allowed Fitz to help him up into the wagon. "General Stuart," he called. Stuart clambered into the wagon and crouched next to the camp bed.

"I can ride if it would be easier," Lee offered.

"Oh, Papa, I don't want it easy. I want you to be safe."

"Then I yield to your wisdom." Lee lay down on the bed.

"Good." Stuart smiled.

"Ah, there it is," Lee said.

"What?" Stuart asked, confused.

"That sunny smile!" He patted Stuart's arm. "I've missed it."

Stuart graced him with another smile. "I have to go."

Lee gripped Stuart's arm. "You're not coming with me?"

"I'll come as soon as I can."

Lee let go of his arm.

Stuart stood but the low canvas ceiling forced him to hunch his shoulders. He kissed Lee on the forehead. "I promise." With a final wave goodbye, he jumped down out of the wagon. "Are you ready, Fitz?"

"Yes, sir!"

Stuart gave the driver the signal to go. The corpsman slapped the reins on the backs of the mules. The animals brayed in protest.

Another slap of the reins produced the desired results. Stuart followed after the wagon, stopping only when he came to Jackson. He reared back, made an unpleasant face, and backed away. "You stink!" He declared.

Jackson smelled his jacket and chuckled. "The Yankees weren't all that concerned about my personal hygiene. Perhaps you could lend me some of that fancy perfume you wear."

"It's cologne and I should think not," Stuart said, appalled by the very idea.

Morrison came to Stuart's rescue. "Don't worry, General Jackson. Jim's waiting for you at the safe house with clean clothes and a hot bath."

"You aren't taking me to Anna?" Jackson asked Stuart.

Stuart gave a small laugh. "No, you can't go hugging your wife stinking like you do. She'd show you the door." Jackson didn't respond. He just stood there with the same confused look on his face. Stuart tried again. "My first priority is to make sure that we're not pursued. Once it's safe, you'll be reunited with your wife."

"But..." Jackson began to protest.

Stuart cut him off with a gesture. "I give you my word. But right now, we have to go before the Yankees find us."

Jackson strode over to Little Sorrel and swung up in the saddle.

"Are you ready, Captain Morrison?" Stuart asked.

"You're not coming with me?" Jackson questioned.

"No, I'm not."

Much to Stuart's relief, Jackson didn't argue anymore.

"When will I see you?"

"I'll come as soon as I can." Stuart gave Little Sorrel a slap on the rump. Jackson followed Morrison down the street.

Stuart watched until Jackson faded from sight. The weight of the world lifted from his shoulders. His friends were safe. He uttered a silent prayer of thanksgiving. God had been more than merciful this morning. General Early should be retreating from Maryland. All that was left to do was find General Rodes and clear out of the city.

Chapter Three

John Reynolds' Office
War Department
Washington City

John Reynolds glanced at the pocket watch sitting on his desk. It was 7:00 a.m. Time for the prisoners to be led from their cells and escorted to the gallows. He pivoted in his chair and stared at the open window. He closed his eyes and listened intently, fully expecting to hear the sound of gunfire. He heard nothing. The streets were quiet. He returned his attention to his paperwork and nervously tapped his pencil on the desk. What had happened to Stuart?

The last message he had smuggled to the cavalry leader warned him that Secretary of War Edwin Stanton would purposely give the newspapers the wrong date for the execution. Stuart should ignore whatever he read. The execution was scheduled for today.

He dared not follow up to make sure Stuart received the message. It was too dangerous. He was being followed. Whether the tail came from Sheridan or Stanton, he didn't know. If he had to guess, he would say that the shadow was courtesy of Sheridan. Reynolds had first seen the tail the morning after he had visited Lee and Jackson in their cell. That same man trailed him home from work. When Reynolds left his boarding house the next morning, he spied a different man loitering across the street. Reynolds tried to give the man the slip but was unable. He was sure that if he looked out the window right this minute, he would see one of the five men who rotated trailing him from the boarding house to the War Department and back to the boarding house.

Reynolds tapped the pencil on the desk again. Did the lack of gunfire mean his message to Stuart had gone astray? He didn't think so. If his note had been intercepted, and Sheridan realized he was helping the Rebs, then yesterday, he wouldn't have been given such a golden opportunity to aid in the rescue.

The commandant of the Washington Arsenal had sent a request to the War Department for extra soldiers to help secure the prison yard during the execution. The request made its way to Sherman's office, and Major Dayton had brought the request to Reynolds.

Sentries had safeguarded the Long Bridge since the war's commencement and had remained long after the surrender. Since the pickets' tour of duty was scheduled to conclude at the end of the month anyway, Reynolds used the pending termination as an excuse to pull the sentries from the bridge and send them to the arsenal. Stuart would be able to ride into the city unobserved, and any guard he placed on the bridge wouldn't be seen except by workers who used the bridge to commute to the city for work.

Another glance at the watch revealed that the hands had barely moved. Reynolds sprang from his desk and crossed to the window. No gun shots, no nothing. Just the normal sounds of morning rush hour. He pounded the window sill in frustration.

"So, you didn't go either." A voice from behind said.

Startled, Reynolds whirled around and beheld William Tecumseh Sherman leaning against the office door frame.

"No," Reynolds said shortly. Sherman was well aware of how he felt about the situation. "I'm surprised you didn't." He didn't bother to hide the contempt in his voice.

Sherman waved his hand. "That circus belongs to Stanton." He straightened up and joined Reynolds at the window. "If I had the power, I would have stopped it." He smiled briefly. "Unfortunately, the only one who had that kind of power was Grant." He sighed in regret.

The unmistakable crackle of gunfire invaded the room.

Sherman gave Reynolds a searching glance. Reynolds was careful to keep his face neutral. "Well, I guess, I was wrong," Sherman

16

laughed. He patted Reynolds on the back. "Someone else has the power to stop Stanton. Stuart?" He quizzed.

Reynolds feigned innocence. "I don't know what's going on."

A grin tugged at Sherman's lips. Reynolds wanted nothing more than for Sherman to leave the office so he could give his full attention to the gunfire. Instead, Sherman sat down on the sill. Reynolds headed toward the door. "Aren't you coming?"

"I'm sure Sheridan will be along soon enough with a report." Sherman gave Reynolds another searching glance. "I won't ask if you had a hand in this." Reynolds sputtered a denial. "Because I really don't care if you did. I know Longstreet is innocent of the charges. If he's freed today, I won't be sorry."

The gunfire increased in intensity.

Reynolds could barely think. Sherman knew he had been aiding Stuart! How he knew, Reynolds couldn't even guess, but there was no doubt – Sherman knew. "If you knew Longstreet was innocent, why did you arrest him?" Reynolds asked, desperate to change the subject.

Sherman scraped the wooden floor with the toe of his boot. "The arrest warrant arrived with the news of Sam's death. At the time, I was too grief stricken to care about Longstreet's fate. And once Longstreet was in Stanton's hands..." A long sigh finished the sentence.

The gunfire ceased.

Sherman glanced out the window. "Well, whatever happened, it's over. One way or the other."

Reynolds prayed Sherman would leave his office before his emotions boiled over and revealed themselves. But Sherman didn't appear to be in any hurry to leave.

Sherman gestured out the window. "Here we go."

Curiosity drew Reynolds to the window. He peered out and beheld Sheridan galloping down the street. Reynolds smothered a smile. Even from this distance, there was no mistaking the anger on Sheridan's face. Stuart had done it!

Sheridan raced up to the building and drew a lathered Rienzi to a sudden stop. He saw the two generals standing in the window.

"You!" Sheridan shouted. His finger stabbed the air. He threw himself off the gelding, ran up the steps three at time, and disappeared into the building.

"General Sheridan doesn't appear to be too happy." Sherman turned from the window and faced the door. Reynolds copied his movement.

Reynolds heard Sheridan running down the hall. The cavalry leader ran past Reynolds' office. He backed up and appeared in the doorway.

"You!" He repeated. This time the finger pointed at Reynolds. "You did this!"

Reynolds met Sheridan's anger with his own. "Get your finger out of my face."

"Do you have any proof?" Sherman asked calmly.

Sheridan sucked in his anger along with a room full of oxygen. He pointed his finger at Reynolds again. "Who else would alert that peacock that the Rebs were going to hang today? Who? Who?" He demanded when Sherman didn't answer.

Reynolds remained outraged. "I don't have to listen to this. Present your proof or take back your slander."

Sheridan hissed. "Oh, I'll find the proof and when I do, I'll make sure you hang alongside your precious Rebs." He scowled at Sherman. "Do I have your permission to hunt down the fugitives?"

Sherman gave permission with a wave of his hand. Sheridan bolted the office.

Sherman patted Reynolds on the back. "Tread lightly around Sheridan. If he's able to prove you aided Stuart, I won't be able to protect you." He followed Sheridan out the door.

Reynolds shut the door behind them and sagged against it in relief.

Chapter Four

Somewhere in the Shenandoah Valley
August 23, 1865
1:00 p.m.

Since leaving the rendezvous point, Morrison had set a steady pace that left Jackson gasping for breath. Prison had severely reduced his stamina, but he wasn't about to ask his brother-in-law to slow down. He felt exposed in the light of day and wanted to reach their destination as soon as practicable.

As they rode, Jackson was devastated by the ruin he saw. The war had levied a heavy toll on the area. Abandoned houses stood guard over empty roads. A light breeze swung doors open and shut allowing a brief glimpse inside. The houses had been hurriedly abandoned before the advancing enemy, who had looted what had been left behind. Remnants of happier times lay faded and strewn across overgrown yards.

On the second day of travel, just as the sun reached its zenith, Morrison left the road and plunged into the wilderness. Even though Jackson had fought up and down the Valley, the paths his brother-in-law rode down were unknown to him.

It was cooler in the woods than on the road. Pinpricks of sunlight pierced the foliage creating uneven patterns of light and dark on the scenery he rushed past. Even here, in the forgotten areas of Virginia, the war had left its mark. It was amazing that the Yankees had foraged so far from the main roads. The small cabins and shacks had suffered the same fate of those nearer the avenues both armies had tramped up and down for four long years.

At night, the two men slept in burned out cellars and filled their canteens from abandoned wells. Jackson lost all fear of being discovered. Since leaving the main road, he hadn't laid eyes on another living soul.

Morrison suddenly turned off the path and charged deeper in the woods. Jackson pressed Little Sorrel to keep up. Morrison climbed a rise. Through pines and scrub trees, Jackson saw a small road.

Morrison dismounted. From his haversack, he removed a pair of fieldglasses. Cautiously, he moved to the edge of the tree line. Careful to remain hidden, he raised the glasses and peered first to the left and then to the right. He lowered the glasses and retraced his steps back to Jackson.

"Coast is clear," he announced. He returned the glasses to his haversack and swung back up in the saddle.

"Can we rest?" Jackson asked, giving into his fatigue.

Morrison shook his head. "It's best we keep riding. We can rest up ahead."

Jackson didn't argue. He followed Morrison out onto the road.

Morrison picked up the pace. Jackson stayed alert, ready to bolt back into the woods if a Yankee patrol suddenly appeared. Up ahead, the road narrowed at a bend. There was a large tree at the bend.

Jackson pulled up on Little Sorrel's reins. A man stood underneath the tree. Morrison rode on. Didn't his brother-in-law see him? The stranger walked out of the shade and into the bright sunlight. There was something familiar about the man, and it stole the warning from Jackson's throat.

Jackson laughed in relief. The mysterious stranger was none other than his aide-de-camp, James Power Smith, the young divinity student from Ohio. Smith saw them and gave a big wave. Once in the tree's shade, Jackson dismounted and held on to Little Sorrel's saddle until his legs stopped shaking.

"General, I'm so glad to see you," Smith declared, a big smile on his face.

"Major Smith, I'm surprised to find you mixed up in such shenanigans," Jackson admonished.

"We're all mixed up in it. Me, Joe, and Sandie." Smith gave Jackson a worried look. "You know we wouldn't let General Stuart rescue you without our help."

"I know, and I'm very grateful." Jackson meant it. The young men had taken a huge risk to aid his escape. If they had been caught, they could have very well ended up hanging alongside him.

Smith drew himself up. "General, it's the least we could do."

Morrison took Little Sorrel's reins from Jackson. "We're going to rest here for a while. Then Jimmie is going to take us the rest of the way."

"Jimmie is going to take us?" Jackson repeated.

"I don't know where this safe house is located," Morrison confessed.

Smith laughed loud and hard. "General Stuart has proven to be almost as secretive as you."

Jackson gave a small smile. "Almost?"

"General Stuart is just being careful," Morrison said. Jackson noted the defensiveness in Morrison's voice. He hadn't realized his brother-in-law had grown close to the cavalry leader.

"General Stuart, Jim, Sandie, and me are the only ones who know where the safe house is located." Smith jerked a pair of saddlebags from his horse. "Just like General Stuart and Colonel Mosby are the only ones who know where General Johnston's hiding. That way if Colonel Mosby is captured, the only information the Yankees could extract from him is the location of General Johnston's safe house. The rest of you would be safe."

"That's very wise of General Stuart," Jackson said. And it was. Only Stuart knew the whole picture. He had to wonder if Forrest did too.

Morrison beamed in pleasure.

Smith pulled a small blanket from one of the bags and spread it on the ground near the tree. He knelt down on the cloth and removed three jars from the other bag. He placed them on the cloth. "We have sandwiches. Are you hungry?"

At the mention of food, Jackson's stomach suddenly growled. He nodded appreciatively. With a groan, he sank down on the blanket. Smith pulled out a napkin-wrapped sandwich. Jackson peeled back the napkin and took a large bite. He chewed and swallowed. Smith handed him a jar. Jackson opened it and smelled buttermilk. He took a large gulp.

"It's good to see you, General," Smith said, tears in his eyes.

Jackson patted Smith on the shoulder. "You don't happen to have another sandwich do you?"

Smith laughed. "Jim was a little enthusiastic in his sandwich making." He looked in the bag and counted. "I have five more."

"Save one for me," Morrison said. "I'm going to go water the horses." He disappeared into the trees.

Jackson chewed on the sandwich and drained the jar of milk. He leaned back on his elbows and glanced up. Overhead, a hawk made lazy circles in the blue sky. "It's good to be out of that cell."

"How's General Lee?" Smith asked. Jackson gave him a puzzled look. "Joe said he was ill."

"He got some medicine from a Yankee doctor, but I'm glad Stuart had Doctor McGuire waiting at the safe house."

Morrison reappeared. "We need to get going."

★★★

The sun was sinking in the sky, and the approaching darkness began to swallow up the path in front of Jackson. Smith's pace was as swift as Morrison's had been. Jackson didn't want to complain, but he was saddle sore and hungry. If they didn't reach their destination within the next hour, he would ask them to stop for the night.

They came to a fork in the path. Smith turned right. They had only gone about five hundred yards when the short pines and elm trees began to diminish. Up ahead, Jackson saw a road. He expected Smith to turn onto the road one way or the other, but Smith rode across it and into the opposite field. Jackson saw a small, weather-beaten clapboard house sheltered in a grove of dogwoods. Smoke puffed from the chimney. The house was completely hidden from the road. If this was the safe house, Stuart had chosen well.

They rode into the yard.

"We're here," Smith announced with a weary yawn.

Jackson dismounted stiffly. The front door opened and Sandie Pendleton appeared on the porch. He caught sight of the riders and dashed across the porch. Before Jackson could speak, Pendleton threw his arms around him and hugged him close.

Jackson grunted in surprise. "Get a hold of yourself, Colonel."

Pendleton let go and backed away, his face bright red with embarrassment. "I'm sorry, that was rude of me."

Jackson squeezed the adjutant's arm. "But very much appreciated."

"We need to get you inside, General," Morrison said.

Smith took the horses' reins and led them around back. Jackson followed Morrison onto the porch. His eyes raked the grounds. They were empty. "Where are the guards?" He questioned Morrison.

"There are none," Morrison replied.

"None!" Jackson exclaimed, stunned by Morrison's declaration. Why would Stuart go through all the trouble of rescuing him, only to leave him vulnerable to recapture?

"The sure way to get noticed by the Yankees is to have a bunch of Confederate soldiers standing around, guarding something."

Pendleton rubbed his upper lip as was his habit when he thought Jackson disapproved of a situation. "You can't see the house from the road."

That was true enough, Jackson thought, but it would only take one person to stumble across this place and betray them to the Yankees. He surveyed the yard again and frowned.

"You need to trust us," Morrison said.

Jim Lewis stepped out on the porch. He caught sight of Jackson and smiled broadly. "General Jackson, the Lord sure has been good to this Virginny man. I prayed every day He'd bring you home safe. And here you are." Jim shook his head in despair. "But General, the Lord done brought you back in terrible condition. Mister Sandie, Mister Joe, let's get the water boilin' in the fireplace, so the General can enjoy a hot bath. How long's it been since you had a bath?"

"The Yankees let us bathe in the horse trough once a week."

Jim clucked disapprovingly. "Go on, boys, do as you're told. They'll be plenty of time to visit durin' supper." Morrison and Pendleton disappeared into the house.

"Give me your jacket," Jim said. Jackson slipped out of the garment and handed it over. "Whew!" Jim's nose wrinkled in disgust. He held the jacket at arm's length. "The only thing this is good for is the fire."

Jackson followed Jim into the house. The lone piece of furniture in the living room was a camp bed. Surrounding the cot were two bedrolls. A large brass tub sat in front of the fireplace. Beside the tub was a low table, which was piled high with clean linen, a clean shirt, and a new pair of pants. A new uniform jacket hung on the doorknob. Its sleeves glistened with gold braid. Jackson chuckled. Stuart had been visiting his tailor again.

Joe and Sandie re-entered the house, carrying dripping buckets in their hands. "Just pour the water in the pot there." Jim pointed to a black pot hanging over the fire. The men dumped the contents of their buckets into the pot. The water flowed dangerously close to the top. They trooped back out for more water.

"Once you're done with your bath, I've got a nice supper waitin'," Jim said. "I know how you like my roast chicken. I was about ready to put some biscuits in the oven when you rode up."

The fire popped and the water hissed. Jim went over to investigate. He smiled. "It won't be much longer."

Arlington, Virginia
August 23, 1865
10:00 p.m.

Doctor McGuire opened the back door and beheld Stuart standing in the shadows of the stoop. He stepped aside and allowed the cavalry leader to enter the small kitchen. McGuire surveyed the backyard. All was quiet. The next door neighbors were tucked away in bed and their house was dark. McGuire shut the door and turned the lock. He took out his watch and made a point of checking the time. "It's late, General," he said reprovingly.

Stuart ignored the reprimand and collapsed in a chair at the kitchen table. "How's General Lee?" He pushed the dishes in front of him to the side.

McGuire put away his watch. "He's resting."

Stuart sighed in relief. He picked up a ceramic pitcher and poured water into an empty cup. "Is there anything to eat?"

"There's stew." McGuire crossed to the stove and ladled the stew into a deep bowl. He picked up a spoon from the counter, returned to the table, and set the bowl and spoon down in front of Stuart.

Stuart took a huge bite. "I apologize for arriving so late, but I had to know if General Lee was okay." He took another bite. "He is okay, right?

"He has a very bad case of influenza."

Stuart dropped the spoon into the bowl. "It's not pneumonia, is it?"

McGuire held up his hand to extinguish Stuart's fear. "No, he just needs good food and plenty of rest."

Stuart accepted McGuire's diagnosis. He turned his attention back to his stew and scraped the bowl clean. "When can he travel? I need to move him as soon as possible."

"Three, four days."

"No sooner?" Stuart drained the cup.

"No sooner," McGuire said firmly. He knew the risks of staying. The safehouse was on the outskirts of Alexandria. Union patrols trotted down the street at regular intervals, but to move Lee too soon could jeopardize his convalescence.

"Can I see him?" Stuart asked.

McGuire shook his head. "He's asleep."

"I won't wake him," Stuart promised. "I just want to check on him."

McGuire relented. "He's in the front bedroom."

★ ★ ★

A noise woke Lee from a sound sleep. He sat up, disoriented. For a moment, he thought that his rescue had been a dream, and he was still in his prison cell. But he couldn't be. There were curtains on the window, and the bed was soft and didn't reek of mildew and wet straw.

In the faint starlight filtering through the large windows, Lee saw a familiar figure sitting in a chair at the end of the bed. "Jeb."

"I didn't mean to wake you," Stuart whispered in apology.

Lee reached over and turned up the lamp. "I've slept enough for one day."

"Sssshhhhh!" Stuart hissed. "Doctor McGuire will chase me out of here if he knows I woke you."

"Doctor McGuire's a fine doctor, but I know what's best for me." He scooted over in the bed. "Come, sit next to me. I can barely see you in the shadows."

Stuart stood with a tired groan and sat on the end of the bed.

"You look so tired," Lee admonished.

"Planning jail breaks is tiring work," Stuart said. Then he smiled.

"That smile is the only medicine I need." Lee readjusted the pillow at his back. "Right before I fell asleep, I was thinking about how you came to visit me every day when I was sick last winter. Your visits did more to cure me than Doctor McGuire's medicines."

"Don't be telling Doctor McGuire that!" Stuart said, scandalized.

"Maybe I should." Lee's smile was mischievous. "Maybe I should just call him in here and insist that you stay with me until I'm well enough to travel."

There was a knock at the door. Lee laughed. "Perhaps that's the good doctor now."

Stuart sprang off the bed and reached the door in two long strides. In the low light, Lee saw that it wasn't McGuire. It appeared to be a courier. Stuart spoke in low tones, so Lee couldn't hear what was being said, but he did catch the names of Mosby and Johnston. The man disappeared down the hall. A few seconds later, Lee heard the back door open then slam shut.

"You're leaving," he said, not hiding his disappointment.

Stuart returned to the small table next to the chair and gathered up his hat and gauntlets. "Mosby spied a suspicious person loitering near General Johnston's safe house. I'm not taking any chances. I need to move him right away."

"Will you send word and let me know that Joe's safe."

"If I can." Stuart slipped from the room.

Near Front Royal
August 24, 1864
2:00 a.m.

Longstreet stretched out on the bed and reveled in his new treasures: feather pillows, whole blankets, and enough water to quench his long denied thirst. He was free. Hidden away somewhere near Front Royal with Forrest prowling about the house. The hour was late, but he couldn't sleep. Too many unanswered questions. With a groan he gave up on sleep and sat up. Maybe there was something left from dinner.

A lantern burned on the kitchen table throwing shadows on the whitewashed walls. The supper dishes had been cleaned up and put away. He smiled in victory! A plate of biscuits sat on the stove. He grabbed one and stepped out onto the small porch. He saw Forrest leaning against the porch rail.

"I thought you'd be asleep by now," Forrest said.

Longstreet sat on the first step. "Couldn't sleep." He looked at the tall trees shrouding the ramshackle little house. "Thank you, Forrest." He popped the last of the biscuit in his mouth.

Forrest was unaffected by the gratitude. "I came for the fight."

Longstreet didn't doubt it. He had never met a more aggressive officer than Forrest.

"But I was glad that the fight was to free you." A long pause ensued. "It ain't the only reason I'm here."

Longstreet stared up at the cavalry leader. Forrest's face wasn't the blank mask he believed it was. "The hangings?"

Forrest nodded. "Sherman put a bounty on my head. It was gettin' harder to hide. Heard what Stuart was up to and thought I could lend a hand."

Longstreet absent-mindedly reached into his pocket for a cigar. When his hand found none, he laughed at his foolishness. His pockets hadn't contained a cigar since the surrender. "You wouldn't happen to have a cigar, would you?"

"Colonel Kelley," Forrest called.

Longstreet glanced down the drive. A horse and rider cantered toward them. As they drew near, Longstreet recognized Kelley.

"Yes, sir," Kelley said.

"Ceegar for the General." With a jerk of his head, Forrest indicated Longstreet.

Kelley hopped down. He extracted a couple of cigars from his pocket and handed them to Longstreet.

"Thank you, Colonel," Longstreet said.

Kelley reached into his pocket again and withdrew some matches. "My pleasure."

"About your business, Colonel," Forrest ordered.

Kelley nodded, remounted, and rode away.

Longstreet struck the match against the porch banister and lit the cigar. A few puffs and the cigar remained lit. He smiled in delight. "How much was the bounty?"

Forrest scowled. "Five thousand dollars."

Longstreet whistled. "For that amount, I may even turn you in." He laughed but Forrest failed to see the humor.

"For that kind of money, many starvin' soldiers would turn me in and not think twice." Forrest glanced down at Longstreet. "I know you think you got a big told you so comin', but I don't regret hangin' them Yankees. They deserved it. You should have let me hang more of 'em. That way, the Yankees will git their money's worth if I'm captured."

Forrest was right. But back when he had ordered Forrest to stop, he had been operating under the delusion that the Yankees were honorable. What he had just endured stripped him of that notion. He slowly exhaled a steady stream of smoke. "Is this my final destination?" He pointed at the ground.

"No, Stuart plans to move you through the Valley like checkers on a board." He made jumping movements with a pretend checker. "Jumping from safehouse to safehouse until it's safe for you to go to some farmhouse hidden in the Valley."

Longstreet was curious. "Have you been there?"

Forrest shook his head. "I ain't privy to all of Stuart's secrets. The only thing I know is that Mrs. Stuart, Mrs. Jackson, and the children are there."

The cigar stopped half way to Longstreet's mouth. "Is my family there, too?" He asked eagerly.

"Your family's in Richmond."

Longstreet felt anger and resentment quickly rising. Why were Stuart's and Jackson's families safe while his family was still in Richmond and in possible peril? "Do you know why my family is not at the farmhouse?"

Forrest walked down the steps and into the yard "You're gonna have to ask General Stuart them questions. That decision was made long before I arrived."

Longstreet stubbed out the cigar. He would most definitely ask Stuart that question the next time he saw the cavalry leader. "Well, the cigar must have done the trick." Longstreet stood. "Good night, Forrest."

Kilkenny Gardens
Near Covesville, Virginia
August 27, 1865
7:00 p.m.

Johnston and Stuart sat in Charles Waterman's dining room eating reheated leftovers. Waterman presided over the table, making polite small talk with the two men who had invaded his house without warning. Johnston had been amazed by the grace in which Waterman had greeted the dusty, tired fugitives. He was even more amazed that Waterman had remembered him. They had only met briefly last May when Johnston arrived at Kilkenny Gardens to help organize the surrender parade Grant had insisted on. Yet, there he was, extending his hand in greeting and opening his home.

The dinner conversation lagged because an exhausted Stuart kept dozing off. Waterman hadn't noticed, but Johnston had. The long, arduous flight from the safehouse to Kilkenny Gardens had been fraught with suspense and sleepless nights.

Johnston had been sound asleep when Stuart burst in on him and told him to get dressed; they had to leave at once. As Johnston pulled on his boots, Stuart relayed Mosby's fears that the Yankees had found the safe house and were preparing to recapture him.

Horses were saddled and brought around to the front of the house. A hurried meal was pressed into haversacks. Mosby went west to draw any patrol after him, while Stuart and Johnston fled south.

As soon as he could, Stuart left the main road and traveled down paths Johnston knew he would never be able to find again. When the trees reclaimed those paths, Stuart pressed through the dense woods. Always headed south. They traveled well into the night. Johnston knew Stuart only stopped because the horses demanded rest. Their punishing pace had even pushed the great Centurion to the breaking point. Stuart allowed no fires. Bedrolls were unrolled in small clearings, and while Johnston wearily lay down to grab whatever sleep he could, Stuart took the watch. Johnston would wake and see Stuart pacing in front of their little camp, alert and straining to hear any noise that would announce the Yankees had found them. As soon as night receded, they were back in the saddle.

Stuart wiped his mouth with his napkin. "I regret having to ask for your help again. You've already been so generous."

"General Stuart, you did right to come here," Waterman assured him.

The dining room door opened, and two boys, the elder no more than fifteen and the younger maybe twelve, came in and sat down at the table. Each boy had a plate of cobbler in his hand. Waterman smiled at them with fatherly pride. "The boys and I can keep General Johnston safe for however long you require." Waterman addressed Johnston. "I should warn you though. Every once in a while, some Yankee will come to visit the library where the surrender happened."

Stuart snapped out of his lethargy. "Then perhaps we should press on to Clover Hill."

Waterman held up his hand. "You know best, but as long as General Johnston remains upstairs during these visits, he'll be safe. The Yankees have only been interested in the library."

"We can always hide the general in the secret cupboard," the oldest boy volunteered.

Johnston didn't like the idea of Yankee visitors or secret cupboards.

"General Johnston, we can keep you safe," Waterman said.

"It's up to General Stuart," Johnston responded.

Stuart took a bite of potatoes and chewed thoughtfully. He swallowed. "Thank you, Mr. Waterman. We'll stay."

★★★

After dinner, Waterman led the two generals up the back stairs to a small bedroom, handed over a wick lamp, and said goodnight. Johnston set the lamp down on the dresser. The room was terribly stuffy. He crossed to the window, pushed back the faded brocade drapes, and threw open the window. The bedroom overlooked the backyard and the stables. He observed Centurion in the corral polishing off his oats. The evening breeze floated into the room. Johnston moved to the next window and opened it. Much better! It wouldn't take the breeze long to drive the stale air from the room.

Johnston sat down on the nearest bed and pulled off his boots. Stuart stood by the door.

"I'll take the watch," Stuart said, suppressing a yawn.

Johnston stood and jerked back the bed covers. "There's no need for anyone to take a watch. We'll have plenty of warning if the Yankees come. You need to sleep."

"I'll sleep when we're all safe at Clover Hill."

That was the second time Stuart had mentioned Clover Hill. Johnston assumed it was a farm somewhere in the Valley and, ultimately, his final destination. He wouldn't do so tonight because he was too tired to care about the answer, but tomorrow, he would press Stuart and find out more about Clover Hill.

Stuart grabbed a slat-back chair and set it in front of the door.

"General Stuart, you're relieved," Johnston teased with a smile.

Stuart didn't receive the jest with humor. Instead, he angrily put his hands on his hips and glared at Johnston.

"Jeb," Johnston said calmly. "I know that since my return from Tennessee, we weren't as close as we once were. But we're still friends, aren't we?"

Stuart's hands slid off his hips. "Of course we're friends."

"Then as your friend, please listen to me. You need to sleep or you'll collapse in exhaustion and be useless to us." Johnston removed his jacket and threw it on the end of the bed. "There's nothing left to do. Our safety is in God's hands."

Stuart relented. He sat down on his bed and pulled his boots off. He flopped back, squirmed until he was under the covers, and plumped the pillow until he was satisfied.

Johnston reached over and drew down the lamp. "Goodnight, Jeb."

Stuart's even breath of sleep was his only answer.

Chapter Five

Clover Hill Plantation
Shenandoah Valley
August 29, 1865
Early evening

Jackson rode up the long, winding driveway sheltered from the warm sun by majestic oak trees with branches weighed down with leaves. At the end of this driveway waited Anna and Julia. But Jackson had ridden a good half mile from the road and the farmhouse still hadn't come into view.

The emerald green hills on Jackson's left and the dense woods on his right were all part and parcel of Clover Hill, a large plantation once owned by Charles Waterman's son, James – a major in one of A.P. Hill's brigades. James had been killed at Chancellorsville during Jackson's assault on the Army of the Potomac's Eleventh Corps.

Another sweep of the driveway didn't reveal the house. It did, however, reveal young Jimmie Stuart standing in the thick clover and throwing a stick for a small black and white spaniel puppy to chase. At the sound of the approaching horses, the little boy whirled about.

"It's ole Stonewall!" He shouted with glee, throwing the stick straight up in the air. "It's ole Stonewall, safe and sound at last!" He sprinted away, shouting at the tops of his lungs. Jackson assumed the small herald was headed toward the still invisible house to announce his arrival to the occupants.

Another turn and Jackson saw two brick chimneys rise above the oaks. He nudged Little Sorrel into a canter, leaving Morrison, Pendleton, and Smith behind.

"Ma! Aunt Anna! Ma! Aunt Anna!" Jackson could hear Jimmie hollering at the top of his lungs.

One more sweep of the driveway and the grand farmhouse came into view. And it was grand! The whitewashed house was situated on a small rise which dominated the fertile landscape. The house consisted of two stories, large bay windows in front, green shutters, a glass paneled front door, and six steps leading to a large verandah. At one end of the porch, a swing chair rocked back and forth in the breeze.

"It's ole Stonewall!" Jimmie screamed with all his might. Then he threw himself down on the ground in exhaustion. The puppy licked the boy's face, causing Jimmie to wriggle and squeal in delight.

The front door opened. Flora Stuart stepped out onto the porch. Wiping her hands on her apron, she came to the top of the steps, raised one hand to shield her eyes from the setting sun, and caught sight of him.

Jackson raised his hand in greeting. She didn't respond in kind. Instead, she whirled about and disappeared into the house. Jackson reined up in front of the steps. The door opened again. This time it was Anna who came out on the porch. She was heavy with child and walked with great difficulty.

Jackson took the steps in two bounds. A yard from his wife, he came to a halt, suddenly afraid to hug her. What if he hurt her or the baby?

"You can hug me," Anna said with a smile. It was uncanny how she was always able to know what he was thinking. "I won't break."

Jackson flushed. He drew her to him and kissed her lightly on the forehead.

"I can't believe you're here!" Anna clutched at his hand and drew it to her heart. "I'm not letting you go this time." Happy tears rolled down her cheek. "I'll fight the whole Union army if I have to."

Jackson gently wiped away her tears.

"General Jackson." It was Flora. Jackson hadn't heard her return. "Isn't Jeb with you?"

"I'm sorry, Flora, I don't know where he is exactly."

Flora paled. "Do you think he's okay?"

Jackson felt guilty about worrying her. "The last time I saw him, he was safe. He told me then he'd come as soon as he could."

Flora twisted her apron in her hands. "Do you know when that will be?"

Jackson shook his head. "It'll be soon."

Anna grasped Flora's hand. "I'm sure he's fine, dear."

Flora took comfort from Anna's words. "You're probably right. I would just feel better if he was here where I could keep an eye on him." She smiled. "Julia's playing in the backyard. I'll let her know that her papa has come home. Anna, dinner is almost ready. If you could tell Jimmie to wash up, I'd be grateful." She went into the house.

"Let's get you seated," Jackson said to Anna. He took her elbow and led her to a long wicker couch covered with cushions. She sat down heavily. He sat next to her. "Can I get you anything?"

She leaned her head against his shoulder and sighed in contentment. "I have everything I need now."

Julia burst through the door. Jackson's heart skipped a beat. How she had grown since the last time he had seen her. He barely recognized her.

"Papa!" She cried, clapping her hands in delight.

Jackson knelt down, scooped her up, and gave her cheek a kiss. "How's my little girl?"

She hugged his neck. "You go away no more!" She scolded.

He felt someone tug on his jacket. He glanced down and beheld Ginny standing next to him, her arms held up high, waiting patiently to be picked up. He laughed, reached down, and scooped her up as well. "How is Ginny?"

"Ginny good," she piped. Jackson gave her cheek a quick peck. As soon as she received her kiss, she started to squirm. Jackson set her down before she fell. Julia wanted down too, though Jackson didn't want to let her go. He gave her another kiss and watched as she took Ginny by the hand and disappeared into the house.

"You'll discover that those two are inseparable," Anna said.

Jackson sat down next to her. "I'm glad Julia has a sister." He put his hand on her stomach. "Because I'm hoping this one will be a brother."

Morrison, Pendleton, and Smith rode up.

Anna burst into tears. "It's Joe!" She exclaimed happily. She tried to rise but the softness of the cushions defeated her.

"You stay and rest," Jackson counseled with a smile. He crossed to the porch rail. "Captain Morrison. Come, give your sister a kiss hello."

Morrison dismounted and hurried up the steps.

Jackson joined Pendleton in the driveway. Jimmie lay in the grass, almost swallowed up by the clover. The puppy lay next to him licking his face.

"Jimmie," Jackson called, "dinner's almost ready. Go and wash up."

The little boy sat up. "Do I gotta?" He pounded the ground in disgust.

Jackson suppressed a smile. "You do if you want to eat."

"Oh, all right." He sprang to his feet. "Come on, Rebel. Ole Stonewall just gave us an order." He trotted off toward the back of the house.

"Jimmie and I will tend to the horses and then be in for dinner," Pendleton said. He grabbed Little Sorrel's reins and followed Smith, who had already disappeared around the side of the house.

"Don't be too long," Jackson said.

Pendleton waved in acknowledgement.

The setting sun painted the skies in brilliant reds and pinks. Jackson glanced about him, taking in the large oaks, the green lawn, the house, Anna and Joe sitting on the porch, her arm through his. He could faintly hear the voices of the children playing in the backyard. He raised his hand and thanked God for His everlasting mercy.

★ ★ ★

War Department
September 4, 1865
7:30 p.m.

"General Sherman! General Sherman!"

Sherman saw Sheridan running down the hall. He stopped and waited for the cavalry leader. When Sheridan skidded to a stop in front of him, Sherman couldn't help but notice that Sheridan looked positively ebullient.

"We got him!" Sheridan crowed. He was literally bouncing up and down in excitement.

"Who do you have?" Sherman asked. He knew it had to be one of the four escaped prisoners. Nothing else could spark this kind of reaction in the little man.

Sheridan suddenly looked about him. Alarmed, but not knowing why, Sherman did the same. They were standing in the intersection of two hallways. Sheridan grabbed Sherman by the arm and led him down one of the corridors. Sheridan gave the hall a final once over. Satisfied they were alone, he spilled his news. "We found Lee."

No wonder Sheridan was excited. "Where?"

"In a house on the outskirts of Alexandria."

Sherman was surprised Lee was so close. Perhaps that was as far as the sickman could travel in his weakened condition. "Is he alone?"

"There's just a doctor with him."

That couldn't be right. "No guards at all?" Sherman questioned.

"No." Sheridan appeared to be equally surprised that Lee's only protector was a physician. "I'm assembling a force now. I'm going to hit the house at midnight."

A predatory gleam filled Sheridan's eyes, which caused a sudden shiver to dance down Sherman's spine. "I want Lee back here in one piece," he ordered.

"Why?" Sheridan barked. His voice echoed down the empty corridor.

"Because I said so!"

"If we bring him back here, we're just opening ourselves up for another rescue attempt. The best course of action is to drag him from the house and string him up in the nearest tree."

Sherman raised one finger and held it before Sheridan's nose. "That's enough."

"But…"

The finger now pressed into the cavalry leader's chest. "Another word, General, and you won't be leading any patrol." Sheridan didn't say anything, but his scowl deepened. "If one hair on Lee's head is harmed, I'll throw you in prison and chain you to a wall."

"You sound more and more like General Reynolds," Sheridan snapped.

Sherman wanted to throttle the man. "I think you should get about your business."

Sheridan gave Sherman a withering glare before hurrying back the way he came. Sherman retraced his steps and headed to his office.

The sound of footsteps faded away. Colonel Rosengarten stepped from the recesses of the doorway that hid him. Lee had been discovered! He hurried to the intersection, careful to look both ways for either Sherman or Sheridan. The hall was empty. It took all his self-control not to run to Reynolds' office.

★ ★ ★

Doctor McGuire heard a sharp rap on the backdoor. He sat up on the couch, threw back the blanket, and turned down the lamp on the table. The house was plunged into darkness. He took up his pistol and crept into the kitchen. From the window above the sink, he saw the shadow of a tall man standing on the stoop. The man knocked again.

McGuire knew it wasn't the Yankees. They wouldn't knock. But he didn't recognize the man at the door and in the weak light couldn't determine if the man was friend or foe.

The door knob turned rapidly back and forth, but the lock held.

"I'm gonna force it," the man said to someone in the yard.

McGuire looked to the right and saw another man standing at the corner of the house. This man he could see plainly and he was a Confederate officer. McGuire relaxed. "Don't force it!"

The man on the stoop looked about him in surprise.

McGuire opened the door and came face to face with the tall man. In the starlight, he saw a large jagged scar on the man's cheek.

"I've come for General Lee," the man barked.

McGuire raised his pistol and pointed it at the chest of the man. "I don't think so."

"It's okay, Doctor."

McGuire didn't lower the pistol. He turned his head and saw Lee, dressed in a black robe, standing in the kitchen doorway.

"General Forrest, what can I do for you?" Lee asked.

McGuire might not have known the man, but he certainly knew the name. He lowered the pistol and allowed Forrest into the kitchen.

"Yankees are on their way," Forrest said. "We ain't got much time."

"You're sure?" Lee questioned.

Forrest withdrew a message from his pocket. "I'm sure."

Lee took the message and walked into the living room. He turned up the flame on the lamp. "This is addressed to General Stuart."

"Stuart ain't around," Forrest said simply.

In the lamplight, McGuire saw Lee pale.

"Is Jeb...General Stuart safe?" Lee asked.

"He's fine far as I know," Forrest answered impatiently.

"Where is he?" McGuire asked.

"He had to move General Johnston to another house. I don't know where." Forrest's impatience increased. "General Stuart appears to be a man who can take care of hisself. But, he would see me drawn and quartered if anything happened to you. So, we need to move before them Yankees git here."

"Of course, you're right," Lee said. He handed the note back to Forrest. "Just let me get dressed." He went into the bedroom. He had only been gone a moment when he reappeared in the doorway. "Doctor, I don't know where Fitz put Traveller, do you?"

"Is Traveller a large gray?" Forrest asked.

"He is," McGuire answered.

"He's in the carriage house along with a bay gelding. My men are having both saddled."

Lee nodded and went back into the bedroom.

"We haven't been formally introduced." McGuire grabbed up his haversack. "I'm Doctor McGuire."

"General Nathan Bedford Forrest."

Lee returned to the living room. He was fully dressed.

"Are you able to ride?" McGuire asked. He quickly tossed medicine into the haversack.

Lee gave a wan smile. "I think I have no choice."

Forrest laughed. "You got a choice. We can stay right here and give them Yankees a fine, Southern welcome when they arrive."

Lee gave Forrest a searching look. "You'd like that."

"Better than Christmas," Forrest smiled. "I brought enough men. I always bring enough men to a fight."

"That's an admirable trait," Lee chuckled. "But I think it best we avoid a skirmish. Our next door neighbors have small children. I'd hate for anything to happen to them."

McGuire drew the flap over the haversack. "Are we ready?"

"We're ready," Lee said.

McGuire blew out the lamp.

★ ★ ★

Sheridan approached the darkened house. His men spread out in the yard behind him, their footsteps heavy on the hard ground. The wind blew through the trees, rustling the leaves. Across the street, a large dog barked, alerting the neighborhood of their presence. A soldier holding the horses' reins threw a stone at the dog. A yelp announced the soldier's aim was true. The street fell into silence.

"Major Stephenson," Sheridan whispered to the man next to him, "Go around back. Don't let anyone escape."

"Yes, sir." The young officer tapped three men on the back and together they disappeared around the side of the house.

Slowly, careful not to make any noise, Sheridan climbed the front steps. A bedroom window faced the porch. Sheridan stared into the window and thought he saw a shape on the bed. Lee! He smiled in satisfaction. He hoped the old man would fight and give him an excuse to shoot him. No quarter to the murderers of Grant.

Sheridan moved to the door. The porch creaked. He froze, held his breath, and waited. The house remained dark. He smiled. It was like shooting fish in a barrel.

He raised his leg and kicked the front door off its hinges. The living room was empty. So was the kitchen. No matter, the prey was in the bedroom. Sheridan burst into the room. Two large strides took him to the bed. He threw back the covers. It was empty. The form he had seen from the window was nothing more than a pillow.

Major Stephenson appeared. "No one!"

Enraged, Sheridan threw the pillow against the wall. It bounced harmlessly to the floor.

Chapter Six

Shenandoah Valley
September 9, 1865
Sunset

Lee weaved through the trees as he led Traveller toward the sound of running water. He stopped to listen. The water source was just a little further to his left. He pushed aside a large pine bough and saw a small stream. He smiled. The stream was deep enough for the gray to get a good drink. He slipped the bit and slapped Traveller on the rump. The gelding trotted into the stream and quenched his thirst.

Lee collapsed on the mossy bank. Away from prying eyes, he gave in to his exhaustion. His hands shook and he fought the urge to lay down in the cool shade and fall asleep. He knew Forrest was impatient to reach the final safehouse, but he didn't know how much longer he could keep up the fast pace. From the moment they had left Alexandria, Forrest had driven them hard. They were in the saddle long before the sun was up and still in the saddle long after the sun went down.

On the third day, Lee's strength deserted him. It took all his determination to remain upright in the saddle. On a rare rest, he drew McGuire aside and asked for a headache powder. It was the wrong thing to do. McGuire mixed up the medicine then went to confront the cavalry leader.

"General Forrest, General Lee needs to rest."

Forrest was in the saddle and ready to move on. "We've already rested fifteen minutes. That's long enough."

"No, it's not." McGuire stood his ground. "General Lee needs at least a two hour nap. He's exhausted."

"We can't be stoppin' in the dead of the afternoon for nappin'. That'll give the Yankees a chance to catch us."

"That's if they're even following us. I haven't seen a single soul for the past two days."

"I'm able to travel," Lee said weakly.

"Well, there you go," Forrest said to McGuire. He nudged the war horse forward.

McGuire stepped in front of King Philip. Exasperated, Forrest drew up the gelding. "I'm not changing my mind," McGuire said. "My duty demands I give my patient the best care I can. Your duty demands you protect us from the Yankees." He smiled. "So, let's both do our duty, and we shall get along splendidly."

From what little Lee had gleaned of Forrest's character during their flight through the Virginia countryside, he expected Forrest to explode in rage. Instead the cavalry leader convulsed in laughter until Lee thought he was going to fall off his horse. "I like ya, Doc," Forrest said through guffaws. "You got gumption." His laughter slowly abated. "You got your two hours."

Lee heard someone approaching. He glanced into the setting sun and saw Forrest leading King Philip.

As King Philip waded into the stream, Lee marveled at the war horse. He was strong, powerful, and his muscles rippled in the sunlight. He was a grand brute and reminded Lee very much of Centurion.

Forrest came and stood next to Lee. "Do you mind if I sit."

Lee shook his head. Forrest plopped down next to him.

"General Forrest, I don't think I've thanked you for all you've done," Lee said. He glanced at the cavalry leader and saw that Forrest's cheeks had turned deep red. "I'm very grateful, but I don't want you to risk your life for my sake. I'm sure you want to get home and see your family."

Forrest grunted. "Surrender weren't my idea." Lee smothered a smile. "And since it weren't, I decided to join General Stuart in his fight with the Yankees up here."

"But still," Lee continued.

"General Lee, I ain't up here just out of the goodness of my heart. Sherman put a price on my head. Five thousand dollars."

Lee refrained from asking what the cavalry leader had done to warrant such attention. A fly buzzed loudly near his ear. He swatted it away with a quick wave of his hand. Out of the corner of his eye, he glimpsed Forrest watching him.

"Don't you want to know what I done?" Forrest blurted out.

"Do you want to tell me?"

"I hung me some Yankees." Forrest flashed a look of defiance. "I hung a lot of Yankees. But they deserved hangin'. They were stealin' from helpless women and children."

"Sounds like an appropriate use of rope," Lee said.

Forrest smiled broadly. He leaned back on his elbows and crossed his legs at the ankle. "That's what I told General Longstreet, but he was concerned that the Yankees would retaliate, so he ordered me to stop. But stealin' from innocent folks who did you no harm is a cowardly act. I thought so then and I think so now." He sat up. "And it was a cowardly act to arrest you in the middle of the night." He tossed a small pebble into the stream. "I hate cowards almost as much as I hate Yankees. So here I am, and I plan to stay until this thing is finished. One way or the other." He added a nod as if to punctuate the conviction of his words. "Well..." He tossed another pebble into the stream.

Lee watched the pebble plink in the stream. Ripples danced briefly before the current washed them away. "Well, what?"

"I'm in Virginia now, and I guess that puts me under your command."

Lee chuckled. "General Forrest, I surrendered the Army of Northern Virginia. I don't have a command anymore."

Another pebble splashed in the stream. "I don't believe that. I've been around your men too long. General Stuart believes you're still his commanding officer. I would like that to, if'n it pleased you."

Lee smiled. "It pleases me just fine."

Forrest stood. "Well, I need to be tuckin' you into bed 'fore that doctor strings me up." He crossed to the stream.

"He'd do it too," Lee teased. He joined Forrest at the stream.

"I ain't afraid of no man, but I'll admit that the doc gives me pause," Forrest confessed.

Lee laughed. "He learned his toughness from Stonewall Jackson."

Traveller waded up. Lee ran his fingers through the gray's forelock before slipping the bit back into the gelding's mouth.

Forrest splashed into the stream; the water lapped at his ankles. He seized the bridle and led King Philip from the stream.

When they reached the clearing, there was a small fire crackling and a coffee pot boiling on the fire. Lee's bedroll was spread out under a large maple. The first of autumn's leaves littered the blanket. Lee brushed aside the leaves and sat down heavily. He struggled with his boots, but they finally slid off. Doctor McGuire stood over him and extended a tin cup. Lee drank down the medicine. He stretched out on the bedroll. "Please wake me when dinner is ready." He closed his eyes and fell asleep.

Clover Hill
September 10, 1865
Early Morning

The riders traveled down a winding driveway Lee thought would never end. At the end of this road was his final destination. There he would remain until... well, that was the question. Lee had been reduced to a spectator in the drama that had become his life. Stuart had the answers, and besides the brief visit his darling boy had paid him two weeks ago, Stuart had kept his secrets. That didn't prevent Lee from mulling on the questions though. What would happen to the four generals scattered throughout the Virginia countryside? Would they have to remain in hiding for the rest of their lives? Would they be able to convince those people of their innocence? Or, was Stuart ultimately planning to spirit the generals out of the country and permanently out of the reach of Federal justice? Lee hoped it wouldn't come to that. He had no desire to live in exile in South America or Europe, even if his family joined him and he spent the rest of his life in peace. He still had to visit Annie's grave and dear Fitzhugh's grave.

Another sweep of the road and the riders came upon an unexpected barrier. Jimmie Stuart stood in the middle of the driveway. From a watering can, he sprinkled water into a shallow hole. A bucket sat on the grass next to the hole.

Lee coveted a hug from his grandson but decided against it. The little boy was covered head to toe in mud. "Hello, Jimmie."

Jimmie's head snapped up. His gaze fell on Lee. "GRANDPA!" He shrieked in joy. A sunny smile erupted on his face.

"What are you doing?" Lee laughed.

Jimmie looked down into the puddle. "I'm trickin' the worms into thinkin' its rainin' so they'll come out of the ground and I can catch 'em. Joe said he'd take me fishin' tomorrow. There's a pond in the woods." He pointed behind him. "Do you wanna go with us?"

"We'll have to see," Lee said. "Is your Pa here?"

Jimmie shook his head. "No, but ole Stonewall is."

The answer brought a mixed reaction. Lee was grateful to the Lord for Jackson's safety, but he wouldn't be able to rest easy until he knew Jeb was safe.

Forrest shifted impatiently in his saddle. "We need to be on our way."

Lee decided to risk the mud. "Jimmie, do you want to ride with me back to the house?"

47

"Better not," Jimmie replied. "I only got two worms so far." He heaved a sigh of disappointment.

Lee chuckled. The son was as dramatic as the father. "I'll see you later then."

"Okay." Jimmie sprinkled the ground with the watering can.

Shenandoah Valley
September 14, 1865
4:00 p.m.

Longstreet stared out of the window at the browning lawn and the trees that were turning from dusty green to dusty brown. He was alone and had been alone since Fitz Lee dropped him off at this isolated location somewhere in the Shenandoah Valley. Well, he wasn't exactly alone. Jim Lewis, Jackson's cook, was here. Lewis had been left behind when Jackson was whisked away to the next square on the board.

The days passed and no one came to check on him. He and Jim had run out of conversation long ago. Now, they just passed the hours in silence. Jim remained in the kitchen doing miraculous things to the chicken that would eventually be served for dinner. Longstreet was left with nothing to do except pace the empty living room and brood about the lack of input he had in the decisions affecting his life.

He heard horses approaching, but he had heard horses approach before. Usually they drew near in the early morning while he lay half asleep. He knew the phantom riders were nothing more than an unrealized desire for someone to talk to.

He collapsed on the camp bed and buried his face in his hands. He must be going stir crazy because the horses were actually coming nearer. He raised his head. These were not phantom riders, unless phantoms spoke with Tennessee accents. Forrest!

Longstreet ran to the door. He threw it open with a bang, which brought Jim from the kitchen shouting "trouble."

Longstreet pointed at the pistol in the cook's hand. "You won't need that. It's General Forrest."

Jim didn't lower the pistol. "I don't know no General Forrest." He tried to pull Longstreet from the doorway, but Longstreet refused to budge.

"He's my General Stuart," Longstreet explained. Forrest had dismounted and was headed toward the house.

"Good man?" Jim asked.

"A very good man."

Jim relented and lowered the pistol.

Longstreet hurried out onto the porch. "Forrest! What are you doing here?" If the cavalry leader hadn't come to rescue him from this God forsaken cabin…

"Come to fetch ya out of here." Forrest removed his hat and wiped the sweat from his forehead with his jacket sleeve.

A smile erupted on Longstreet's face. "It's about time. When do we leave?"

"Day after tomorrow I reckon."

The smile faded abruptly. "Two days!" Longstreet groaned in dismay.

"Yes, sir." Forrest plopped the hat back on his head. "Any sooner and we may come across the Yankees."

"Since when did you start hiding from the Yankees?" Longstreet asked.

Forrest's eyes narrowed. "You callin' me a coward?"

Longstreet heard the challenge in the cavalry leader's voice. "I know better than that." He was conciliatory. He had no intention of angering Forrest and ruining his chances of escaping this hell. Thankfully, Forrest let the matter drop.

"Where am I going this time?" Longstreet asked. Since the only seat in the house was the camp bed, Longstreet sat down on the porch step. Forrest collapsed next to him.

"Last stop. You're going to the farmhouse."

That was a relief. "Do you have any news about my family?"

"I asked General Stuart that very thing when I saw him. He told me your family is safe in Richmond. Custis Lee, is that right?" Longstreet nodded. "He's there watching over General Lee's family and over yours also."

"What does that mean exactly?"

"I don't rightly know, but you can ask General Stuart when you see him." Forrest removed his hat and wiped his forehead again.

"When will that be?" Longstreet snapped.

"He should be at the farmhouse when you get there," Forrest said.

Finally, he would get some answers to his questions.

Forrest's stomach growled loudly. "Do you think my men and I could get something to eat?"

"That is something I can do." Longstreet stood and walked into the house.

★ ★ ★

Shorter days announced summer's eventual end. There wouldn't be too many days left where Lee could sit on the swing chair at the end of the porch and enjoy a warm evening. He considered the swing his private oasis. After dinner, he loved to sit there, rock back and forth in the evening breeze, and watch the sun set over the green fields. He always had company. Tonight, it was Flora. Jackson was in the nursery reading a bedtime story to the girls. Lee didn't know the whereabouts of Jimmie or Rebel. Anna was in bed: Doctor McGuire's orders. The baby was due any time.

Flora sat on the couch, mending one of the girls' dresses. A large basket of mending sat at her feet. Lee watched the needle dart in and out of the dress and was transported back to Arlington House. In the evenings, his girls would always have a needle in their hands. Whether it was fine embroidery when guests were present or mending when they were alone, a flashing needle was a familiar and comforting sight.

Lee rocked the swing back and forth and listened to Flora's concerns over the children's clothing. All three were growing like weeds, and with winter coming, Flora didn't know how she and Anna would manage to dress them warmly enough to ward off the cold. The current plan was to give Ginny Julia's coat and Julia Jimmy's coat. Anna had come across a coarse blanket in the back of the linen closet. Flora hoped to create a coat for Jimmie from the blanket, but she didn't know if she could fashion it without a pattern. While she talked, the needle flitted in and out of the faded calico.

Around the driveway's final bend came two riders. Lee recognized the easy gait of Centurion. Flora was bent over her needle and didn't see her husband's approach. Lee reached over and laid a gentle hand on her arm. Flora looked up at him in alarm. Lee smiled. "Jeb's home," he whispered.

Flora dropped her mending on the seat next to her. She stood and raised a shaking hand to her mouth. Joyful tears spilled down her cheek. She ran down the steps and into the yard, her faded skirts streaming behind her.

Stuart saw her and hurried Centurion along. As he neared, he reined up and threw himself from the thoroughbred. He caught Flora in a hug and whirled her about.

Lee glanced through the living room window and saw Jimmie sitting by the fireplace brushing burrs out of Rebel. "Jimmie." Jimmie looked about. He smiled when he spied Lee in the window. "Your Pa's home."

Jimmie sprang to his feet. He sprinted from the room and hit the door at full speed. He dashed down the steps with Rebel barking at his heels. "Pa! Pa!"

Stuart snatched up his son and threw him high in the air. Catching him, Stuart hugged him close.

The other rider was Joe Johnston. He dismounted and wearily climbed the steps.

"So, this is our home for the present." Johnston looked out at the grounds. "I couldn't think of a prettier piece of land to hide out on."

"I'm glad to see you safe," Lee said.

Johnston sat down on the couch and carefully laid Flora's mending in the basket. "I'm just happy to have arrived. I was beginning to feel like a pea in a shell game. How long have you been here?"

"Almost a week."

"Anyone else here?"

Jackson came out of the house. He smiled when he saw the happy reunion in the front yard.

"General Jackson!" Johnston hailed.

Jackson walked over and leaned against the porch rail. "It is good to see you, General. I've prayed for your safe return."

"Thank you." Johnston closed his eyes.

"You must be exhausted," Lee said.

Johnston's eyes opened. "We were in the saddle before dawn." He stretched his arms over his head and yawned.

"Are you hungry?" Jackson asked.

"I'm too tired to eat," Johnston confessed with another yawn.

"Let me show you to your room." Lee stood. There were steps behind the swing leading to the side yard. He stopped at the steps. "There's a guest house in the backyard," he explained. "Your room is there."

With a grunt of pain, Johnston rose and followed Lee into the side yard.

Jimmie ran up on the porch and over to Jackson. "My pa's come home," he exclaimed happily, scrunching his shoulders up around his ears in excitement.

"Jimmie, come get your puppy. It's time for bed," Stuart called.

"Coming!"

Stuart gave Flora another kiss. "Tell my girls I'll be in to kiss them goodnight in a minute."

Flora ushered both son and puppy into the house.

Stuart loosened the cinch on Centurion's saddle and stripped the thoroughbred of saddle and blanket. Next came the bridle. Stuart slapped Centurion on the rump. The stallion dashed across the lawn. Stuart repeated the steps to Johnston's mare. Free from her restraints, she trotted into the clover to graze.

Stuart sat down on the bottom step. "Forrest should be on his way with General Longstreet."

Jackson joined him. "What do you think about this General Forrest?"

"I like him. He's the kind of man you want in a fight."

Jackson dropped his head. "Are we going to be in a fight?"

It was a long minute before Stuart replied. "I don't see any other way."

Jackson raised his head. Neither did he.

Chapter Seven

Clover Hill
September 19, 1865

Jackson gazed up the stairs and heard Anna's muffled groans. The baby was coming. Any minute according to Flora, who made it a point to check in with the impatient father every quarter hour or so.

Earlier this morning, as the sun's first rays invaded the bedroom, Anna had shaken his shoulder and whispered that she needed Flora right away. One look at his wife's pale face and Jackson knew that before the day ended, he would be a father again.

He hurried down the hall and pounded on Stuart's bedroom door. The door flung open. Stuart stood dressed in a nightshirt, his LeMat in his hand. When he saw Jackson, he lowered the pistol. "I thought you were the Yankees," he laughed.

"The baby's coming," Jackson stammered.

Stuart waggled the LeMat. "I guess I don't need this." He set it down on the dresser.

Jackson looked past Stuart but he didn't see Flora anywhere in the room. "Where's Flora?"

"She's downstairs feeding the children."

Jackson started down the hall.

"Wait," Stuart called after him. "I'll get her."

Jackson stopped.

Stuart came out of the room, stuffing his shirt tails into his pants. "What are you doing standing in the hall. Go, sit with your wife and do whatever she asks. Don't question her. Just obey."

"Just obey," Jackson repeated.

"Immediate obedience even if the orders are contradictory. Understand?"

Immediate obedience! Contradictory orders! What was Stuart babbling about?

Stuart gave him a push. "Go on! I'll get Flora and Doctor McGuire."

Jackson hurried back to his bedroom.

That had been eighteen long hours ago. And during those hours he had wrestled with an overpowering dread that this pregnancy would end the same way Ellie's had – both mother and child dead.

He knew they were fearful thoughts for a man who strove never to take counsel of his fear. But they were also fearful thoughts for a man who not only believed in God's sovereignty but in His goodness. He had spent many sleepless nights in prison, praying for the safe delivery of this baby and the protection of his wife. He believed those prayers had been heard. As the execution day neared, great peace had flooded his heart. He wondered if this fear, overwhelming him now, was a betrayal of that peace. Would God hold his weakness against him?

He knew better. He served a loving, merciful Father and not a vengeful God; a Father who knew how the loss of a wife, son, and daughter had scarred his heart and made him anxious for his family.

Jackson heard another moan of pain. He raced halfway up the steps before he stopped. He would just be in the way. McGuire was with Anna, and Jackson trusted the young doctor implicitly.

"General Jackson, come and sit with us," Lee called from the living room. "Staring upstairs will not hasten the baby's arrival."

Jackson relented and walked into the living room. Stuart met him with a cup of coffee. Jackson took the cup and sat on the couch next to Lee. He sipped the coffee slowly. It was hot and strong.

The brightness of the room bothered him. Stuart had every candle and lamp in the room burning bright. Jackson reached over and turned down the lamp sitting on the end table. It made little difference. The room was ablaze with light.

He heard voices coming from the porch: Smith, Pendleton, and Morrison. They had spent the early part of the evening pacing the living room until Stuart shooed them out with a cry of "too many bodies." For a moment, Jackson thought Stuart was going to shoo Johnston from his chair by the fire, but he didn't. Obviously, when babies came, Stuart liked it bright and calm and with plenty of strong coffee.

"General Jackson," Lee said, "have you settled on a name?"

"James Ewell Brown Stuart Jackson," Stuart volunteered before he could answer.

Jackson smiled at Lee. "That would be a fine name."

"Long at least," Johnston quipped.

Jackson laughed. "If it is a girl, we will call her Eugenia, after Anna's and Captain Morrison's sister. We're having a slight disagreement on the boy's name though. Anna wants to name the baby after me."

"What's wrong with that?" Stuart asked. He struggled out of his chair and crossed to the end table. "Do you mind if I turn this up?" He pointed at the lamp. "It's a little dark in here." He didn't wait for an answer, but twisted the lamp's knob as far as it would go.

"I don't know if I want to saddle a son with my name," Jackson confessed.

"Why did you use the word saddle?" Lee asked.

Jackson flushed. "I just don't think it's fair that this child won't have his own identity. When he tells someone his name, for better or worse, I'll be silently standing there with him. I want him to feel that he has the freedom to rise or fall on his own merit." He reached over and turned down the lamp.

"He will," Lee said. "I was away when Rob was born and didn't know Molly planned to name him after me. At first I was angry. After a while though, I began to cotton to the idea. It's a special legacy. He'll carry my name wherever he goes. I hope he goes farther with it than I ever dreamed of going."

"Does Rob ever feel burdened by the name?" Jackson asked. The young man had big shoes to fill. What if he could never fill them? What then? Would Rob grow to resent his name, his father, his heritage? He didn't want that future for his son.

"I've never asked him," Lee said. "What do you think, Joe?"

Johnston smiled sadly. "I never had the privilege of having children, though I loved my nephew Preston as if he was my own." He sniffed back his tears. "I'm sorry; it's the one regret of my life. If I had a son, I think it would have been a fine notion for him to carry on my name."

"Jimmie will only be saddled with my name if I don't leave him a legacy of faith, honor, and integrity," Stuart said. "That's my burden, not his. If I leave him that inheritance, I'll have left him something far more valuable than money or land."

"My dear Stuart, when did you grow so wise?" Jackson asked.

"You don't have to act so surprised," Stuart said. "I'm a deep thinker."

"Custis was no more than eight when he and I went on a hike," Lee said. "The snow was so deep that I had to plow through it. Custis fell behind. When I looked back for him, he was literally walking in my footsteps. I knew then that I had to be careful how I walked because he was watching me closely. I have tried to walk as straight as I could, for all my sons' sake."

Johnston leaned forward. "General Jackson, if I may be so bold. I've known you for four years. In all that time, the path you've blazed has been straight and true. Your son will be honored to walk in your footsteps."

Jackson colored deeply at the compliment. "Thank you," he stammered.

Upstairs, a door opened and Jackson heard two pair of footsteps echo down the hall toward the staircase. The stairs squeaked. The baby had to be here! Jackson rose in anticipation. McGuire entered the room. From the tired smile on the doctor's face, Jackson knew everything had gone well. Behind McGuire, Jackson saw Flora holding the baby wrapped in a towel.

"Congratulations, General Jackson, you have a son," McGuire announced.

At his words, tears of happiness flooded Jackson's eyes. "How's Anna?"

McGuire patted him on the back. "She's fine."

"Can I see her?"

"She's sleeping right now, and I want her to rest. In the meantime, would you like to meet your son?"

Jackson didn't feel the floor beneath his feet as he walked toward Flora. Though the baby was practically suffocating in the towel, Jackson caught a glimpse of a bright red forehead and a tangle of black hair.

"He's a beautiful boy," Flora said. With care, she transferred the baby into Jackson's waiting arms.

Jackson pushed back the towel and stared down at his sleeping son. He raised his eyes toward Heaven. *Lo, children are an heritage of the Lord: and the fruit of the womb is His reward,"* he quoted from the Psalms. "Thank you, Lord, for this great blessing." He kissed the baby on the forehead. "Joe, come and meet your nephew."

He heard footsteps clattering noisily across the porch and then in the hall. Joe appeared in the room; Pendleton and Smith at his shoulder. He tiptoed over to Jackson and peered at the baby. "What's his name?" He whispered.

Jackson smiled and held the baby up so the occupants of the room could see him. "Meet Thomas Jonathan Jackson, Jr."

★ ★ ★

"Folks are in there," Forrest said. He pointed up the front steps and to the closed door of the plantation house. "I'll be 'round back if you need me."

Longstreet dismounted and stretched. He handed the gelding's reins to Colonel Kelley and climbed the stairs. The front door was unlocked. It squeaked slightly when he pushed it open. The boards in the foyer squeaked as well. To the right was the living room; it was empty. The door on his left was closed. Where was everyone?

Longstreet walked down the hall, past the staircase, and into the large dining room. China plates were stacked on the sideboard. He heard a noise in the kitchen. He pushed through the swinging door and beheld a little boy standing on a chair in front of a counter. Longstreet caught sight of an open bread box.

"Can you help me?" The little boy pointed toward the bread box. "I ain't allowed near the knives, so can you cut me a slice of bread."

Longstreet crossed to the boy and lifted him down off the chair. "Where are the knives?" The boy pointed to a drawer on Longstreet's left. He opened it and withdrew a knife. When the boy smiled his thanks, Longstreet saw a miniature version of Stuart. The only problem was that he couldn't remember the boy's name, so he asked.

"Jimmie." The little boy sat down at the kitchen table.

Longstreet cut a slice of bread. In the cabinet to his right he found a plate. He served Jimmie his breakfast.

"There's jam in the larder," Jimmie informed him.

"Where is everyone?" Longstreet asked from the larder. He spied a jar of grape jelly on a high shelf.

"Aunt Anna had her baby last night."

Forrest had told him that Jackson's wife was due to have a baby any time. He grabbed the jar. It was sticky.

"A little boy named Tom," Jimmie said in a sing-song voice.

Longstreet set the jar on the table and went to the sink. Fortunately, the kitchen was equipped with a pump. Cold water splashed into the sink. He washed his hands and grabbed a cup from the counter. "Do you want some water?" He glanced over at Jimmie. There was jelly everywhere. He grabbed the towel. "Come here."

Jimmie held up his hands. Longstreet vigorously applied the towel.

The kitchen door opened. Stuart walked in. He caught sight of Longstreet. "General Longstreet, how long have you been here?"

"Not long."

"General Longstreet helped me get my breakfast," Jimmie announced. He had the jelly jar in his hand.

"Let me do that," Stuart laughed.

Jimmie surrendered the jar. Stuart crossed to the drawer and took out a knife. He scraped jelly across his son's bread. "There you go." Stuart filled the coffee pot from the pump. He stoked the fire in the stove and set the pot on the burner. "Coffee should be ready in a moment."

"Jimmie was telling me that General Jackson has a new son," Longstreet said. He sat down across from Jimmie.

"A baby boy born early this morning."

"It makes me wonder where my family is." He gave Stuart a level stare.

Stuart met his gaze. "Your family's in Richmond along with General Lee's family."

"Why?"

At the bark of his voice, Jimmie dropped his bread on the plate and turned frightened eyes on his father. Longstreet felt bad about scaring the boy, but his question had waited long enough.

Stuart smiled at Jimmie. "I'm going to take Centurion for a gallop. Would you like to go?" Jimmie's head bobbed up and down. "Then go get dressed. Ask your Grandpa if he wants to come."

Jimmie ran out of the kitchen.

"Aunts and uncles and grandpas." Longstreet angrily crossed his arms. "What a happy family you've all become since I left."

The coffee pot boiled over. Stuart hurried to the stove and lifted the pot from the burner. "Do you want a cup?"

Longstreet was tired of Stuart's evasions. "What I want is for you to tell me why your family is safe and mine is in Richmond."

Stuart slammed the pot on the counter. "First of all, your family is safe. I have men watching over them. The same is true with General Lee's family and Lydia Johnston. By the time I heard that you had been arrested, it was too late to get your family out of the city."

"I don't believe that."

Stuart picked up the coffee pot and poured himself a cup. "What don't you believe?"

"That you can't get my family out of Richmond." Longstreet was ready to shake Stuart to get the truth from him.

"You're right. I can get your family out," he confessed, surprising Longstreet with his candor.

Now, they were getting somewhere. "Then bring them here."

Stuart shook his head.

Longstreet fired up. "I'll make it an order."

Stuart held his ground. "I don't know where you get the idea that Clover Hill is some safe haven. My family lives in an armed camp with the very real fear that the Yankees will fall upon them at any time. None of us will be safe until we're free."

Longstreet only heard the defiance in Stuart's voice. "Bring my family here," he ordered.

Lee walked into the kitchen. He was dressed for a ride. "General Longstreet, I thought I heard your voice."

It was a reprimand, except Lee no longer had authority over him. "This doesn't concern you!"

Lee ignored him. "Jeb, Jimmie is out front and ready to go. Why don't you go upstairs and finish getting dressed. I'll show General Longstreet to his quarters."

Longstreet couldn't believe it. Lee was dismissing him like a junior officer. "Not until I get an answer to my question."

"Go on, Jeb," Lee said firmly. Stuart bolted the kitchen.

Longstreet stood. "He and I were not finished."

Lee smiled. "Yes, you were." He opened the back door. "Let me show you where you'll be staying."

Because he had no choice at the present time, Longstreet followed Lee out of the main house and toward a small guest house in the backyard. The symbolism wasn't lost on him. He was being shunted to the rear once more. But he would not silently remain there. After all, he had commanded two armies and Lee only one. If anyone was going to lead the next phase, whatever it turned out to be, it would be him, not Lee or Jackson or Stuart.

Chapter Eight

Forrest surveyed the ground around him. To his immediate left were dense woods. On the right, the ground rose for 100 yards before leveling off into another dense wood. He made his decision. "Set the line here." He gestured across the main road leading to Clover Hill. Soldiers dismounted and disappeared into the trees. A few moments later, they reappeared pulling, tugging, and carrying any brush, limb, or other building material they could lay their hands on. Quickly, fortifications were erected

A half hour ago, Stuart's spy, posted in a farmhouse about five miles from the plantation, had thundered up to Forrest with a report that a large Union patrol had passed the farmhouse and was headed down the road toward Clover Hill. A second courier arrived five minutes later with the same ominous report. Forrest sent the courier on to Stuart, but wasted no time in preparing the defenses. This was the fight he had been praying for since he arrived in Virginia. He'd beat the Yankees on this line, pursue them, and tear them apart.

"General Forrest," Colonel Kelley yelled, "here comes General Stuart."

Forrest waited as Stuart galloped up on that great black stallion of his. He wasn't alone; Fitz Lee was with him.

Stuart threw himself off Centurion and after a brief hello to Forrest surveyed the defenses. He shook his head. He jogged off the road and up the rise. Not understanding what Stuart was up to, Forrest chased after him. A third of the way up, Stuart turned and faced the road. He tugged on his beard while his head pivoted from the road to the top of the hill and back down to the road again. Forrest paced impatiently behind him. Stuart sure was taking a long time to make up his mind.

"Alright." Stuart pointed to the top of the hill. "Let's move the defenses up there."

"What for?" Forrest asked in exasperation. "The men are building a perfectly good breastwork on the road."

Stuart ignored Forrest's exasperation. He ran up the hill with Forrest in hot pursuit. He didn't stop when he reached the top but plunged into the woods. "Forrest..."

"I'm right here," Forrest said between gulps of breaths.

"When the Yankees attack at the top of the ridge, we'll fall back to a stronger position in the woods." He furrowed his brow in thought. "Let's say about 200 yards in."

"I don't see the need for that," Forrest declared. Stuart was over thinking the situation. It was much easier to meet the enemy head on and whip 'em.

"This is the Yankees' first patrol down this road," Stuart explained rapidly. "They could easily be headed to Staunton or Waynesboro. Either we hold our breath while they pass the plantation and hope they don't notice us, or we can fight them there," he pointed back toward the defenses, "and alert them to the fact that this road is important to us. I think a better option is to convince the Yankees that we're worried about them discovering something in the opposite direction."

Stuart was right, but that didn't prevent Forrest from giving him an annoyed look before starting down the hill.

"Oh, don't worry," Stuart hollered after him. "I'll set the line in the woods."

★ ★ ★

The sound of gunfire drew Jackson from the house. He stood on the porch and listened, trying to determine where the gunfire was coming from. Longstreet appeared around the side of the house and joined him.

"What do you think?" Longstreet asked. "About a mile away to the south?"

"A mile and a half."

The front door opened. "Two miles," Lee corrected.

Jimmie dashed from the woods, Rebel at his heels. "Ole Stonewall! Ole Stonewall!" Tears coursed down his cheeks. "Is it the Yankees?"

Jackson hurried down into the lawn. Jimmie ran over to him. With a tremendous heave, Jackson picked him up. Jimmie buried his face in Jackson's neck. "Are the Yankees comin' to get us?" He sobbed.

"They have to get past your Pa and General Forrest first," Jackson soothed. He patted Jimmie on the back. "They won't be able to do that."

Jimmie searched Jackson's face. "I wish you were there. Everyone knows that Yankees are scared of ole Stonewall."

Jackson smiled at Jimmie's confidence. "It's better that I'm here to protect you." Jimmie hugged him tight.

Flora burst from the house. "Where's Jimmie?" She cried, panic in her voice.

"I have him!" Jackson shouted. He took two more steps then set Jimmie down. "Run to your Ma."

Jimmie did as he was told.

"Flora, take the children, and you and Anna hide in the cellar," Lee said.

Flora took Jimmie's hand and pulled him up the steps. Johnston, Pendleton, Smith, and Morrison poured out the front door. Jackson's aides were armed with rifles. Jimmie saw the rifles and struggled against Flora's attempts to drag him into the house.

"I want to fight!" Jimmie yelled as he tried to pry Flora's fingers from his wrist. "I want to fight the Yankees with ole Stonewall and Grandpa!" He appealed to Morrison. "Tell her, Joe. Tell her I can fight."

With a jerk from Flora, Jimmie and his protests disappeared into the house.

"Major Smith, I need you to do me a favor," Lee said. "Go in the basement and wait with the women and children."

"Yes, sir," Smith said. He followed Flora in the house.

Around the bend, on the double quick, marched the fifteen or so soldiers that comprised the plantation's guard.

"What do you think?" Longstreet asked Jackson. "Should we post the men at the bend?"

"No." It was Lee who answered. Longstreet visibly angered over the correction. "Let's set the line in the woods. At least the men will have some cover."

Jackson volunteered to take command of the men. He trotted down the driveway and waved the soldiers over to him.

"Are we going to let General Jackson have all the fun?" Longstreet asked. He went down the steps.

"After you," Johnston said to Lee.

Lee followed Longstreet into the yard.

★ ★ ★

Jackson leaned against a tree. With the woods muffling the sound of gunfire, he had lost all sense of the battle, but he wasn't concerned. Stuart would drive the Yankees back. And if Stuart failed, well, then what could he and fifteen men do against a Yankee patrol?

Jackson checked his watch. An hour had passed since he had first heard musket fire. He handed his rifle to Morrison and stepped from the woods. Quiet reigned. The skirmish must be over. He turned back to the kneeling soldiers. "I think we're safe."

Lee gestured and the woods emptied. He dismissed the men to their camps. Pendleton volunteered to retrieve the women and children from the basement. Morrison went with him.

"Well, that was exciting," Johnston said.

Lee laughed. "It certainly broke up the monotony of the day. But you'll excuse me if I have no desire to repeat the exercise anytime soon."

Johnston took Lee's rifle. "I could use a glass of lemonade. How about you, Robert?"

Longstreet remained behind with Jackson. "General Lee may not want to repeat the exercise, but we should come up with a plan just in case the Yankees break through Stuart's pickets. I don't relish the idea of fighting from these woods. We could be easily trapped in there and defeated."

Jackson's grunt was non-committal.

Stuart, Forrest, and Fitz Lee rode around the bend.

"Are the Yankees dispatched?" Jackson asked.

"Of course," Stuart replied. "They didn't prove to be a worthy adversary."

That explained Forrest's glum face, Jackson thought.

"What are your plans for their return?" Longstreet was serious.

"They won't be comin' back," Forrest said unhappily. "This one's – he pointed at Stuart – plan had a built-in diversion. The Yankees think you're hiding somewhere in the direction of Harrisonburg."

"That diversion won't last long," Longstreet said.

"I don't know about that. Them Yankees received quite a lickin'," Forrest said.

Longstreet shook his head. "No, they'll be back double the strength they were today." He swept the lawn with his hand. "We need to turn this place into an armed fortress."

"That sort of defeats the purpose of makin' this place appear abandoned. If soldiers are suddenly patrollin' all around, it will alert the Yankees to our presence," Forrest said.

"At least we'll be prepared when they do find us," Longstreet insisted.

Forrest glared at Longstreet. "You can dig in like you did all through Georgia. That worked out so well for us."

Longstreet swelled in anger. "That's enough out of you!" He barked.

Forrest threw himself off King Philip. Jackson quickly stepped in between the two men. So did Stuart, who threw an arm across Forrest's chest, but directed his anger at Longstreet. "I believe the system we have in place is effective. We're able to receive advance notice when the Yankees are coming and meet them miles from here."

Jackson knew Longstreet wasn't convinced, but the Georgian let it go for now. He excused himself and strode angrily away. Jackson wondered if he was going to plead his case to Lee, since Lee would be the only one who could get Stuart to change his mind.

An uncomfortable silence fell on the group, no one knowing what to say.

Stuart nudged Jackson in the ribs. "You should have seen it."

Jackson laughed. Here came the blow-by-blow account of the skirmish. It was almost like old times.

"Yes, you should have," Forrest chimed in. "It was a thing of beauty."

Chapter Nine

Summer disappeared overnight. The occupants woke to a frost covered lawn and trees furiously shedding their leaves. Summer clothes were stored away and heavy woolens liberated from trunks. The old farmhouse was drafty, so Jackson put Morrison, Smith, and Pendleton to work chopping firewood, while he and Stuart hauled the wood up to the various bedrooms. Lee wanted to help, but Doctor McGuire prohibited him from participating in physical activity. He was still weak and not recovering as quickly as McGuire would have liked.

Feeling less than useful, Lee walked the 100 feet to the house where Longstreet and Johnston resided. Forrest had a room there as well, but the cavalry leader found the idleness of hiding too much to bear. He stormed into the big house one morning and announced to Stuart that he would be taking responsibility for the vedettes surrounding the property and the various camps spread throughout the Valley. Since Forrest was unfamiliar with the countryside, he roped Fitz into being his guide. At first, Morrison had volunteered to show Forrest around, but Anna wouldn't hear of it. She wanted her loved ones under her watchful eye. Pendleton and McGuire moved into Forrest's room giving Morrison and Smith a room to themselves. Longstreet's return meant that Jim Lewis reigned over the kitchen. Both households shared meals around the large dining room table, and the custom was to come and go in the two houses without knocking.

The last days of summer had passed peacefully, but the chill in the air and the change of season produced a restless spirit in more than Forrest. Hiding from the Yankees was not a long term solution to their predicament.

After dinner, one chilly evening, when Anna had retired upstairs to put the baby to bed, and Flora was in the living room with the children, the subject could no longer be avoided. It was Longstreet who brought it up and when he did, no one objected.

Jackson settled back in his chair. He had already reached the conclusion that the only way they would gain their freedom was to fight it out. He knew Stuart and Forrest agreed with him.

"The way I see it, we have two options, we hide or we fight," Stuart said, pouring a cup of coffee.

"We could also leave the country," Johnston volunteered.

"And go where?" Longstreet gestured toward the coffee pot. Stuart scooted it over.

Jim appeared from the kitchen. "I have some peach cobbler fresh from the oven. Can I interest anyone in a piece?"

Jackson raised his hand. "You can interest me."

Jim brought out the dessert. From the sideboard, Stuart collected plates and forks and set them in the center of the table. He handed Lee a large serving knife before returning to his seat.

Lee cut a piece, plopped it on a plate, and handed the plate to Johnston. "Where would we go, Joe?"

"They want officers in the Mexican army. Or we could retire to South America. Or Europe," he added swiftly when Longstreet frowned at him.

Longstreet accepted a plate from Lee. "So, we have three options. Hide, fight, or run."

Jimmie dashed in from the hall. "CCCOOOBBBLLLEEERRRR!" He shouted, waving his arms over his head.

Jim met him at the kitchen door. "Jimmie, now you hush. Them men are discussin' important things. They don't need loud little boys interruptin' them, screamin' about dessert. Now, come git your cobbler and some milk and keep ole Jim company while I clean up."

Jimmie dropped his head. "Sorry, Jim."

Jim retreated into the kitchen with Jimmie at his heels.

Longstreet's fork clattered on his empty dish. "Fight or leave. I don't care which. I just don't want to spend the rest of my life in hiding."

"The rest of our lives may be an exaggeration," Lee said. He passed some cobbler to Jackson. "There's an election in little over a month. McClellan has said that if he is elected, he would re-evaluate the evidence against us. If he finds we've been falsely convicted, he will commute our sentences and let us go home in peace."

Jackson took a bite of the dessert. The cobbler was hot, and he quickly took a gulp of water.

Johnston pushed away his plate. "McClellan also says we have to turn ourselves in while he reviews the evidence. And under no circumstance will I put my fate in the Yankees' hands. I don't trust them and that certainly goes for McClellan. He's a politician now, and if it served his ambition, he would renege on that promise in a heartbeat and see us hung in broad daylight on the Capitol grounds. No, surrendering is not an option I will voluntarily choose."

Stuart reached over and dragged the cobbler pan to him. He cut a large piece and dumped it on his plate. "Besides, we would all have to surrender. The Yankees' list of most wanted keeps growing. Me, Forrest, Fitz, Mosby, Generals Early and Rodes, we're all on it."

The group fell silent. Stuart's fork scraped his plate.

"We could always leave the country," Johnston brought up again.

"So, we go and, maybe after a year, we can earn the money to bring our families to wherever we are." Longstreet gestured between Lee and himself. "That's a long time to be away from your wives and children."

"You haven't seen your family since you went west," Stuart said. He wiped his mouth with his napkin. "Is another year too great a price to pay for freedom?"

"You say as your family is safe by your side," Longstreet snapped.

Furious, Stuart reared back. "I risked my family to save your hide," he barked. Jackson placed a hand on Stuart's arm. Stuart turned and glared at him.

"General Longstreet," Lee said in reproof.

At first, Jackson thought Longstreet wasn't going to back away from his statement, but he did. "I know you risked your family to save us."

Stuart accepted the apology, but his anger didn't abate.

Jackson gestured across the table toward Johnston. "I agree with General Johnston. I won't turn myself in."

"If we head toward Mexico, do you think we could make it?" Lee asked Stuart.

"You would need to ask Forrest," Stuart said tightly. "He has the contacts in Tennessee and Mississippi. But do we really want to be officers in Maximilian's army? I don't. I would rather fight."

"How many men could you gather?" Jackson asked.

"Two, three thousand. Maybe more," Stuart said.

"We would need ten times that amount," Johnston said in despair.

"I don't think so," Stuart said. "According to the newspapers, the Army of the Potomac has been sent home and so has Sherman's Grand Army of the Republic. Most of the army is either in the West fighting Indians or occupying the South. The Yankees just have a skeleton force in Washington. If General Lee issues the call, we could raise enough men to capture the city."

"I won't issue that call," Lee said.

Dumbfounded, Jackson stared at Lee. With that refusal, Lee had decapitated any hope of them gaining their freedom. Jackson could issue the call, but the number of soldiers who would respond would pale in comparison to the number who would come if Lee summoned them.

"What? Why not?" Stuart asked. His voice was a mixture of surprise and anger.

"For me, fighting is not an option."

Stuart slammed his hand on the table, rattling the dishes. "I can't believe what I'm hearing."

"Stuart," Jackson reproved. The last thing he wanted to do was back Lee into a corner. He was convinced that if he presented Lee a promising battle plan, Lee would reconsider his opposition to fighting.

"Fitz, Forrest, General Rodes, all of us. We were willing to die to set you free," Stuart said.

Lee remained calm. "And we've thanked you for that." He indicated his fellow prisonmates.

"I don't want your thanks," Stuart spat out. "When Captain Morrison found me, I could have gathered up my family and disappeared. But instead, I risked..."

"Jeb!" Lee interrupted. He was no longer calm. A red flush had crept into his cheeks. "You don't have to keep reminding us of your sacrifice. All of us sitting here are cognizant of it and know we can never repay you for what you did." Lee's voice rose. "But I refuse to be emotionally blackmailed by it every time you don't get your way."

Stuart stood up so fast that his legs raised the table a couple of inches. It slammed back to the ground. "Emotional blackmail! Is that what you think?"

"At this moment, yes I do," Lee said. "And it must stop. Now, sit back down." It was the most direct order Jackson ever heard Lee issue.

Stuart stiffened his shoulders. "I won't sit down. The war is over. I no longer report to you."

Jackson stood and raised his hands. "I think we all need to calm down. Fighting with each other isn't going to solve our problem."

Stuart turned on Jackson. "I don't need you to remind me of my manners."

Jackson needed to get out of the room before he said words that could not be taken back. "We're done here." He gathered up his dishes.

"Yes, we are." Stuart headed toward the hall.

"Where are you going?" Jackson asked.

"Out!" Stuart took three steps before turning back and pointing an angry finger at the stunned generals. "There's only one answer and that's to fight. If y'all can't summon the courage to do it, then the rest of us will just have to do it for you." Then he was gone. The slamming front door the exclamation point to his anger.

The sound faded away. Lee folded his napkin and laid it on the table. "Good night, gentlemen." He rose and pushed his chair under the table. He left the room.

Jackson glanced at Johnston and Longstreet. Both looked absolutely shell-shocked. Truth be told, so was he. He had never seen Lee and Stuart angry at each other before. He sat back down and took another bite of cobbler. He did know of another way out of the impasse, but before he pursed it, he needed to make sure of something first. He set his fork down, crossed to the kitchen, and pushed the door open. "Jimmie, can you come here?" He returned to his seat.

Jimmie burst out of door. "What do you need, ole Stonewall?"

He motioned for the boy to come closer. Jimmie marched over to Jackson's chair. "I have orders, soldier." Jimmie came to attention. Jackson picked up his napkin and wiped a milk moustache from the boy's upper lip. "Go to the little house and tell Captain Morrison I need to see him."

"Yes, sir." Jimmie gave a quick salute and dashed out of the room.

General Johnston picked up the coffee pot and shook it. "I need more coffee. Anyone else?"

Longstreet indicated he would like some. Johnston and the coffee pot disappeared into the kitchen.

"What do you need Captain Morrison for?" Longstreet asked.

With his fork, Jackson poked at his cobbler. "I want to play a hunch. If I'm right, we may find a way out of this mess without fighting."

"Tell me," Longstreet said.

"Stuart had a person high up in the War Department who aided him in our escape. I'm hoping Captain Morrison knows who it was. If we can contact that person…" Jackson's voice trailed off.

"Then what?" Longstreet pressed.

"I don't know exactly, but this man, whoever he is, may be able to help us. At least it's worth a try."

Johnston returned with the coffee pot. Morrison was with him.

"Have a seat, Captain," Jackson said. Morrison slid into Stuart's chair. "When we were rescued, Stuart already knew General Lee was ill. How did he know that?" One look at his brother-in-law's face and Jackson knew Morrison knew the identity of Stuart's spy. "Joe, it's important."

Morrison took a long look at Longstreet then Johnston, as if he was taking their measure. "Stuart did have a contact that kept him informed of what was happening in the prison. He never told me who it was."

"But you're sure he had one," Johnston said.

"Yes," Morrison mumbled.

"Did he tell anyone who it was?" Johnston pressed

"I believe he told General Forrest."

Jackson gave Morrison a level stare, but his brother-in-law dropped his eyes and refused to look at him. "You believe?"

Morrison exhaled. He was clearly uncomfortable. He looked longingly toward the kitchen door and freedom. "I saw General Stuart hand General Forrest a note."

"A note," Longstreet said incredulously. "You saw Stuart give Forrest a note."

"I was close enough to catch bits and pieces of their conversation. The note was from the spy."

"Well, if Forrest knows, he'll tell me," Longstreet said confidently. "I'll just go and ask him." He pushed back his chair.

"Hold on," Jackson said. He doubted Forrest would tell.

"It's not right to ask General Forrest to betray General Stuart's confidence," Morrison said heatedly.

"Then you tell us," Longstreet pushed.

Morrison appealed to Jackson. "Don't make me. General Stuart has trusted me far more than any other man ever has. And that includes you."

"Okay, Joe," Jackson relented. "I'll ask Stuart myself."

"No, no, no," Longstreet exploded. "I'm sick and tired of sitting on the outside while decisions are made that affect me." He pointed his finger at Morrison. "General Jackson asked you a question, Captain. If you know the answer, tell us."

Johnston held up his hand. "I believe Jeb will tell General Jackson."

"No he won't," Morrison blurted out.

"Why not?" Longstreet barked.

"Because if it got out, that person could be hung for treason."

"You do know who it is, don't you," Longstreet accused.

"General Stuart doesn't know that I know." Morrison folded his arms across his chest and sat back in his chair.

Jackson leaned forward to protect Morrison from Longstreet's anger. "Joe, I understand your concerns, but the man's identity is safe with us. That person is responsible for saving our lives. We'd never betray him."

"But secrets get out. That's their nature. I'm not saying you would tell on purpose, but what if you let it slip. I couldn't live with myself."

"Will you tell me?" Jackson said.

Morrison nodded.

Longstreet slammed his hand on the table. "No! I'm not going to be shunted to the background any more. We're in this together. No more secrets. No more one person making the decisions." He pointed his finger at Morrison. "If you trust your brother-in-law, you can trust me and General Johnston."

Morrison's struggle was clearly written on his face. Jackson wanted to spare him from further agony, but Longstreet wasn't wrong. They all had a right to know. If Morrison declined, then Jackson would ask Stuart and share the answer with Longstreet and Johnston.

"It's General Reynolds," Morrison whispered. "I recognized him from Gettysburg. When Sandie and I brought him and General Grant to see you."

The name didn't surprise Jackson.

"Can I go now?" Morrison asked. He was half out of his chair.

"Go on," Jackson said.

Morrison fled the room.

Chapter Ten

Lee heard the front door open and close. He sat up and threw back the bedcovers. The floor was cold to his feet, but he didn't care. He looked out the window and saw Stuart standing at the bottom of the porch steps, facing out into the yard. A small figure darted past Stuart's feet. It was Rebel.

Lee quickly dressed and grabbed his uniform jacket. When he stepped out onto the porch, the cold seized him and he shivered. The puppy was running circles around Stuart.

"Just go, you mangy mutt," Stuart muttered.

"Jeb," Lee called. Stuart stiffened. "Where did you go?"

"I visited Forrest."

Lee groaned. If Stuart was in a fighting mood, visiting the aggressive Forrest was like pouring oil on a fire.

"I would like to talk about what happened tonight." Lee came down the steps.

"I think we made our positions very clear." Stuart avoided Lee by walking out into the lawn. "Here Rebel, here boy!" The puppy stopped for a moment then went tearing down the driveway as if he was being chased. "Oh, for crying out loud!"

"Jeb," Lee said.

Stuart whirled around. "What do you want, General Lee?"

"We're not doing this, Jeb."

"Doing what?"

Rebel came dashing back up the driveway. Stuart made a grab at him, but the puppy evaded his grasp. "I'm going to put you on a rope the next time I bring you out," he grumbled.

Lee took a deep breath. "It seems to me that the only way I can be your papa is if I never disagree with you." He could no longer keep his anger in check. "No, I'm sorry. You need to make a decision. Do you want to be my son or not?"

Stuart didn't say anything. The puppy came over to him, sat down, and barked. He scooped Rebel up. "It's late. I'm going to bed."

"If you walk away from me without answering my question, you can continue to call me General Lee, for that is the only name I will answer to."

Stuart stopped. Lee could feel Stuart's glare even if he couldn't see it in the dark. Suddenly, Stuart deflated. "When I said I risked my family, I wasn't emotionally blackmailing you. I was trying to tell you that there wasn't anything I wouldn't risk for you. I would restart the war to make sure you're safe and reunited with your family." Stuart sat down on the steps and released the puppy. Rebel ran up the steps and barked at the front door.

There was no anger in Stuart's voice. Only anguish at being so misunderstood.

"I'm sorry I accused you of such a callous thing. I should have known better," Lee said.

The puppy was still barking. "Rebel! Be quiet!" Stuart commanded. The puppy gave one last bark before lying down.

Lee crossed to the steps.

Stuart looked up. "Papa! All I want to do is keep you safe, but you seem dead set against the idea. I don't understand why."

Lee sat down next to Stuart. "I'm not dead set against the idea."

"Then why don't you help me?"

"When I signed the surrender terms, I surrendered for all my men. If I break the terms, the men who served under me could be subjected to arrest or worse."

"The Yankees broke the terms when they arrested you without cause."

"That's true," Lee conceded, "but the Yankees did that. I'm afraid that if I lead an army, no matter the size, against Washington or any other city, the Yankees will be able to say that it was me who broke the terms and take their vengeance out on all the men. My soldiers have given enough for the Cause. I can't ask them to sacrifice what little they have left for me."

Stuart leaned back against the steps. "Fighting may be our only option."

"If it is, then General Jackson or you can lead whatever force you gather."

Stuart shook his head. "It's not the same. The men will want to know why you're not in command."

"Tell them my duty is to protect those who decided not to fight."

The door opened and Jackson appeared. Rebel leapt to his feet and raced into the house. "I heard the puppy barking and thought that he had been locked out." He looked down the steps. "Stuart, glad to see you back."

"I apologize for being rude to you," Stuart said contritely.

Jackson sat down on the step above them. "No hard feelings." He gave Stuart's shoulder a slight shove.

Lee exhaled; surprised at the freedom the breath gave him. He felt as if he had been holding his breath since Stuart exploded at him in the dining room.

"Stuart," Jackson said, "I want you to arrange a meeting with General Reynolds."

"General Reynolds?" Lee asked. He glanced at Stuart, but Stuart was glaring up at Jackson. "What can General Reynolds do for us?"

"Did Forrest say something?" Stuart's voice was like a whip.

"He didn't have to. I suspected you had a highly placed source."

Jackson's statement sent Lee reeling. "You did?" He said to Stuart.

"Didn't you ever wonder how he knew to have Doctor McGuire waiting for you at the safe house?" Jackson asked.

"I never thought of it," Lee said. "Jeb?"

Stuart was still staring at Jackson. "But you have the name. Only Forrest and I knew who it was."

"Captain Morrison knew," Jackson said. "He told us."

"Us?" Stuart practically shouted. He jumped to his feet.

Jackson remained seated. "It's not fair to keep General Johnston and General Longstreet or the two of us – Jackson gestured between he and Lee – out of the decision making. All of us need a say in whatever happens in the future."

Stuart's anger rekindled. "How did Captain Morrison know it was Reynolds? I never told him."

"Joe was present at your meeting with Reynolds and he recognized him from Gettysburg. He escorted Reynolds and Grant to see me about the bounty Sheridan had placed on your head. Remember?"

Stuart's lips compressed in anger. "I don't know what you expect Reynolds to do," he finally said.

"Maybe nothing, but he's the only chance we have to resolve this peacefully," Jackson said.

"It isn't going to be resolved peacefully," Stuart insisted. "You know that."

Lee glanced back at Jackson and saw that Jackson agreed with Stuart.

"Reynolds says he has no influence with Stanton," Stuart continued angrily. "So why put his life in danger if he can't help us."

"He's doing it so I won't have to make the call." Lee smiled at Jackson. When Jackson ducked his head, Lee knew his faithful lieutenant was blushing at being caught in such a kindness.

Stuart flung himself down on the porch. "I don't even know if I can get a message to Reynolds. He's only ever contacted me."

"Will you try?" Lee asked.

Stuart shook his head. "He can't help us."

"Will you try?" Lee asked again.

"Don't ask me," Stuart whispered.

Lee fought the urge to let Stuart off the hook. But he couldn't. If there was another way out of this mess besides restarting the war, they had to take it. "For me," he said.

Stuart capitulated. He would do his best to get a message to Reynolds. Lee didn't ask Jackson what would happen if the message went astray or Reynolds refused to meet with them. That was a question for another day.

★★★

A knock on the door brought Reynolds from his paperwork. He closed the file he was auditing and called for the person to enter. Colonel Rosengarten slipped into the office.

"When I was leaving my hotel this morning, there was a young boy waiting for me on the sidewalk. He gave me this." The adjutant held out a slip of paper.

Reynolds took the paper and glanced at the signature. He gasped in surprise. "It's from General Jackson."

"How can you be sure?" Rosengarten questioned. "It could be a trick to trap you." He fell into the chair next to the desk.

"At the bottom, here. The postscript." Reynolds showed Rosengarten the bottom of the note. "He thanks me again for the blankets and the Bibles."

"What does he want?"

Reynolds quickly read the message. The surprises kept coming. "He wants a meeting."

"Stuart told him about you! He had to!" The adjutant railed.

Reynolds opened a drawer and fished out a pair of scissors. Jackson had been careful not to address the letter to a specific individual, but the bit about the blankets and Bibles made it clear that the note had been intended for him. He snipped the postscript from the note. "Let's go see General Sherman."

Rosengarten jumped to his feet. "You're not meeting anyone. It's not worth the risk."

"If I thought I was in danger, I would destroy the note and forget all about it." He waved the paper. "Jackson's seeking a peaceful resolution. I don't have the power to see that done, but Sherman does."

"Sherman isn't going to help," Rosengarten scoffed.

Reynolds snatched up his jacket. "Sherman's more sympathetic than he lets on."

★ ★ ★

Sherman looked up from the note. "You're sure it's from Jackson."

"I am," Reynolds said. "What should we do?"

"Do?" Sheridan snapped. "Tell the Rebs we'll meet them and when they show up, arrest them."

Reynolds glared at the cavalry leader, who was seated in the opposite chair. "If that's your only input, you don't have to be here."

Sheridan scowled at Reynolds, the same scowl Reynolds had seen countless times. He shook his head. He still couldn't fathom why Grant hadn't cashiered Sheridan the first time the cavalry leader back talked his superior officers.

"What do you suggest, General Reynolds?" Sherman asked. He folded the note.

"I think it's a good thing. One of these days, General Sheridan's patrols will finally get lucky and stumble upon the fugitives' hiding place…"

"Oh, I'll find them," Sheridan growled "And when I do, I'll drag them back in chains."

"Strong words for so little results," Reynolds mocked. He smiled when Sheridan's face fell into its familiar wrathful lines.

"What's your point, General?" Sherman said, annoyed at Reynolds.

"According to General Sheridan's latest report, he estimates that Stuart has about 300 men under arms. So, President Hamlin needs to consider how a battle, costly in lives, will play in the newspaper this close to the election?"

Sheridan glared at Reynolds. "When I whip Stuart, Hamlin will be able to brag to the newspapers about the successful capture of the fugitives."

Sherman leaned back in his chair. "I could care less about the politics of the situation. That fight is between McClellan and Hamlin. What I care about is preventing another war." He turned his attention to Sheridan. "I know how you feel. You've been breathing vengeance since Sam died." He unfolded the note, read it again, and sighed. "Unfortunately, Stanton has the only say in any terms we could offer the Confederates."

Reynolds let out a slow breath. "So, what do we do?"

"We take the note to Stanton and see if we can come up with a plan that will satisfy both him and Jackson." He gave Reynolds a level stare. "But I do know this much. They're going to have to surrender. There's no way to avoid it."

Reynolds made a face. "I know."

Chapter Eleven

Manassas Battle Field
October 12, 1865

From the safety of the trees, Jackson watched Stuart and Forrest ride across the wide meadow to the crest of Henry House Hill where Reynolds and Sheridan were waiting for them. He wasn't happy that Sheridan was one of the participants in the hastily arranged meeting. The little man's presence bode ill for any hope of a peaceful resolution.

Memories washed over him and he shivered. It was on Henry House Hill, during the war's first battle, that he had been transformed from an unknown professor of natural and experimental philosophy into Stonewall Jackson. A name he didn't deserve but couldn't shake.

A year later, he had made his stand at an unfinished railroad cut not far from here. When his men had run out of ammunition, they had thrown rocks at the Yankees until Longstreet finally unleashed an artillery barrage that sent the Yankees scurrying back to Washington. Then last year, he had driven the Yankees from Bull Run Creek for a third time. Now he had returned to this hallowed ground as a beggar beseeching the Yankees for a favor.

Ten days after Stuart had started Jackson's letter on its way to Reynolds; an answer had made its way back to Clover Hill. Two lines on a half piece of foolscap indicating the location and time for the meeting. A separate postscript signed by Sherman promised the Confederates safe passage to and from Bull Run Creek.

Longstreet vouched for Sherman's veracity. Forrest did not. His opinion of the Union general was blunt and not very flattering. Jackson weighed the two diametrically opposed views and came down on the side of Longstreet. He had known Longstreet longer and believed Forrest's quick temper colored his perception.

It was decided that Stuart and Jackson would travel to Manassas and Stuart would meet with Reynolds. They would travel light: just a small guard and a wagon for supplies. Jackson was more than happy to sleep on the ground and eat hardtack, but Stuart didn't want to sleep outdoors in the rain or what other surprises October might throw at them.

On the morning of their departure, Jackson looked out his bedroom window and observed Pendleton, Morrison, Smith, Jim, and Doctor McGuire all packed and ready to go. He bounded down the steps and out the door, practically tripping over Rebel, who now made it a habit to sit by the door and dart out the moment it opened.

"Rebel!" Jackson snapped angrily.

The puppy dashed down the steps and into Morrison's waiting arms. Morrison scooped him up and headed toward the house. Jackson met him at the bottom of the steps. "Where do you men think you're going?"

"We're going with you," Morrison replied. "We always go with you." He gave the squirming puppy a pat on the head.

"Not this time. I can't allow you to come. It's too dangerous." Morrison started to laugh. "Did I say something amusing, Captain?"

"During a battle, you never hesitated to send us into a hail storm of bullets to deliver a message. Now, that was dangerous. Riding with you to Manassas, piece of cake." Morrison laughed again. "If you'll excuse me, I'll bring Little Sorrel around." Still laughing, he headed toward the back of the house.

Pendleton approached. "General Stuart just left. He said he would meet us on the road."

Jackson gave in. He gestured toward his aides. "I can almost understand why you three want to go, but why are you coming, Jim?"

"'Cause General Stuart gets hongry when he travels." Jim threw a large set of saddlebags over his horse. "And I was asked."

"Well that explains Jim." Jackson faced McGuire. "Why are you coming?"

"I was feeling left out," McGuire confessed with a grin. He pulled the cinch tight on his saddle.

"Is Anna okay to be left alone?" Jackson queried impatiently.

Morrison appeared puppyless and leading Little Sorrel. Jackson drew on his gauntlets.

"Anna's fine. As for young Tom, I've never seen a healthier baby," McGuire said. He swung up in the saddle.

"I've lost control of all of you," Jackson fumed.

"Your absence was quite liberating." Morrison took out his watch. "We need to go. General Stuart's expecting us." He swung up on his mare, gave her a nudge, and cantered down the driveway.

When they reached the rendezvous point, Stuart wasn't alone. Forrest was waiting with him. Jackson groaned when he saw the man. "Stuart." He frowned at the cavalry leader. "We agreed that it would be just you and me."

"Thought you could use an extra hand," Forrest said. "Just in case General Sherman's word ain't all General Longstreet believes it is."

"You promise to behave."

Forrest gave King Philip's neck a quick pat. "You don't have to worry none about me, General Jackson. I ain't lookin' to pick a fight. But I don't trust Sherman. I don't care what General Longstreet says. A man who would turn his soldiers loose to terrorize women and children ain't the type of man to be trustin' with your life. So, I'm going, just in case."

Jackson refocused his glasses. Stuart and Forrest had arrived at the rendezvous point. Stuart's instructions were not to agree to any terms. If the Yankees demanded an answer today, then Jackson had permission to speak on the fugitives' behalf. But if the Yankees could wait, the offer was to be brought back to the farmhouse for discussion and group consensus. Jackson thought that part of the plan a bad idea. Too many cooks in the kitchen, so to speak.

The meeting was under way. There was nothing to do now but wait.

★ ★ ★

"General Reynolds." Stuart greeted the Union general with a smile and a handshake. A short distance away Sheridan remained mounted and glowering. Stuart was only too happy to ignore him. "May I introduce to you Nathan Bedford Forrest?"

Reynolds was gracious as usual. "General Forrest, your exploits have been bandied about Washington since the Grand Army of the Republic returned to the capital."

"General Sherman don't much like me," Forrest said with a shrug. "I spent most of my time disrupting his supply lines. There was little he could do about it."

"Something like that," Reynolds laughed.

"What's his problem?" Forrest pointed at the scowling Sheridan.

"That's General Sheridan," Reynolds said as way of explanation.

"What do you have for us?" Stuart asked.

Reynolds hesitated.

"Told you," Forrest said to Stuart. He wrapped the reins around his hand and prepared to swing up on King Philip.

"Hold on," Stuart ordered. "General Reynolds didn't bring us out here on a wild goose chase. Let the man speak."

Forrest huffed in exasperation.

"I'm going to give you the bad news first," Reynolds said. He reached into his pocket and brought out a slip of paper. "You'll have to surrender."

"Absolutely not," Stuart said.

"We're wasting our time," Sheridan hollered over.

Reynolds whirled and faced the belligerent man. "It's my time to waste."

Sheridan dismounted and strode over to the clutch of men. He didn't say anything. He just stood with his hands on his hips and a scowl on his face.

"And you will have to restand trial," Reynolds continued.

Stuart fired up. "These are your terms? You brought us all the way here to tell us that we have to surrender, only to be railroaded and hurried to the gallows. No, thank you. Let's go, Forrest."

"Wait a minute!" Reynolds said. "There's more."

"What difference does it make if there's more?" Stuart railed, still angry. "Once we're in your hands, there's no guarantee you'll keep your word. No guarantee at all."

"This is going to have to take some trust. The plan has the approval of General Sherman and President Hamlin."

Stuart tugged on his beard and thought for a moment. He did trust Reynolds, but he was the only Yankee he trusted. A look at the glowering Sheridan was proof enough of the danger they faced in surrendering. Well, it wasn't his decision to make. That responsibility belonged to Jackson. Stuart would certainly make his objections known. "What else?"

"Like I said, you'll get a new trial and a jury of your peers. I'll be the jury foreman. Others on the jury will include General Blair, General Howard, General Cooke..."

"My father-in-law!"

"General Thomas and General Garfield. I know that General Howard was your roommate at West Point."

"He was," Stuart conceded.

"And your father-in-law will be on your side."

At one time, Stuart had had great respect for Flora's father and had even named his son after the man. Then the war came and Cooke had chosen to stay with the Union. A grave mistake that had angered Stuart so much that he changed his son's name from Phillip St. George Cooke Stuart to James Ewell Brown Stuart, Jr. Flora had been devastated by the breach with her parents, but Stuart didn't care. The man was a traitor to his State and to the Cause and deserved their scorn.

"And General Thomas is a Virginian," Reynolds said.

Stuart took no consolation in that fact.

"You have to admit that these men will be fair."

"What good is fair if all the witnesses are drunks and liars," Forrest said.

"They'll be none of that. Secretary Stanton has promised to present his evidence. You'll also be able to present witnesses and evidence too," Reynolds said. "And have attorneys present."

"A fair trial?" Stuart asked.

"Absolutely," Reynolds encouraged. "Guaranteed by the president. And to make sure that the terms are followed, they'll be sent to the newspapers. Reporters from all the large papers will be present in the courtroom. Everything will be above board and in broad daylight." Reynolds handed over the paper.

Stuart read the terms quickly and was impressed. Reynolds was offering them a way to clear their names and return home. "How about the other men on your ever growing list? Fitz Lee, Colonel Mosby..."

"If they lay down their arms and agree to live by their paroles, they'll be left alone to live in peace."

Stuart stowed the terms in his pocket.

"There's just one more thing," Reynolds said.

Stuart's heart sank to his stomach. He knew the terms were too good to be true. "What?" He barked.

"General Forrest will have to surrender and stand trial for the hangings of our troops in Georgia."

Forrest reared back. "I'd rather die first."

"That can be arranged." Sheridan was snide.

"Let's you and I go right now, little man." Forrest placed his hand on his pistol.

Sheridan swelled up. "With pleasure."

Stuart grabbed Forrest's hand. Forrest released the pistol.

"Stop it!" Reynolds barked at Sheridan. The little man scowled but backed down. "General Forrest, this comes from General Sherman."

Stuart saw nothing but regret in Reynolds' face.

"You can refuse, of course, and ride away. But either General Forrest surrenders at the same time you do or the deal is off the table."

Stuart was flabbergasted. "I've no control over General Forrest."

"I'm sorry," Reynolds apologized.

"When do you need an answer?" Stuart asked.

"As soon as possible. President Hamlin would like to have this over before the election."

"Of course he would," Stuart said. "General Jackson is here with me. I'll take this to him and let him decide. We can meet back here tomorrow at dawn, and I'll give you either a yes or no."

"Tomorrow at dawn then."

Stuart nodded. He swung up on Centurion and waited while Forrest settled in the saddle. He wheeled the great stallion and headed back toward Jackson.

★ ★ ★

Jackson watched Forrest's hand fly to his pistol. He sucked in his breath. He knew Forrest was volatile, but he didn't expect a duel to break out during negotiations. Good, Stuart seemed to have resolved it peacefully. Jackson exhaled slowly.

The two cavalry leaders mounted up and headed back. Forrest rode stiffly, angrily. Stuart's body language was harder to discern. Now Reynolds and Sheridan were riding away.

A gunshot rent the silence and echoed over the quiet battlefield. Surprised by the unexpected sound, Jackson dropped his glasses. They bounced heavily against his chest, bruising it. He fumbled, found the glasses, and raised them. Both generals had put spurs to their mounts. Centurion was gobbling up the ground with his customary speed.

91

King Philip trailed behind, but Forrest's war horse had great speed also.

Jackson swung up on Little Sorrel and rode to the small clearing where they had set their camp. He would meet Stuart and Forrest there.

Pendleton greeted him in a high state of agitation. "I heard a gunshot!" He exclaimed. "Do you know where it came from?"

"I don't," Jackson replied. He peered down the path. What was keeping Stuart?

"Maybe it was just a hunter. What do you think?" Pendleton asked.

Jackson grew exasperated with the young man's questions and silenced him with a sharp sweep of his hand. Stuart and Forrest were coming now.

"Is everyone okay?" Jackson asked.

Forrest dismounted quickly. "That shot came from the Yankees." He pulled his rifle from his saddle boot.

"The Yankees!" Pendleton said. "Joe! Jimmie! Get your guns!"

"No one needs any guns," Jackson said. If the shot came from the Yankees, then this meeting was a carefully orchestrated ambush and his aides, armed or not, would not be able to protect them.

"That might not be a bad idea," Forrest said. Pendleton dashed toward his tent.

Jackson noticed Stuart was still in the saddle. "Stuart, are you okay?"

Stuart looked down at his shirt front. Jackson's heart stopped. His gaze followed Stuart's. The shirt was still white. His heart resumed beating.

Slowly, Stuart dismounted. When he did, the color drained from his face. Jackson started toward him. Two steps and Stuart collapsed. Jackson caught him, but Stuart was heavy and falling. Jackson fell to the ground, careful to cradle Stuart in his arms. "Stuart!"

Stuart said nothing. Jackson held him close. There was blood on his jacket sleeve where it had come in contact with Stuart's back. "Get Doctor McGuire!"

"I'll go," Forrest said.

Jackson heard Forrest sprint away. "Hold on, Stuart. Hold on. Doctor McGuire's coming." Stuart's head fell back against Jackson's shoulder. His eyes were closed and there was blood in the corner of his mouth. "No, no, no, no, no. Don't you leave me! You stay here with me!"

"Can't," Stuart coughed. His spittle was filled with blood.

Stuart was dying! Jackson could barely comprehend it. All that life and laughter was fading away before his eyes. Death was here. Jackson could feel it. He raised his eyes toward Heaven. "No!" He pleaded. "No!"

"Flora," Stuart whispered.

"Don't worry, Jeb. I'll care for her and the children like they're my family. I promise." Tears flowed down his cheeks. Where was Forrest? What was taking so long?

Stuart opened his eyes. "Goodbye." He smiled.

"Goodbye," Jackson choked out. Stuart hadn't heard him. Jackson gently closed the lifeless eyes. "We'll meet again in Heaven." He gathered the cavalry leader in his arms. Sobs tore through his body. He placed his forehead on the top of Stuart's head and wept.

"General Jackson."

Jackson raised his head and gazed down at Stuart's face. His dear Stuart was at peace.

"General Jackson."

It was Pendleton. He wished his adjutant would go away and leave him alone. Pendleton knelt down, put his hand on Jackson's arm, and tried to loosen Jackson's grip on Stuart. Stunned by the act,

Jackson jerked his arm away. Stuart shifted. Jackson tenderly drew him close again.

"Please, General Jackson," Pendleton pleaded. "Please." Once more he tried to loosen Jackson's grip.

"Leave us alone." He flung Pendleton's hand away.

Pendleton didn't give up.

"I said leave us alone," Jackson yelled. He looked up and saw his aides and McGuire standing around him.

McGuire knelt down in front of him. "We need to take General Stuart back to his tent."

Jackson was appalled. They wanted to take Stuart and bury him in the ground, forever out of his reach. His tears began anew. "You're not taking him anywhere!" He placed his forehead on Stuart's head again. "I won't let them take you."

"He's gone and lost his mind," Jackson heard Pendleton hiss.

"No, it's the grief talking," Smith replied.

Jackson glared at them. "Stop talking about me like I'm not here. Just go away and leave us alone. That's an order."

McGuire was still kneeling in front of him. "General Jackson, please."

He pushed McGuire away. The doctor fell back in the leaves and dirt. Jackson would fight before he would let them take Stuart away. "No!"

McGuire rose and dusted himself off. "Sandie, go fetch Jim."

Jackson heard footsteps running away.

"It's okay." McGuire put his hand on Jackson's shoulder. "We'll just stay here with you until you're ready."

Jackson shivered. The air was colder and so was Stuart. Jackson needed to warm him. He wrapped his arms tighter around his brother. He heard footsteps approaching.

"Now, General Jackson..."

The familiar voice that spoke was kind and gentle. Jackson looked up and saw Jim. Tears traced their way down Jim's cheeks. Jackson took comfort in the tears. It proved just how much Jim loved Stuart. Why, Jim had only come on this trip because Stuart didn't want to go hungry.

Jim knelt down and clasped Jackson's hand lightly. "You know General Stuart as well as I do. He wouldn't want to be laid out in a soiled jacket and them worn pants. No, he'd want to be dressed in his fancy uniform. The one he wore to the surrender. I found it at the bottom of his trunk, and I got it all laid out nice and ready." Jim squeezed Jackson's hand. "But General Jackson, I need him so I can wash and dress him." He shifted and sat next to Jackson. He slid one arm under Stuart's body. "Now, you give him to ole Jim. I'll take good care of him."

Jim was right. Stuart would want to be laid out in his fancy uniform, the one with all the braid. How Stuart loved braid! He loosened his grip and allowed Stuart to slip from his grasp. Jim laid him tenderly on the ground.

Jackson sobbed. Stuart looked so forlorn. He bent over and kissed the cavalry leader on the forehead. "Goodbye," he whispered again. He scooted away.

Jim stood. He gestured toward the young men. "Sandie, Joe, Jimmie, come help me."

The three men lifted Stuart from the ground.

"Gently," Jackson commanded. "Watch his head."

Sandie shifted his arm and cradled Stuart's head. Slowly, they headed back toward the camp.

"Put him in my tent," Jackson said to Jim.

Jim assured him that he would. Jackson dropped his head into his hands.

"Is there anything I can do for you?" McGuire asked.

Jackson had never heard such concern in the young doctor's voice. "No." He withdrew his bandana and wiped his eyes. "I haven't lost my mind, just in case you're wondering."

"I know you haven't," McGuire said. He reached down his hand. Jackson allowed McGuire to pull him to his feet. His legs were numb and his arms were cramping. He looked around. "Where's General Forrest?"

"He's making sure the perimeter is safe. To tell you the truth, he's pretty torn up. I think he found a kindred spirit in General Stuart."

The feeling returned to Jackson's legs. He took a few stiff steps. His eyes burned and he had a pounding headache. "Do you have any headache powders?"

"In my tent." McGuire put an arm around Jackson's shoulder. Together, they walked back to McGuire's tent.

Chapter Twelve

Jim had done a splendid job. Stuart was dressed in his finest jacket with his yellow sash tied securely around his waist. The thigh-high boots Jackson had given Stuart for Christmas in Harrisburg had been polished and now glistened in the low candlelight. All of Stuart's shirts had been dirty, so Jackson had given Jim his last clean one. Stuart would have been very pleased with the way he had been laid out.

In the jacket's pocket, Jackson placed Stuart's small field Bible. The last time Jackson saw it had been along the Potomac. Stuart had been reading it when Jackson told him it was time to break the Union flank and give the besieged Confederates time to escape over the river. Stuart had been his usual superb self that day, proving what Jackson had known since the moment Stuart had galloped into Harper's Ferry – he was the greatest cavalry leader this country had ever produced.

Jackson covered Stuart's body with a blanket. Death was changing him, further stealing him away. The pain in Jackson's heart was all he had left. And once the pain was gone, how long until the memories faded?

He forced himself to stop looking at his camp bed. Every time he did, he blubbered like a baby and his eyes burned too much for any more tears. Doctor McGuire's powders failed to make a dent in the pounding headache that made him feel like his forehead was being squeezed in a vice.

To keep his eyes from the bed, he went through Stuart's trunk and wept every time his hand held something familiar. Then he came across the letters. There was one for Flora and one for each of the children. There was one addressed to Lee. When Jackson saw his name, he choked back a sob. He turned the letter over and over in his hands, but couldn't bring himself to break the seal and read it.

From outside, he heard Morrison call his name.

"What is it, Captain?" Jackson asked, annoyed. He had left strict instructions not to be disturbed.

Morrison came into the tent. "General Reynolds is here."

Surprise flooded away the grief. Then he grew angry. Reynolds and his meeting was the sole reason his dear Stuart was dead. "Tell him to go away."

Morrison flushed. "Sir, I don't think he's going to do that."

Jackson clenched his fists. "Fine! Show him in."

Morrison started to leave when his eyes fell on Stuart. "I'm going to miss him."

Jackson eyes filled with tears. "About your business, Captain."

Morrison fled the tent. Jackson slipped the letter into his pocket.

The Union general entered. He didn't say a word but stopped at the camp bed and stared down at Stuart.

Stuart's LeMat was in the trunk. Jackson snatched it up and pointed it at Reynolds. "Give me one reason why I shouldn't kill you right now."

Reynolds didn't move. "Because you're not that kind of man."

Jackson waved the pistol. "You don't know what kind of man I am."

Reynolds gave him a kind smile. "I know you're not a cold-blooded killer."

No, he wasn't. Jackson returned the gun to the trunk. "I'm sorry. I'm sorry." He collapsed in his chair. "Why are you here?"

"I heard the gunshot and saw that Stuart had been wounded. I came to make sure he was okay. Even if it meant challenging one very angry General Forrest."

That admission caught Jackson totally unaware. He had no idea that Stuart had been wounded until he collapsed. How did Reynolds know? Unless it was Sheridan. Of course, Sheridan! Why hadn't he thought about that loathsome little man sooner? "Did Sheridan have anything to do with this?" If the cavalry leader had played even a small part in Stuart's murder, Jackson would track him down and extract vengeance.

Reynolds shook his head. "No, Sheridan was just as surprised as I was when we heard the shot."

"Are you sure?" Jackson questioned.

"He's not that good of an actor. I questioned him for about twenty minutes until I was satisfied he had no hand in it." Reynolds motioned toward the stool sitting in the corner of the tent. "May I?" Jackson yielded. Reynolds sat down. "I don't know who it was yet, but I ordered my adjutant, Colonel Rosengarten, to find out."

"What's going to happen to the man who murdered Stuart?"

"Once Colonel Rosengarten identifies him, I'll make sure he's court-martialed and sentenced appropriately."

Jackson laughed bitterly. "Don't lie to me. Not here. You and I both know that nothing will happen to him."

Reynolds started to protest.

Jackson erupted in anger. His hand reached for the LeMat. "Spare me your empty promises. Don't forget, I know first hand about Yankee justice." The intensity of his fury frightened him. He was angry enough to do murder. "Help me, Lord. Help me," he prayed silently. He threw the pistol back into the trunk and slammed the lid closed with a bang.

Reynolds flinched at the sound but quickly recovered his composure. "What I'm going to say next is going to sound callous, but you can't let General Stuart's death stand in the way of accepting the deal President Hamlin has offered."

Jackson knew about the deal. Forrest had explained it while they waited for Jim to finish preparing Stuart's body. Jackson had barely heard what the cavalry leader was saying, but he heard loud and clear that Forrest would never surrender to the Yankees.

"The terms allow you to be cleared while giving Hamlin and Stanton a way to save face. You can't turn it down."

"I have to discuss it with the others," Jackson stalled.

Reynolds leaned forward. "Stuart said you had the authority to make the decision. You need to make it. Tonight."

Jackson felt his anger overpowering him again. He tried to fight it down but it was winning. If Reynolds didn't leave his tent, he would retrieve the LeMat and shoot him. "I don't need to do anything but tell Stuart's wife that she is now a widow and his dear children that their pa won't be coming home. That is all I need to do, General Reynolds."

Reynolds stood. "Of course. Is there anything I can do?"

"Are you a Christian man?"

Reynolds was surprised by the question. "Yes, I am. Why do you ask?"

"You need to go," Jackson said, his whole body shaking with rage.

"Please urge the other generals to accept the deal. It's only a matter of time until Sheridan finds you. And when he does, I can't protect you."

"Just go!" Jackson said tightly.

Reynolds exited the tent.

★ ★ ★

Lee sat on the swing reading a book to Julia and Ginny. They listened intently as he expounded on the trials of the main character: a lost kitten in search of his mother.

Anna came out onto the porch. "Come on girls, dinner is ready."

The girls climbed down off the swing chair.

"Where's my reward for reading the story?" Lee asked. He bent down and received a kiss on the cheek from Julia first then Ginny. The two little girls ran across the porch and disappeared into the house.

Anna came over to him. "I thought they'd be back by now."

"I never knew how hard it was to be the one waiting at home," Lee said.

Anna sat down on the couch. "Are you sorry you stayed?"

Lee smiled. "Only because I'm curious to know what's happening."

"Me, too," she confessed. "Do you think this meeting with General Reynolds will do any good?"

"It can't hurt," Lee said. He closed the book and set it next to him.

She stood. "Dinner will be ready in about fifteen minutes."

"I'll be in. I just want to enjoy this warm sun for a moment longer."

Lee rocked the swing. It swayed gently back and forth, the chains squeaking in protest. The sun began to slip behind the trees. Another day of waiting had come to an end. No, he didn't like being the one left behind.

The swing came to a slow halt. He crossed the porch but stopped at the steps. A noise had caught his attention. Horses! Jackson and Stuart were returning. In anticipation, he went down the first step and stopped. Jackson came around the driveway's bend. Right behind him was Forrest.

Forrest's appearance caught Lee by surprise. Jackson hadn't told him that Forrest had been invited to go along. Lee raised his hand to wave, but stopped. He could tell by the rigidity in Jackson's body that something was wrong. Perhaps the meeting had gone badly. Pendleton, Smith, and Morrison now appeared and Doctor McGuire was right behind them. He didn't see Stuart. Had he stopped to check in with the pickets surrounding the farmhouse?

A wagon came around the bend. Lee saw Centurion tied to the back of the wagon. The stallion pulled against his tether, desiring to be free. Had Stuart taken Virginia with him also? No, Virginia was in the corral with Traveller.

Then Lee saw the coffin in the back of the wagon. The marrow froze in his bones, and a sob escaped his throat. He found himself at the bottom of the stairs not even knowing how he got there. Jackson dismounted and walked toward him, careful to avoid his eyes. Another sob escaped Lee.

"Tom," he breathed. Jackson came over to him. "Is it my darling boy?"

Jackson nodded.

Lee's strength deserted him. He staggered backward, his ankles coming in contact with the bottom step. He fell back hard on the stairs.

"Where's Flora?" Jackson asked.

Jackson's voice sounded muffled in Lee's ears. "She's in the kitchen feeding the children."

Jackson walked past him. Lee reached up and grabbed Jackson's hand. Jackson stopped and looked down. "Did he suffer?"

"He went quickly."

Lee released Jackson's hand. Jackson went up the steps and into the house.

The wagon arrived in front of the porch. Forrest halted it. He untied Centurion. The stallion strained against the cavalry leader, but Forrest held on.

Lee felt disconnected from the scene. Everything happening around him seemed to have a dreamlike quality. Only the rough hewned coffin was real.

A scream rent that dream. It continued – hysterical and heart rendering. Jackson had told her. Flora, who used to telegraph Lee's headquarters after every battle demanding to know if Stuart was alive. Flora, who had lived four years terrified that her beloved cavalier would be taken from her. The thing she had feared the most had come upon her. Her husband was gone.

The screaming stopped. Lee wanted to go into the kitchen and comfort her, but he couldn't make his body obey his desire. Jackson was there and so was Anna. And Johnston and Longstreet. They'd have come from the little house for dinner. There were enough bodies to offer sympathy and get in the way.

But there was no one with his darling boy. Stuart was alone. Unsteady now, Lee stood and walked over to the wagon. He caressed the rough wood with his hand. "I'm here, Jeb. I won't leave you."

Forrest slipped around the house leading Centurion and King Philip. Jim followed with the rest of the horses.

McGuire came over to the wagon. He placed a gentle hand on Lee's back. "How are you feeling?"

Lee knew McGuire meant his heart. After all, he had collapsed after Fitzhugh's death and then again last year. McGuire was being a vigilant doctor, but right now, the question just sounded ridiculous. How was he feeling? Like the world had suddenly stopped spinning, that's how he was feeling.

But McGuire didn't seem to need an answer. "I'll be inside, if you need me."

Jackson's aides milled about, staying a respectful distance away. Lee glanced at them. Each one seemed devastated, but Captain Morrison was destroyed. Lee wanted to speak comforting words, but he couldn't bring himself to do it.

The front door opened. Lee looked over his shoulder and saw Jackson. Stiffly, Jackson came down the steps and joined him at the wagon.

"Flora?" Lee asked.

Tears sparkled in Jackson's eyes. "She fainted. Doctor McGuire and Anna are with her."

Lee reached down and gently caressed the rough pine as if stroking Stuart's cheek. That was something he always loved about his dear boy. Whereas he had to beg Fitzhugh for a kiss or a hug, Stuart never seemed to mind a father's need to express his love to his son.

Tears splashed, wetting the wood. Lee made no attempt to stop them. This was the worst blow of his life. Far more injurious than Fitzhugh's death or even the surrender. The sun had set and would never rise again. No more would his darling boy ride up to his tent filled with joy and laughter to pour them out like a warm spring shower upon Lee's tired soul. "I'm fifty-eight years old. But I've lived an hour too long." His throat tightened and he couldn't speak.

"Don't talk so," Jackson said sternly. "You were his beloved Papa, and he wouldn't want you to grieve."

Lee wiped at his tears. "He told me once that if I came to Lexington, he would look after my happiness forever."

Jackson reached into his breast pocket and withdrew a letter. "He left you this."

Lee recognized Stuart's handwriting. How many notes, messages, and reports had he received from Stuart during the war? This would be the last one he would ever receive. He didn't want it to be the last. He refused to take it.

Jackson stood there for a moment with his hand extended. Finally he placed the letter on the coffin. "He wanted you to have it."

Lee reached over and placed his hand on the letter to keep the wind from blowing it away.

The front door exploded open, banging hard against the house. Jimmie raced out, running so fast, he was almost out of control. Rebel nipped at his heels. He stopped when he saw the wagon. His eyes enlarged at the sight of the coffin sitting in the wagon. He raised his arm and pointed his finger at the coffin. "Is my Pa in there?" He shrieked in terror.

He stared first at Jackson and then at Lee. Suddenly, he tore off, running down the driveway. Rebel raced in front of him.

"Jimmie!" Jackson called. "Jimmie!"

"I'll go after him," Lee said.

"No, I'll go." Jackson headed down the driveway.

★ ★ ★

It was growing dark. The trees in the surrounding fields were slowly turning into a solid black monolith – void of shape and form. So far, the little boy was ignoring his calls. He'd search for another ten minutes. If he hadn't found Jimmie by then, he would go back to the house, fetch his aides, and set them searching.

"Jimmie! Jimmie! Please answer me."

Only silence greeted his calls.

He headed toward the house. As he went, he brushed against the limbs of a large pine. He heard a rustling sound.

"Be quiet, Rebel." Jimmie's loud whisper came from the depths of the tree.

Thank you, Lord, for that wonderful puppy. "Jimmie, come out."

At the sound of Jackson's voice, Rebel whined.

"Ssssshhhhh!" Jimmie hissed.

"Jimmie, I know you're in there," Jackson said.

Nothing.

Jackson squatted down and lifted up a large branch. Jimmie sat with his back against the tree trunk. He had his knees drawn up to his chest, his arms wrapped around his shins, and his cheek resting on his knees. He was weeping. Rebel lay at his feet.

Jackson fell to his knees and crawled in. The branch returned to its place, enveloping the two of them in a dimly lit cocoon.

Jackson leaned back against the tree trunk. The bottom branch brushed against the top of his head. Rebel came over and put his head on Jackson's shin. He stroked the puppy's head. Jimmie hadn't acknowledged him. He just sat and wept quietly.

"I was a little older than you when my mother got sick. One day there was a knock on the front door. It was my Uncle Cummins. He had come to take my sister and me to his home at Jackson's Mill. I didn't want to leave my mother, so I ran out of the house and hid under a tree, just like this one."

"What happened to your mother?" Jimmie sniffed.

"She died."

Jimmie stared up at him with tear filled eyes. "Were you sad?"

"Very, very sad."

"As sad as me?"

"As sad as you."

Jimmie's body shook as he wept. Jackson remembered the fear and uncertainty that had overpowered him that day as he hid under the pine tree praying that he would never have to leave his mother.

"I know you have baby Tom," Jimmie said in between sobs. Jackson could barely understand him. "And I know he probably takes up all your love. But do you think you might have a place in your heart for a second little boy. I won't take up much room. I promise."

"Why?" Jackson asked, fighting back tears.

"Because I'm no one's little boy now." His voice was so small and frightened. Jackson's heart broke.

"I'll always have enough room in my heart for you." He gathered the boy in his arms. Jimmie fell against Jackson's chest and wailed. "I promised your pa that I would take care of you. You're as dear to me as Tom and Julia."

"Ginny, too?" Jimmie yowled.

"Ginny, too."

That seemed to mollify him and his weeping slowly ceased. He looked up at Jackson. "Is my Pa in Heaven with Jesus?"

Jackson smiled "Yes, he is."

"I should be happy, but I just want my Pa back." He burrowed closer to Jackson.

"Me, too."

★★★

Anna stood over a large pot on the stove. The water was finally coming to a boil. At the table, Jim ground the last of the acorns into powder. It was the only thing Anna could find to dye Flora's dresses black.

As she watched the bubbles rise in the pot, all she could think of was what if the situation was reversed, and the pot being prepared was to drown her in perpetual mourning. She couldn't even fathom all the feelings that would be washing over her if Tom had been murdered. She just knew those feelings would be like suffocating ocean waves during a winter storm. The loss wouldn't just be a husband, but a comforter, provider, friend, and father to her children. Flora's world had been turned inside out and upside up down, never to be put back together the way it was before. All Flora could do was move on from here, but Anna wondered where she would get the strength.

"The powder's ready," Jim announced. He wiped tears from his cheeks with his sleeve. "Do you want me to tell Miss Flora?"

"I'll do it," Anna wiped her hands on her apron. "Could you keep an eye out for General Jackson? He went to find Jimmie and hasn't returned yet. It'll be dark soon, and I'm getting worried."

"I will," Jim assured her. He crossed to the stove and stirred the powder into the water.

Anna wearily climbed the stairs. She peeked into the nursery. The girls were playing quietly. She hurried from the doorway before they saw her. They were too young to understand the tragedy that had befallen the house. She envied them their innocence.

Flora's trunk was emptied and bright splashes of red, green, blue, violet, plaid, and flowered prints created a colorful bedspread. Flora sat on the floor with one of Stuart's calico shirts in her hands.

Anna flew to her side. "Darling!"

Flora buried her face in the shirt. "How will I live without him? He was my world."

Anna pulled her close and let her cry.

"Do you know what's so ironic?" Flora whispered through her tears.

"What?"

She plucked at the hem of dress behind her. "Jeb loved me in bright colors and used to chastise me not to wear black." She smiled at the memory.

"Then don't dye the dresses."

Flora stared at Anna, a scandalous look on her face. "I couldn't do that. It would be disrespectful to his memory." Tears flowed freely. "Oh, Anna, I don't know how I go on from here. I'm estranged from my family, and we don't have any money saved. I guess I could live with my brother-in-law."

Anna hushed her fears. "You don't have to think about that right now."

"I can't think of anything else," she tearfully confessed. "I'm so afraid."

"You don't need to be. You'll stay with us."

"I don't want to be a burden."

Anna squeezed Flora's hand. "You could never be a burden. I love you like a sister."

Jim appeared in the doorway. "The dye is ready."

"Jim, do you know if Jimmie came back?" Flora asked.

"General Jackson found him. He's fine," Jim said.

Flora broke out in renewed tears. "I don't even know what to say to him."

Anna untangled herself. "Flora, Jim and I'll take care of the dresses. I want you to rest."

Flora protested, but Anna insisted. She gathered up the dresses and handed them to Jim. "I'll be down in a minute."

Jim closed the door behind him when he left.

★★★

Lee sat alone in his bedroom, staring at Stuart's letter, still unopened, still unread. On the nightstand was a glass of buttermilk. Jeb used to tease him about his favorite cure all. But this was one wound buttermilk couldn't cure, even if he drowned in it.

The grandfather clock in the hall struck two. The house was quiet. He had tried to sleep, but the letter called to him. For the last hour or so, he had just stared at the handwriting on the front of letter. He couldn't avoid it any longer. He turned it over, broke the seal, and opened a small piece of white paper, unlined, with a watermark that read "Delarue & London" within a shield decorated with scrolls.

My dearest Papa,

If you're reading this, it means God has decided my time on His earth has ended. Please do not grieve since I know nothing now but unspeakable joy in the presence of our Savior. I'm with my darling Flora, and I know no more tears. You're the finest man I've ever had the honor to know and even though it was only for a short time, I enjoyed being your son very much.

Please know I'm sorry I had to leave you. Goodbye, my dear papa. I love you.

Your loving son,

Jeb

Lee turned the small piece of paper over. The back was blank except for the blob of red sealing wax. Lee read the letter again then refolded it. He placed the letter in his Bible, blew out the candle, and lay down on the bed. He reached over and lifted the Bible from the nightstand and pressed it against his broken heart. He gave into his grief and wept.

Chapter Thirteen

Two days ago, after a simple funeral officiated by Jackson, Morrison and Pendleton had set out for Lexington. Jackson had decided to bury Stuart in his family plot in the cemetery not far from his house. It was temporary, of course, unless Flora decided to make it permanent. Morrison and Pendleton would deliver the body to Reverend White, Jackson's pastor, who would arrange for the final interment. Fitz had gone along as protection. The round trip should take six days, and Lee knew they would be anxious days for the household.

For Lee, the large house suddenly felt claustrophobic. He purposely avoided the living room where Jeb's coffin had rested. He knew he wasn't the only one avoiding the room. Flora had refused to participate in the funeral arrangements, had refused to do anything but remain in her room and weep.

There was a knock on his bedroom door. Lee looked up from the book he was reading. "Come in."

Longstreet entered. "Do you have a moment?"

"Of course." Lee rose and gestured for Longstreet to sit in the chair he had just vacated. Longstreet fell into it. With no other place to sit, Lee sat on the bed. "What can I do for you, Pete?"

"We need to talk about the meeting Stuart had with General Reynolds." Longstreet adjusted the doily on the arm's chair.

"General Jackson says we'll do so tonight after dinner."

Longstreet grimaced. "I don't know if General Jackson is in the right frame of mind to judge the Yankees' deal."

Lee gave Longstreet a level glance. "What are you trying to tell me?"

Longstreet held up his hands. "I'm not sneaking around…"

"It feels like it," Lee snapped. He reached over and grabbed his Bible from the nightstand. He opened the book to the page that contained the letter and stared down at Stuart's handwriting.

Longstreet stood. "I'm sorry to have bothered you."

Lee closed the Bible. He was being unfair. "Pete, sit down." Longstreet sat stiffly in the chair. "None of this has been easy," he said as a way of apology. "Especially for a man who is accustomed to being in command."

Longstreet relaxed. "I'm just frustrated."

Lee gave a small smile. "You're not the only one. Most of the time, it feels like the walls are closing in, and I don't have the strength to push them back. And how I want to push them back."

Longstreet laughed. "I thought I was the only one who felt like that."

"I think we all feel like that to different degrees," Lee said with a sweep of his hand meant to include all the inhabitants of the house.

The wind blew rain drops against the window. Longstreet shivered. "It's cold in this room."

"I don't mind the cold. It keeps me alert." Lee crossed to the fireplace and stoked the fire. The embers blazed to life. "It should be warm in just a moment."

Longstreet smiled his thanks. "I wanted to talk to you. Actually, I've wanted to talk to you since Atlanta fell." He fell silent and fiddled with the doily.

"About what?" Lee prompted. Longstreet started to speak but stopped and shook his head. Lee gave Longstreet an encouraging smile. "We're friends, Pete. At least I think we are. You can tell me what's bothering you."

When Longstreet looked at Lee, his eyes were moist. "I don't know how you did it. I don't know how you made the decisions you made, came up with the strategies you did so quickly, and fought so successfully."

"Well, I had your strength, General Jackson's fearlessness, and General Stuart's cavalry." He gave a small chuckle. "You all made my job very easy."

Longstreet held up his hand. "No, that's not true. We all looked to you."

"And I looked to you." Lee smiled. "You were my war horse. Jackson, my right arm. Jeb, my eyes and ears. Commanding isn't a solitary task. I didn't have to have all the answers. I listened to everything I was told and decided accordingly."

Longstreet rose and crossed to the window. "Ever since the Peninsula campaign, I wanted independent command. And I was willing to do anything to get it."

"Oh, I knew that."

"You did?" A shocked Longstreet asked the window.

"Subtlety is not one of your virtues, Pete."

Longstreet still gazed out the window. "I was slow in obeying your orders to return from the Suffolk region because I didn't want to come back. I felt like I was drowning in your shadow."

Lee went over to the fireplace and poked at the logs. "How did you find independent command?"

"Very lonely. I had no war horse, no right arm, and no eyes and ears." Longstreet was rueful. He left the window and sat down. "I did have General Bragg though. He was a rock. But I was stubborn and hard to move off of my ideas. I think my stubbornness cost me Atlanta."

"Tell me why you think that." Lee gave the logs a final poke and returned to the bed.

Longstreet recounted the moment when Thomas had marched away and Forrest had counseled attack. And how he had hesitated, and, by morning, Sherman had pulled back across the Chattahoochee. "If only I had attacked, I could have won the war."

"And you've been tormenting yourself ever since." Lee was compassionate. "The war was lost on many fronts and not just along the Chattahoochee."

Longstreet remained unconvinced. "You wouldn't have hesitated."

"You don't know that."

"Well, Jackson wouldn't have."

Lee laughed. "No, he probably wouldn't have. But sometimes it was my job to restrain all that aggression."

"I guess." Longstreet was unconvinced.

"Pete, we lost our independence because we were out manned and out supplied," Lee said sternly. "I don't know what happened in your army at the end, but mine dissolved out from underneath me."

Longstreet let out a deep sigh. "We were just overwhelmed. I couldn't ask the men to sacrifice any more."

Lee understood that sentiment. "Is that a decision you can live with for the rest of your life?"

"It's going to have to be." Longstreet shifted in his chair.

There was a loud rap on the door. "Grandpa!"

"Come in, Jimmie."

The door flew open and Jimmie and Rebel entered on the run. Jimmie hurled himself on the bed. Lee gave the boy's stomach a tickle. Jimmie collapsed in laughter and rolled about. Rebel jumped up on the bed next to his young master and waited patiently for his turn to be tickled. Jimmie sat up, gasping for breath. "Hey, General Longstreet."

"Hi, Jimmie," Longstreet said.

"Jim says dinner's ready. General Johnston is already at the table. Now, if you'll excuse me, I need to tell ole Stonewall." With that, Jimmie jumped off the bed and dashed out of the room.

Longstreet pointed at the retreating figure. "Is it me or when he smiles, he's the mirror image of his father."

"He is that. Are you ready for dinner?" Lee asked. He grabbed his uniform jacket and headed toward the dining room.

★★★

Once more the dishes had been cleared away and the generals sat around the dining room table ready to discuss their futures. Forrest sat in Stuart's usual place. It unnerved Lee to see him there. By rank and experience, Forrest was the natural successor to Stuart, but in his grief, Lee only saw him as an interloper. He knew he was being unreasonable, but tonight, he couldn't help it.

Jackson withdrew a sheet of paper from his breast pocket. "I know you've heard the terms. I have spoken of them briefly and General Forrest more so."

"May I see them?" Johnston pointed at the paper in Jackson's hand.

"Of course," Jackson said.

Johnston read the paper. When he finished, he smiled. "It seems to me that if we surrender, we're almost guaranteed an acquittal. Robert, we know most of these men. They wouldn't find us guilty unless they were presented with strong evidence. Plus, we can cross examine any witness the Yankees put on the stand. We should see this for what it is: a way out."

"But General Forrest will have to surrender and stand trial for his extra-curricular activity in Georgia," Lee said. He glanced over at Forrest, but the cavalry leader didn't seem to be interested in the conversation. He had already made it perfectly clear that he wouldn't surrender. Perhaps he didn't see the need to repeat himself.

"Maybe we can negotiate that point," Johnston suggested. He laid the paper on the table.

"I don't think we're in a position to negotiate." Longstreet pointed at the paper. "General Reynolds has been very generous. Those are good terms."

Lee put his elbows on the table and leaned forward. "I don't think the terms are the issue we should be discussing."

"Then what should we be discussing," Longstreet interrupted angrily.

Lee exhaled loudly. "We need to be discussing the election." He sat back in his chair. "From what I can discern from the newspapers Fitz brings us, Hamlin's motive for offering us this deal was to stop McClellan from using our arrest and escape to gain political points. After the election, Hamlin loses his incentive to retry us."

"Then we should surrender right away," Johnston said.

"What happens if we're in prison on Election Day?" Lee asked.

Johnston dropped his head into his hands.

"I can't live trapped here anymore," Longstreet lamented. "If McClellan wins, we'll have to wait five months to find out if he'll honor his pledge to overturn our sentences. I can't do it."

"You're free to leave," Forrest said to Longstreet. "No one here will stop you. I'll even escort you to Richmond if you want. Shave off that beard and the chances are pretty good them Yankees won't even recognize you." Longstreet glared at Forrest. "I'll take you right now if you want." He stood. "Let's go." He waited.

"Sit down," Longstreet said.

Forrest sat down. He threw up his hands. "You know what? I'll just go. You can tell the Yankees that after I heard the terms, I skedaddled back to Tennessee."

Johnston raised his head. "We could try that."

Lee disagreed. "I couldn't think of a more ungracious way to thank General Forrest for all he has done for us. As far as I'm concerned, he's earned our friendship and loyalty."

"You, sir, are a gentleman," Forrest said to Lee with a smile.

Lee turned toward Jackson. A chill raced down his spine. Jackson's face was thunderous. "General Jackson?"

"They murdered him." Jackson's voice was like a lash. "They shot him in the back like cowards. They have showed us who they are. I'll never trust them again."

Lee had heard Jackson angry and frustrated before, but never had he heard hate in his Second Corps Commander's voice. But he heard it now and it frightened him.

"If you'll excuse me." Jackson pushed back his chair and left the room. A few seconds later, the front door opened and shut.

"Perhaps it was too soon to discuss what to do," Lee said. "Jeb's death is still a raw wound."

Forrest left the generals still discussing their options and walked down the hall. He stopped when he reached the front door. He didn't like the way the conversation had gone. There didn't seem to be any fight in any of the generals. They were passive and quite satisfied to leave their fate in the hands of others. The only one who possessed any fire was Jackson. Forrest wondered if he could stoke that fire into a fight. Well, standing on this side of the door wasn't going to get him what he wanted. He stiffened his spine and walked out onto the porch. Jackson was there, leaning against the rail and looking out into the yard. Forrest stepped to the rail.

"If we want to be free, we're going to have to fight," Jackson said as soon as Forrest reached his side.

Forrest smiled. "When?"

"Can you keep us safe until spring?"

"Spring!" Forrest groaned. "I think it's a bad idea to wait. We need to go now."

"No, the Yankees will be expecting us to do just that. When we attack, we have to catch them by complete surprise." Jackson turned and rested his back against the rail. "Besides General Lee hasn't come to the realization that we're going to have to fight, and we're going to need him."

Forrest didn't like the fact that Jackson was going to yield any decision to Lee. He didn't believe Lee a coward, but Lee had shown very little aggression since his rescue. "How long do you think it'll take him to come to that realization?"

"I think he already knows. But he'll wait first for the election then the inauguration. When McClellan reneges, and McClellan will, he'll be ready."

Forrest absorbed the news without a word.

"How many men do you need to protect Clover Hill?" Jackson asked.

Forrest did some quick calculations. "One hundred."

Jackson folded his arms across his chest. "Can it be less?"

"No," Forrest hissed. "You asked, and I gave you the right answer."

Jackson bit his upper lip and thought. "Campfires in the winter will be a signal fire alerting the Yankees to our presence."

A cool breeze blew. Forrest shivered. "We have minimum men located near the house. Most of the pickets are situated in the farmhouses and the small towns surrounding the plantation. The men are hidden in plain sight. If the Yankees were to fall on us, they would have to come down the roads that go through those towns and past those farmhouses. We would receive word well in advance."

Jackson smiled. "Whose idea was that?"

"Stuart's originally, but I changed it a mite."

"Impressive," Jackson acknowledged. "Can you feed them?"

Forrest hesitated. "So far we have been able to, but spring's a long time away."

"We're in the Breadbasket of Virginia. If you ask, you'll find the people of the Valley to be quite generous."

"Maybe, but it would be more advantageous if you do the asking."

Jackson nodded in agreement. "One hundred men. Ask for volunteers. Send the rest of the men home."

Sending the men home made no sense to Forrest. Why send the army out of your reach? "How will we get the men back?"

Jackson smiled. "They'll come when General Lee calls."

"I'll get right on it." Forrest headed down the steps.

117

Chapter Fourteen

Sherman's Office
War Department
October 19, 1865

Reynolds slumped in a chair and rubbed a tired hand over his mouth. The journey from Manassas had been interminable. The meeting with the distraught Jackson still haunted him. He couldn't believe that Jackson had actually pointed a gun at him! He was pretty sure Jackson wouldn't have fired, but the act revealed the level of betrayal and anguish the Confederates were feeling. The careful deal Sherman had crafted, a deal meant to assuage Southern fear about surrendering, had been destroyed by a distraught private who decided to avenge the death of his older brother at Shippack Creek.

Camp had barely broken when Sheridan lobbied to have the prisoner released from his bounds. Reynolds listened to Sheridan jabber for an hour before shutting him down and ordering him never to broach the subject again.

Upon their return, Reynolds made a full report to Sherman. The flag of truce had been shattered, Stuart was dead, and Jackson was filled with grief and rage. The last part alarmed Sherman. He put the city on alert, expecting Jackson to take his rage out on the capital. Troops scattered around the city were reassigned to the southwest trenches to protect the capital from an attack via Centreville.

All through the night, the sound of marching feet and rumbling artillery bounced between the buildings. Helpless citizens gathered on street corners and gossiped about what it all meant. Were they at war again? Concerned politicians sent an avalanche of messages to the War Department demanding Sherman meet the impending threat at

Centreville, at Bull Run Creek, or in the Valley. Anywhere but the capital. An angry Stanton railed against Reynolds for failing to bring the Confederates in when he had them in his grasp at Manassas. He demanded Sherman cashier Reynolds and send him home to Pennsylvania in disgrace. The election hung in the balance and such incompetence could not be tolerated.

Sherman ignored the citizens, threw away the politicians' messages, and endured Stanton's tantrums, but Reynolds could see the strain was beginning to tell. Seven days had passed – seven days of sleep-robbing tension.

"So?" Sherman questioned impatiently.

Reynolds sat up. "Nothing today." Sherman's fist pounded his desk. "But it's only been a week." Reynolds was conciliatory.

"There's no more time!" Sherman barked in a display of temper.

"Has President Hamlin changed his mind about the agreement?" Reynolds asked alarmed. What if all he had done so far had come to naught?

Sherman leaned back in his chair. "With the capital on full alert and the newspapers disparaging Hamlin's failures to capture the fugitives day after day, why should he continue to be generous?"

Reynolds threw up his hands in disgust.

Sherman cleared his throat. "One more thing. Sheridan has been nagging me about the soldier who shot Stuart. He doesn't believe the man deserves a court martial."

"That's because Sheridan doesn't have any morals." Reynolds was livid at Sheridan for going behind his back.

Sherman sat up. "Well, I do have morals and I agree with him. The man shot a fugitive. Most think he was doing his job." Reynolds dropped his head. "John, you're not crazy like Don Quixote, but all the same, you're tilting at windmills. If the Rebs had taken our offer at Manassas, you could have shepherded them out of Washington Arsenal and back to Lexington or wherever they wanted to go by the end of the week. Face it, there's nothing more you can do."

Reynolds' laugh was bitter. "I can always vote for McClellan."

Sherman picked up a pencil and twirled it between his fingers. "McClellan won't be able to withstand Stevens, Sumner, and the rest of the Radicals. He's never been able to withstand pressure in his life and you know it. They'll force him to renege on his campaign promise to see justice done. The war hasn't even been over for six months. So don't be confusing McClellan's election as a mandate for forgiveness and reconciliation toward the South. All it means is that Stanton overplayed his hand, and Hamlin will be the one to pay the price."

Reynolds was tiring of the conversation. "How long does General Jackson have to answer?"

"Time is up. I can't keep the city on alert any longer." Sherman dropped the pencil on the desk. "Either we get an answer by tonight, or it won't matter anymore."

"Understood." Reynolds waved a hand and left the office.

McClellan's Home
Trenton, New Jersey
November 7, 1865

Telegraph wires snaked through the study, making it difficult for McClellan to pace the room. The first election results had brought nothing but bad news, stretching McClellan's nerves to the breaking point. Hamlin had won his home state of Maine before capturing the rest of the New England states. That meant McClellan was 30 electoral votes behind, and the night had just begun.

He had already started the election in a hole the depth of a grave. Two weeks before the election, southern legislatures had defied the Radicals by refusing to ratify the 14th and 15th Amendments. The 15th Amendment, giving the vote to the former slaves, was the linchpin of the Radicals' design to dominate the affairs of state for decades. Within hours, Thaddeus Stephens forced the Reconstruction Act through the House, and Charles Sumner whipped up the necessary votes for passage in the Senate. Before the sun set, Hamlin signed the bill. The new law effectively dissolved the Confederacy and divided it into military districts. Soldiers were stripped of their votes. Any person who supported the rebellion, whether on the battlefield or at home, was denied due process under the law. That meant no legal rights and no recourse through the courts. The South was at the mercy of whatever master the Radicals placed over it.

The state legislatures were dismissed and in their place ruled military administrators. Sherman recalled troops from the West to occupy southern cities. State treasuries were flung open so that carpetbaggers, scalawags, and agents of the Freedman Bureau could plunder what wealth remained.

Today, only former slaves, Union soldiers, and those vultures that had left the North at the war's conclusion to pick clean the South's bones were able to cast a vote for president. To guarantee that the former slaves obeyed their new master, the Freedman Bureau and the Union League bullied, bribed, and used physical coercion to deliver the vote to Hamlin and the Republican ticket. By the time the polls closed at sunset, the Radicals would control all aspects of southern life right down to the county tax collector.

"New York's coming in now," Henry Bicknell announced. The nervous small talk that filled the room ceased. If Hamlin won New York and the state's thirty-three electoral votes, then the election was over. All that would be left was the size of the defeat.

The telegraph machine chattered excitedly, almost as if it was proclaiming good news. McClellan fought back his anticipation. The machine had chattered the same way when he lost Connecticut and Rhode Island.

The operator slowly read the long strip of paper.

"If we lose New York, is there any way I can win?" McClellan asked.

"I don't believe you've lost New York," Bicknell replied.

"You didn't believe I would lose New Hampshire either." The words came out sharper than he had intended.

The operator wrote quickly on a piece of foolscap and held it up in the air. "General."

McClellan took a step forward and tripped over a wire. "There are too many wires in this room!" He shouted. He didn't apologize for his rudeness. If he did so every time he gave in to his nerves, he would spend the night apologizing. He was sure Bicknell understood and didn't really care if the operator and the rest of the well wishers, party bigwigs, and news reporters gathered in the room understood or not.

He took the paper and held it in a tight fist. Here it was – his moment of truth. He shouldn't be worried. After all, it was his destiny to save this country. God had spoken this truth to him in so many ways. All he had to do was open the paper to confirm what he believed in his heart to be true.

He couldn't do it. He held the paper out to Bicknell, who unfolded it and read it quickly. A smile erupted on Bicknell's face. McClellan felt a surge of overpowering happiness. He had won his first state.

The telegraph machine began to click and clack. The operator gathered the tape and began to transcribe them.

"Who is it this time?" McClellan demanded. He was losing patience with the operator's dawdling. Bicknell had assured him that the operator was quick and accurate, but McClellan had yet to see any evidence of it. "Who? Who?" He shouted.

Annoyed, the operator glanced up from the tape filled with dashes and dots and glared at McClellan. "New Jersey."

McClellan flung up his hands in disappointment. He had put New Jersey's electoral votes in the win column early this morning.

The next hour saw Maryland and Delaware fall into his column, while Hamlin claimed the Carolinas and Florida.

James entered the room bearing a large silver tray. "I brought coffee and sandwiches." He set the tray on the low table. "Is there anything else I can get you."

"You can get me Pennsylvania," McClellan snapped, watching his guests gobble down the food and empty the coffee pot.

"Will you be satisfied with Georgia?" Bicknell asked. "And it's nine electoral votes?"

"Georgia!" McClellan exclaimed. Miracles of miracles! He had won a southern state. What further proof did he need that winning the election was his destiny?

The operator handed Bicknell another slip of paper. "We lost Tennessee."

McClellan's euphoria evaporated. He crossed to the table and shook the coffee pot. He heard liquid sloshing about. He quickly poured himself a cup of coffee and took a sip. It was unsatisfying. He set the cup down.

The machine went still. Pennsylvania, Ohio, Michigan, Indiana, and Illinois. Their polls closed hours ago, but no word had been heard from the party chairmen supervising the vote count. McClellan needed these states to counterbalance a defeat in the South. Last night, his chairmen assured him that he would win, but the inactivity of the telegraph key seemed to be writing a different story.

McClellan paced the room, tripped over wires, and drank unsatisfying cup after cup of coffee. Bicknell waited by the machine, his fingers drumming on the table. The operator yawned from boredom. The wellwishers kept up a steady stream of babble that drove McClellan up the wall. He finally ordered them out of the study and closed the door behind him. He fell against the door in relief and reveled in the calm.

The sudden clacking of the machine caused him to jump in surprise. The key clicked and clacked. Pennsylvania? No, it was Ohio, and he had won the state. Indiana and Illinois followed within minutes. The hour concluded with another victory in the South. He had won Alabama. He smiled triumphantly. The Radicals' grip on the former Confederacy wasn't as absolute as they believed.

Behind the desk, Bicknell was adding up the electoral votes. "Only thirty-one to go."

Midnight came and went and Hamlin closed the gap. In quick succession, Mississippi, Louisiana, Arkansas, Missouri, and Iowa fell into the Republican's column.

McClellan breathed easier when the results came in from Michigan, Wisconsin, and Minnesota. He won two and lost one, but moved twelve votes closer to claiming the prize.

The machine began to chatter. "It's Pennsylvania," the operator announced.

Here it was. The moment of truth. If he won Pennsylvania, he won the election. The good news was that he no longer needed Pennsylvania to win. Any combination of the remaining states could deliver the election into his hands.

Bicknell read the results. Inscrutable was not a word McClellan would usually employ to describe the little man, but right now Bicknell was a sphinx.

"Well?" McClellan questioned.

"Mr. President, you've won Pennsylvania."

McClellan's heart did a flip, then another. "Did you say Mr. President?"

"I did indeed." He handed the slip of paper to McClellan.

Pennsylvania – McClellan was all it said. Two simple words that erased the stink of the jail cell and the sting of his enemy's scorn. His exile had ended with a laurel wreath upon his head. He may be a mere mortal, but tonight, Heaven had come to earth and graced him with supernatural power. He would not betray the trust God had placed in him. He would restore the Union, bind up the divisions that had caused the war, and bring healing to the weary nation.

He smiled at Bicknell. "Would it be greedy if I still want to win the western states too?"

★ ★ ★

Four days later, Fitz Lee galloped up the driveway. He threw himself off his mare, and took the steps three at a time. A quick knock to announce his presence, and then he opened the door and entered the living room. The only one present was General Johnston.

"General Lee," Johnston said. "What's the matter?"

Fitz held up a newspaper. "Election results."

"Let me get the others. They should hear it also." Johnston strode toward the hall. He turned back to Fitz. "Was it McClellan?"

Fitz smiled and nodded.

Chapter Fifteen

Winter winds brought changes to the household. Sandie Pendleton had been the first to leave. When he returned to Lexington to deliver Stuart's body to Reverend White, he had discovered that his wife was expecting a baby, and she had kept the pregnancy a secret from him. He was torn between his duty to his wife and his duty to Jackson and wrestled between the two all night. As dawn was breaking, he settled on a compromise. He would stay in Lexington for two weeks and then return to Clover Hill. The baby wasn't due until after the first of the year. Hopefully, by then, everything would be settled and Jackson would be free. He wrote Jackson a note of explanation and gave it to Morrison to deliver.

Jackson read the letter, sat down, and wrote a letter of his own. He ordered Pendleton to remain by his wife's side. He never believed his aides should have been mixed up in this mess. It was long past time for the young men to get on with their lives. He knew the letter would cut Pendleton to the quick, but the hurt would dissipate with time. In the meantime, Pendleton would be safe from arrest or worse.

Next, Jackson practically bullied Smith into resuming his studies at Union Seminary in Richmond. Smith didn't want to go, listed a thousand reasons why he should stay, but in the end, Jackson won the argument.

"Mr. Smith, you have a great call on your life. One I wish I had." Jackson stood with Smith on the porch, waiting for Jim to bring Smith's mare around.

"I've never deserted your side in the middle of a fight," Smith pleaded. "I don't want to do so now."

Jackson's smile was compassionate. "You're not."

"Well, Joe thinks there will be a fight in the spring. I'll come back then," Smith said firmly.

Jackson shook his head. "No. I want you to stay in school."

Smith started to protest, but Jackson cut him off. "The one thing you can do for me is to pursue the call God has placed on your life."

Jim came around the house, leading the mare. Smith's shoulders slumped in defeat. He walked down the steps.

Jim handed over the reins. "I packed enough food to last until you get to Hoge's house."

"Thank you."

Jackson came down the steps.

Smith started to swing up in the saddle, but stopped. For a moment, Jackson thought his aide had finally come to the realization that the war was over, and he no longer had the authority to order him to return to Richmond.

He faced Jackson. Tears fell from his eyes. "I'll make you proud of me." His voice wavered.

Jackson swallowed back his own tears. "Jimmie, I've always been proud of you."

Doctor McGuire was the next to leave. With Lee recovered and the baby healthy, McGuire paced the house in boredom. One night, after dinner, he announced that he would be leaving by week's end. He was going to Staunton to open his long delayed medical practice. Jackson took solace in the fact that McGuire would be close by in case one of the children came down with a fever. Jackson reluctantly waved goodbye and didn't go back into the house until McGuire disappeared around the bend.

That left only Morrison, but his brother-in-law stubbornly refused to return to North Carolina to rebuild Cottage Home.

"Everyone else is deserting you. I'm not going to." Morrison was defiant.

Jackson recognized the statement as the opening salvo of a tough skirmish. He settled back on the couch. "Sandie and Smith didn't desert me. They're just getting on with their lives. Something you should be doing." He pointed his finger at the obstinate young man.

Morrison refused.

"So, what are you going to do?" Jackson demanded. "Just hang out here this winter, stare down the driveway, and pray the Yankees don't come? Or are you going to make like Forrest and pray they do. I can think of a better use of your time." Jackson gave the young man his most withering stare. In the past, it had reduced generals to stuttering, quivering messes, but it failed to work its special power on his brother-in-law.

"It's my time," Morrison replied. Then he smiled. "Besides, in the spring, you're going to need me."

"Why is that?" Jackson asked, knowing perfectly well what Morrison was referring to.

Morrison gave another small smile. "Because I think you've come to the same conclusion General Stuart had. We're going to have to fight to win our freedom."

Jackson shook his head. "It's not your fight. It never has been."

There came a clatter from the hallway. Jimmie dashed by the living room with Rebel in hot pursuit. The front door opened before slamming closed again.

"That's where you're wrong," Morrison continued once silence reigned in the house again. "There are not yours and my fights. You're in trouble and need your family around you. I'm your brother. Let me help you."

Jackson rose and walked over to the window. Jimmie had piled leaves high in the yard, and he and Rebel were running through the pile, scattering leaves over the lawn again. "Alright, Joe, you can stay."

"General Jackson, I don't need your permission."

He had never heard such steel in Morrison's voice before. He whirled and faced his brother-in-law. This wasn't the star-struck teenage boy Jackson had met while courting Anna, or the naïve young cadet at VMI before the war. Here was a man well able to make his own decisions. "No, you don't need my permission. Sandie didn't need it to leave; and you don't need it stay."

"I guess it's too much to ask for you to be glad I'm staying," Morrison said.

Jackson turned back to the window. "No, it's not too much at all."

★ ★ ★

Snow fell during the second week of December. Just a dusting, but it was enough to make Jimmie positively giddy with joy. Anna insisted he eat breakfast before venturing outside, and he danced in his chair while he gobbled down his oats. Finally, he ate enough to be dismissed. Hat, coat, and mittens on, he dashed outside. He made a few small snowballs and plucked a can out of the trash to use for target practice.

Lee sat in the swing chair and cheered the little boy on. After an hour, Jimmie ran over to the porch. "Hey, Grandpa!" He flashed Lee a sunny smile. "Do you think Traveller can go for a gallop today?"

"I was thinking of taking Traveller out for a gallop. I was going to wait until the snow melted."

Jimmie huffed in disappointment. "How long do you think that'll take?"

Lee searched the sky. The sun was up, and he could feel the air warming. "Not long."

The little boy brightened. "Do you think I can ride with you?"

"I think that would be a wonderful idea."

Jimmie came up the steps and sat down next to Lee. His nose was running. Lee took out his handkerchief and held it over Jimmie's nose. "Blow!" He ordered. Jimmie obeyed. "You're a good boy," Lee praised.

Jimmie gave Lee a sideway glance. "You know what I'd like to do?"

Lee hoped it wasn't fishing. He had no desire to sit on a cold creek bank. "What?" He hoped the little boy didn't see his grimace.

"Learn how to ride. So I can go ridin' by myself."

"Jimmie," Lee scolded, "you've ridden by yourself."

"But not like you ride Traveller, or Pa used to ride 'Turion. I can just walk in a circle if someone is leading the horse." He folded his arms across his chest.

"I understand your frustration," Lee said sympathetically. "But we don't have a pony for you to learn on."

Jimmie smiled again. "Little Sorrel is almost a pony."

"Little Sorrel is General Jackson's horse."

"Do you think ole Stonewall will let me ride him?"

"I don't know. Why don't we ask him?"

Jimmie leapt from the chair and dashed to the door. He threw it open and hollered down the hall. "Ole Stonewall, can you come here!" He turned to Lee, flashed a smile then scrunched his shoulders in excitement.

Lee heard Jackson come down the hall. "Jimmie, there's no need to holler. We don't live in a barn. You come inside and find me if you want me."

"Sorry," Jimmie blurted out, but Lee could tell he wasn't sorry.

"Now what can I do for you." Jackson sidestepped and allowed Rebel to pass. The puppy ran down the porch and jumped in the swing next to Lee.

"Grandpa and I want to ask you somethin."

Jackson closed the door behind him and crossed to the swing. Rebel held up his paw. Jackson gave him a scratch behind the ears. "What can I do for you?"

"I want to learn how to ride," Jimmie explained quickly. "But Grandpa says we don't have a pony. But Little Sorrel's a pony."

"I should think Little Sorrel would be insulted to be considered a pony. After all, he's a brave war horse."

Jimmie laughed. "No he's not. King Philip is a war horse. That's what General Forrest says."

Jackson shivered. "What do you think, Grandpa?"

Jimmie turned large pleading eyes on Lee.

"I think Little Sorrel is gentle enough. We could probably jury rig one of Jeb's saddles to fit."

Jackson rubbed his arms to warm them. "I think it's a fine idea."

Jimmie tugged on Lee's hand. "Let's go, Grandpa."

"Yes, let's go, Grandpa," Jackson said with a laugh. "I'm going back inside. How about you, Rebel? The fire's warm."

Rebel declined and ran ahead of Lee and Jimmie as they headed toward the back of the house and the corral.

Chapter Sixteen

The first riding lesson had been a crowning success. Not only did Jimmie ride Little Sorrel by himself, but the lesson had lured Johnston from the little house. He stood next to Lee and offered up helpful suggestions and compliments. Lee was only too happy to let him to do so. Since the rescue, Johnston had walked about as if the weight of the world was on his shoulders. In the hour that Jimmie rode circles around the corral, that weight had lifted and Johnston's laughter filled the air. Anna called them into lunch, and Johnston was still laughing as he followed Lee and Jimmie into the house.

Anna had just set a bowl of soup in front of Lee when the back door burst open and Forrest entered with some papers in his hand.

"General Forrest, how are you this fine afternoon?" Johnston spread a napkin in his lap.

"Guess what, General Forrest," Jimmie piped. "Grandpa and General Johnston are teaching me how to ride."

"That's right nice, sonny," Forrest said. He waved the papers at Anna. "Mrs. Jackson, I can't bear any more of these lists. I ain't Santee Claus."

Jimmie dropped his spoon. His head swiveled toward Forrest. "Do you know Santa Claus, General Forrest?"

Anna gave Forrest a small shove on the back. "Let's discuss your concerns in the living room."

"Do you, General Forrest?" Jimmie called. "Do you think he knows?" He asked Lee and Johnston.

Johnston quickly returned the conversation to horses.

Anna and Forrest burst in on Jackson, who was sitting on the couch reading his Bible. He hastily closed the book.

"You need to be more careful," Anna scolded Forrest.

"What's going on?" Jackson asked.

"Nothing, dear," Anna said sweetly.

It didn't look like nothing. Jackson stood, prepared to defend his wife from Forrest.

"You're sending me lists." Forrest shook the papers at Anna. "Lists of presents to buy for you."

Anna gave Forrest a smile. "That's because you're the only one for the job."

Forrest scoffed. "Don't sweet talk me, little lady."

Jackson huffed in exasperation. "Someone better tell me what's going on."

Anna patted Jackson on the chest. "General Forrest and I are just having a little disagreement."

"I can see that." He didn't know if he should be angry or even who he should be angry at for that matter. "What about?"

Now Forrest shook the papers at Jackson. "Your wife has mistaken me for Santee Claus."

"General Forrest, please," Anna reproved. "There are little ears in this house that hear more than they should."

"I don't have time to protect you and do your shoppin'."

Jackson glanced at his wife, but she didn't seem the least bit intimidated by Forrest's bluster. Instead, she gave Forrest a smile meant to charm him. "Flora and I just want to make sure the children receive some presents."

Forrest dealt six pieces of paper into Jackson's hand. Jackson glanced at them. They were filled with lists of toys, clothing, and other presents. "These ain't some presents. I would need two sleighs to haul 'em all back."

Jackson had to agree with Forrest. He was a cavalry leader, not one of Santa's elves. "Anna, maybe it's too much to ask General Forrest to go on a shopping spree."

Forrest nodded in agreement.

"A few gifts are hardly a shopping spree," Anna laughed. Jackson stared at his wife in disbelief. She was behaving like a coquette. "I just want the children to have a wonderful Christmas." She gave Forrest another sweet smile.

Jackson watched as Forrest wavered. "I can probably have my men pick up a few items for the kiddies. But just the kiddies," he emphasized.

"Oh, General Forrest, I don't know how to thank you," she flirted like a belle with a beau.

Forrest snatched the lists from Jackson and thrust them at Anna. "Just whittle it down some."

Anna plucked the papers from Forrest's hand. "Thank you so much." She kissed his cheek.

He grunted and departed via the front door. Anna turned toward Jackson and flashed him a triumphant smile.

★ ★ ★

Jim was convinced there was a turkey for Christmas dinner in the woods, so he rousted Morrison from a nice warm bed and pleasant dreams and shoved him out the door toward the tree line. Morrison had only gone a few hundred feet when he was hailed. It was Longstreet.

"Thanks for coming with me," Morrison said. It was the first words that had passed between them in about an hour.

"Glad to get out of the house," Longstreet remarked. "Have you actually seen a turkey in these woods?"

Morrison nodded. "About another hour in, Rebel scared up a rafter when Jimmie and I were hiking through the woods."

Longstreet smiled. "Energetic little boy with an energetic puppy."

"A puppy that lives constantly underfoot," Morrison complained. "I'm surprised General Jackson hasn't insisted on some type of obedience training." He blew out his breath. White puffs floated into the air. "Anyway, I didn't have my rifle with me, otherwise we would have had a feast that night. My mistake was telling Jim." He stopped, squatted down, and searched the ground for tracks.

Longstreet leaned against a nearby tree. "I'm going to ask you a question, and I hope you'll answer truthfully."

Morrison stood. "Of course I will. Well, if I know the answer," he hastily qualified.

"I've tried to let this go, especially after Stuart's death, but I just can't." Longstreet shoved his hands in his coat's pockets. "Why is it that Stuart managed to get his family and your brother-in-law's family safely out of Richmond, but not mine?"

There was an accusation in Longstreet's voice that Morrison didn't care for. He had heard it before in Longstreet's many laments to Johnston. Morrison still abode with Longstreet and Johnston in the little house and the walls were paper thin. Nothing Longstreet or Johnston said remained between them. Longstreet had been unhappy since the day he had arrived. At first, he had taken that frustration out on Stuart. After Stuart's death, his frustration had been turned on Jackson. Morrison never confronted Longstreet over his unfair attacks. To do so would be to admit that he had overhead conversations that weren't meant for him. "What did General Stuart say?" Morrison parried.

"That by time he found out about my arrest, it was too late," Longstreet said angrily.

"But you don't believe that." Morrison was careful to keep his voice neutral.

Longstreet walked away. "I just never felt like I was receiving a straight answer."

Morrison caught up to Longstreet. "Flora and the children weren't in Richmond when the arrests happened. They were in Perkinsville. And it wasn't General Stuart who got Anna out of Richmond, it was me."

Longstreet was thunderstruck. "Why didn't Stuart just tell me that?"

Morrison thought back to the days of wandering after Jackson had been arrested. Wasted days before Stuart decided on a course of action. Valuable time had been lost by then. The Yankees had Lee's family under surveillance as well as Lydia Johnston in the hopes that they could capture Stuart if he tried to spirit the families out of Richmond. "Because he felt like he should have known the families would be in some danger. But it wouldn't have mattered anyway. By time we found out that you had been imprisoned, the Yankees were already keeping a close eye on your family."

Longstreet gestured forward. "If you're going to bag a turkey, we need to keep moving." He started walking. Morrison hurried to keep up.

They walked along in silence.

"I'm sorry you're so unhappy," Morrison finally said.

Longstreet shook his head. "I'm not unhappy. I'm just frustrated. I have no control and no say in my life. It makes me feel trapped."

Morrison shifted the rifle into the other arm before jumping a gully that had appeared in the weeds. Longstreet made the leap and continued to walk.

Morrison wanted to slap some sense into Longstreet. "You're alive. That's more than General Stuart."

Longstreet stopped short. "General Stuart was my friend long before you joined General Jackson's staff. So don't you dare try to make it seem like I don't care what happened to him."

Morrison fired up. "Then try to be grateful at least. You're not trapped; you're alive. Every day that follows your rescue is a gift. Stuart could have gathered up his family and just kept going. But he didn't. Because he was your friend. And your constant bellyaching is hard to take because it smacks of ingratitude for all he did for you." He stalked off.

"Wait up!" Longstreet called.

Morrison slowed down but didn't stop. He could hear Longstreet jogging toward him. When Longstreet reached his side, Morrison didn't let up. "And Forrest did the same, and you know how you repaid him. You tried to convince him to give himself up so you could go free."

"You can stop upbraiding me now." Morrison glanced up at Longstreet, but Longstreet's face revealed nothing about what he was thinking. "I've been a cad. General Johnston has been trying to tell me the same thing for a long time."

Morrison came upon another gully. He jumped over it and waited for Longstreet to do the same. But Longstreet just stood on the other side and stared at Morrison.

"Are you coming?" Morrison questioned.

"You would think as a commanding general of two armies you would be able to exercise some control over the events that are happening. But you don't. They just unfold and you react, hoping that sooner or later what you're doing will have some kind of effect on those events. Since the surrender, I've been shuttled from house to house to house."

"For your safety!" Morrison practically shouted.

"You're right." Longstreet was contrite. "But I couldn't see it that way. It was just another situation where I wasn't in control. And the longer we stayed here, the angrier I became and the more trapped I felt. And when you feel trapped, all you care about is escape. The terms were the escape; Forrest was the obstacle. Remove the obstacle and be free. Not making an excuse for my behavior. Just explaining it. But I am sorry."

Morrison held out his hand and helped Longstreet across the gully. "I didn't have to fight to leave. I had to fight to stay. General Jackson wanted to send me home for my own good. But my place is here."

Longstreet chuckled. "We're a contradiction in terms."

"To say the least," Morrison agreed with a laugh.

They tramped along in silence once more.

"You're right," Longstreet said. "McClellan won. That's only good news for us. We could be free by summer."

Morrison wondered if he should tell Longstreet of Jackson's belief that they would have to fight for their freedom. He decided against it.

Longstreet stopped and held up his hand. Morrison halted and looked in the direction of Longstreet's point. "Turkeys!" Longstreet whispered.

Longstreet was right. Six hens scratched the ground approximately forty yards to their left. Jim would be pleased. Morrison raised his rifle and fired.

Chapter Seventeen

The afternoon sun lit up the happy room, warming it in spite of the cold wind outside. Jackson sat on the couch, holding a sleeping Tom. From the kitchen wafted the aroma of roasting turkey. Jim had been hard at work on dinner since the breakfast dishes had been washed and put away.

Christmas had come early to the house, drawing everyone to the living room to watch the children ransack their candy-filled stockings before turning sticky fingers on their presents. For the girls, there were dolls and yards of fabric for new dresses, which were desperately needed. Ginny was wearing one of Julia's old dresses and the dress Julia wore was too small for her. Flora and Anna sat in the corner with a new pattern book, plotting dressmaking strategies.

Jimmie's box had been filled with school supplies and books. Jackson was glad to see the books. He had listened to Jimmie read the same book about some lost kitten searching for his mother for the past three months. Jackson had the story memorized, and he suspected Jimmie did too. Now, there were enough books to last five nights before they would have to reread one. The little boy lay on his stomach in front of the fireplace, writing his ABCs on his new slate. Rebel lay next to him, crunching a large bone.

Lee, Johnston, and Longstreet were huddled in a corner, drinking cup after cup of Jim's eggnog and discussing why Napoleonic strategy was a failing one during the war. Morrison sat next to them, listening to the animated discussion. He had nothing to contribute, but that didn't stop him from drinking liberally from the pitcher. Lee tried to entice Jackson into the debate, but Jackson used the baby to fend off their entreaties. He smiled down at his son, who slept peacefully, unaware of all the activity percolating around him.

Anna sat down next to him. "Happy darling?" She threaded her arm through his.

He smiled at her. "Very." He gave a small chuckle. "While I sat in prison, I used to despair that I would never see you again. How I praise God for His bounty of blessings. For here I am. My wife is sitting by my side, looking pretty as a picture." He kissed her cheek. "My daughter is happy and healthy. And my son…" He stroked the baby's forehead with his fingertip. "I have always regretted missing so much of Julia's life. Her first steps and her first words. I don't plan to miss them in my boy. He may be the only son I have, and he needs to know his father."

"Anna, come look at this pattern," Flora called. "I think it would be perfect for Julia."

"Coming," Anna said. She kissed Jackson's cheek and whispered "I love you" before joining Flora.

Jackson watched her go. His gaze fell on Jimmie. The little boy was no longer writing. He sat ramrod straight, staring at Jackson with tear filled eyes. The expression on his face was a mixture of shock, betrayal, and immense sorrow.

Jackson knew he had made a terrible mistake! How many times since Stuart's death had Jimmie sought reassurance that he was still Jackson's little boy? Yet Jimmie had just heard him tell Anna that Tom may be his only son.

"Jimmie," Jackson said.

"No!" Jimmie shouted. He sprang to his feet and bolted the room. Rebel scrambled after him.

The room fell silent. A concerned Lee glanced over at Jackson.

"Jimmie," Flora scolded, "you come back here." Jimmie's footsteps could be heard running up the steps. "That boy doesn't listen to me anymore." She stood and dumped the yard goods she was measuring on her chair.

"Flora, let me," Jackson said.

"Are you sure?" She asked.

Jackson gently laid the baby in the small cradle by the couch. "I'm sure."

"Thank you."

Jackson headed upstairs.

★ ★ ★

Jimmie had fled to Flora's room. When Jackson peered around the door, he saw the boy sitting before Stuart's trunk. The lid was open. He held something in his hand and was murmuring softly to Rebel.

Jackson walked into the room. "Jimmie."

Jimmie pivoted so his back was to Jackson. "Don't you have to get back to Tom?"

Jackson sat down next to the little boy. "Tom is sleeping." He gestured at Jimmie's hand. "What do you have?"

Jimmie's hand closed around the object. "I'm allowed to hold it. Ma said."

"I know." He pointed at the object again. "May I see it?"

Jimmie pivoted back around, extended his arm, and slowly uncurled his hand. The hidden object was Stuart's watch. How many times had Jackson seen the watch in Stuart's hand? He fought back the tears that flooded his eyes at the memories. "That's a mighty fine watch."

"It was my Pa's." Jackson noticed Jimmie emphasis on the word "my." "Ma says I can have it on my 18th birthday."

"That will make a fine present."

Jimmie opened the case and looked at the hands. "What time does it say?" He held the watch up to Jackson. The watch had stopped long ago.

"It says ten minutes past five. See, the big hand tells you the minutes and the little hand tells the hour."

Jimmie closed the watch case and with a tenderness that Jackson didn't think the boisterous little boy was capable of, laid it back in the trunk. He gave it another pat. "It's okay if you just want Tom to be your only little boy," he sobbed loudly. "I understand." Tears dripped off his chin.

"It's not okay with me," Jackson said.

Jimmie stared up at him. "But you said Tom was your only son."

"Oh, Jimmie, I'm sorry. I didn't mean..." he stopped. Jimmie didn't say anything but continued to stare up at him. "Whose son are you?

"I'm my Pa's son," Jimmie wailed. "I want my Pa!"

Jackson tried to hug the boy, but Jimmie extended his arm and held him back. "My father died when I was still a baby. I really never knew him, but I missed him all the same. A pa and his son have a special bond that can never be broken. Never, ever. You share that bond with your Pa, and I share it with Tom. But after my father died, my Uncle Cummins asked if I would be his little boy."

"Did you say yes?" Jimmies voice shook with sobs.

"I did."

"What happened?"

"Uncle Cummins loved me and raised me and took good care of me. He wasn't my pa, but I loved him almost as much." Jackson reached over, put his finger under Jimmie's chin, and gently lifted up the boy's tear stained face. "You're General James Ewell Brown Stuart's son. That will never change. But when I agreed to let you be my little boy that promise was forever."

Jimmie's tears stopped. "Promise, promise?"

"Promise, promise." Jackson lowered the trunk's lid. "Now, give me a hug and forgive me for upsetting you on Christmas." Jimmie complied.

There was a knock on the door. Jackson looked and saw Lee framed in the doorway.

"Is everything alright?" Lee questioned.

"We've been missing Stuart," Jackson explained.

A cloud passed over Lee's face. "Yes, we've been missing him all day." The cloud passed. "Jim says dinner is ready."

Lee stood at the front door and debated whether or not to interrupt Jackson's solitude. After dinner, conversation had turned from McClellan's promise of amnesty to reminiscences of Stuart. Jackson had abruptly fled the living room. Lee wasn't surprised by Jackson's sudden retreat. He seemed always to untangle himself from any conversation where Stuart was the topic. The only time Lee heard Jackson speak of Stuart was to answer a question from Jimmie. But Jackson had been gone a good hour and Lee was worried.

He opened the door, slipped out onto the porch, and saw Jackson sitting on the swing. Lee shivered. The night was chilly, especially when the wind blew. "Are you okay?" He crossed to the couch and sat down.

Jackson gave him a puzzled look. "I'm fine, why?"

"You just seemed ill at ease in there."

Jackson smiled. "I didn't mean to worry you."

"Well, you did," Lee confessed. He shivered again.

Jackson stood. "It's cold. We should go in."

"No, I'm fine." Jackson sat back down and began to rock the swing. "Tom, can I speak frankly?"

The swing came to an abrupt stop. Jackson gave Lee another puzzled look. "Of course."

Now that he had Jackson's permission, Lee didn't know how to begin. He sucked in his breath and just got about it. "I've noticed that you avoid any conversation when Jeb is the topic."

The swing started up. Back and forth it went without Jackson commenting. Slowly, the swing came to a stop. "I just can't." Lee was sympathetic. It was hard for him, too. "The Yankees murdered him, and someone should have had to pay for that crime. General Reynolds promised me that the murderer would be punished, but according to the newspapers Fitz brought last week, the murderer was released from prison with just a slap on the wrist."

At the mention of Reynolds, Lee turned shocked eyes on Jackson. "When did you speak to General Reynolds?"

"The night Stuart died. Reynolds came to pay his respects." Jackson's voice hardened. "I held Stuart's pistol on him and it took all my self-control not to shoot him."

Lee was unnerved by the fury in Jackson's voice. "I've never heard you speak so."

Jackson looked out into the lawn. When he faced Lee again, Lee saw anguish in his eyes. "Love your enemies, the Bible commands us," Jackson said hoarsely. "Pray for them that spitefully use you. I cannot do it. I've prayed for grace to forgive what was done, but all that happens is I grow angrier with every day that passes."

"It's natural to be angry," Lee said. "I was angry after Fitzhugh was killed."

"Did you have murder in your heart?" Jackson asked. "Because I do, and I'm choking on it." His voice began to rise. "And I don't understand why General Longstreet and General Johnston believe they can trust the people who murdered their friend." He held up his hand. "I can't."

"General Longstreet's just keen to be reunited with his children." Jackson jerked to his feet and paced away from Lee. "Surely, you can understand that."

"Of course I understand," Jackson snapped.

Lee pressed the point. "McClellan's promise of amnesty gives everyone a chance to go home."

Jackson threw himself in the swing. It rocked back and forth wildly. "It galls me that we will be beholden to the very ones who murdered Stuart."

"You can't go on like this," Lee chided. "This hatred will eat you up. Jeb wouldn't want you so tormented."

"Do not begin to tell me what Stuart would or wouldn't want," Jackson hollered. "I knew him better than you."

Lee felt the back of his neck heat up. "That's enough! I will not be talked to like that," he rebuked. He didn't feel guilty over his harshness. At the moment, Jackson was a stranger.

Jackson stared at Lee for a long, terrifying moment. He lowered his head. "I'm sorry." His shoulders heaved in a silent sob.

Lee's anger went out. Had he been too preoccupied with his own grief to notice just how much Jackson was suffering? "You may have known Jeb better…"

"I should have never said that," Jackson whispered. "I didn't mean to diminish your love for him. I'm sorry."

"Will you allow me to say that I do know Jeb wouldn't want you suffering so? He would want you to take the deal so you could home."

The wind blew suddenly. An icy blast that snatched Lee's breath away. He shivered.

"You should go in, before you catch cold," Jackson said.

"In a moment."

Jackson stood, leaned against the porch rail, and stared out at the lawn. Lee wondered what he saw in the darkness. "I can't accept the deal. Not today."

"The good news is that you don't have to accept the deal today," Lee countered. "Consider the next three months a gift of grace."

"I guess," Jackson sighed.

Lee joined Jackson at the rail. "McClellan's policy was to always prosecute the war in such a way that would allow the states to reunite peacefully without acrimony."

The door opened and Anna appeared. "There you are. I've been looking everywhere for you. Jim has cut the gingerbread. Come in and get a piece."

"Coming." Jackson headed for the door. He didn't wait for Lee.

Lee watched Jackson disappear into the house. The conversation had been a revelation. He had no idea Jackson was so angry and grief-stricken, for only anger or grief could make Jackson forget himself and speak in such a disrespectful manner. What comfort and counsel could Lee give? Right now, he didn't know if words alone could ease Jackson's suffering. Another blast of arctic cold cut through his jacket. He shivered again and hurried into the house.

Chapter Eighteen

McClellan stood at the window that overlooked the streets of Washington and peered into the darkening skies. March had come in like a lamb bringing with it blue skies, white clouds, and temperatures soaring in the 60s. Tomorrow promised more of the same. The streets were teeming with revelers, all here to celebrate his inauguration – or, as he had been referring to it in the privacy of his home, his coronation. For his plans included another run at the end of this term and another run four years after that. He had come into the world for such a time as this. He wouldn't waste the opportunity God had given him. He knew his mission. He was to bind up the brokenhearted; pour a healing balm upon the sectional and economic divisions within the nation; and restore the South to her former glory.

He smiled at his poetic brilliance. Right now, in front of the Capitol, a statue to honor Grant was being erected. He even heard of plans for a grander monument for that fallen fool Lincoln. Well Lincoln could have his monument. For McClellan knew that when his reign was over, statues would be erected to his glory in every city and town throughout the country.

His first order of business was to consolidate power. The election's popular vote had wound up too close for comfort. He had won Pennsylvania by less than 6,000 votes. The South was firmly in the hands of the Republicans. The Radicals had swiftly exacted their revenge on Georgia and Alabama by levying punitive taxes. Taxes the Radicals knew the destitute citizens couldn't pay. Farms and plantations were surrendered to clear the tax bills. The population began a migration from the country to the cities where only despair and poverty waited. McClellan knew that as long as former Confederate soldiers and officials were denied the vote, the Republicans would always be able to steal any election out from underneath him.

The closeness of the race meant he had come to Washington without a mandate. The Republicans controlled the House and Senate and had enough votes to override any legislation he might veto. This made enacting his agenda both treacherous and difficult. He would need to win his battles with Congress in the newspapers. During the war, he had raised up a magnificent army. He would do so again. This time it would be a civilian army who would make it impossible for members of Congress to ignore their constituents. The Republicans may not want to enact McClellan's policies for the policies' sake, but they would enact them to keep their seats and power. For a politician, the prize was always power. McClellan gave a casual shrug. In that aspect, politicians really weren't that different from generals.

Tomorrow, in his inauguration speech, he would announce his plan to grant amnesty to the fugitive generals, including the scoundrel Forrest. At the end of the year, he would lift Reconstruction and return the vote to all citizens. Furthermore, he would make sure that any congressman or senator sent from the South in a fair election would be seated. Claims for wanton destruction of personal property during the war would be considered and, if proven valid, paid.

It was a recipe designed to make him the South's savior. Yes, the South would always honor the Gray Fox and Old Jack, his former West Point classmate, but the South would never forget that it was he, McClellan, who had lifted it from the bitter ashes of defeat. The people would remember him at the polls in four years. In fact, McClellan believed they would continue to vote for him no matter how many times he ran. Southerners were a generous and gracious people: loyal to those who showed them kindness.

In the window's reflection he saw James approach. "What?"

"Sir, Congressman Stevens and Senator Sumner are here."

His enemies were coming to supplicate themselves at his feet. At the moment, he wasn't in the mood for such worship. "Tell them to make an appointment with Mr. Bicknell."

"They said it couldn't wait."

Couldn't wait! These arrogant men must be taught a lesson they wouldn't soon forget. And now was just as good a time as any to begin their schooling. "Show them in."

The revelry in the streets lost its appeal. Now, it was just bothersome noise. McClellan crossed to a large chair and settled in. He would punish these interlopers by keeping them standing. To give himself an air of supreme indifference, he picked up a newspaper and began to read. The door opened and Stevens and Sumner entered.

"Mr. President-elect," Sumner hailed.

McClellan didn't answer but continued to read the newspaper. He could feel anger emanating from Sumner at the snub. It gladdened his heart.

Stevens didn't say anything. He sat down on the couch. "Do you think we could get some coffee?"

McClellan jerked his head up and stared at the bewigged Stevens.

"Well?" Stevens asked. "Oh, Charles, do sit down. You're making me nervous."

Sumner glanced around him, spied a chair, and sat down.

Stevens was staring at McClellan. "Coffee?" He asked again.

These two men had not been in the room for five minutes and they had seized control from him. He needed to snatch it back, but not by being spiteful and denying them hospitality. "James!" The butler appeared in the doorway. "Could we have some coffee?"

"Yes, sir, right away." James shut the door behind him.

McClellan fixed his glare on both visitors. "Now, what is so important that you had to see me tonight?"

Stevens smiled and McClellan suddenly felt wary, like the fieldmouse does when the hawk flies overhead. He steeled himself. "We're concerned about a portion of your speech tomorrow," Stevens said.

"How do you know what's in my speech?" He questioned angrily. Only Bicknell and his new cabinet had been given copies.

Stevens smiled again. "General..."

"You mean Mr. President-elect," McClellan corrected harshly.

Stevens bowed his head slightly. "My apologies."

"How did you get a copy of my speech?"

"There are no secrets in Washington." Sumner settled back in the chair. "And you can't be making any policy concerning the South without input from Congress." He banged his cane on the floor for emphasis.

"You mean the Radicals," McClellan sniped.

"Same difference," Stevens said.

A knock on the door announced James' arrival with the coffee. He placed the silver tray on a low table in front of the couch. Stevens reached over and poured a cup. He added cream, picked up a spoon, and leaned back on the couch. He stirred the coffee, tapped the spoon on the cup's edge, and placed it on the saucer. He took a small sip. "There are many in the North who believe the South has not fully paid for her rebellion." He took another sip of coffee.

McClellan stiffened. "The South is in ruins. Her people destitute. Her cities burned and her plantations destroyed. What more can she pay?"

"By hiding the fugitives, the South has proven that she is unrepentant and unreconstructed," Sumner said. The cane banged on the floor again.

McClellan shifted slightly in the chair and straightened the magazines on the side table. "Gentlemen, that kind of hyperbole might work in the Radical caucus, but it doesn't work with me. What Hamlin and Stanton did in arresting and trying the Confederate generals was unjust and unworthy of a great nation."

Sumner scoffed.

"My election shows that the people agree with me." McClellan was pointed.

"Yes, that's true," Stevens said. He set the cup on the table. "But it's not the people who pass your agenda. It's us. And if you grant the fugitives amnesty, we'll make sure any legislation you send up to the Hill is dead on arrival. All of it. Dead."

"I won't sit here and let you threaten me." McClellan's voice was a whip.

Stevens smiled again and McClellan felt a shiver go down his spine. To hide his discomfort, he picked up a magazine and flipped through it.

"It's not a threat when you have the votes to carry it out," Stevens replied. He poured himself another cup of coffee.

Politics had destroyed his military career. He had been cast into prison, been forced to resign his commission, and been humiliated when his name became a national joke. Under no circumstance was he going to let that happen again. "We can't hang men we know are innocent," he battled back.

"They're not innocent," Sumner barked, his cane banging rapidly on the floor. "They're responsible for thousands of deaths."

How do you argue against such stubbornness? McClellan changed tack. "You do realize that I'm trying to avoid another war."

Sumner laughed. "That's what you said after Stuart was killed. Not a peep from the Rebels."

Sumner was right. After Stuart was killed, all Washington stood on alert, waiting for the gray horde to attack. After a week of sleepless nights, Sherman quietly cancelled the alert. But that false alarm didn't mean the South still wouldn't fight to keep the fugitives safe.

"I agree. It's foolish to risk war," Stevens said. "So we alter President Hamlin's plan. The fugitives surrender and get a new trial."

McClellan was wary. "What's the change?"

"We do away with General Reynolds' lenient jury," Sumner said. "No new evidence is introduced, and the Rebs don't get to cross examine the witnesses."

Drunk witnesses! McClellan shook his head in disgust.

Stevens' spoon went round and round making waves in the cup. "I don't understand why you would risk your presidency to save this nation's enemies."

Right now, McClellan wondered the same thing. His destiny wasn't to save Lee and Jackson. It was to save the nation. But if he backed down after being threatened, he would spend his whole presidency backing down.

Stevens quit stirring his coffee. The spoon once more tapped the rim of the cup. "In the military, things are very black and white. That's not the way it is in Washington. We operate mostly in the gray."

Sumner leaned forward. "We want to give you every opportunity to succeed. But the South must pay. Her spirit must be irrevocably broken. Amnesty is out of the question."

McClellan stroked his forehead. "If I give in on amnesty and say that the fugitives must surrender, then I want Hamlin's whole plan to stay in effect. We can't allow them to be convicted by drunken scoundrels who could barely stick to the script Stanton wrote for them. No, if we have the evidence that they participated in Lincoln's assassination, then we show it to the nation – both North and South. And the Rebs can challenge our evidence and present evidence of their own."

Stevens' spoon made circles in his cup. Round and round it went. McClellan stared at Sumner, but the Senator had gone mute. Stevens stopped stirring. "The jury comes from Congress. Other than that, your proposal is acceptable." He set the cup on the table and stood.

Sumner struggled to his feet. "I wish you nothing but success tomorrow."

The two made their goodbyes and left.

★ ★ ★

McClellan sat behind his desk feeling the effects of last night's balls. He had danced too many waltzes and sipped too much champagne. He wasn't a drinker, but last night was a special occasion and he had over indulged his joy. He was no longer president-elect. He was now the President of the United States. He had reached the pinnacle of success. He wanted to spin around in his chair in gleeful exuberance, but stopped himself. It wouldn't be dignified. He had already met with his Cabinet. That meant he only had one meeting left for his first full day in office. Once the meeting concluded, he planned to take a nap and sleep off his headache.

A knock preceded the door opening. Henry Bicknell entered.

"Good morning, Mr. Bicknell," McClellan said cheerfully.

Bicknell tugged on his jacket. "General Sherman is here. General Reynolds is with him."

"I'll see them now."

The generals entered. "Gentlemen, please be seated." McClellan gestured toward the chairs opposite a large couch. He fell gracefully on the couch and crossed his legs. "Lieutenant General Sherman," he laughed breezily. "That is a rank Lincoln made sure he withheld from me."

Sherman smiled. "You've risen much higher than lieutenant general."

"So could you, if you ran for the office. But not too soon. I plan to be here for a while."

"No thank you," Sherman laughed. "I've had my fill of politicians."

"I hope you don't include me in that group," McClellan chided playfully.

"You'll always be a military man to me." Sherman sat down.

"John, it is good to see you again," McClellan said to Reynolds.

"Mr. President."

McClellan waited until Reynolds was seated. "I won't waste your time. I wanted to let you know that I won't be granting amnesty to the fugitives."

"I don't understand," Reynolds stammered. He clasped his hands together. "You campaigned on amnesty."

McClellan glanced at Sherman, but Sherman didn't seem surprised by his announcement. "It was a promise I couldn't afford to keep." McClellan gave a shrug. "The deal you offered the Rebs in October will be offered to them again. The only change will be to the jury. Instead of generals who might be sympathetic to their plight, the jury will be made of members of Congress who won't be."

"They won't come in," Reynolds insisted. "They'll fight."

McClellan waved his hand dismissively. "No, they won't."

"How can you know for sure?" Sherman asked.

McClellan glared at Sherman. "General, in the past, you've had a tendency to overstate Confederate strength and intentions." McClellan noted that his pointed comment had hit its mark. Sherman sat ramrod straight in his chair. "I believe you've done so now. You put Washington on high alert after Stuart was killed. Not one Reb came to avenge his death."

"Which proves?" Reynolds asked.

"The South has no interest in avenging her fallen heroes." McClellan rubbed his head. It was pounding. He wanted to bring this conversation to a quick end and crawl off to bed. "If they had an interest, General Sherman's hysteria last fall would have been justified."

Sherman's jaw tightened. He glanced at Reynolds. So did McClellan. The Pennsylvanian appeared to be shell-shocked.

"You're making a mistake," Reynolds said wearily.

McClellan stood. "Thank you for telling me your concerns. But the decision has been made. Now, if you'll excuse me."

★ ★ ★

The morning was dark and drizzly and it perfectly matched Reynolds' mood as he and Sherman exited the Executive Mansion. His greatcoat did nothing to keep the chill out. He shivered, but knew the shiver was from more than the cold.

"Can you believe that ass," Sherman fumed. "Bringing up Kentucky in hopes of intimidating me? Hysteria! The only thing that kept me from punching him in the jaw was respect for the office because I have nothing but contempt for the man."

Reynolds no longer knew why he was fighting. The Rebels certainly weren't. Sherman wasn't the only one who had expected Jackson to march on Washington. When he hadn't come, Reynolds lost all heart. Well, no longer. He wouldn't waste any more tears, prayers, or arguments saving men who didn't want to save themselves. "I'm finished."

His announcement caused Sherman to forget his tirade. He stared at Reynolds in confusion.

"I'm going to resign, go home, and marry my fiancée. She's waited long enough."

Sherman put a hand on Reynolds' arm and brought him to a quick halt. "You're not going to let McClellan run you off, are you?

Reynolds pointed back toward the mansion. "I knew he couldn't withstand the pressure brought to bear on him by the Radicals. But I did expect him to hold out a little longer. He didn't even last a day."

Sherman let go of Reynolds' arm. "No, he didn't."

"There are only two scenarios. Either the fugitives come in or they restart the war."

"No, those aren't the only scenarios. Those just happen to be the two you've fixated on."

Reynolds laughed and shook his head. "You didn't hear the iron in Stuart's voice when he said he would restart the war."

"Stuart's dead," Sherman said flatly, "and as McClellan so bluntly stated, my hysteria resulted in nary a Rebel to be seen."

Reynolds walked out of the gate and onto the sidewalk. He stopped when he reached the street. He turned to say something but changed his mind. What was the point? He plowed across the street. The drizzle had turned the top layer of the road to mud. He slid slightly but regained his balance. He reached the other side and stopped to scrape the mud off his boots on the curb.

"What were you going to say?" Sherman asked.

"I was going to launch into another chapter and verse on how wrong it is to sentence innocent men to hang just so that the Radicals can keep the South prostrate."

"So your answer is to resign." Sherman took out a cigar and bit off the end. He spat it into the street.

Reynolds stammered to put his thoughts into words but failed. "It's the only option left," he finally said.

Sherman lit the cigar and puffed out white smoke. "I despise words like only. They're very limiting, and I don't think you should limit your options."

"I don't know what else to do. I can't be a part of whatever the Radicals are plotting." He started to stammer again. "I just can't," he choked out.

Sherman examined the glowing end of his cigar. "I think it is an extreme measure – resigning. I can transfer you to any post you want. Do you want to go west? Or would you rather have one of the southern posts?"

Reynolds didn't want to go either south or west.

Sherman puffed on the cigar. "Take a leave of absence."

Reynolds shook his head. "I don't want a leave of absence. I have fought my war. Now it's time to go home."

"You still have one more battle in you."

He didn't. He shook his head again. "I'm tired of fighting for men who don't seem the least bit interested in fighting for themselves."

Sherman threw the cigar into a small puddle. It sizzled before going out. "It's chilly. Let's keep moving." He started down the sidewalk.

Reynolds walked along in silence. Suddenly, he sighed. He knew he couldn't walk away from this fight. He owed it to Sam to make sure the paroles he had signed were honored. He surrendered with another sigh. "I'll take a leave."

"Good," Sherman smiled. "When this finally comes to a head, I'll send word."

Chapter Nineteen

Clover Hill
March 10, 1866
Afternoon

Forrest took the front steps three at a time. He threw the front door open with a bang, stepped into the hall, and looked in the living room. He waved at the startled ladies and continued down the hall. The dining room was empty and only Jim was in the kitchen. From the backyard, he heard voices.

"Welcome back, General Forrest," Jim said. He reached into the oven and pulled out a loaf of bread.

"Thank you, Jim." Forrest opened the door and went out on the back porch. He saw Jackson and Longstreet sitting under the sycamore trees. On a low table sat a pitcher of lemonade. Johnston, Lee, and Morrison were leaning against the corral watching Stuart's son ride Jackson's Morgan around the corral.

"Forrest!" Longstreet hailed. Forrest went down the steps and across the lawn. "How are you on this fine spring day?"

"I could be better," Forrest said. He flung himself into one of the empty chairs.

"What has you all abuzz?" Longstreet asked. He held up his glass. "Lemonade?"

Forrest declined. He reached into his haversack and withdrew a newspaper. "This." He passed it to Longstreet.

Longstreet unfolded it and read the headline. Without a word, he handed it to Jackson.

"Are any of us surprised?" Jackson asked after reading the headline.

"I am. A little bit," Longstreet admitted. "I guess it serves me right for believing a politician." He laughed ruefully and held out his hand. Jackson surrendered the newspaper. He began to read the article.

Forrest heard footsteps rustling in the grass. He squinted into the sun and saw Lee approaching.

"Jimmie looks good up there," Jackson said.

"He is his father's son," Lee said. "General Forrest, it's good to see you."

"General." Forrest smiled. He liked Lee. Ever since meeting the venerable general, he had thought Lee the perfect Southern gentleman.

Lee pointed at the newspaper. "I can tell by your faces that the news must not be good."

"Cavalry's not coming," Forrest said. He changed his mind about the lemonade. He vaulted from the chair and poured himself a glass.

"Translation," Lee chuckled.

"McClellan has decided that we won't be granted amnesty," Jackson explained.

Forrest returned to his seat. He took a sip of lemonade and smacked his lips in delight.

Lee sat down. "It was always a fool's hope," he said wearily.

Longstreet looked up from the paper. "The news isn't all bad. McClellan is essentially offering us Hamlin's terms. We surrender, get a new public trial, and a jury of our peers. If we are acquitted, we go free."

Jackson rose suddenly and left the group. Forrest watched him cross the yard and join Johnston at the fence.

"Forrest, did you see this?" Longstreet held up the paper and pointed at an article in the bottom left corner.

"You know I don't read real good."

Longstreet folded the paper so the article was on top. "It seems you've been granted a reprieve."

Forrest leaned forward in the chair "What do you mean?"

"The War Department has issued a blanket amnesty for all crimes perpetrated against Union forces in Rebel territory during the war."

Forrest frowned. "I ain't been convicted of no crime."

"You're included on the list as is Colonel Mosby." Longstreet passed the paper to Forrest and pointed to a section of the paper.

Forrest concentrated on the article and read it slowly. He understood enough to realize that Longstreet was right. The Yankees were no longer looking for him. He could go home in peace and see his family. He smiled.

"Congratulations, General," Lee said.

Jackson returned. He took the seat next to Forrest and with a gesture requested the newspaper. Forrest complied. Johnston had come too and sat opposite Lee. Forrest glanced at the corral. Morrison was unsaddling Little Sorrel, while Stuart's son dashed into the small stable.

"Why are congratulations in order?" Johnston asked. Clearly, Jackson had told him the news.

"The Yankees have called off their search for Forrest," Longstreet said.

Forrest glanced at the general. Longstreet seemed genuinely pleased that he was free to return home.

"That is good news," Johnston said. "But it's good news for us, too. With General Forrest in the clear, we can take advantage of McClellan's offer." No one said anything. "We were all for it last October. What's changed?"

"Nothing," Lee said. He leaned back in his chair.

Jackson shook his head. "The Yankees can't be trusted. Once they have us in custody, there's nothing to prevent them from hanging us."

Longstreet frowned. "It's going to take a bit of trust..."

"Based on what? What has happened in the last year that would make you – he pointed at Longstreet – trust the Yankees?"

Longstreet appeared flummoxed by Jackson's question. "What choice do we have?"

"We can fight," Jackson said.

Jackson's answer sent a thrill of hope dashing down Forrest's spine. This was the first Jackson had spoken of fighting since that long ago night on the porch.

Longstreet laughed in derision. "Who? The four of us?"

Forrest raised his hand. "Five. It's the fight I've been waitin' for."

"But you can go home." Johnston was shocked.

"Today I can go home," Forrest replied. "What happens when the Radicals change their mind and decide that it's good politics to hang me? No, thank you."

"We can raise an army," Jackson said. "Stuart thought he could rally 2,000 men."

Johnston stared at Jackson in disbelief. "How do you plan to go about raising this army?"

"General Lee will ask them to come," Jackson replied matter-of-factly.

Longstreet laughed again. "I never thought you were a fool, Jackson."

If Longstreet had spoken like that to him, Forrest would have decked him. But Jackson's only reaction was a tightening of his jaw.

"General Lee has already stated that he won't take part in any fight." Longstreet was snide.

"I can speak for myself, Pete," Lee said tightly.

Longstreet threw up his hands in exasperation. "Surely, you don't agree with this madness."

"Why is it madness?" Forrest interjected. Longstreet would never agree to go on the offensive, no matter what size army Jackson raised. "Ain't it more madness to walk back into prison?"

"But we'll have an agreement," Longstreet insisted.

"Yeah, and the Yankees ain't never broke an agreement before," Forrest scoffed.

Longstreet appealed to Johnston. "Help me out here, Joe."

"I don't like the idea of fighting. I don't think it's realistic," Johnston said.

Was Jackson the only general who had a spine? Forrest glared at Johnston. "Why not?"

"Supplies, logistics, ammunition, and manpower," Johnston reeled off, holding up a finger for each item he mentioned.

"But the Yankees have sent all their men home," Forrest said. "There's probably no more than 4,000 soldiers in Washington City."

Longstreet stared at Forrest as if the cavalry leader had lost his mind. "You want to seize the Federal capital?"

"You got another city in mind?" Forrest retorted. He turned his palms up and invited Longstreet to offer up the name of another city.

Instead Longstreet turned toward Jackson. "You shouldn't encourage him."

Forrest bristled.

"Let's all calm down," Johnston said. "Turning on each other isn't going to solve anything." He gave Forrest a disapproving look. "Now, we're all agreed that we can turn ourselves in, fight, leave the country, or continue to hide."

"I'm done hiding." Longstreet folded his arms across his chest.

"When you turn yourself in, the Yankees will hang you," Forrest said.

Longstreet pursed his lips together and glared at Forrest.

"They killed him," Jackson said, his voice low and menacing. "They shot him in the back. They promised us safe passage, and we were fools enough to believe them. Shame on us if we believe them again."

Shocked, Forrest stared at Jackson. He never believed Jackson was capable of such anger. His opinion of Ole Stonewall shot up.

"You talk like you want vengeance," Johnston said.

"I want justice," Jackson said.

Lee searched Jackson's face. "Are you sure that's all you want?" Forrest heard concern in Lee's voice.

"I'm sure," Jackson growled.

"I don't believe you," Longstreet snapped.

"I don't care." Jackson stood. "I won't surrender." He strode away.

Forrest watched him go. "I agree with General Jackson."

"Of course you do," Longstreet sneered.

Forrest clenched his fists. "I don't know why you're so quick to trust the Yankees."

"Because we can't win," Longstreet lectured as if Forrest was too simple to understand the reality of the situation.

"Stop it!" Johnston ordered sharply. "I'm tired of the constant bickering that goes on." Forrest never heard Johnston raise his voice before, and the sound shocked him into silence. "General Jackson is grieving and it's interfering with his thinking. I know him. He isn't serious about fighting."

Lee shook his head. "General Jackson is right. The Yankees murdered Jeb. We just can't ignore that fact."

"Who's ignoring it?" Longstreet leaned forward. "There's nothing we can do about it. We aren't in a position of strength. That's the only thing that matters."

"So, we run up the white flag and give ourselves up," Forrest said.

Longstreet jerked back in his chair; his face a mask of rage. "This conversation doesn't concern you. So why don't you pack up and go home and leave the decision to those it does affect."

Forrest bolted to his feet. "Is that what you want?"

"Sit down, General." Lee gestured at the chair. "We're going to need your services."

Forrest sat down and smiled triumphantly at Longstreet, but Longstreet was staring at Lee.

"You're going to side with Jackson again." Longstreet didn't give Lee a chance to answer. "You always take his part. He's not right here. He's going to kill us all."

A shocked Forrest watched Lee give Longstreet a gentle smile instead of a swift belt to the chops. "It's not about sides. If we decide to fight, I'll issue the call."

"What about your high ethical stance of not breaking the surrender terms."

"I haven't changed my mind," Lee responded. "General Johnston or General Jackson can lead any force that is raised."

"No."

Forrest whirled around and saw Joe Morrison leaning against a tree. Morrison straightened up and came over to the group.

"I'm sorry to interrupt," Morrison said.

"No need to apologize, Captain," Lee said. "You've every right to speak."

Morrison sat down in the chair Jackson had vacated and put his hand on Lee's arm. "When General Stuart made the decision to rescue you, he only issued a one sentence appeal: 'General Lee needs you.'" Lee put his hand over Morrison's hand. "There's not one man who won't come when you call, but if they come, they'll want you at the head of the army."

"General Jackson..." Lee began.

"No," Morrison repeated. "If you call the men, you must lead them."

Lee nodded then smiled at Morrison. "Thank you for your honesty." He stood. "If you'll excuse me, gentlemen." He headed toward the house.

Forrest leaned back in his chair. He couldn't have been more pleased with the way the conversation had gone. Jackson was determined to fight and it appeared Lee would support that decision. Hadn't Lee even said that Forrest's services would be needed?

Longstreet stalked off without saying a word.

"What do you think?" Forrest asked Johnston.

Johnston was distraught. "I'm not eager to fight, but if General Lee decides that it's the right course of action, then he can count on me." With that, he stood and started back toward the corral.

★ ★ ★

Lee came around the side of the house and saw Jackson standing in the lawn, throwing a stick for Rebel to chase. The spaniel raced after the stick, brought it back, and dropped it at Jackson's feet. Jackson gave it another heave. He didn't acknowledge Lee when he approached. Rebel brought the stick back and once again dropped it at Jackson's feet. He sat down and waited for Jackson to throw the stick.

"You took away our choices back there," Lee said.

Jackson threw the stick down the driveway. Rebel chased after it. This time he didn't bring it back. He was content to lie in the spring grass and chew on his prize.

"I need to ask a question," Lee said, "and I need you to give me an honest answer."

"Have I ever lied to you?" Jackson questioned sharply. He headed toward the porch and sat down on the bottom step. Lee sat down next to him. "Ask me your question."

Lee hated pressing Jackson, but he had to know what Jackson was thinking. "Why are you so insistent on fighting?"

"I don't trust the Yankees."

That answer was too simplistic. "You don't trust the Yankees because of what they did to Jeb?"

Jackson didn't look at Lee. "Yes, but that's not the whole answer."

"Then tell me the whole answer."

Jackson sighed. Lee didn't hear anger, but frustration. "You already know it. Have you forgotten the trial?" Of course Lee hadn't, but he held his tongue and allowed Jackson to make his case. "Now, they're saying, 'trust us.' Why in Heaven's name should we?"

Lee still wasn't convinced that Stuart's death wasn't the sole reason for Jackson's decision to fight. After all, Jackson had arranged that fateful meeting with Reynolds in the hopes that they might find a peaceful resolution. The only thing that had changed since that fall day was Stuart's murder. "You're saying all the right things…"

Jackson frowned. "But…"

"I think Jeb's death fuels your desire to fight more than you're willing to admit."

Jackson dropped his head. "I wish I could tell you that I've won the struggle over my anger, but I can't. I don't trust my own heart despite my many prayers to forgive Stuart's murderer."

It was as Lee thought. "If you don't trust yourself, then why should we trust you?"

Jackson raised his head. "Because I honestly believe that my motive is not based on vengeance." He reached behind him and gathered up the newspaper Forrest had given him. "Have you read the reports about the carpetbaggers and the Freedman Bureau?"

Lee nodded.

"By surrendering, we unleashed a scourge worse than locusts on our people."

Lee pulled hard on his cuff. "Are you blaming me for surrendering?"

Jackson appeared genuinely shocked by Lee's question. "No! Why would you think that?"

Lee didn't answer. Instead he gestured toward the newspaper. "If I knew what the Yankees had in store for us, I would have never surrendered."

"None of us knew," Jackson said, still shocked by Lee's accusation. "But General Johnston and I both agreed with your decision."

Lee chuckled. "Jeb didn't."

"No, he didn't," Jackson laughed. "But he didn't know what the Yankee politicians had planned for us either. We've been isolated on this farm. We can only read about the Yankees' thievery. But Forrest has witnessed it first hand. Don't you think it's interesting that he urges us to fight?"

"General Forrest is a fine man, but I feel he's too quick to want to engage in battle. So, I would take his urgings with a grain of salt."

Jackson stared down at the newspaper. "Reading these reports, I think Forrest's eagerness is understandable."

Lee gestured at the newspaper. "Do you think the reports are exaggerated?"

"No, I don't," Jackson said.

Lee sighed. "General Longstreet insists that the Yankees hold all the cards, and we're too weak to do anything but surrender."

"General Longstreet isn't wrong," Jackson said.

Lee sat back in surprise. If Jackson believed Longstreet was right, then why was he holding on so tightly to the idea of fighting?

"If we surrender ourselves, we do so from a position of weakness," Jackson continued. "We're forced to beg the Yankees for mercy." Lee heard anger creep back in Jackson's voice. "Mercy for what? A crime we didn't commit, and they know we didn't. It makes no sense to me."

In truth, it made no sense to Lee either. There was no earthly reason to trust the Yankees. Longstreet's desire to accept the deal emanated from his weariness of hiding. That was a foolish reason to surrender.

Rebel ran up with the gnawed stick and dropped it at Lee's feet. Lee obliged the spaniel and tossed it into the yard. With a bark, Rebel was off to the chase.

Lee addressed another concern. "Where are you going to get the men for your army?" He asked, knowing full well what Jackson was going to say.

"You're going to have to ask the men to pick up their arms."

Rebel returned with the stick. This time Jackson threw it high into the air. Rebel didn't budge. With a yawn, he plopped down and went to sleep.

"If we follow General Longstreet's course, at least we have some idea of how it'll turn out," Lee said. "We either go free or we hang, but we don't plunge Virginia back into war. We don't risk the lives of men who should be home sowing their crops or tending their businesses. I have to admit that appeals to me. I don't want to ask the men to sacrifice what little they have to save me. I can't be selfish with their love for me."

Jackson held up the paper. "I'd never ask the men to do that. It's bad enough I couldn't convince Captain Morrison to return home, but the thought of dragging Mr. Pendleton away from his new baby or Mr. Smith from his studies is anathema to me." The paper waved back and forward. "If we fight, we must fight to bring an end to Reconstruction and win the vote back for our men."

The decision came down then to surrender or fight, and if surrender was foolish and fighting was a battle they couldn't win, they were truly in an untenable position. Sitting next to him was the conqueror of the Valley, who had fought and won against overwhelming odds every time. If anyone could beat the odds of the impossible, it was Stonewall Jackson. "Do you have a plan?" Lee asked.

Jackson frowned. "Not a fully developed one."

"But you've been working on one."

Jackson smiled. "Yes."

Lee faced Jackson. "Is it a winning one?"

Jackson didn't hesitate. "It will be."

Lee made his decision. "What do you need me to do?"

Chapter Twenty

Sherman's Office
The War Department
March 28, 1866

Sherman turned off the lamp. The long day was finally over. He had standing reservations at one of Washington's finest restaurant where a stiff drink, a good cigar, and a lovely lady were waiting for him. He grabbed up his jacket and headed toward the door. Sheridan burst into the office. Sherman held up his hand. "Whatever it is, it can wait until tomorrow."

Sheridan pushed by him. "No, it can't."

"Sheridan, I'm not in the mood…"

Sheridan fell into a chair and withdrew an envelope from his jacket pocket. "You will be when you see this."

With an exasperated sigh, Sherman returned to his desk, threw his jacket on his chair, and turned up the lamp. "Make it quick. I have dinner reservations."

"We captured a Reb courier."

Sherman reached over the desk and took the envelope. He withdrew the letter and glanced at the signature. It was from Lee to General Early.

"Lee's asking Early how many troops he thinks he can raise." Sheridan's eyes gleamed with anticipation. "They're going to fight."

Sherman scowled. Sheridan may be giddy over the prospect of slugging it out with the Rebs again, but Sherman thought the whole idea repugnant.

"You don't seem pleased," Sheridan accused.

"No," Sherman barked, "and you shouldn't be either."

Sheridan leaned back in his chair. "We licked the Rebs once. We can lick 'em again."

"At what cost in life?"

Sheridan leaned forward. "You know, we could stop this fight before it got a proper start."

"We could?"

"Yes. We hit the Rebs hard and send them a message."

Sherman reread the letter. Everything inside him rebelled at the idea of having to go back into the field again. "What do you have in mind?"

Sheridan smiled – a predatory smile. "All you need to do is give me a free hand."

"Okay, but make it count."

Sheridan jumped to his feet. "I'll make it count." He ran from the office.

Sherman turned down the lamp. He could still make his reservation. He knew Sheridan's lesson would be costly to the Rebs in life and loss of property, but his conscience didn't bother him about what he had just unleashed. If Sheridan could extinguish Lee's hope of restarting the war, any action, no matter how severe, was justified.

Lexington, Virginia
April 2, 1866
11:30 a.m.

Pendleton stood in his father's attic supervising five students as they worked out the algebra problem he had written on the chalkboard at the front of the classroom. Since his return from Clover Hill, he had divided his life between his new son, Alexander Swift Pendleton, Jr., who was the delight of his life, and his teaching position at his father's school.

During the war, he had felt the call to preach the Gospel, but there wasn't enough money to move his family to Richmond and join Smith at the seminary. At first he had tried to save his salary by living with his parents, but that hadn't worked out very well. The small house was filled to the brim with relatives and in the cramped environment, Kate felt her mother-in-law was constantly criticizing how she was raising the baby. To keep the peace, Sandie moved his family into a small boarding house about three blocks from his parent's residence, but rent and the spiraling cost of food ate away his small salary every month.

His thoughts often returned to Clover Hill. Even though Jackson had sent a letter ordering him to remain in Lexington, obeying that order had been the hardest thing he had ever done. He felt like a traitor deserting the general just when the general needed him the most. But his family needed him also. He had received another letter from Jackson congratulating him on the birth of little Sandy and wishing him well. The letter only served to increase his guilt. On the ride to Lexington with Stuart's body, Morrison had shared Stuart's belief that the generals would have to fight to win their freedom. When the fight began later this spring, he planned to be by the general's side, where he belonged. Even if he had to do so over the Kate's strenuous objections.

The usual quiet of the afternoon was punctured by shouts and gunfire. His students looked up from their slates and craned their necks toward the windows. Pendleton rapped the desk with his hand. The young men reluctantly returned to the algebra problem. Pendleton crossed to the window. He saw a large mob heading in the direction of Washington College and the Virginia Military Institute.

Curiosity seized him. "Class, I'll be right back. When I return, I expect that problem to be solved."

He hurried down the stairs, the hall, and onto the front stoop. The mob was armed and angry.

"What's going on?" He questioned.

"Colonel," a man said. Pendleton was dressed in his faded Confederate uniform that had been recently shorn of its insignia. After seizing control of Virginia's government, the Yankees had demanded that all uniforms be stripped of military rank. Kate had cut the three stars from his collar, but they were plainly visible because they were the only spots on the uniform that hadn't been faded by the sun and road. "The Yankees are here. They've forced the cadets from the Institute and are planning to burn it down. We're going to stop them."

Pendleton was unarmed but he leapt from the porch and joined the group. The mob turned on Washington Street. He couldn't believe his eyes. The Yankees were burning houses and businesses all along the street! Women and children stood on the sidewalk pleading with the Yankees to spare their homes. The soldiers refused to listen. Pendleton counted five buildings already ablaze.

The crowd's cohesion fell apart. Many fell out and joined the men and women who were trying to put out the fires. About a third still moved toward the Institute.

Jackson's house! It was just down the street!

"Let me have your pistol," Pendleton said to a man next to him.

The soldier didn't hesitate. "What do you plan on doin'?"

"General Jackson's house is about a block away. I'm going to protect it."

"I'll come too."

Pendleton agreed and the two men threaded their way through the crowd. Up ahead, Pendleton could see Jackson's house. He breathed a sigh of relief. There were no Yankees anywhere near it.

"Go around and protect the back," Pendleton ordered the soldier.

"Yes, sir," the man said. He disappeared around the corner of the house.

Pendleton climbed the steps and posted himself between the two front doors that faced the street. He could see the soldiers moving his way. Hatred suddenly froze his bones. Sheridan stood in the middle of the street directing the action. Pendleton checked the pistol. He had six shots and he would need them all.

"That's Jackson's house! Burn it!" Pendleton heard a voice shout. Five soldiers ran toward the house, the flames on their torches expanding and diminishing as they ran. Pendleton stood at the end of the porch, by the second door, and waited patiently until the soldiers were about fifteen yards away. He raised his pistol and fired it in the air.

For a moment the street went quiet. Only the roar of flames could be heard. But it was only for a moment. The Yankees drew their pistols and leveled them at Pendleton. "You best get down, Reb. We plan to burn this house."

Pendleton aimed his pistol at the speaker. "I won't let you," he barked.

"Jackson's a traitor! Now move away!"

Pendleton refused. "I'll shoot anyone who comes on this porch."

There was a window on the side of the house near where Pendleton stood. One of the soldiers threw a torch through the window and into Jackson's study. Pendleton leaned across the railing and fired. The soldier fell back on the ground. He was dead.

Pendleton fired at the gang's leader. His aim was true and the soldier collapsed.

Gunfire roared in his ears. Pendleton slammed against the door and slowly sank to the porch.

Forrest rode up to the plantation house. He dismounted but lingered in the driveway. He had no desire to deliver his news. He gazed upward. The sky was blue and punctuated with puffy white clouds. In the oak tree to his left, he could hear mockingbirds arguing loudly. Spring was in the air. The weather was warm and so was the breeze. He sighed in despair.

"General Forrest!" Lee hailed from the porch.

Forrest took a deep breath and climbed the steps. Lee, Jackson, and Jackson's wife were sitting on the porch. The baby was lying on a blanket at Mrs. Jackson's feet. He was growing like a weed. It wouldn't be much longer until he was crawling all over the place. Forrest heard girlish giggles. He smiled. The two little girls were having a tea party at the opposite end of the porch.

He stopped at the top of the steps and took another breath. "One of our couriers was captured."

Jackson stiffened. "Do we need to move?"

Forrest waved his hand. "No, sir. The courier doesn't know of this place. He was to get your letter – Forrest gestured at Lee – to General Early."

"Is my bad old man okay?" Lee asked.

Forrest hoped Lee was referring to Early. "Yes, sir. He's in hiding."

"So we're safe?" Jackson questioned.

"Yeah, but I'm increasing the pickets for the next week or so." Forrest was aware that Lee was watching him very closely. "The Yankees..." he hesitated.

"I think it would be best if you just told us," Lee said.

Forrest thought the advice sound. "The Yankees descended upon Lexington and burned it."

"Oh, no!" Anna gasped. "Is our house okay?"

Forrest shook his head. "I'm sorry, ma'am, but it's been burnt up."

Anna began to weep. Jackson gathered her in his arms. "Oh, Tom!" She sobbed. "I can't believe it."

"The whole town is gone. Even Washington College and VMI."

"Why?" Jackson choked out.

"To send us a message," Forrest said, praying that the Yankees' bullying tactics wouldn't sap the courage from Jackson. "If we continue to organize troops, other cities and towns will probably suffer the same fate." He faced Jackson. "There's one more thing. Your adjutant..."

The color drained from Jackson's face. "Sandie?"

"He was defending your house from the Yankees."

Anna stopped crying and sat up. She looked at her husband; terror filling her face.

"Is he alright?" Jackson questioned.

Forrest forced himself to say the words. "Sir, them Yankees kilt him dead."

Anna broke into renewed sobs. Jackson jerked to his feet. Without a word, he brushed past Forrest and disappeared around the side of the house.

Anna fled into the house.

Lee stood, his face stormy with emotion. "Excuse me; I'm going to check on General Jackson."

"Want me to come with ya?" Forrest asked.

"No." Lee went down the steps.

★ ★ ★

Jackson walked blindly but headed in the direction of the clump of chairs under the sycamore trees. He stumbled over a root and hit the ground hard. The pain in his heart violently stabbed at him. Whatever possessed Sandie to think that a house was worth his life?

"I don't understand, Lord," he whispered as tears coursed down his cheeks. He felt as useless as a beaten out willow. He had always sought the Lord's direction on the decisions he made and believed he had received it, but those decisions had led to Stuart's murder and now Sandie's death. "Why?" His mind screamed. "Why?" There was no answer, just the agony of his loss.

"General Jackson? What's wrong?"

Jackson looked up and saw Longstreet standing above him, but his throat was too constricted to speak.

"Here!" Longstreet stretched out his hand.

Jackson reached up and allowed Longstreet to help him to his feet. He sank down into the first chair he came to.

"What's wrong?" Longstreet asked again. He handed Jackson a large bandana.

"The Yankees intercepted General Lee's letter to General Early." Jackson wiped his eyes. "In retaliation, they burned Lexington. Sandie Pendleton was killed trying to defend my home." His sobs choked him.

"Oh, no," Longstreet gasped. Jackson looked up and beheld genuine sorrow on Longstreet's face. "I liked that young man very much."

"It's my fault," Jackson said, giving expression to the accusing voice in his head.

"How is it your fault?" Longstreet asked gently.

There were a million reasons why it was. "I should have just let the Yankees hang me. Then Stuart and Sandie would be alive. My selfishness has caused this." His heart once more cried out to God, asking questions that desperately needed answers.

"None of what has happened since the surrender has been your fault," Longstreet insisted. "So, you must stop blaming yourself." Jackson wept hot tears. "The Yankees are responsible."

No, that wasn't true. Reynolds had offered them a way out and his fury over Stuart caused him to refuse the deal. That was on him and not the Yankees. He wanted justice – no, he wanted revenge. But vengeance belonged to the Lord. He started weeping again. What if the Lord was punishing him for the hatred in his heart?

"We didn't surrender…" Longstreet continued.

"Because I was angry," Jackson interrupted

"You only felt what we should have all felt."

Jackson wiped his eyes again. "You didn't. You wanted to surrender right away."

"That was because I was selfish," Longstreet insisted. "I would have sacrificed Forrest and all of you to be reunited with my family.

When I helped carry Stuart's coffin into the living room, I should have realized that we were dealing with people who couldn't be trusted. Stuart was my friend, too."

"We shouldn't blame ourselves for not knowing what to do in this impossible situation." Jackson turned his head and saw Lee standing there. Jackson hadn't heard him approach. "None of us have ever been in these circumstances before. Surrender? Fight? We had to figure it out and that takes time. And it meant that we might make a wrong decision or two as we felt our way through this trouble."

"But that doesn't excuse the Yankees from burning Lexington or killing Mr. Pendleton," Longstreet said. He laid a hand on Jackson's shoulder. "And you're not responsible for that."

"Sandie shouldn't..."

Lee sat next to Jackson. "Sandie did what he did because he loved you."

"General Lee!"

Jackson looked toward the source of the shout and saw Forrest standing in the side yard, frantically waving his arm. Had the Yankees found them? He rose and with Lee and Longstreet hurried toward Forrest.

"It's the Doc!" Forrest hollered again.

McGuire? What was he doing here? Jackson thought as he hurried toward Forrest. Had he come because he had heard about Sandie? The two had been tentmates during the war, and McGuire had stood up with Sandie at his wedding.

"The Yankees have burned Staunton," Forrest announced.

Jackson came around the corner of the house and saw a weary McGuire sitting on the porch step drinking a glass of lemonade. Morrison was seated next to McGuire, clinging to the banister as if it was the only thing keeping him from flying off the earth.

Jackson walked over to the steps. McGuire and Morrison stood as he approached.

"I just heard about Sandie," McGuire said. Tear stains marred his dust covered face. "I'm so sorry."

Jackson didn't want to talk about it. If he did, he would start crying and not stop. "Tell us about Staunton."

"The Yankees rode in about dawn. They ordered us from our homes. Some men refused and were killed defending their property."

"How many?" Longstreet asked.

"I had twenty-five dead and over sixty wounded in my hospital before I was forced to evacuate it," McGuire said in a voice void of emotion.

Forrest slammed a fist into his palm. "I say we go track down them Yankees."

This produced a faint smile from McGuire. "I was hoping you would say so. I have fifty men ready to ride."

"You didn't bring them here, did ya?" Forrest demanded.

Jackson stared at McGuire, hoping the doctor hadn't inadvertently revealed their hiding place.

McGuire shook his head. "I left them with the pickets. I traveled east before doubling back. They've no idea where I disappeared to."

"Good," Forrest said. "I'm gonna after the Yankees." He looked at the generals. "Any objections?"

Jackson had none. These Yankees needed to be gotten after.

"I'm going with you," Longstreet said.

Forrest pointed a finger at Longstreet. "I've no plans to dig in when I find 'em and wait for 'em to attack. I'm gonna hunt 'em down, fight 'em hard, and kill 'em all. You got a problem with that?"

"No, I don't."

McGuire came down the stairs. "I'm going, too."

"So am I." Morrison shook with rage. His face was bloodless and he clenched and unclenched his fists.

"Are you sure?" Jackson said.

Morrison turned his anger on Jackson. "You can't order me to stay behind. Sandie was my friend."

"I would never do that," Jackson insisted. "But have you considered your sister's feelings?"

The color returned to Morrison's face in rush. "I'm going." He turned his attention to Forrest. "If you'll have me."

Forrest glanced surreptitiously at Jackson, who nodded in permission. "Of course, I'll have you. Be prepared to leave in fifteen minutes."

Jackson addressed Morrison and McGuire. "You be careful. I couldn't bear to lose you both."

Morrison ran into the house.

McGuire swung up in the saddle. "General Forrest, I'll meet you where I left my men."

"Have them in their saddles and ready to go," Forrest said.

McGuire cantered down the driveway.

★ ★ ★

Forrest stripped Clover Hill of most of its guards. Even after combining the men McGuire had brought, Forrest had less strength than the Yankees. His strength declined even further when some of the men couldn't keep up with his swift pace. Longstreet counseled Forrest to slow down, but the cavalry leader wouldn't hear of it. He told Longstreet that if he was the only man who arrived at the Yankees' camp, he would engage the enemy.

Last night, Forrest had finally run the Yankees to ground south of Front Royal. The sun was setting when his scouts returned with news that the Yankees were settling in for the night.

"Fine," Forrest said. "We attack 'em at daybreak." He slipped his fieldglasses from their case. "I'm going to reconnoiter the ground."

The reconnaissance revealed that the Yankees were not expecting any confrontation. Sheridan had a few pickets posted, but the soldiers didn't seem to believe that they were in any danger. In fact, when Forrest reconnoitered the ground again at 3:00 a.m., the pickets were fast asleep. Forrest slipped back through the trees and grabbed a quick nap.

He awakened as the black night gave way to a gray dawn. He sat up and glanced around. Longstreet, Morrison, and McGuire were already awake. He stood and stretched. He'd like nothing more than a hot cup of coffee but he had forbidden all campfires. He didn't want the smoke to alert the Yankees of their proximity. The men had groaned in protest, but a sharp word had squelched all complaints.

Longstreet walked over. "Good morning."

"Morning." Forrest was too anxious for small talk. He wanted to get the men in position so he could bring off his attack while the Yankees were still in their beds. He glanced up into the sky. It was growing lighter, but not fast enough to suit him. "Do you know where you're goin'?"

Longstreet nodded and headed off toward the thick woods on his right. Forrest had put him in charge of the Staunton contingent. The men followed after him. Surprisingly, so did McGuire. Forrest gulped. He ran after the tall doctor and caught up with him just as he reached the tree line. "Where do you think you're goin'?"

McGuire gave him a puzzled look. "I'm going with my men."

Forrest wrapped his hand around McGuire's forearm. "No, you're not. You're a doc, not a soldier." He tried to pull McGuire back, but the doctor didn't budge.

McGuire chuckled. "I'll have you know that I mustered in as a private in the Virginia militia. I know my way around a battlefield."

"Really? What battles did you fight in?" Forrest questioned.

McGuire gave another chuckle, but this time it smacked of guilt. "I never actually fought..."

"That's what I thought." He gave another tug on McGuire's arm. "And you ain't fightin' now. General Jackson would draw and quarter me if I allowed another one of his family members to git kilt."

McGuire smiled at the compliment. "General Forrest, I would feel less than a man..."

"No guiltin' me into it. You're a fine doctor. When all this is done, the Yankees' are gonna need your services."

"Alright," McGuire relented.

Forrest let go of his arm. "Now, I can count on you not to sneak into the woods once I turn my back."

McGuire's look was one of pure innocence. "Of course."

Forrest didn't believe him. "Well, if you get yourself shot, don't come cryin' to me." With that he stalked off toward the men waiting for him.

Forrest glanced back toward the woods. McGuire was nowhere to be seen. Forrest saw Morrison standing by himself, pistol in hand. He could send Morrison to babysit the doc, but what if that got Morrison killed. How could he face Mrs. Jackson? He shook his head. War in Virginia was far more complicated than war in Tennessee. He would leave the doc in Longstreet's hands, while he watched over Morrison.

Forrest peered through his glasses. Some of the Yankees were already awake: stoking fires and putting coffee pots on the hot embers to percolate. But the majority remained in their warm bedrolls. Forrest raised his pistol and fired it in the air. With that the men sprang forward as one.

Chapter Twenty One

Executive Mansion
Washington City
April 17, 1866
9:30 a.m.

Henry Bicknell ushered Sherman into McClellan's office. The president stood facing the window, looking out on Pennsylvania Avenue. His back was to Sherman and when Bicknell closed the door, McClellan didn't acknowledge Sherman's presence in the room. The moments dragged by, and Sherman's anger began to creep toward boiling.

"Well?" McClellan finally barked to the window.

"After we intercepted Lee's letter, I gave Sheridan permission to send the Rebs a message."

"And from what I hear, the message was the equivalent of poking a wasp's nest. How many men did Sheridan lose at Front Royal?"

"Forty wounded and twenty dead. The rest of his men escaped unharmed."

McClellan turned from the window. "This entire situation has been mishandled from the beginning, and I blame you."

Sherman stiffened in anger. "I wasn't the one who ordered the Rebs arrested. That was Stanton."

McClellan returned to his desk. "I find your constant excuse making tiring." He slapped his hand on his desktop. "Fix it!" He shouted.

Sherman gave a small laugh. "That's easy. Just give the fugitives their freedom."

McClellan's face turned bright red. "I don't have that luxury. The Radicals have made it clear that the arrest of the Rebs is non-negotiable. So, I'm turning to the army to resolve this matter. If you can't accomplish your orders, then I'll have your resignation and..."

"You can have it," Sherman almost shouted. He bit his tongue and choked as the words caught in his throat. The perks of the job far outweighed the occasional unpleasant meeting with this popinjay and his phony outrage. "I've sent for John Reynolds."

McClellan appeared to be pleased. "That's a good start. Reynolds has a rapport with these Rebs. They'll listen to him." McClellan pointed his finger at Sherman. "But make no mistake, General. If I see Lee's columns descending upon this city, I'll exact my vengeance on you." He sat in his chair. "You're dismissed." He waved his hand.

Sherman stalked from the room and slammed the door behind him.

United States Military Academy
West Point, New York
April 17, 1866
3:00 p.m.

Reynolds walked across the plains toward his office in the library. The spring wind was cold. Cadets hurried by, saluting as they passed, determined to get out of the wind. He looked about him and smiled. He loved West Point. When the war began, he had been the Commandant of Cadets, but now, thanks to General Sherman's generosity, he had been promoted to superintendent. Of all the posts in the army, it was the one he had coveted the most. He knew Sherman had only secured the job for him to keep him tethered to the mess with the Rebels. He should be angry at being so manipulated, but he couldn't bring himself to be. In coming back to West Point, he had come home.

His life had taken on bright colors. A wedding and a honeymoon made him forget all about fugitive generals. His days were filled with students. In the evening, he returned home to a waiting wife, dinner on the table, and pleasant conversations he wanted to have.

"Good morning, General," a cadet hailed, his New England accent prominent. He snapped to attention as Reynolds passed.

"Cadet Taylor," Reynolds replied, returning the salute.

The cadet continued on his way. Reynolds watched him go. Taylor was a symptom of one of the major problems plaguing the Academy this term. He was supposedly from Louisiana, but his accent gave away his Boston birthplace. Taylor's father ran the Freedman Bureau in New Orleans and had gained the appointment for his son from his congressman, who just happened to be his brother – another carpetbagger selected for the House of Representative in the aftermath of the dissolution of the southern states. Reynolds was fully aware that the carpetbaggers' corruption was out of control, but that reality shouldn't deny southern students their rightful place at the Academy.

He would have to change the practice. No longer would young men from Ohio, New Jersey, Pennsylvania, or Massachusetts fill the seats that should go to students from Virginia, Texas, Alabama, and Mississippi. Starting next school term, the students would have to prove that they were raised in the states and districts which appointed them or be denied admittance.

Reynolds knew his policy faced stiff opposition from the Radicals, who continued to push their oppression of the South daily through the Congress, but he would pit his war record and popularity against the Radicals any day.

He entered his office. On his desk, he could see his mail. Warm in his great coat, he listlessly sorted through the envelopes. There was a knock on the door. "Enter!"

The door opened and a cadet appeared. He marched over to the desk and stiffly handed a telegram to Reynolds. A salute followed. The cadet exited as swiftly as he entered.

Reynolds reached across his desk and plucked up his letter opener. He slit the envelope and withdrew the telegram. It was from Sherman. He sighed in despair. The first word on the telegram was Sheridan. If the cavalry leader was involved then what followed next could only be bad news.

Each word caused his heart to drop further into his stomach. Lexington and Staunton had been burned and Jackson's adjutant had been killed trying to protect Jackson's house. What new outrages must Jackson be feeling right now?

Sherman was recalling him temporarily to Washington. Hopefully, Sherman wasn't obtuse enough to expect Reynolds to try to negotiate some type of deal with the fugitives. It was too late for that. Reynolds had warned Hamlin, Stanton, Sherman, and McClellan until he was blue in the face that a day of reckoning was fast approaching, but politics and retribution had outweighed compassion and commonsense.

He didn't want to leave West Point or his new wife, but Sherman hadn't given him a choice. He stripped off his coat, circled his desk, and took a seat. After rereading the telegram, he savagely wadded it up and slammed it into the wastebasket. No, his presence wouldn't change a thing.

Chapter Twenty Two

Sherman's Office
War Department
April 19, 1866

Reynolds dropped his valise by the door of Sherman's office. His great coat followed. He saw Sherman sitting at his desk sorting through a mountain of paperwork that was stacked high on the corner of his desk. Sheridan was slouched in the chair opposite the desk. Both men looked toward the door.

A look of relief swept over Sherman. "You made good time."

"I left as soon as I received your telegram." Reynolds didn't wait to be given permission to sit. He fell into the chair next to Sheridan. He was bone tired. The train ride from West Point had been uncomfortable, and he had been unable to sleep.

"The news isn't good." Sherman glared at Sheridan.

"I wouldn't expect it to be," Reynolds replied. He shifted in his chair and glanced at Sheridan. The cavalry leader remained unfazed by Sherman's anger. "Do you think I could get some coffee?" What he really needed was a nice, soft bed.

"Major Dayton!" Sherman bellowed. The aide appeared in the doorway. "Coffee, please." Dayton disappeared without a word. Sherman turned his attention to Reynolds. "Besides Forrest's successful attack…"

That brought a snort of derision from Sheridan.

"That's enough from you, mister," Sherman hollered, his voice echoing throughout the small office.

Reynolds noted with displeasure that the look of defiance remained on Sheridan's face.

"You got licked," Sherman continued. Sheridan's scowl deepened. "I don't care whether you admit it or not, you still got licked." Once more, Sherman turned his attention to Reynolds. "The Valley has been quiet of late," he said, finishing his thought. "We don't have any reports of men readying themselves to march on Washington, but as you can imagine, the place is a powder keg." He glared at Sheridan again.

"I could dissipate that anger if you would just let me finish what I began," Sheridan snapped.

"Shut up!" Sherman thundered. "You've done enough."

Sheridan didn't back down. "No I haven't and that's the problem." Reynolds rolled his eyes. Sheridan bolted up in his chair and glared at Reynolds. "You got something to say?"

Reynolds' laugh was bitter. "I knew you were trouble from the moment you came East."

"I disagree," Sheridan replied coldly.

"That's because you're a fool," Reynolds said, his voice just as frosty as Sheridan's.

The cavalry leader jumped to his feet. "I refuse to sit here and be insulted by the likes of you!"

"Sit down," Sherman said with a low voice.

"No!" Sheridan was defiant. "This man has been in bed with the Rebs since day one. He's a traitor."

This time Reynolds' laugh was boisterous. "Are you still chasing that old bone?"

Sheridan narrowed his eyes. "You don't fool me. I know you were behind the peacock's rescue."

Reynolds laughed again. He purposely turned his back to Sheridan.

"I told you to sit down," Sherman repeated.

Sheridan retook his seat.

Reynolds stifled a yawn. "You've brought me a long way. I hope it wasn't so that I could be insulted by Phil."

This time, Sherman glared at Reynolds. "I brought you here because I need your help. Phil's insulting because he doesn't know any other way to behave. But he's here at my request."

Reynolds couldn't think why Sherman would need Sheridan's advice on anything. After his unprovoked attack on Lexington, Sheridan should have been cashiered. But he wasn't, and Reynolds could only assume that Sherman, despite his present display of temper, approved of Sheridan's strong armed tactics.

Reynolds gestured between himself and Sheridan. "He and I are unsuited to work together."

Sherman placed folded hands on his desk. "I'm hoping you'll help me out of this impossible situation. Despite Phil."

"I don't know what I can do," Reynolds said.

Dayton returned. He carried a tray filled with coffee cups, pot, sugar bowl, and creamer. He set it on the desk. "Is there anything else?" He asked Sherman.

"No, thank you," Sherman said in dismissal.

Dayton shut the door behind him. Reynolds poured a cup of coffee. He took a sip. It was nice and strong. He took another sip. "I don't know what I can do to help," he repeated.

"The president has ordered me to fix this mess and to prevent an outbreak of fighting. He's leaving the how up to me."

It was the first good news Reynolds had heard since his arrival. "Declare a blanket amnesty and let me return to West Point."

Sherman frowned. "That was my suggestion."

Reynolds' heart dropped. "And?"

Sherman's frown deepened. "My hands are tied. I have pleaded with my brother, with Senator Sumner, and Congressman Stevens. There'll be no amnesty. The fugitives will have to surrender and stand trial."

"Those terms are non-starters."

"I don't think so," Sherman said.

Reynolds stared dumbfounded at Sherman. Surely, Sherman didn't believe that Lee and Jackson would come in after the destruction of Lexington and Staunton. With a clatter, Reynolds set his cup on the tray. "You can't be that deluded."

Sherman drew his hand through his hair before holding it up at Reynolds. "I have two options. The first is to give Sheridan a free hand. The second is to have you contact General Jackson and convince him to surrender."

"Jackson has no reason to trust me."

Sherman learned forward. "Jackson's a soldier. Make him understand."

Reynolds jerked to his feet and began to pace. He knew from the moment he received the telegram that this was Sherman's end game.

"You're my only hope," Sherman said, his voice constricted. "If you won't arrange a meeting with Jackson, then I'll have no choice but to employ Sheridan's strategy."

Reynolds faced Sherman. "Are you blackmailing me?"

Sherman stiffened in anger. "I would never do that. I'm just out of options. One way – he pointed at Reynolds – or another – he pointed at Sheridan – I'll fulfill my orders. Because if I don't, McClellan will find someone who will."

"I don't even know how to contact Jackson."

"Just do what you did all the other times you fed Stuart information," Sheridan sniped.

Reynolds pointed his finger at Sheridan, but directed his comment to Sherman. "You need to get him out of here before I shoot him."

"You're dismissed," Sherman said to Sheridan with a jerk of his head toward the door.

Sheridan stood. Before he left, he threw Reynolds a hateful look.

"I don't know if I can get a message to Jackson. And if I can, I can't predict if he'll respond favorably," Reynolds said.

"Just do your best, John," Sherman said.

Reynolds stood. "Right now, my best is to get some sleep. I assume you made a reservation for me at the Willard Hotel?"

"I did," Sherman said.

"Good." Reynolds stood. He picked up his greatcoat and valise and exited Sherman's office without saying goodbye.

★ ★ ★

As the last bites of dinner were being consumed, Forrest appeared in the dining room. He held up an envelope and announced that it was from Reynolds. He gave the message to Jackson, who turned it over in his hands. He glanced around the table and smiled. "This can wait until we're finished." He set the envelope next to his plate.

The rest of dinner was a strained affair. Conversation dwindled away. The only sounds were utensils scraping against plates. Flora suddenly dropped her fork on the table. "If you'll excuse me." Her voice shook. She fled the dining room. Anna excused herself and followed.

Jackson felt all eyes in the room on him. With a sigh, he picked up the envelope, broke the seal, and read it out loud. Reynolds was asking for a meeting. He couldn't come up with one good reason why he should go. From the looks on the others' faces, neither could they.

"So, we're in agreement," Jackson said.

"Unfortunately," Lee said. He folded his napkin and laid it on his empty plate.

The room was silent except for Forrest's spoon stirring his coffee.

"Do you think we should at least hear what General Reynolds has to say? Don't we owe him that courtesy?" Johnston asked.

"No, we don't." Longstreet snagged the last biscuit from the basket. "The time for dealing and terms and surrender are over. Only one course of action is open. I think we've known that for a while. Some of us just reached that conclusion faster than the rest of us." He grinned at Jackson. "But now that we are all on the same page, we need to start preparing before the Yankees can put up a defense or burn any more cities."

"General Forrest, I'll take some coffee." Jackson held up his cup. Forrest lifted up the pot and filled the cup. Jackson took a sip.

"But you don't know why General Reynolds wants to meet with you." Jackson saw Anna standing in the hallway. "Do I get a say in your deliberations?"

Lee turned in his chair and faced Anna. He smiled gently. "Of course, dear."

Anna came to the table and slipped into her usual seat. "I wonder if you have considered all the consequences of your decision to fight."

"I think we have, ma'am." Forrest was sharp.

Anna fixed her gaze on her husband. "You have a daughter and a baby boy. And then there are Jimmie and Ginny. For all intents and purpose, you are their father now. I don't think Jimmie could survive losing you." She turned to General Lee. "And you are his beloved Grandpa. It's Grandpa this and Grandpa that. You owe it to them to hear what General Reynolds has to say."

"Anna," Jackson said softly, "if we surrender, the Yankees will hang us."

"Ma'am, are you sure you just don't want your husband to go off to fight?" Forrest asked. He was still sharp.

"General Forrest," Lee reproved.

"It's okay." Anna put a gentle hand on Lee's arm but addressed Forrest. "I have made my peace with the Lord about the possibility of my husband's death since that long ago day he led the cadets of VMI to Richmond. This isn't about my fear of losing Tom, but my worries for the children. Two of them have already suffered the loss of their father."

"We all have wives and children, ma'am," Forrest replied. Jackson noted that his tone was gentler.

"And I believe I speak for them as well," Anna said. "General Forrest, I'm not asking you or my husband to surrender to the

Yankees. I'm just asking that you meet with General Reynolds and hear what he has to say."

"It's a waste of time." Longstreet popped the rest of the biscuit into his mouth.

"It could be, but you don't know that," Anna said. "Surely, General Reynolds understands the state of affairs. Yet, he has asked for a meeting. Maybe he has a new offer. But unless you go, you won't know for sure."

"It's a delaying tactic," Forrest said. He emptied his coffee cup.

"I agree." Longstreet gave Jackson a piercing stare.

Jackson rubbed his cheek. He really didn't believe that Reynolds had anything new to offer, but Anna was right. He owed it to Jimmie and Julia, Ginny and little Tom to at least hear the man out. After all, Reynolds had risked his life and reputation on their behalf. "Okay, Anna, I'll meet with General Reynolds."

He watched his wife sigh in relief and his conscience panged him.

"I'll go with you and keep you safe," Forrest said.

Jackson opened the letter and read the last paragraph. Reynolds had set the meeting for three days from tonight. The crude map drawn on the bottom of the page was a crossroads near Front Royal. He refolded the letter and handed it to Forrest. "In the meantime, we go forward with our plans. If Reynolds offers us no new terms, then we haven't lost any time. But if he has come with a new proposal that benefits us, do I have your permission to accept that offer?"

"Yes," Johnston said. Lee agreed.

"As long as it's not surrender," Longstreet said.

Jackson nodded. He glanced at his wife. "Is that okay, Anna?"

She smiled. "If it comes to fighting, at least you'll know that you've done everything possible to avoid it. I can't ask for anything more. When will you be leaving?"

"Tomorrow at dawn," Forrest said.

★ ★ ★

Near Front Royal
April 27, 1866
4:30 p.m.

Reynolds sat underneath the shade of a large tree at the top of a hill. Below was the road that Jackson would approach on, if he accepted the invitation at all. Hidden behind him, in the trees, was Colonel Rosengarten. The one thing Reynolds had hated about leaving Washington was saying good-bye to his adjutant. After he had awakened from his nap, he searched the War Department until he found Rosengarten squirreled away in the building's bowels, unhappily shuffling discharge papers for the last remnant of the Army of the Potomac. When Reynolds burst through the door, Rosengarten's smile was one of rescue. As long as Reynolds was in Washington, Rosengarten would remain by his side.

Reynolds slipped his watch out of his pocket and glanced at the time. Jackson was late. "We'll give him another fifteen minutes and then we'll head back."

"Okay."

Reynolds returned the watch to his pocket and lifted his face to the warm, spring sun. The trees were leafy green and the grass on the hill a lush green carpet. He heard horses approaching. He stood. "Someone's coming." In response, Rosengarten pulled back the hammer on his pistol.

Reynolds gathered the reins of his mare. He swung up in the saddle and began to walk slowly down the hill. Halfway down, he stopped and waited. He didn't have to wait long. He recognized the rider on the small horse as Jackson. But the Confederate general wasn't alone. Forrest was with him.

Forrest spied him first, turned from the road, and headed up the hill. Jackson followed.

"General Forrest," Reynolds greeted.

Forrest didn't reply. He turned his attention to Jackson, who dismounted. Reynolds followed suit. He extended his hand, but Jackson didn't extend his. Reynolds dropped his hand. Already, the meeting didn't promise a successful ending.

"General Reynolds." There was suppressed fury in Jackson's voice. "Last time we met, you promised me Stuart's murderer would see justice. According to the papers, the man received a slap on the wrist, a discharge, and a hero's welcome home."

"General Jackson." Anger tinged Reynolds' own voice. He resented being taken to task by the very men he had risked his reputation and life to save. "I did my best to see that the young man received his punishment, but my recommendations were ignored."

Forrest put his hand on his hips. "You ain't got nothin' new for us, do you?" Reynolds shook his head. "Let's go, General Jackson."

Reynolds felt Jackson's eyes rake him.

"Why did you want a meeting?" Jackson questioned.

"Because General Sherman's other option was to send Sheridan back into the Valley."

"Well, thank you for that, at least." Jackson stripped his gauntlets from his hands.

"It's only temporary. When I return to Washington, Sherman will unleash Sheridan."

Forrest stamped about. "Sheridan will find the towns well defended this time." He jerked on Jackson's arm. "We need to go."

"In a moment."

Forrest stomped off down the hill.

"The terms have changed since I last met with General Stuart and General Forrest," Reynolds said.

"Of course they have!" Forrest shouted from down the hill.

"How have they changed?" Jackson questioned.

"Before, I was able to give you a jury I believed would set you free. Now, you'll be tried in the Senate and the jury will consist of hand-picked Radicals."

"Guaranteed to convict us." Jackson exhaled. Reynolds thought it was the final punctuation mark on the conversation. But it wasn't, for Jackson gave him a slight smile. "General Reynolds, I do want to apologize for holding a pistol on you the last time we met. You didn't deserve that."

Reynolds smiled. "You were angry."

"I was furious, but it was still wrong."

"Let's go, General Jackson," Forrest repeated.

Jackson gazed down the hill deep in thought. When he returned his attention to Reynolds, there was a serious glint in his eyes. "General Reynolds, as my Christian brother, what would you do if you were in my shoes?" Reynolds hesitated. "As my Christian brother," Jackson repeated.

"I'd fight."

Chapter Twenty Three

Jimmie stood on the porch peering through Lee's fieldglasses. The glasses darted this way and that. Every once in a while, he would wave his hand in front of the lenses. Rebel had already been inspected from head to tail. Now, the glasses were turned on Lee, who was sitting in the swing.

Jimmie reached out his hand. "You're so close, I can touch you." He exclaimed to Lee. A song bird tweeted in the oak nearest the house. Jimmie whirled the glasses toward the tree and bird. "It's a bluebird," he announced.

The glasses began to bob up and down in an erratic fashion. Lee peered out into the lawn. He saw a butterfly flitting across the lawn.

Longstreet came up on the porch and crossed to the swing. "Can I have a word with you?" He asked.

Lee gave permission and Longstreet fell onto the couch. Jimmie turned the glasses on Longstreet. He giggled. "General Longstreet, you're a giant!"

Rebel bounced up and down in front of the Georgian, demanding attention. Longstreet ignored the dog. Rebel reached up to the arm of the couch and barked. Longstreet pushed him away. Rebel fell back, but renewed his attempts to be noticed.

"You know, if you pet him, he'll go away," Lee reproved. He didn't understand why Longstreet ignored the spaniel. A simple pat on the head was usually all Rebel required.

Longstreet scratched Rebel on his head. Satisfied, the spaniel retreated down the porch and lay down in front of the door.

"What can I do for you, Pete?" Lee asked.

Longstreet wasted no time. "I want to know why you seem determined to give Jackson command of the army."

At the name Jackson, Jimmie whirled the glasses toward the men. Lee gestured toward Jimmie with his index finger. "Little ears," he said softly.

Longstreet smiled at the boy. "Jimmie, I bet if you take those glasses in the backyard, you could see all kinds of birds, squirrels, and insects."

Jimmie lowered the glasses and stared at Longstreet with wide eyes. "What kind of bugs?"

"I saw some grasshoppers just a few minutes ago."

"Can I, Grandpa?" Jimmie appealed to Lee.

"You promise to be careful," Lee admonished.

"Very careful," Jimmie promised.

Lee gave permission. Jimmie ran down the stairs.

"Careful," Lee called. He laughed as Jimmie slowly walked around the side of the house. He knew the moment the boy was out of sight, he would be running again before the bugs got away. Rebel glanced up, saw that Jimmie was gone, and shot off like an arrow after his master. Lee sighed in resignation. "Go on with your thought, Pete."

"I don't understand why you're abdicating command of the army to General Jackson."

Lee laughed. "Pete, I think your concerns are premature."

Longstreet frowned. "I don't think so. Stuart told us he could raise a force of 2,000 men. I'm sure with his death and the destruction in the Valley, the number of men who will answer any call has grown significantly."

Lee sighed. Why was Longstreet pressing this point now? Before Jackson returned from his meeting? Before they knew how many men would actually come? "Even if you doubled the men Jeb said would come, we're talking less than division strength. We hardly need an organized command structure. Especially since we will be awash in generals."

Longstreet leaned forward. "Someone needs to be in overall command."

"I don't want it to be so, but I think it has to be me," Lee said reluctantly, thinking back to Morrison's words under the sycamore trees the afternoon they found out that McClellan had reneged on his promise of amnesty.

Longstreet slammed back in the couch. "That's a mistake."

Lee was flabbergasted at the comment. "Why is that a mistake?" The back of his neck grew hot.

"Because you're going to listen to Jackson like you always do."

"Like I always do?" Lee demanded.

Longstreet didn't back down. "Jackson is too aggressive. He'll throw that division at the Yankees and pray God grants him victory. We can't afford that strategy. Not now."

"I disagree with your assessment of General Jackson's strategy," Lee said tightly.

"Of course you do," Longstreet snapped.

Lee rocked the swing with the heels of his boots. This was a conversation he no longer wanted to participate in. The back of his neck burned, and he could feel the heat rising in his cheeks.

"We must use the men wisely," Longstreet insisted. "We'll only get one chance at winning our freedom."

Lee didn't answer. The chair's chains squeaked in the silence.

"I believe I'm the right man for command," Longstreet announced.

The swing came to a sudden stop. "You do." Lee didn't hide his disapproval.

"I know that both you and General Johnston outrank me on the seniority list."

Lee stared at Longstreet in disbelief. Seniority list? Outrank? "Pete, the Confederacy is dead. There isn't a seniority list anymore. When those men come, they'll come out of loyalty..."

Longstreet waved his hand in interruption. "Then it shouldn't be taken for granted that you're in command."

"I don't think it's being taken for granted." Lee looked around for some reason to leave the porch.

"General Jackson believes you're in command."

Lee heard the same contempt in Longstreet's voice that his old war horse always used when speaking of Jackson. "General Jackson is just being deferential to an old man."

"Don't patronize me," Longstreet snapped. With one hand he gripped the arm on the couch. His knuckles turned white.

Wanting to bring the conversation to a close, Lee stood. "I'm not."

Longstreet jumped to his feet. "No, Robert, I've been ignored long enough. I've commanded two armies. I stayed in the field longer than you. I've proven my worth. I believe that whatever action we take, I should be in command. I've earned it."

"I've no doubt that you are more than able to lead whatever force we gather." Lee didn't keep his voice from rising in anger.

"But," Longstreet barked.

"The soldiers who answer our appeal will be Valley men. The fight will most likely happen in the Valley. Who better to lead those men in that theater than Jackson?"

Jimmie came around the side of the house. He stared at the two men. "Is everything okay, Grandpa?"

Lee sat down on the swing. He swallowed his anger and smiled at his grandson. "Everything is fine. Are you done with my glasses?" Jimmie nodded. "Can you put them in my room for me?" Jimmie nodded again. He climbed the steps. "I'm going to take Centurion for a gallop. Do you want to come along?"

Jimmie's mouth flew open. "Can I?" He scrunched his shoulders up around his ears.

"Ask your mama," Lee said. Jimmie flew into the house. When the door banged shut, Lee let his anger rekindle. "I understand how frustrated you've been since you've arrived. But this conversation is needless. No one is trying to steal a command from you. We've one chance to win our freedom. One chance! So, any decision will be made by all of us. But I will tell you this. I have no fear in letting General Jackson determine our strategy. Just like I would have no hesitation to follow your strategy or General Johnston's if it was the correct one. We're in this together, and our situation is so dire that I can't believe you would give in to ego and ambition."

"Is that what you think I'm doing?" Longstreet's voice cracked like a whip.

"Yes, I do," Lee retorted. "I'm sure when the time comes, everyone's ideas will be taken into consideration."

Jimmie raced from the house. "I'm ready, Grandpa." He had on his fighting jacket, his cape, and his plumed hat.

"So am I. If you'll excuse me, Pete." He didn't wait for an answer. He grabbed Jimmie's hand and hurried down the steps.

★★★

Lee looked around the dining room. It was filled to bursting with generals. He wanted to poke Longstreet and say, "I told you so," but General Mahone sat between he and Longstreet. Mahone had arrived early this morning. By nightfall, Jubal Early, Harry Heth, Robert Rodes, and John Mosby had all been brought in by Fitz. The dining room couldn't contain them all. Rodes, Mosby, and Heth sat in the hallway. Captain Morrison was seated on a stool behind Jackson's chair. Jedidiah Hotchkiss stood in the corner waiting. His cache of maps spread out on the table.

To tell the truth, Lee had been shocked when he saw Heth following Fitz up the long driveway. He didn't think his letters had been circulated outside the Valley. Yet, one had reached Heth all the way in Chesterfield County. When Forrest arrived with Mahone, another general not from the Valley, Lee asked Forrest just how far his letters had been sent. "As far as they needed to go," was the cavalry leader's cryptic reply.

Lee sat in Stuart's old seat next to the kitchen door. He stood. "Last call for coffee or lemonade." A pitcher and a coffee pot made their way to him. He grabbed both and slid through the kitchen door, coming face-to-face with Jimmie dressed in his nightshirt and robe. Rebel sat next to him. After dinner, Flora had pulled the protesting boy from the dining room and sent him on to bed. Obviously Jimmie and his dog hadn't stayed there. At Lee's appearance, Jimmie put a finger to his lips. Rebel began to whine. Jimmie tapped the spaniel on the nose. "Ssshhh!" He hissed.

Lee smiled and set the pot and pitcher on the kitchen table. Jim turned from the dishes and saw the containers.

"The men sure are thirsty," he remarked. He grabbed the coffee pot and filled it with water. He set it on the stove to boil. The pitcher of lemonade was replaced by one of water. "It's all that's left," he said. "I'll bring out the coffee once it's ready."

Lee gestured toward Jimmie, who was scrunched up against the counter.

"He arrived about ten minutes ago," Jim reported.

"If he gets underfoot, send him to bed." He fixed his gaze on Jimmie. "Do you hear me?"

"Ooohh, Jim ain't gotta worry about me. I'll be good. But Grandpa, you remind ole Stonewall that I'm a soldier, too."

Lee laughed. "I'll remind him." He held up the pitcher. "Thank you, Jim." He exited the kitchen. "Only water now. Coffee will be out in a moment."

His words made little impact on the men. He set the pitcher on the sideboard and retook his seat.

"General Lee," Forrest said.

The news must be good, Lee thought, for the usually gruff cavalry leader was practically jovial.

"Your letters did the trick. Latest count from Colonel Kelley is about 700 men, but that trickle is quickly enlarging into a pretty fair size stream," Forrest continued happily. "When we're ready to move, you can count on double that easy."

"How are we going to hide them all from the Yankees?" Johnston questioned.

"We ain't," Forrest said. "Well, not for long. Especially if we double in size in the next week."

"Do you think the Yankees already know what we're up to?" Heth asked.

"I suspect so." Forrest was his usual blunt self. "Keepin' this place a secret from the Yankees was easy, but what happens next will have to be done in plain sight."

"How many camps have we established so far?" Rodes asked.

Morrison stirred. "Fifteen right now." He was responsible for assigning the men to the different camps scattered throughout the Valley. Morrison employed the same system Stuart had created last summer.

Forrest turned to Jackson who was sitting in his usual seat at the head of the table. "So, whatever you're plannin', you need to git about it quick."

Lee chucked. That was the Forrest he had grown to know.

Jackson cleared his throat. "I agree with General Forrest's assessment. The Yankees are fully aware that our strategy is to capture Washington City."

An unhappy buzz filled the room.

"Then why do it?" Rodes questioned.

"I agree," Heth chimed in.

Jackson smiled. He gestured to Colonel Hotchkiss, who pulled out a map from the pile and laid it on top.

"Richmond!" Longstreet exclaimed when he saw the map.

"There's no reason to think we can surprise the Yankees. Last October after Stuart's murder – Lee never heard Jackson refer to Stuart's death as anything but murder – the Yankees went on high alert. Since the capture of our courier, the Yankees are once more on alert. So, I'm going to use their assumptions against them."

Longstreet puffed out his cheeks in disagreement but didn't speak.

"We distract them," Jackson continued, "and make them believe we have another objective in mind."

Rodes stood and squeezed between Johnston and Heth so he could see the map.

Jackson continued. "According to the newspapers Fitz brings us, we know Richmond is headquarters for Military District Number One, which encompasses Virginia, North Carolina, and Eastern Tennessee. If we can take Richmond, we can sever the hold the Yankees have on this territory. Free Richmond and you literally free soldiers from Virginia and North Carolina to join our cause."

"So, we're taking Richmond to raise an army," Early said.

Jackson nodded. "We advertise that fact – so loud and clear that the Yankees in Washington can't help but hear us."

Lee was impressed. A force moving toward Richmond under those circumstances would be almost impossible to ignore. But there was a large garrison of Yankees in Richmond and a smaller one in Raleigh according to the newspapers. A small diversionary force would never be able to take the city, and the Yankees would know that too.

"It also keeps the Yankees in Richmond occupied. We won't have to worry about them arriving via the trains in our rear as we move on Washington." Jackson sat down.

"How many men do you plan to send to Richmond?" Lee asked.

"At least a third of what we gather, plus cavalry."

Longstreet sat up straight. "That's risky."

"Yes, but any less won't draw the Yankees' attention," Jackson replied.

Longstreet scoffed. "Not even you are foolish enough to believe you can take Washington with less than 1,500 men."

"I'll have less than that," Jackson responded.

"Less!" Longstreet protested. "Are you planning another diversion?"

"Actually, I am."

Lee glanced around the room. The only one who seemed to be upset over Jackson's announcement was Longstreet. The rest were content to wait until Jackson finished before commenting.

"Where is this one headed?" Longstreet asked. "Atlanta?"

Forrest glowered. "Why don't you let the man speak?"

The kitchen door banged against Lee's chair. It must be Jim coming in with the coffee pot. "Just a moment." Lee stood and pushed his chair in. The door swung open. Jim appeared in the doorway with the coffee pot in his hand. Behind him, Lee saw Jimmie sound asleep on the floor. Rebel was curled up next to him. Lee grabbed the pot. "Do you mind putting our little soldier to bed?"

At Lee's words, Jackson leaned back in his chair and peered into the kitchen. His eyes met Lee's and he smiled.

"No, sir, I don't mind," Jim said. "Will there be anything else?"

Lee shook his head. He set the coffee pot on the sideboard. "Gentlemen, the kitchen is closed until tomorrow morning."

Johnston squeezed past the chairs until he made it to the sideboard. He poured a cup of coffee. "General Jackson, where is the second force going?"

"Bull Run Creek," Jackson replied.

Johnston took a sip from his cup. "You're going to make the Yankees believe we're attacking Washington via Manassas and Centreville."

"Right." Jackson quickly sorted through the maps and pulled out one of northern Virginia and Maryland. "In the meantime, the main body will attack through Maryland and take Washington City from the north."

Early laughed. "While the Yankees are looking south and west." He slapped his hand on the table. "Brilliant!"

"According to our spy..." Jackson gave each of the fugitive generals a glare that warned them to keep the spy's identity to themselves. The other generals in the room appeared curious, but held their tongues and didn't ask. "There's a strong Union presence in Front Royal, which the force designated for Manassas will defeat. The other stronghold is Harper's Ferry. Now, we can easily avoid Harper's Ferry, but that will take us miles out of our way. Or we can send a force under General Forrest, capture the garrison there, and use the telegraph to send misinformation to the Yankees in Washington. We'll strip both towns of weapons. General Forrest, once you secure Harper's Ferry, you'll join the march to Washington."

"I'd like to be in command of the force headed for Richmond," Longstreet volunteered.

"I think that would be an excellent idea," Lee said swiftly. Jackson frowned at him, clearly not pleased. Lee didn't know who Jackson had tasked for the job, but Lee was afraid that if Longstreet marched with the main force, the possibility existed that he would resort to his old habit of slowly obeying any order he disagreed with.

"Are you sure?" Jackson asked Lee.

Lee nodded.

"It's settled then," Longstreet said. He turned to Forrest. "General, I believe your place is with me."

"No," Forrest replied sharply. "I'll go with General Lee and General Jackson.

"I'll go with you, General Longstreet," Fitz volunteered with a raise of his hand.

Lee leaned forward and put his elbows and his clasped hands on the table. "General Longstreet, I don't think it would be a bad idea if you actually took Richmond and raised that army just in case the battle goes against us in Washington."

Longstreet smiled and nodded. Lee was glad to see the smile.

Johnston had returned to his seat. "I'm very familiar with the ground at Bull Run Creek. I'll be more than happy to command the force assigned there."

Mosby stood. "My men and I will go with General Johnston."

The rest of the generals were given their posts. Rodes and Early would go with Jackson and Lee. Mahone would go with Longstreet. Heth with Johnston.

Overall, Lee was pleased. It was a good plan and had every chance of success.

The meeting was breaking up. The officers would remain guests of the plantation until it was time to depart. Johnston volunteered to show Heth, Mahone, and Early to the little house. Morrison had given up his room and moved a camp bed into the nursery with the children. Forrest, Mosby, and Fitz returned to the pickets. Rodes and Hotchkiss would be bunking in the living room. Jackson shepherded them down the hall.

That just left Longstreet in the room. Lee was instantly on guard.

"Thank you for backing me for the Richmond command," Longstreet said.

"You're the best man for the job." Lee began to clear the table, stacking the cups on the sideboard.

Longstreet handed Lee two cups. "I can't be the third wheel in your command structure. I am better than that. You know it and I know it. But for some reason I cannot fathom, you seem determined to place all your trust in General Jackson. I don't think he deserves it, yet he has it."

Lee wondered if Jackson saw Longstreet as a rival. He didn't think so. Jackson was a servant to his God and his duty. If that duty meant being number two to Longstreet, he would do so. Jackson gave his honest opinion about any situation, then accepted and obeyed the orders given him. That was his strength.

"I listen to all my commanders," Lee said, "but in the end, I listen to that small voice that knows the right course of action. If you want to be angry with anything, be angry with that voice."

Longstreet's face tightened. "I know you believe that. But tonight, the only plan offered was Jackson's."

Lee stared at Longstreet. "Where was your plan, Pete?"

"I didn't create one."

Lee slammed the cup down on the sideboard. "Then don't fault General Jackson because he did." He leaned over the sideboard and reined in his anger. "You and I have beat this dead horse for all its worth. I don't care if you don't believe me." He straightened. "Good night." He strode from the dining room.

Chapter Twenty Four

Anna slipped her arm through Jackson's. She had demanded and received an hour of her husband's time. In the last four days, she had seldom seen him alone. Preparations were escalating so that Longstreet, Mahone, and Fitz could leave tomorrow morning at first light. Their march on Richmond would initiate the opening salvo in a battle that, hopefully, would bring their hiding to an end. Even though she didn't want her husband fighting again, she knew there was no other choice. At least, by taking the fight to the Yankees, the hope existed that they could win their freedom.

To make sure they weren't disturbed, she insisted that the hour be spent walking through the woods away from prying eyes and couriers' messages.

"Darling." She squeezed his arm. "I made a promise to myself that I wouldn't look ahead, but be content in today. I'm going to break that promise. When all of this is over, I want to return to Lexington and rebuild our house."

"We could go anywhere. Back to North Carolina if you want."

She squeezed his arm again. "But you were happy in Lexington."

Jackson covered her hand with his. "I was, but I've been happy here, too. Perhaps we can go west to the Indian Territory and have a farm like this one."

Anna shook her head. "I don't know if Flora would want to go back west."

Jackson stopped. "Flora?"

Anna looked up at his face. He quickly turned away. "We can't leave her. You have to honor your promise to Stuart."

Jackson reached down and plucked a wildflower, smelled it, and gave it to Anna. "I don't know if we should bring Flora and the children into our family. I believe I can fulfill my promise to Stuart by making sure Flora is comfortably settled in whatever life she chooses, whether it's with her parents or with Stuart's brother."

His words stunned her. Since Stuart's death, she had taken it for granted that Flora and the children would live with them once they were free to resume their lives. She had welcomed the idea. She loved Flora like a sister and considered Jimmie and Ginny to be her children. She knew that Flora felt the same about Julia and Tom. "What has changed?"

"I just don't think it would be wise to complicate our lives by introducing Stuart's family into it."

Anna knew him well enough to know that there was something more to this sudden reticence than any complications that might be introduced into their lives. He had fallen silent again. She nudged him with her shoulder, but he remained silent. She walked along, hoping that he would reveal his secrets. When he didn't, she spoke her concern. "You seem to be searching for a way to break your promise to Stuart."

"I'm torn in two," he confessed with a sigh. He stared down into her face. She was surprised to find tears in his eyes.

"What's the matter?" She gripped his arm harder.

"I want to honor my promise." He battled back his tears. "But it's only a matter of time until Flora's grief eases, and she begins to think of forging a new life on her own. And when she does, she'll take that little boy with her, and it will be like losing Stuart all over again."

She embraced him and held him close.

"I can't do it a second time," he confessed. "Jimmie is such a comfort and a joy. I would rather him go now than live in constant fear of losing him." He broke away. "I'm a selfish beast."

She reached up and cupped his cheek with her hand. "You're not selfish. Who can blame you for not wanting to suffer another loss?" He took her hand and kissed it lightly. "But Tom, even if Flora only stays with us for a couple of months before moving on, Jimmie wouldn't be gone forever. He can come visit us during the summer or during any of his school vacations."

"That's true," Jackson replied gloomily.

Anna smiled. He was afraid that Jimmie wouldn't want to come to visit. That was nonsense, of course. "You are his ole Stonewall. He'll visit you anytime you ask."

Jackson shook his head. "Jimmie just misses his father. That's all."

Anna threaded her arm through his again. "I wish you could see what I see. When you left to meet with General Reynolds, he was at a loss. Every sound in the driveway brought him racing down the hall hoping you had returned. And the disappointment that followed when it wasn't. My stars! His father will always have a place of honor in Jimmie's heart and life. He'll consider it a source of pride to be Jeb Stuart's son. But he adores being your little boy."

Tears flooded Jackson's eyes again. "I'll make sure he never forgets his father."

Anna smiled. "Sometimes I forget how much you miss him."

"Every day."

She took his hand. "Then my darling, keep your promise and trust me when I say that Jimmie and Ginny will always be a part of our family no matter what Flora decides in the future." He squeezed her hand. "In the meantime, I have less than two days with you, and I demand your full attention."

He drew her near. "You do?" He smiled.

"I do."

He leaned down and kissed her.

★★★

Jackson stood on the porch, drinking a cup of coffee, and watching the frantic, last minute preparations of Longstreet, Mahone, and Fitz. The sun was not up yet, so the dim light slowed their movements.

Jackson heard a horse galloping up the driveway. From the frantic pace, the rider could only be Forrest.

Fitz turned from cinching his horse's saddle and hailed the approaching horseman. Jackson was correct. It was Forrest. He drew up King Philip and threw himself from the saddle. "General Jackson," he called. "It's a beautiful morning, don't you think."

Jackson just laughed.

Longstreet exited the front door. "Good morning, General Jackson, General Forrest." Longstreet had been terse since the strategy meeting. In fact, Longstreet hadn't said more than three words in a row to Jackson since that night. Jackson found the brusqueness unsettling. He knew Longstreet was angry. Jackson just didn't know what he had done to make him so.

Jackson sat on the porch rail. "General Longstreet, I promised you a third of the men that we assembled in the Valley. I'm going to have to change that."

Anger radiated from Longstreet like heat from a stove. "And how am I supposed to convince the Yankees that I'm serious about taking Richmond?" He slapped his gauntlets against his thigh. "Perhaps, you should take the Richmond assignment. That way you could mystify and mislead the enemy with hand shadows."

"That's unnecessary," Forrest snapped.

Longstreet glared at his cavalry leader.

Jackson pursed his lips to keep angry words from escaping. "Six hundred men will ride with you," he said when he had his anger in check.

"Six hundred men!" Longstreet slapped his gauntlets on the porch rail. "Unbelievable!"

Jackson ignored Longstreet's tantrum. "Custis Lee sent word. He has been approached by men asking what they can do to assist you. He instructed them to slip away from the city at the first possible chance and rendezvous with you at the juncture of Three Notched Road and Rockfish Gap Turnpike. Where both cross Meachum's River.

The men will arrive tomorrow at noon. If you're not there by two, they have been instructed to scatter and reform closer to Bull Run Creek. So, don't be late."

"I don't intend to," Longstreet barked. "Did Custis tell you how many men I should expect?"

Jackson took another sip of coffee. "The estimate is 150 to 200 men."

"So, I should expect half that," Longstreet snapped again.

"Why? Can't Custis Lee count?" Forrest asked.

"He finished first in his class at West Point," Jackson said. "So, I think he can count past 100."

"Fine." Longstreet went down the steps and crossed to his gelding.

Forrest shot Jackson a look of solidarity. "Is there any more coffee?"

"Jim has a pot on the stove." Jackson handed him his empty cup. "If you ask nicely, he may wrangle us up a stack of flapjacks."

Forrest smiled. "I'm always nice." He headed into the house.

Jackson sighed and went down the steps to where Longstreet was conversing with Mahone.

"General Jackson," Little Billy said.

Even though Mahone had commanded a division in the First Corps, Jackson had always admired Mahone's quick decision making and attention to detail.

"Do you mind if I speak to General Longstreet for a moment?" Jackson asked Mahone.

Anger radiated from Longstreet once more. He excused himself to Mahone and traipsed after Jackson.

"It's good to be going to battle with you again," Jackson said.

Longstreet reared back as if he had been slapped. Then a stricken look appeared on his face. "Why would you say something like that to me? Especially after I've been raging about here like a wounded bear for the past couple of days."

Jackson smiled slightly. "I've been meaning to ask if I've offended you somehow?"

"Yes," Longstreet said.

Jackson's eyes flew open. He quickly searched back over his interactions with Longstreet but nothing stood out. "How?" He blurted out.

"By being a genius," Longstreet said. Then he laughed.

Jackson stood with his mouth agape. He didn't know what to say or even if he should say anything at all.

"I'm, sorry, Tom, but these last couple of days, I've been an ass. I've been jealous of you for a very long time." He removed his hat, snatched a bandana from his pocket and wiped the hatband. He stuffed the bandana back in his pocket. "And when you presented your strategy at the meeting, my jealousy got the better of me and that's why I fought you."

Jackson heard the words Longstreet was saying, but didn't really comprehend their meaning. Why would a battle plan bring about a confession of jealousy? "I don't understand."

"I was jealous because I couldn't come up with a strategy of my own. I did try." He laughed bitterly. His bandana made another appearance and once more he wiped his hatband. "My first campaign in the west was a huge success. But it was my only one. I know I was sabotaged by General Polk twice, but in reality, when the pressure was on, I couldn't think. The ground, the line, the retreat were all accomplished by General Bragg. When he died, I was lost. After Atlanta fell, I retreated because it was the only thing I knew how to do."

"I'm sorry," Jackson said because he didn't know what else to say.

Longstreet flushed again. "I believe your plan will work."

"If God is merciful to us," Jackson said.

The front door opened and shut. Lee walked out on the porch. Longstreet waved. Lee came down the steps. "Well, General Longstreet, it's about that time."

Longstreet smiled. "Yes, sir, it is. If I can take Richmond, I will. But either way, I'll keep the Yankees pinned down south. Your rear will be secure."

"I know," Lee said.

Longstreet put on his hat and crossed to his gelding. "Let's go!" He swung up in the saddle. "I'll be praying for you," he said to Jackson. He tapped the gelding and cantered down the driveway. Mahone and Fitz hurried after him.

Chapter Twenty Five

Meachum's River
Central Virginia
May 1, 1866
11:45 a.m.

L ongstreet arrived at the rendezvous point early. From the road, he could hear the roar of the river. It was filled with spring rains and was running fast. But that was not all he heard. He recognized the low rumbling of men gathered together and excited with the anticipation of battle. He had heard that sound countless times before. A chill danced down his spine. Behind him, making a great show for the Yankees, strode a long column of men, still marching with the quiet confidence of the Army of Northern Virginia.

Earlier this morning, he had sent a courier dashing back to Clover Hill to advise Jackson that his numbers were growing. Longstreet didn't know where the men were coming from, but every hour more and more soldiers joined the column.

Longstreet called a halt. Ordering Mahone to join him, he left the road and picked his way through the trees toward the buzz. Up ahead, through the thinning oaks, he could see a large clearing. A smile erupted on his face. The clearing was filled with men. Custis had underestimated the number. There had to be over 300 men waiting.

The men caught sight of him. The buzzing ceased. Longstreet felt exposed and vulnerable. Did the sudden silence mean that the men were disappointed that it wasn't Lee or Jackson emerging from the trees? He desired nothing more than to flee.

"Hurray for General Longstreet!" He heard a lone soldier cry. The sentiment brought him very little comfort. One happy cry in a sea of dumbstruck voices.

"Hurray for General Longstreet!" The cheer was taken up. Soldiers pressed forward, crowding the gelding, and reaching up their hands to him. He clasped the first hand, then a second, and a third. The cheer continued. It was deafening.

He dismounted and waded through the men. During his sojourn in the west he had never received this kind of welcome. Not once had the men even raised their voices when he passed. How many of the men present in this clearing were from the First Corps: his men, who had followed him from the Peninsula, to Maryland, and back to the Rappahannock.

His cheeks hurt from smiling, but he couldn't stop. He shook hands until his own ached and shouted hello until he was hoarse. His heart thumped inside his chest and tingles ran up and down his spine. The men hadn't forgotten him, and they still loved him.

Mahone brought him his horse. One day, he would have to name this beautiful gelding Stuart had given him. He swung up in the saddle and addressed the men. "We're going to Richmond and liberate it from the Yankees. Once Richmond is free, our orders are to march on Raleigh and capture the Union garrison there."

"We can do it!" Some of the men shouted.

"Of course we can!" Longstreet agreed.

He turned the gelding and headed toward the road.

"Columns of four!" Longstreet heard Mahone cry out.

The men fell easily into place.

Sherman's Office
War Department
May 2, 1866

Sheridan burst into Sherman's office without knocking. He waved a telegram high in the air. "From Colonel Simpson in Charlottesville."

Sherman watched the telegram as it whirled about in the air. It was making him dizzy. He stood and snatched the piece of paper from Sheridan's hands.

"We need to move, right now," Sheridan insisted.

Sherman read the telegram. He was flabbergasted. He looked at Sheridan in disbelief. "Is this correct?"

Sheridan blew out his breath. "Colonel Simpson is tracking the column."

"Twelve hundred men!" Sherman shouted. "And cavalry!"

Sheridan paced to the window. "We need to launch an attack on that column before it reaches Richmond."

Sherman stared at the telegram. Why Richmond? It made absolutely no sense since the city represented no feasible gain for the Rebels. Plus, there were over 3,000 Union soldiers in the former Confederate capital and another 1,500 men within easy call at Raleigh. He could have those soldiers in Richmond in less than twenty-four hours. "It's a demonstration. It has to be."

Sheridan spun from the window. "A 1,200 man demonstration?"

A feeling of dread slowly made its way up Sherman's chest. "How many former Reb soldiers are in Richmond?"

"About 6,000, give or take."

The dread reached Sherman's heart. He sat down hard in his chair and put his head in his hands. Last fall, he had stretched the Washington defenses to its limit to receive a blow from a force he believed would consist of 1,500 men. What would he do against a force close to 10,000? Lee could easily overwhelm the city.

"Do you want me to go to Richmond?" Sheridan asked. He was standing in front of the desk.

Sherman shook his head. George Thomas was in command of Military District One and was well up to the task of defending the city. He would do more than hunker down behind breastworks. He would meet the enemy and smash them. "I want you to stay put."

Sheridan shifted impatiently. "I can do more good in Richmond."

"You want to do good?" Sherman demanded. Sheridan scowled at Sherman's tone, but nodded. "Then I need a plan on my desk by the end of day that details how we defend Washington against a force of between 10,000 and 15,000 men."

★ ★ ★

Clover Hill
May 3, 1866

Johnston threw his saddle bags over his horse's rump. Harry Heth had just disappeared in the early morning dark to prepare the men for the march to Front Royal. Heth wouldn't have to work hard to get the soldiers to fall in. Last night, Johnston had spent a little time with the men, who had eased back into camp life. They were excited to be on the march again and especially eager to strike a blow against the Yankees. Johnston was glad for the excitement. That way he didn't have to answer questions on just how risky this venture truly was.

Yesterday afternoon, while he was going over the final details with Heth, Jackson had arrived with distressing news. He could only spare 400 men for the demonstration at Bull Run Creek. Johnston waited until Jackson left before he wilted. Four hundred men! That wouldn't be enough to hold the creek, let alone harass the Yankees if they suddenly retreated to Washington to help defend the city against Jackson's attack.

Then salvation! A courier arrived late last night from Longstreet with a message that produced wild excitement in the house. Men were joining Longstreet's march, not in drips and drabs, but in the hundreds. Longstreet had left with 600 men and now his ranks numbered 1,200. He expected a force close to 2,000 by time he reached Richmond.

Hope revived in Johnston's heart. If his column could be the magnet Longstreet's column proved to be, then the odds increased that he could put up a real defense against whatever force the Yankees sent to Bull Run Creek. Not only that, but with enough men, he could actually defeat the Yankees and move on Washington and cooperate with Jackson's attack.

He adjusted the bags, securing them behind the saddle. The front door opened and Rebel dashed out followed by Lee. The spaniel darted toward the bushes and disappeared under the leafy branches.

"Robert!" Johnston called softly.

Lee searched for the body that belonged to the voice. Johnston moved out of the deep shadows of the tree. Lee spotted him and came down the steps. Rebel reappeared and dashed after Lee.

"This is not the profession for old men," Lee said with a laugh.

Johnston joined in the laughter. "No, it's not. But it's the only profession I was made for."

Rebel sniffed around before trotting down the driveway.

"I know the situation is bleak," Lee said.

In the faint light, Johnston saw Lee's face. His old friend appeared to be gloomy this morning, which surprised Johnston, for Lee had always sounded upbeat during their many meetings.

"I'm not sending you on a suicide mission," Lee continued. "If you can't hold against whatever force those people send against you, retreat back to Front Royal, scatter the men, and return to the farmhouse."

"The only time I left my post was at Seven Pines and that was because I was carried from the field." Johnston expected Lee to laugh, but Lee's face remained in its sad lines. "What's wrong, Robert?"

Lee dropped his head. "I don't know. I can't shake this feeling of doom that has settled on me this morning."

"Are you unsure of the plan?" Johnston asked.

"No." Lee's reply was swift.

At least Lee's rapid answer revealed confidence in the strategy. So, something else had to be troubling his old friend.

Johnston heard footsteps approaching from the side yard. He had to wait until the figure was almost upon them before he recognized Jackson.

"Are you ready?" Jackson asked.

"Just waiting for Mosby," Johnston replied.

Jackson was all business this morning. Johnston took that as a good sign. Lee might be despondent, but Jackson certainly was not.

"General Forrest will leave tomorrow morning. I've asked him to march with you until Front Royal. I would rather hide his force from the Yankee garrison, but if you need him, he's instructed to join in the fight."

This last minute change bothered Johnston. The original plan had called for Forrest to use the fight at Front Royal to bypass the city and the Yankee garrison stationed there unseen.

"Are you having second thoughts about my move on Manassas?" Johnston asked.

"No. Why would you ask?" Jackson queried sharply.

"You seem to be changing strategy at the last minute."

Jackson looked down. "Actually, I'm disappointed in the number of men who've come. I expected to have at least 600 guns for you. I asked Forrest to be ready to make up the numbers. Just in case."

"If Pete's experience is indicative of what we should expect as we march, I'll have more than 600 guns before I reach Front Royal."

"Then send Forrest on his way," Jackson said.

Mosby rode up. "General Johnston, the men are ready."

"You better get going," Lee said.

Johnston swung up in the saddle. Lee came over and extended his hand. "Be careful, Joe. Remember what I told you."

"I will," Johnston smiled again, but Lee didn't respond.

"We're six hours behind you," Jackson said.

"I plan to make thirty miles a day," Johnston said.

Jackson gave the mare a pat on the rump. Johnston gave a small salute and headed down the driveway. Mosby cantered after him.

★ ★ ★

It was time. Jackson walked across the backyard and headed into the kitchen. Jim was busy putting together a haversack of food for the trip. Jim had wanted to come, but Jackson had asked him to stay behind and watch over the women and children. His agreement came, but it came reluctantly. Jackson watched as Jim stuffed more food into the sack, stressing the seams.

"Are you sure you don't want me to go along?"

Jackson saw hope flicker across the cook's face. "Jim," he said slowly, hating to disappoint him. "It would set my mind at ease to know that you're in charge. Jimmie can run a little wild, and he needs a strong hand."

"Yes, sir." Jim pulled the flap down over the bulging sack. "I'll keep the young man in line." He did a poor job hiding his displeasure from Jackson.

Jackson patted him on the shoulder and headed toward the dining room door. He turned back. "Oh, don't let Jimmie tell you that he has permission to ride Virginia or Centurion. He doesn't. He wasn't happy when I told him that, so…"

Jim cut him off. "I'll remember."

Jackson pushed against the door. "Pray for us. We're going to need Providence's intervention if we're to win our freedom."

There was no disappointment in Jim's smile. "I will, sir."

"I'll say goodbye before I leave." Jackson pushed on through the door. As he walked down the hall, he glanced in Lee's bedroom. The room was empty, but Jackson recognized the well-traveled valise sitting on the bed.

He climbed the stairs. He heard Flora's and Anna's voices coming from his bedroom. He entered the children's nursery. Jimmie wasn't there, but Julia and Ginny were sitting on the floor, playing with their Christmas dolls.

"How are my girls?" He knelt down and extended his arms. Julia dropped her doll and ran over. She threw herself into his arms and allowed Jackson to kiss her cheek. Jackson saw Ginny hanging back. "Don't I get a kiss from my Ginny?"

A smile spread across her face. Her smile was more reminiscent of her mother and not the sunny smile of her father. She approached shyly. Jackson held out a hand. Ginny grasped it and allowed Jackson to draw her close.

"Papa, are you leavin'?" Julia asked.

He picked them up and sat down on Jimmie's bed. "Yes, I am."

"I don't want you to go." Julia burst into tears. The moment she did, Ginny started to cry also.

"Oh, no tears," Jackson cajoled. "I won't be gone long. I promise." He kissed each girl on the forehead. "Now, I want each of you to draw me two pictures while I'm gone. Can you do that for me?" Through their tears, they nodded. "Do you promise to obey your mamas?" Again they nodded. "Can I have another kiss?" Julia kissed his cheek. Ginny followed suit.

Jackson stood. "Now, go find your Grandpa and kiss him good-bye." He lifted them from the bed and with a slight swat on their bottoms sent them in search of Lee.

He watched as they ran down the hall then turned in the opposite direction and went into his bedroom. His own valise was on the bed and Anna was packing a shirt. When he appeared in the door, she began to weep.

Flora handed Anna a pair of socks. "I'll leave you two alone." She touched Anna's arm. "Do you want me to take the baby?" Tom was sleeping in his crib. Anna glanced at Jackson, who shook his head. "Okay, then" She crossed to the door and squeezed Jackson's arm. "You be careful and come back."

Jackson smiled. "I will. Have you seen Jimmie?"

"Not since breakfast. He was helping General Lee pack." She squeezed Jackson's arm again and exited the room, closing the door behind her.

Anna placed the socks in the valise. She sniffed back her tears.

Jackson crossed to the bed. "I thought we agreed that there would be no tears," he admonished, but his tone was gentle.

"I'm sorry." She collapsed in his arms and buried her face in his chest. "They started when I said goodbye to Joe. I can't believe I have to watch you march off again."

He didn't say anything but held her close until her sobs ceased. "I prayed for another way out of this."

She untangled herself from his embrace. "I know. The Yankees have left you with no other choice."

"Just put your trust in the goodness of God. I know that He'll give us both a hope and a future."

She turned her tearful face to him. "I will."

He gathered her close and kissed her.

★ ★ ★

All the goodbyes had been made. Except for Jimmie. Jackson hadn't seen the little boy since last night. He stood on the front porch and called, but Jimmie didn't appear. Jackson checked his watch. He couldn't wait any longer.

Behind him, Lee was making his final farewells. Kisses for Anna and Flora and hugs and kisses for Julia and Ginny. With one final goodbye, Lee joined Jackson at the top of the steps.

"I see Captain Morrison is ready," Lee said, pointing at the young man already in the saddle.

Jackson surveyed the yard again. "I'd have liked to have said goodbye to Jimmie, but he must be pouting over my refusal to allow him to ride by himself in our absence."

Lee laughed. "He tearfully appealed to me for permission, but I supported your decision."

Jackson headed down the steps. He grabbed Little Sorrel's reins from Jim and swung up in the saddle. When Lee was set, Jackson turned and headed down the driveway. Lee and Morrison followed.

"WAIT! WAIT!"

Jackson turned Little Sorrel back toward the house. Jimmie burst from the woods. Jackson dismounted and waited for the little boy to approach.

Jimmie stopped a few feet away. Tears spilled down his cheeks. "Don't go! Don't go, ole Stonewall!" He begged between sobs.

"I have to." Jackson started to walk toward the sobbing child, but Jimmie sprinted away.

"Just go then!" Jimmie yelled. "Go and leave me. I don't care."

Lee joined Jackson. "Jimmie," he called.

"I don't want you to go," Jimmie whimpered.

"We'll be back," Lee said. "Now, come and give us a hug goodbye."

Jimmie stood frozen in place. Lee knelt and held out his arms. Jimmie slowly walked over to Lee and allowed Lee to embrace him. He turned his tearstained face up to Jackson. "Don't leave me, ole Stonewall," he whispered.

Jackson felt a sword pierce his heart.

Lee stood. "When we come back, we'll buy you a pony so you can ride by yourself. Won't we, General Jackson?" Jackson nodded. The peace offering did little to assuage Jimmie's tears. "Now, give General Jackson a kiss goodbye."

Jimmie folded his arms across chest. His lower lip protruded and he shook his head in refusal.

Jackson kissed the boy on the top of his head. "Goodbye." He started back toward the horses.

Jimmie suddenly wrapped his arms around Jackson's waist. "Goodbye, ole Stonewall."

Jackson scooped the boy up, hugged him close, then threw him onto Little Sorrel's saddle. He swung up behind Jimmie and cantered down the driveway toward the farmhouse. Rebel chased after them.

Chapter Twenty Six

Thomas' Headquarters
Richmond, Virginia
May 3, 1866
2:30 p.m.

When Thomas first received Sherman's telegram warning him of the approaching Confederate force, he didn't believe it. What good would it do for Lee to attack Richmond? Then the reports came in from Charlottesville and Perkinsville that a good size force, growing with every mile the Rebs marched, was moving toward the city.

A second telegram from Sherman three hours later revealed the general's belief that the Rebs hoped to raise an army by taking Richmond. Once that new army was raised, the Rebs would move on Washington. Thomas' orders were to defeat the Confederates, take the fugitive generals into custody, and disperse the soldiers.

Thomas' immediate problem was that Richmond was filled with Reb soldiers. What if they revolted against the martial law he had imposed upon his arrival, and he found himself suddenly fighting a two front battle? That would never do. From his adjutant, Thomas requested a list of all Confederate generals in the city. The list he received was a who's who of the Army of the Northern Virginia: Pickett, Armistead, Garnett, Ewell, and Custis Lee, plus a wagon full of colonels, majors, and captains. Any one of them capable of rallying the Rebs.

He sent word to General Birney in Raleigh to put half his force on the trains north immediately. Birney's reply wasn't what he had hoped for. Thomas had expected to have the additional men before the Rebs reached Richmond. Birney's telegram told him to expect his men in seventy-two hours. No reason was given for the delay, and Thomas' demands for an explanation went unanswered. The Rebs would be at the city's limits before Birney's men arrived.

He set his men to refortifying the defenses the Confederates had built during the war. He would confront the Rebs in the trenches west of the city. That left him two days to neutralize the Reb leadership within the city.

In the wee hours of the morning, he sent troops to round up the generals. Pickett, Armistead, Garnett, and Ewell were pulled from their beds and thrown into Libby Prison as was one of Jackson's aide-de-camps, who was seized on his way to class at the Union Seminary. Unfortunately, the sweep didn't net Custis Lee. By the time his men reached the Lee house on Franklin Street, Custis had vanished. Thomas hurried a message to the various checkpoints posted throughout the city to be on the lookout for Lee, but for the time being, it appeared Custis Lee was in the wind.

Thomas wasn't ready to panic. Not over Custis Lee. The son was not the father. His next sweep filled Libby Prison with more Reb officers. He slowly encircled the city with an iron curtain. Once Libby Prison was stuffed to the rafters, he filled the warehouses by the river with prisoners. He didn't care if he had to imprison all 6,000 ex-soldiers. When the Rebs arrived, they would receive no help from within Richmond.

Sherman's Office
War Department
May 6, 1866
3:45 p.m.

There was a knock on Sherman's door. Before Sherman could bid entrance, the door swung open and Major Dayton stood framed in the doorway. He looked as if he had just survived an artillery barrage. "We were wrong!" He choked out.

Sherman gestured his adjutant into a chair. As Dayton made his way across the office, Sherman wondered if the man would even make it to the chair for his legs were visibly shaking.

"Now what has you all shook up?" Sherman asked.

Dayton leaned forward and laid the telegram on the desk. "This is from Major Perry at Front Royal. The garrison was attacked by a Confederate force this morning."

Sherman grabbed up the telegram. It was very short on details. Perry stated that the attack came from the southwest.

Running footsteps echoed down the hallway. Sherman knew the footsteps belonged to Sheridan. Hopefully, the cavalry leader had received additional information. Sheridan burst into the room.

"We've lost Front Royal and its supplies. That means over 500 rifles and two batteries of artillery. The Rebs had both infantry and cavalry. Our men were marched to Linden where they were tied up and left at the railroad depot," Sheridan reported breathlessly.

Sherman wadded up the telegram and threw it across the room. "So Richmond is just a diversion!"

"Not necessarily," Sheridan replied.

Sherman closed his eyes. "Explain."

"We've always believed that the Rebs were coming here. Front Royal puts their march through Thoroughfare Gap." Sheridan collapsed in a chair next to Dayton. "If the Rebs manage to take Richmond, it means 6,000 soldiers are on the trains and in Manassas by the end of the day. And the trains keep coming." He sat up. "You were right. The main attack is from Centreville."

Sherman's eyes popped open. "The Rebs could be through the Gap and across Bull Run Creek as early as tomorrow."

"That's good news," Dayton piped up.

Sheridan glared at him. "How is this good news?"

"General Thomas reports that as of this morning, the Rebs haven't attacked."

Sherman took a deep breath. If or until the Rebs took Richmond, there would be no troops coming from the south. So, the immediate danger was the column approaching Manassas.

A thrill danced down Sherman's spine. He was about to do battle with the vaunted Robert E. Lee. He clapped his hands in anticipation. "Did Major Perry give us the strength of the Reb column he encountered?"

The question appeared to confound Dayton.

"Well?" Sherman barked.

"It was in the telegram," Dayton stammered.

Sherman spied the telegram lying on the floor behind Sheridan. He pointed impatiently. "It's there. Behind you."

Dayton whirled about. He tried to reach the small slip of paper from the chair, but couldn't. He stood, bent down, and scooped it up. He unwrinkled the paper before squinting at it. "It's hard to read now," he qualified.

"Do your best, Major," Sherman snapped.

"Seven hundred guns."

Sherman rubbed his forehead. The Rebs could easily have 1,000 men or more by time the column reached the creek. He dragged a piece of paper from his drawer. He began to write. "I'll lead…"

"No, no!" Sheridan declared. "You can't lead anything."

Sherman laughed. "I beg your pardon."

"Your job is to hold the politicians' hands and assure them that the Rebs aren't going to murder them in their beds. I'll go."

Sheridan was right. Once McClellan heard the news, he would be sure to summon Sherman to the White House for lectures and recriminations. "Since we don't know the Rebs actual numbers, take half the men in the Washington defenses. I'll move the rest to the southwest perimeter, just in case."

Sheridan's scowled. "Don't insult me!"

Sherman jerked his thumb toward the door. "The faster you get going, the faster you'll forget about my insult."

West of Richmond
May 7, 1866
8:00 a.m.

Longstreet peered through his fieldglasses. The trenches in front of him were filled with blue uniformed soldiers. He smiled at the irony. He spent his whole career avoiding a frontal attack on an entrenched position, yet here he was, about to attack an entrenched position. He wished Forrest could see him now. He was sure the cavalry leader would be thoroughly impressed, though he would crack wise about how it was too little, too late.

"General Longstreet."

Longstreet turned and saw Lee's oldest son standing in the shadows. Custis had come into camp last night and brought with him tales of the Yankees rounding up Confederate officers and imprisoning them in Libby Prison. Not only that, the Yankees had thrown a cordon around the city and set a curfew. Anyone in the streets after dark was arrested and thrown into prison.

Lee's revelations explained why the stream of men joining his column had been reduced to a trickle. Before the curfew, over 400 men from Richmond had joined his ranks, but throughout the night and the early morning, only five men had come.

"What is it, General Lee?"

"We're ready when you are," Custis said.

Longstreet smiled. When Custis realized that his father wasn't with the column, he had a difficult time hiding his disappointment. But it seemed Lee's son had recovered his equilibrium. "Custis, how's my family?"

"They miss you terribly, but other than that, they're fine."

Good, Custis knew where they were living. "Tell General Mahone to go when he's ready."

There was no finesse to Longstreet's plan. He had compacted his men into a tight line, almost into a fist, and he would drive that fist right at the Yankees. If they were able to punch through, he would roll up the Yankees' left flank. If not, he would disengage. He was only supposed to make a demonstration. Lee emphasized that the loss of life was to be kept at a minimum. He just hoped the attack would be enough to convince the Yankees that he was serious about taking the city.

The drum began its long roll, jarring him. It had been almost a year since he had heard that once familiar sound. He laughed. He never realized what beautiful music it was. He raised his glasses and watched as the gray lines surged forward.

Richmond, Virginia
Union Trenches
May 7, 1866
10:45 a.m.

Thomas stood at the point of the Rebels' penetration into his line. They had managed to empty the trenches and drive his men back about 100 feet, but he had sent in reinforcements and easily pushed the Rebs back. The Confederates had retreated, leaving a smattering of dead and wounded on the field. His medics had taken the wounded to the hospital, and Thomas set a small burial detail to haul the dead to Hollywood Cemetery to be interred with the rest of the Confederate dead.

Thomas watched two soldiers haul one of the dead Rebs to a wagon and scratched his cheek. This morning, during breakfast, a telegram arrived from Sherman informing him that a column was marching toward Washington via Thoroughfare Gap and the attack on Richmond was just a diversion. Until this morning's attack, Thomas would have vigorously disagreed. But the Confederate assault was half-hearted, designed to spare men rather than capture the city. Six had been killed and twenty had been wounded in a sharp skirmish that had lasted fifteen minutes and was over before it began.

Now, Thomas didn't know what to think. After the attack, the Rebs had disappeared from his front. He had sent out scouts to find them, but after making a brief reconnaissance, the scouts reported the Rebs were gone.

So where had they gone? Had they retreated back up the road to Charlottesville and disbanded? Were they sliding around the city, preparing for another attack? Or was he worried over nothing? Even if the Rebs did attack, they would have to put more heart into their next assault than he witnessed this morning.

An orderly approached and slipped Thomas a note. He read it quickly. Birney's men had finally left Raleigh and would be here by tomorrow evening. When this was over, Thomas promised himself a good long talk with Birney about the expediency of obeying orders.

In the meantime, he ordered his pickets to keep a watchful eye just in case the Rebs reappeared. He headed back to the city. He needed to alert Sherman that the Rebs seemed more interested in demonstrating then seizing the city.

Chapter Twenty Seven

Harper's Ferry
May 9, 1866
Dawn

F orrest stood on Schoolhouse Ridge and gazed through his
fieldglasses at Boliver Heights where the major portion of his
cavalry were waiting for his bugler orderly to give the signal for
the attack on the Union garrison.

When Forrest accepted the assignment to capture the small
outpost, he had asked the cartographer, Hotchkiss, for his maps of the
area. Hotchkiss only had one and gladly handed it over. Morrison
observed Forrest pouring over the map in the little house's kitchen and
let it drop that Jackson's first post was at Harper's Ferry. Not only that,
but during the Maryland campaign, Jackson had attacked and
captured the town.

Intrigued, Forrest shook Hotchkiss awake and asked if he had the
maps Jackson used for the attack. Hotchkiss didn't. That sent Forrest
flying up the steps to Jackson's bedroom door. He rapped on it until
an irritated Jackson flung the door open.

"You had better be bringing me news that the Yankees are
attacking," Jackson barked.

"I need all of your maps of Harper's Ferry," Forrest replied. He
peered into the room and saw Mrs. Jackson comforting the wailing
baby.

"I don't have them," Jackson said. "Check with Colonel
Hotchkiss."

"My first stop," Forrest said.

"Then check with Captain Morrison. If I do have them, they'll be in
my trunk. Now, if you'll excuse me." He slammed the door shut.

The maps weren't in Jackson's trunk, and Captain Morrison had no idea where else to look. Johnston overhead the conversation and during breakfast carefully described the physical geography of the region, giving insight to Forrest on why Harper's Ferry was hard to defend. Forrest wasn't satisfied. Johnston had evacuated the outpost without really being threatened. Jackson had conquered the garrison. Forrest would give Jackson the morning to cool off before approaching him again.

After lunch, Forrest found Jackson sitting in a chair under the sycamore trees reading his Bible. "Let's talk about Harper's Ferry." Jackson gave him a perturbed look. Forrest refused to feel remorse for his pre-dawn invasion of the bedroom. "How do I take it?"

Jackson closed his Bible. "The key is Maryland Heights. Get cannon up there and Harper's Ferry becomes untenable."

That was totally unhelpful. The Confederates didn't have any cannon. He said so.

"We have the battery Mosby liberated from Fort Monroe."

Forrest had forgotten about those cannon. But it wouldn't be enough, for now Jackson was talking about putting cannon on Loudoun Heights to the east of the town.

"Where am I supposed to be gettin' all these cannon?" Forrest demanded.

"Hopefully from the garrison at Front Royal." Jackson made it a point to stretch and yawn.

Forrest ignored the display. "Ain't General Johnston goin' be needin' 'em?"

"Probably, but there aren't enough cannon to go around. Take the cannon from Front Royal…"

"If there are cannon," Forrest exploded.

"Let's have faith in God's ever kind providence that there will be," Jackson replied. He stroked the Bible cover.

Forrest waited for Jackson to either laugh or give some indication he was teasing, but Jackson seemed to be done talking. "Well, let's." Forrest was skeptical.

Jackson smiled. "You'll have to drag those cannon up Maryland Heights by hand. There's no other way around that. But don't leave them up there. I'll need them for my assault."

There had been two batteries of artillery in Front Royal. Forrest seized them over Johnston's protest and headed toward Harper's Ferry on the gallop.

He arrived yesterday afternoon just as the sun sank below the horizon. He sent Colonel Kelley up Maryland Heights to see if the Yankees had a signal station or outpost on the large edifice. Kelley returned around midnight and reported no Union presence. That made getting the guns across the Potomac and up on the heights easier. But Jackson was right. The guns were dragged up the hill by brute force.

Forrest sent 100 men and four guns up to Loudoun Heights. Troopers sealed off the Shenandoah River at the bottom of Bolivar Heights. The screen ran west of Maryland Heights. Another screen was positioned between Loudoun Heights and Maryland Heights, straddling the Potomac River. Jackson's orders were precise. Seal off the area and don't allow anyone to escape.

By dawn, all was ready. The gunners were told to keep up a rapid fire. Between the two positions, they had twelve guns. Not threatening by any means, but a rapid enough fire to keep the garrison pinned down long enough for his troopers to storm the city. He sent Captain Baker to cut the telegraph.

Forrest's heart began to thump in anticipation of battle. He gave the order to his bugler. The clear, sharp notes of the bugle pierced the quiet. The guns on Loudoun Heights opened first, followed by a barrage from Maryland Heights. The range was true. He knew the town was his. He peered through his glasses and waited for a white flag to be hoisted.

Jackson's column experienced the same phenomenon Johnston's and Longstreet's had experienced on their marches. He left Clover Hill with 700 men, but by time Forrest's message arrived that he had successfully taken Harper's Ferry, there were close to a thousand men in the ranks.

Jackson marched the column hard, pushing the men to make thirty miles a day. Those who had marched up and down the Valley with him at the beginning of the war were used to the quick pace. Jackson strictly kept to his practice of marching the men three miles in an hour and resting them for ten minutes at the end of the hour. He made each man lay down in the thick clover, because, as he told Lee, who questioned the necessity of having the men lay down, "when a man lies down, he rests all over." Lee hid his smile and led Traveller to the cool waters of the Shenandoah.

As they neared Harper's Ferry, Jackson suddenly turned east. He would cross the Potomac at Point of Rocks. Once across the Potomac, he believed he could reach the Union capital in two days. The men would be pushed to their limits, but they had done it before under more trying circumstances than these.

He got the men up and on the road. They were about six miles from the Potomac. He planned to spend the night in Virginia and cross into Maryland at first light.

★ ★ ★

Harper's Ferry
May 9, 1866
3:30 p.m.

"Colonel Kelley." Forrest dropped his gauntlets on the table. Kelley looked up from his cup of coffee. "The men and I are headin' out now. I'm leavin' you enough men to keep the Yankees in their makeshift jails. But if they try to escape, don't hesitate to kill 'em."

Kelley smiled. "We took their shoes and their guns, so the chances of them escaping are slim." Forrest frowned. "But I'll take your advice to heart."

Forrest was satisfied. "Now, I know I done told you this ten times, but it's important that you telegraph Washington every three hours."

"I know," Kelley replied. There was no tension in his voice. Forrest was just being thorough.

"If you get a telegram from the War Department you don't understand, get that colonel fella to advise you. Tell him it'll go a lot easier on him if he cooperates."

Kelley laughed. Colonel Davis seemed to be a reasonable man. He had surrendered the small town within minutes of the first artillery barrage. Ever since, he had bent over backward to cooperate with the Confederates. Kelley didn't foresee that cooperation drying up just because Forrest left.

"General, when will we know you were successful?" Kelley asked. He poured another cup of coffee.

"If you don't hear from me in four days, I think it'll be safe to assume that we've lost."

Kelley sipped the hot liquid. "What should we do?"

"Go home," Forrest said. "You've been gone from your families long enough."

It was an answer Kelley hadn't expected. "Are you sure?" He stammered.

"If this gamble don't pay off, then I'll be out of your reach." Forrest was matter of fact.

Kelley set his cup on the table. "But you think it'll work."

"If this plan had been conceived by any other man than Stonewall Jackson, probably not." Forrest smiled at the adjutant. "But just in case, you've been an exemplary officer. Your loyalty to your country and to me won't be forgotten. Thank you."

"You take care, General." Kelley choked back his emotions.

"No need for that," Forrest admonished. He smiled again. "Good-bye, Colonel."

"General."

Forrest grabbed his gauntlets and headed outside.

Point of Rocks
May 10, 1866
3:40 a.m.

Jackson stood on the Virginia side of the Potomac and watched as the men waded through the waist high water. Forrest had splashed across an hour before and set a picket on the river bank to keep away the inquisitive. Jackson had deliberately chosen the early hour because most occupants of the small households dotting the riverbank would be tucked safely in their beds.

Lee joined him. "Good morning, General Jackson." He handed Jackson a tin cup filled with strong, black coffee.

Jackson took the cup. "Thank you." In the moonlight, Jackson noted that Lee looked tired. "Sir, you could have slept a while longer."

Lee laughed. "Have I grown so old since the surrender that I can't be up when the men are?"

Jackson felt his cheeks heat up. "I meant no offense."

Lee laughed harder. Jackson's cheeks burned. "One of these days, you'll realize when I'm teasing you."

Jackson stammered wordlessly. He always knew when Stuart was poking fun, but he never knew with Lee. He heard a horse splashing across the river. As the rider came near, Jackson recognized Forrest.

"We ain't been discovered yet," Forrest reported from the water's edge. "About half the men are across." He looked up into the sky.

"Two hours of darkness left. We should be clear of the river and well down the bank by then."

"Thank you, General Forrest," Lee said.

"I've instructed my men to set a screen on either side of the river. We'll keep you hidden," Forrest said.

For Jackson, it was unsettling to hear that Tennessee accent explain things that were once the purview of Stuart. How he longed for Stuart's boisterous laugh, more now than at any time since his death. This was where Stuart excelled, and though Jackson could find no fault in Forrest's actions, he just wasn't Stuart. He cleared his throat to rid himself of the memories crowding him. "Rest the men for a half hour at dawn."

"I'll tell General Rodes. If'n you'll excuse me." He turned King Philip and dashed back across the river.

"I could use another cup of coffee," Lee said. "How about you?"

Jackson agreed and followed Lee back to the campfire.

Chapter Twenty Eight

West of Fairfax, Virginia
May 11, 1866
2:45 p.m.

The men trudging behind Sheridan on the thirty mile trek from Washington to Bull Run Creek were not the seasoned veterans of the Army of the Potomac or even his division from the Army of the Cumberland. Those men were back behind counters in their stores, behind plows on their farms, or behind desks at their businesses. These soldiers – and Sheridan used the term loosely – were the last draftees of the army. They signed their papers last May and were twenty days from being discharged and sent home.

Sheridan knew Sherman must have his reasons for filling the Washington defenses with these "soldiers." After all, the war was over and the South was defeated and prostrated. When Jackson didn't storm Washington after the peacock's death, the assumption of safety increased. There was no reason to send for seasoned warriors from the west or the south just to have them stand around in trenches.

He could hear the soldiers murmuring behind him like a hive of angry bees. Their laments grew hourly. They had blisters on their feet, heat rashes from their uniforms, and their shoulders were rubbed raw by heavy packs. They were hungry and thirsty, having already consumed two days worth of rations and drained their canteens dry. The column had marched six miles in the last four hours, and one would think they had been double-quicked for a week through the thick spring mud without a rest. Speaking of rest breaks, they were becoming more frequent and longer in duration. At this rate, they wouldn't reach Bull Run Creek until sometime next month. And who

239

knew how many ex-Confederates would have joined the Reb army by them.

"Major Elliott!" He hollered. The major rode up and gave a very sloppy salute. "Major, we need to pick up the speed."

"Sir..." The major's voice was apologetic.

"Pick it up!" Sheridan stormed. "We're making Centreville even if we have to march all night."

Elliott wilted slightly. "Yes, sir." He turned his horse and headed back to the column.

Sheridan shook his head. If these recruits couldn't even march, how could they stand against the veterans waiting for them at creek? He scowled. If the Rebs weren't at Richmond, he could have demanded troops from Thomas, or if he had another couple days, he could have ordered the Pennsylvania militia down from Harrisburg. At least the Pennsylvanians had experience after combating the Rebs during Lee's invasion of the Keystone State.

Behind him, the murmuring increased. He didn't care. He had less than ten miles to whip them into some kind of semblance of an army.

North along the Virginia Central Railroad
May 12, 1866
2:30 a.m.

After being turned back in his first attack, Longstreet had a choice to make. He could continue with the demonstration and keep pulling back at the first sign of opposition, or he could get about the business of taking the city. He knew the parameters of his orders. He had fulfilled them. Not one Yankee had marched north from Richmond.

Yesterday afternoon, he had reconnoitered down the Virginia Central Railroad all the way to where the rail line crossed the Meadow Bridge and saw very little Union activity. The outer defenses were empty. Unfortunately, he couldn't say the same about Academy Hill on the right or Maddox Hill on the left. Infantry and, more importantly, artillery were clearly visible. He couldn't force the hills. It would be a slaughter.

Supper found him pouring over maps of the city, trying to find a way in. As the candles burned low, he finally found the answer. In the dark, he could march the men down the railroad, past the hills, and take both from the south. It's the last thing the Yankees would expect. He could then turn the batteries on the city and bombard the Yankees into submission.

Longstreet leaned back in his chair with a satisfied grin on his face. The plan was worthy of Jackson. He called for Custis Lee and Mahone. Both men staggered into the tent.

"Yes, sir." Mahone rubbed sleep from his eyes.

Custis swayed on his feet.

"Let's get the men up."

That woke Custis up. "Sir, it's the middle of the night."

"I know what time it is," Longstreet snapped. He gestured at the map and explained his plan.

Bull Run Creek
May 12, 1866
7:00 a.m.

Johnston raised his fieldglasses and peered over Bull Run Creek and down the road north toward Centreville. The road was empty. He wasn't expecting the Yankees. Not this early. But he was expecting Mosby to return from Centreville and let him know which road the Yankees were marching down. As he did when he commanded the army during the first battle that had been fought along this creek, Johnston fully expected the Yankees to attack at Mitchell and

Blackburn fords. Of course, back then, the Yankees had surprised him by sending the main force over Sudley Ford on a flanking move against his lightly defended left flank. The Yankees could employ that same flanking movement against him this morning. They could march down Warrenton Pike and flank his line at either Lewis or Farm ford.

Johnston didn't have enough men to picket the entire creek bank from Lewis to Blackburn fords. Of course, if he had cannon, he could have defended the approaches from the Warrenton Pike with canister, but Forrest had confiscated the cannon seized at Front Royal.

According to Mosby's scouts, who had spent the night skulking around the Yankees' bivouac, the Yankees numbered approximately 2,000 and seemed to be, from all the complaining the scouts overheard, raw recruits who didn't relish the idea of fighting this close to their discharge from the army. Mosby had reiterated that fact when he met with Johnston at three this morning.

Raw recruits. Johnston smiled up at heaven. His columns had swelled to around 1,200: all battle-tested men who were eager to engage the enemy. As long as the Yankees didn't split their column and try to surprise him from the left, he should be able to hold the creek.

The men were waking up. It was only a matter of minutes until the cook fires were stirred to life, the coffee pots were steaming, and what little the men had for breakfast would be frying in pans. Johnston's stomach growled. He could stand a cup of coffee. Hopefully, Heth was awake so they could plan for the day. All that was needed was for Mosby to return with his report.

North of Richmond
May 12, 1866
7:30 a.m.

Longstreet sat on his gelding, now named Victory. Next to him, Fitz Lee was peering through his fieldglasses as his cavalry demonstrated below Academy Hill. Fitz's force was so small that the demonstration was the equivalent of jumping up and down, waving your arms, and shouting "look at me." The good news was that it was working. The small show of bravado had captured the Yankees' full attention.

Longstreet hadn't heard from Mahone since he led the long column down the Virginia Central Railroad. Before the men moved out, Mahone had laid down the law. No noise. Little Billy might be small in stature, but he was mighty in authority. When the column moved out, the only sound that could be heard were the soldiers' steady footsteps.

As the wait dragged on, Longstreet battled back his impatience. The sun had been up for an hour and a half and nothing. What was taking Mahone so long? The column was vulnerable in the daylight. "Come on! Come on!" He muttered.

Fitz lowered his glasses. "Did you say something?"

Longstreet shook his head. He raised his glasses and peered past the troopers. There was movement. The crack of gunfire rolled over the hills. The attack was on. Confederate troops poured over the crest of Academy Hill and quickly overwhelmed the defenders. The battle was won before it began. Mahone ordered the cannon turned south.

Longstreet nudged Victory in the ribs and headed toward Maddox Hill. Hopefully, Custis Lee had the hill in his possession and was preparing to move immediately on Union Hill to the east. Once that stronghold was taken, Longstreet would command all the roads north. Fitz rode alongside. "Fitz, take your troopers and capture Fort Jackson." Longstreet didn't expect Fitz to meet any resistance. From the ease that his men had taken Academy and Maddox hills, it was clear that Thomas had expected Longstreet to attack from the west again. "If you need help, let me know."

Fitz spurred Nelly Gray and raced away.

Longstreet smiled. Once the fort was in Confederate hands, Longstreet would control the railroads Thomas needed to get his troops north to Washington. The Yankees could still escape, but only to the south. His next step would be to cut the railroad to Petersburg as quickly as possible, before reinforcements arrived from North Carolina.

Bull Run Creek
May 12, 1866
8:30 a.m.

The blue sky was cloudless. The temperature was beginning its ascent toward the eighties. Johnston glanced about, half-expecting ghosts to rise from the ground. Three battles had been fought on this sacred and hallowed ground. Now, a fourth, and hopefully final battle would soon begin. A dust cloud moving in from the north meant Mosby was returning. The Yankees must be on their way.

"Harry!" Johnston called.

Heth set aside the book he was reading and joined Johnston.

Mosby splashed across the creek and threw himself from the saddle. He slipped the bit on his rangy gelding and allowed the horse to return to the water for a drink.

"One column marching right for us," Mosby announced with a smile.

"How long until the Yankees arrive?"

Mosby laughed. "At the rate they're marching – next Tuesday."

Johnston didn't laugh. "A more realistic answer, Colonel."

Mosby sobered. "Two hours maximum."

Johnston made his decision. "Harry, take responsibility for the left flank. Anchor it on the Flat Run. General Mosby, take your men to Henry House Hill. Keep an eye on the Warrenton Pike." Mosby protested. "Just in case. If any Yankees do appear and the force is small enough for your troopers to engage, do so. If not, fall back and join up with General Heth's men." Johnston turned his attention to Heth. "Harry, if that happens, let me know right away. I'll be at Blackburn's Ford." He smiled at the two men. "You have your orders."

Thomas' Headquarters
Richmond, Virginia
May 12, 1866
10:00 a.m.

Thomas listened as shells from the hills to the north whistled over his headquarters and splashed harmlessly in the James River. He looked out of his office's window at the crowd gathering in the street. Each shell that screamed overhead was greeted with the Rebel yell, waving Confederate flags, and a rousing rendition of Dixie. Just another sign that order was breaking down. The checkpoints had already been swept away. Former Reb soldiers were pouring through the streets on their way to Academy and Maddox hills. An hour ago, his men had abandoned Plow Hill. The Rebs now surrounded him on the north, east, and west.

The roads south were packed full with carpetbaggers, scalawags, and members of the Freedman Bureau. All fleeing from the much deserved wrath of the Confederates. Good riddance to bad rubbish, Thomas thought, but their flight made the roads south impassable.

His men still held Libby Hill, so that meant that the railroad to the south remained open. Birney's men should be arriving sometime before dawn.

But until Birney's men arrived, he had no other option but to make his stand on Libby Hill. Hold there and the city remained in his hands.

Blackburn's Ford
Bull Run Creek
May 12, 1866
11:00 a.m.

The Yankees moved slowly, unpracticed, into a sloppy line of battle. Johnston recognized the general sitting on horseback behind the line. It was Sheridan. Hatred churned his stomach. That little man was the reason for all the wrong in his world and while Jackson may call what they were doing justice, right now, good old fashioned revenge would suit Johnston just fine. Revenge for his imprisonment, for having to climb up the scaffold, for having his legs and hands bound and the black hood dragged over his head, and, most of all, revenge for Stuart.

The Confederate line erupted in gunfire. Acrid smoke rose into the air, burning Johnston's eyes. He heard ramrods rattle in rifle barrels. His men leveled their muskets and fired again. Johnston raised his glasses. The Yankees' front line had been decimated. Blue uniformed bodies lay still in the spring clover. Screams and cries from the wounded rose above the gunfire like some type of demented aria. The Federal line closed ranks. Rifles were lowered and shook with nerves. Before they get off another shot, his men fired. The Union line splintered. About half of the Yankee fled to the rear. Johnston wished he had a ten pound Parrot. One blast of canister would have sent the Yankees running all the way back to Washington like scared rabbits.

"First line fire only," Johnston ordered. "Second line, wait for my command."

The first line fired. Johnston raised his glasses. The Yankees were in complete disarray. "Second line! Fire!"

Bullets dropped the dead to the ground like sacks of feed. The new recruits had suffered enough death. Not even Sheridan's threats could force them to stay. They turned and ran back to Centreville.

A Rebel yell rose above the noise of battle. Tears streamed down Johnston's cheeks at the sound. Another yell rose higher than the first. This time he joined in. They had held the creek and won the day.

Chapter Twenty Nine

East of Rock Creek
Outside Washington City
May 13, 1866
4:00 a.m.

Jackson's column had arrived north of the Federal capital without alerting the city of its approach. That didn't mean the long line hadn't been spotted in the hard march through Maryland. Right now, about 50 of Forrest's troopers were babysitting those unfortunate farmers, merchants, and fishermen whose path had brought them into close proximity to the Confederates. Forrest ordered his men to hold the prisoners for seventy-two hours then release them.

Johnston's diversion at Manassas had paid off. Two days ago, the northern defenses were emptied of one-half their strength. How Jackson had come to know this little tidbit of information, Forrest wasn't sure, but he didn't think the news had come from Reynolds. Washington had been a seecesh city during the war. Perhaps a former spy had slipped the news past the Yankees.

Last night, Forrest had joined Jackson in a reconnaissance of the northern forts that made up the Washington defenses. They were lightly manned. But that didn't mean the assault would be easy. The forts were packed with artillery and those cannon could easily keep Jackson's forces at bay until help arrived.

With that in mind, Forrest volunteered to enter the city as soon as the attack began to stop any reinforcements coming from the west or south. Jackson shook his head. When Forrest pressed for a reason, Jackson shared his concerns. If the attack should fail, Forrest would find himself cut off and trapped between two hostile forces.

"Then I'll charge 'em both ways," Forrest declared.

"Cavalry." Jackson shook his head in amusement. "You think you're indestructible because you ride a fast horse." But he gave permission.

By Jackson's orders, there were no fires so there was no coffee. The lack of the strong beverage plus the sleepless nights Forrest had endured since leaving the farmhouse had eroded his patience and humor. He stood alone from his men, staring up at the star filled sky, not wanting to make small talk.

General Early didn't know his moods and that's why Lee's bad old man, a nickname Forrest now fully understood, brazenly approached.

"Good morning, General Forrest." Early was cheery. Forrest grunted in reply. "My men are waking now. I'll have them along the banks of Rock Creek within the hour."

Forrest gave the night sky one final perusal. All the pieces were in motion. But would it be enough? When the stars faded and the black sky turned gray, he would have his answer.

Willard Hotel
May 13, 1866
5:00 a.m.

Reynolds sat up in bed. Cannon! Had the Confederates broken through at Manassas? He listened intently. Something was wrong. He threw back the covers. The artillery was coming from the poorly defended north! Not taking time to turn on the lamp, he dressed as quickly as he could in the dark. He was pulling on his boots when he heard a loud thumping on his door.

"Coming!" He grabbed his coat and swung the door open. It was Sherman.

"Good, you're dressed." Sherman pivoted and started down the hall. Reynolds locked his door and trotted down the hall to catch up.

Sherman took the steps two at a time. The lobby was filled with panicked hotel guests, dressed in nightclothes, all demanding answers from the two generals as to the source of the loud thumping that filled the pre-dawn sky.

Reynolds pushed through them without answering and escaped into the street. He took a deep breath. He didn't see the out-of-control wagon bearing down on him until a shout from Sherman alerted him to the danger. He dashed back to the safety of the sidewalk. The wagon careened by. With a shaking hand, he grabbed Sherman's arm and dragged him into the lobby of the nearest restaurant.

"We need to get Sheridan back here," Sherman said.

Reynolds agreed. "In the meantime, I'll take command of the garrison at Fort Stevens and try to coordinate a defense."

"Keep them back, John. You've got to give Sheridan enough time to return from Virginia. I'll send you reinforcements as soon as I can."

Through the window, Reynolds saw a horse tethered to a post. He sprinted from the restaurant, untied the horse, threw himself into the saddle, and threaded his way through the chaotic streets.

Fort Stevens
May 13, 1866
8:00 a.m.

In the end, it wasn't the thousand men who marched with Jackson that made the difference, but fifteen southern sharpshooters. As the Union batteries worked their guns; the sharpshooters worked their scoped rifles. Men fell dead with every shot. Within minutes, the Union artillery slowed their fire. A few cannon even fell silent. Jackson moved his men forward, covering yardage in short bursts under the cover of Confederate artillery and the deadly aim of the sharpshooters.

Ten minutes ago, his men had clambered over the fort's earthen walls. Jackson peered through his glasses. The battle was now hand-to-hand. His men were driving the cannon crews from their perches. He nudged Little Sorrel forward.

Lee quickly threw his arm across Jackson's chest. "No, it's not safe."

Jackson didn't argue. He raised his fieldglasses and watched the events unfold. The U.S. flag fell to the ground. The fort was theirs.

"Let's go," Jackson said to Lee and Morrison. This time, he didn't give Lee time to stop him.

They galloped to the fort. The cannon had been removed from their placements. Morrison led Lee and Jackson up over the earthen walls and through one of the gun openings. They stopped on the gun placement scaffold. Down below, on the fort's floor, the Confederates were rounding up the Union soldiers, disarming them, and sitting them down against the east wall.

"Captain Morrison," Jackson said. "General Forrest should be in the city by now. You take command of the infantry and join him." Morrison stared at Jackson dumbfounded. "Go on, Joe. You've earned it."

A joyful smile broke out on Morrison's face. "I'll rendezvous with General Forrest." He hurried down into the fort's floor, calling for those soldiers who had been assigned to move into the city. The men lined up quickly.

Jackson and Lee followed Morrison down into the fort.

"General Lee! General Lee!"

A courier threaded his way through the mass of soldiers. He saluted quickly. "General Rodes reports that Fort Slocum has fallen. He is preparing to take Fort Totten."

"Thank you, Major," Lee said.

Jackson rode over to the wall and raised his glasses. He searched west for some sign of battle from Early. The sky was clear of smoke and no sound of gunfire reached his ear. Jackson lowered the glasses.

Behind him the Union cannon had been limbered up and sat ready to join the troops moving through the city.

Morrison rode up. "We'll be moving out now."

"Tell General Forrest that General Early doesn't appear to be under attack, so he should expect reinforcements from Rock Creek."

"Yes, sir."

Morrison gave the order. Jackson watched with satisfaction as the gray wave rolled into the city.

A Union colonel slowly approached. "General Jackson."

Jackson was surprised that the colonel knew his name. "What can I do for you, Colonel?"

"I'm Colonel Rosengarten." Lee joined them. "I'm General Reynolds' adjutant. General Lee, I was the one who warned General Stuart that General Sheridan had discovered your safe house in Arlington. General Jackson, I was in the woods when you and General Forrest met with General Reynolds for the last time. I heard him tell you that he would fight."

"Why are you telling me this?" Jackson demanded.

"So you would know who I am and feel safe coming with me. General Reynolds needs to see you right away."

Lee shook his head. "That meeting is going to have to wait."

Rosengarten closed his eyes. When he opened them, they were filled with tears. "Sir, it can't wait. He's been wounded. He's dying."

Rosengarten's words sent Jackson reeling back in the saddle as if he had been punched.

"Take us to him," Lee said.

Rosengarten set off across the fort. Lee and Jackson followed the adjutant to a small hut just inside the fort's gate. "He's in here." Rosengarten opened the door and went inside.

Jackson dismounted slowly. He rested his head on his saddle, trying to gain control of his emotions. Lee touched his shoulder. Jackson pushed away from Little Sorrel and followed Lee into the hut.

It was dark inside. The only light came from the doorway. Against the far wall, Jackson saw Reynolds lying on a small pallet. Rosengarten leaned down and spoke softly to the dying man.

"General Lee." Reynolds' face contorted in pain.

Lee sank down on the small stool next to the pallet and took Reynolds' hand. "General Reynolds, what can I do?"

"You can trust me one last time." His voice shook with pain. "Is General Jackson with you?"

"I'm right here," Jackson said.

The pain in Reynolds' face eased and he smiled briefly. "I'm sorry I couldn't prevent this. I want you to know that I tried."

"I know you did," Jackson said.

Lee squeezed his hand. "We do trust you."

"Good." His breath came in gasps.

Rosengarten placed a wet rag on Reynolds' forehead.

"Let me send for Doctor McGuire," Jackson said. "He can help you."

Reynolds smiled again. "We have good doctors in the Union army too. There's nothing more that can be done. I just…need…to…" He began to cough.

Rosengarten poured a cup of water and knelt next to Reynolds. "Here." He raised Reynolds' head off the pallet and held the cup to Reynolds' lips. He drank just enough to wet his lips.

Jackson stared down at Reynolds. He was sinking fast. "What can we do for you?"

Reynolds closed his eyes and allowed a small groan of pain to escape his lips. "I need you not to overreach."

"I don't understand," Lee said. He appealed to Jackson for some help, but Jackson had no idea what Reynolds was saying.

"I'm sorry." Reynolds' body convulsed in pain. "I'm so hot," he whispered. Rosengarten removed the rag and resoaked it in a bowl of water that sat on a small, rickety table next to the bed. He wrung out the rag and replaced it on Reynolds' head. "General Lee, my soldiers believe they won the war." His words came out in spurts. "If you demand your country, McClellan will have no problem raising an army to deny you that very thing. My men defeated you once; they'll defeat you again. Of this, they are sure and so am I." He stopped speaking and closed his eyes.

Jackson stared at Lee. Was Reynolds saying that no matter what they did, they would never be free?

Reynolds opened his eyes. "If you demand the surrender terms…"

"We plan to demand the repeal of Reconstruction," Lee said.

Reynolds smiled then closed his eyes. "That is a wise course. Most soldiers believe Reconstruction is wrong. If you do this, the people will back you." Reynolds' voice faded in and out, making it hard for Jackson to follow what Reynolds was saying. "McClellan always chooses the easiest path. If he thinks he will be hailed as a hero for righting the wrong done to you and the South by the Radicals, he'll do it." Reynolds fell silent. He opened his eyes again. "Promise me, not to overreach."

"I promise," Lee said.

Reynolds' relaxed. "I'm fading fast." His eyes found Jackson's. "Pray for me, General Jackson. As a Christian brother."

Fighting back his tears, Jackson nodded.

"I will too," Lee said, squeezing Reynolds' hand again. "As a Christian brother and your friend."

Jackson would never get use to that holy, somber moment when a soul passed from this earth to stand before the Savior. He bowed his head and uttered a prayer.

Chapter Thirty

Sheridan's Headquarters
Centreville, Virginia
May 13, 1866
9:30 a.m.

Sheridan stood on the narrow stoop of the house he had commandeered last night as his headquarters and watched his so-called army drag themselves from their coffee pots and line up in columns of four. His adjutant handed him a slip of paper. He glanced at it. Fifty-five men had deserted last night. He tore up the note and scattered the pieces on the ground. He glared at the men in their sloppy column. If he didn't need them so badly, he would court martial the lot of them for dereliction of duty, imprison them five years in the foulest prison he could find, and when they had finished their time, drum-march them from the service.

"General Sheridan! General Sheridan!"

Sheridan saw a horse galloping down the street. The rider was waving his hat and shrieking at the top of his lungs. The column of men scattered out of the way. It was the fastest Sheridan had seen the men move since they left Washington. The courier pulled up and the horse slid in the dust at the bottom of the stairs. "General Sherman needs you to return immediately."

Sheridan shook his head. "I haven't defeated the Rebs yet.

"The Rebs are in Washington."

Stunned, Sheridan stood rooted in place. The Rebs couldn't be in Washington. They may have defeated him yesterday, but he knew they hadn't gotten past him in the night.

"Sir, the Rebs attacked the city from the north. General Sherman says get back as quickly as you can."

As quickly as he could! With these marchers!

"Colonel Kellogg," Sheridan called to his adjutant. "Get this man – he pointed at the courier – a fresh horse. Then get the men ready to march." His adjutant jumped down the steps. Sheridan spoke to the courier. "Tell General Sherman, I'm coming with all haste."

Richmond
Union Hill
May 13, 1866
9:30 a.m.

The boom of artillery filled the air. Longstreet smiled. Fitz Lee had opened fire from Fort Jackson. Longstreet focused his fieldglasses and saw the ground on Libby Hill explode in a volcano cloud of dirt and rock. The artillery behind him belched, shaking the ground under his feet. Longstreet raised his glasses again and waited for impact.

U.S. Capitol Building
May 13, 1866
10:30 a.m.

General Early dismounted at the bottom of the wide staircase that led up to the capitol building. He smiled. The staircase was filled with people, all frozen in place like terrified statues, staring at the Confederates pooling at the bottom of the steps. Early climbed the first two steps. The spell broke. The crowd stampeded into the building. Early continued up the stairs, past the columns and the marble statuary to the large wooden doors. He looked back and over the heads of his men and observed more Confederates pouring down the street headed toward the Executive Mansion. He smiled. The final act was about to unfold. He threw open the door and entered the building.

"Captain Morrison," he called as Morrison entered the gas lit hallway. "The House chamber is that way." He pointed south down the hall. Morrison sprinted away. A large force chased after him. Early turned north and stopped when he reached the doors of the Senate chamber. He waited until his men were in position. He turned the handle and walked in.

At the front of the chamber, Early saw red velvet curtains draped over and around a raised platform. The chamber sloped gently toward the platform. Down at the front of the room, senators huddled together speaking in distressed voices that echoed throughout the room. They hadn't noticed the Confederate general when he entered the room.

Early raised his pistol and fired a shot into the ceiling. Plaster dust showered the carpet. The huddles splintered apart. Men hit the floor and crawled on their bellies under the first row of desks to hide. Early walked down the sloping aisle and stopped.

"Good morning, gentlemen," he said pleasantly. "My name is Jubal Early. I am a major general in the Army of Northern Virginia." At his friendly greeting, a few heads popped up over the desks to stare. Early gestured at them with his pistol. "You're all my prisoners."

Pennsylvania Avenue
Near the Executive Mansion
May 13, 1866
11:00 a.m.

Forrest reunited with Lee and Jackson. With a choked voice, Lee recounted the death of Reynolds. Forrest's sorrow at the loss of the good general quickly turned to anger when Lee said that he agreed with Reynolds' final words. Forrest drew King Philip up so sharply that the war horse reared. When the gelding's hoofs struck the ground, Forrest erupted, not at Lee, but at Jackson. "I thought we were doin' all this so we could win our independence."

It was Lee who answered. "General Forrest, if I thought that we could trust those people, I would roll the dice and demand our independence. But I believe General Reynolds is correct. To do so would turn the public against us."

"Who cares what the public thinks?" Forrest raged. "We have independence in our grasp. Don't let some dyin' Yankee general talk you out of what's right."

"We may have independence in our grasp at this hour, but can we keep it?"

"We'll fight!"

"We tried that." Lee nudged Traveller forward, leaving Jackson and Forrest in the street. The troopers trailing in their wake stared at both generals in shock. Jackson urged Little Sorrel on.

Forrest caught up with Jackson. "Do you agree with him?" He pointed at Lee's back.

"I trust General Lee implicitly."

It wasn't an answer. Forrest narrowed his eyes and gave Jackson the once over. How had he misjudged these generals so badly?

"General Forrest," Lee called.

"What!" Forrest snapped.

Lee drew up. "We don't have time to argue, so humor me for a moment. Let's say that General Reynolds is correct, and I coerce our country from McClellan. He'll give in to whatever we demand today. He's a rarity. He was a born without a spine."

Forrest leaned forward in the saddle. "I don't see that as a negative."

"Because in the short term it's not," Lee said.

This conversation made little sense to Forrest. He glanced at Jackson, but Jackson sat motionless in his saddle, thoroughly earning his sobriquet. "Then demand the country."

Lee smiled. "Oh, General, you're not a short-term thinker. We were right to fight the war. We couldn't stand by and allow our rights to be trampled and our states invaded. We were also right to surrender. I don't know how it was in Georgia, but in the end, my men ate once every five days. They were so weak during that final march; they couldn't even carry their rifles. My army dissolved out from underneath me. If General Reynolds is correct, and the men who defeated us come to secure their victory, where do we find the men, the supplies, the weapons, the wagons? Where?"

Forrest didn't have an answer. He just didn't like the idea of giving up so easy.

Lee pressed his boots into Traveller's ribs. "When we surrendered, we were promised to be restored into the Union, not reconstructed into it. We didn't surrender so carpetbaggers could devour us. And we certainly didn't surrender so that we would lose the vote and be subjected to a military occupation in which we have no rights. General Reynolds says that the soldiers, and they are the only ones who really matter, will not re-enlist to keep the South prostrate under the heel of the Radicals. They see what is happening to us as a grave injustice. So, let's right that injustice, go home, and honor the men who fell on the field. Do you agree?"

Up ahead the white brick walls of the Executive Mansion came into view. "Yeah, I agree," Forrest said crossly.

Lee gave Forrest a searching glance. "That will do for right now." He smiled at Forrest like a father does at a wayward son.

Forrest scowled in protest.

"Forrest," Jackson said. "If you were General Sherman…"

"I'd shoot myself," Forrest said.

Lee burst into laughter.

Jackson continued as if he hadn't been interrupted. "And you needed reinforcements, where would you get them?"

Since the Confederates were slowly gobbling up soldiers as they swept south through the city, there was only one place. Sherman would have to recall the force he had sent to Manassas. But Manassas was a hard day's march away. That force wouldn't arrive until it was too late. The city would belong to the Confederates. He said so.

Jackson disagreed. "As long as McClellan and Sherman believe reinforcements will arrive and defeat us, they won't be in a bargaining mood."

"Well, someone needs to get on the road to Centreville to prevent that from happening," Forrest said.

"Do I have a volunteer?" Lee asked.

"How many men can I have?"

Jackson made his decision quickly. "Five hundred."

"That ain't near enough."

"General Johnston will be in pursuit."

Forrest gestured ahead. Union soldiers had set up a barricade in front of the Executive Mansion. "Let's win this battle first."

Chapter Thirty One

McClellan had turned his office into a command center and snatched responsibility for the Washington defenses clean out of Sherman's hand. When Sherman complained about the breech of protocol, McClellan pulled rank by rudely reminding Sherman that as president, he was also commander-in-chief. Sherman's contribution to the defense of Washington was sitting on the couch and listening while a panicked McClellan ordered troops designated for the relief of John Reynolds redirected to the Executive Mansion for guard duty.

Then an hour ago, disaster struck. A telegram arrived from General Thomas. He would surrender Richmond to General Longstreet at noon.

When Mr. Bicknell read the telegram to the room full of advisors, who were doing very little advising, Sherman could only sit astounded by the sheer audacity and speed of Lee's strategy.

The terms of surrender would allow Thomas to march his men from the city as long as he went south. Thomas planned to travel to Fort Monroe and from there ferry his troops back to Washington.

Sherman heard footsteps running down the hall. The knock on the door was just a courtesy. The door opened and in fearful expectation, all the advisors pivoted toward the harried clerk framed in the door way.

"The Rebs have broken through! They're coming up the drive!"

McClellan fell into his chair. "Can I get out?"

Sherman wasn't the only one in the room who noted the "I." The clerk shook his head. McClellan quickly recovered his poise. He turned and faced Sherman. "What do you suggest we do?"

261

Now, after the battle was lost, McClellan was returning command. "I suggest you prepare for visitors," Sherman said with all the sarcasm he could muster.

★ ★ ★

Thomas' Headquarters
Richmond, Virginia
May 13, 1866
Noon

Longstreet, the two Lee cousins, and Little Billy rode down Clay Street on their way to President Davis' former home. Crowds spilled onto the tree-lined street making it difficult for the horses to make their way. Longstreet glanced over at Mahone. Little Billy was waving his hat in joy. Behind him, he could hear the Lees shouting to the crowd.

Up ahead, a young widow stepped into the street and called out his name. Longstreet drew up. She handed up a package. "For you, General!"

Longstreet put a finger to his hat and nudged Victory. He looked down at the package. It was a Confederate battle flag made from a handkerchief. Allowing the celebratory atmosphere to wash over him, he unfolded the small scrap of material, and waved it in the air.

Mahone unleashed a Rebel yell. The soldiers in the crowd followed suit. The yell escorted them down the street.

Thomas was waiting for them on the front porch. In the driveway, his somber staff stood, all formally turned out in dress uniforms. A young orderly held the reins to Thomas' gelding.

Longstreet dismounted and climbed the steps. Mahone and the two Lee cousins waited in the street at the bottom of the hill. "Good afternoon, General Thomas. I'm General Longstreet. We've battled each other through Kentucky, Tennessee, and Georgia. It's ironic that we finally meet in Virginia. You're not too far from home."

Thomas' smile was sour. "It is good to meet you." He got right down to business. "My men and I will be marching to Fort Monroe. I've sent a wire to General Sherman alerting him of my surrender."

"Sir, is there anything you need," Longstreet said.

"No. My men have been directed to the rail depot where they will leave their weapons and all army supplies. Is there anything I can do for you?"

"No." Longstreet saluted.

Thomas returned the salute.

With more dignity than Longstreet could have summoned if the roles were reversed, Thomas walked down the steps. When he did, the Confederate generals saluted. Thomas returned the salute. The streets interrupted in catcalls and jeers at the southern man who had stayed with the Union and had fought against their men. Thomas didn't flinch. He took the reins from the young man and swung up in the saddle. He wheeled about and trotted down the street. His aides followed.

"General Lee," Longstreet called. Both Lees looked up. "Custis," he corrected.

"Yes, sir," Custis said.

"Where's my family?"

Executive Mansion
May 13, 1866
Noon

For Sherman, the waiting was worse than death. McClellan stood at the window, spinning desperate scenarios that, if enacted, would surely get them all killed. Besides no one in the room had any weapons except for Mr. Harrison, who grasped a palm pistol in his shaking hand.

This time the footsteps coming down the hall were different. Void of panic, they were measured and victorious.

"Where should I be?" McClellan blurted out. "I know," he said, answering his own question. "I'll sit behind my desk."

He crossed to the desk and sat down. Then stood up. Then sat down again. He looked down at the desktop and prepared himself. When he looked up, he was scowling in angry defiance.

The door opened and a tall man entered with a pistol clutched in his hand. Sherman stifled a gasp of surprise. It was the devil himself!

"My name is Forrest," the devil announced. He waved the pistol menacingly.

McClellan rose from his seat. "I am President McClellan."

Forrest was staring at Sherman, hatred flashing in his eyes. "You must be Sherman."

Sherman heard the challenge in the Reb's voice. "I am." His voice was ice.

Forrest glared for another moment before directing his attention to the rest of the men. "Any of you armed?" Harrison raised the palm pistol into the air. Forrest gestured with his gun. Harrison approached the fearsome cavalry leader as if Forrest would murder him where he stood. Forrest wrenched the tiny gun out of the advisor's hand. With a careless wave of his pistol, he sent Harrison scurrying back to the safety of the other advisors. As a group, they shrank back into the corner.

Without taking his eyes off the room, Forrest backed up to the door. He turned his head slightly. "Room's secure," he called out.

He moved out of the doorway. Lee and Jackson came into the room. Sherman recognized them from the trial. Lee had lost his sickly pallor. Instead, he wore an air of genteelness and aristocracy as casually as he wore his uniform jacket. Jackson, on the other hand, was all steel and fire. Whatever the three Rebels wanted, they weren't going to take no for an answer.

Lee's gaze raked the room. "I am General Lee." He indicated Jackson. "This is General Jackson."

McClellan smiled. "Yes, I recognize my old West Point schoolmate. How are you, Tom?"

Jackson stiffened. "I'm fine, Mr. President."

"Good." McClellan returned to his seat. "Now, gentlemen, you've come a long way to see me. What can I do for you?"

Lee directed his attention to Sherman and smiled. "I don't think I know you."

Sherman stood. "I'm General Sherman."

Lee's gaze flitted toward Forrest before returning to Sherman. "It's good to finally meet you." This time Lee didn't smile. "You've been responsible for so much death and loss since the war ended."

Lee's words hit Sherman like an artillery barrage, but he refuse to let Lee see that he was rattled. He stiffened his spine and met Lee's gaze.

"I don't know if you're aware of this, but General Reynolds is dead," Lee said.

A tidal wave of recriminations swept over Sherman at the news. He collapsed on the couch. Why hadn't he just left John at West Point where he was happy? He swallowed hard. "I'm sorry to hear that."

Lee turned to Forrest. "On your way, General Forrest."

Forrest nodded and exited the room. When his footsteps faded, Lee addressed Sherman. "General Forrest is on his way to intercept your small force returning from Bull Run Creek. Now, I've noticed the absence of General Sheridan today. Am I safe to conclude that he is leading that force?"

Sherman grimaced. "He is."

"General Johnston is giving pursuit."

Sherman sank back into the couch. The news that Sheridan was walking into a trap was the final blow to any hope of rescue.

"What do you want?" McClellan asked. "Hopefully, it's something I can provide."

"For your sake, I hope it is," Lee said.

McClellan heard the steel in Lee's voice and wilted. "I don't have the authority to give you your country," he stammered nervously. "The Congress wouldn't stand for it."

Lee laughed. "Perhaps I'll leave them in General Early's custody a while longer. He can be quite persuasive." He crossed to a chair and sat down. "But don't worry, we don't want our country."

"What?" Sherman exhaled in surprise.

"You still don't understand us," Lee said. He crossed his legs and pulled on the cuff of his sleeve. "We're more than willing to live by our paroles."

"Your actions say otherwise," McClellan said severely. "You've attacked a peaceful city. Your General Longstreet seized Richmond. And you say you're willing to live by the surrender terms." He waved his hand dismissively. "I don't believe you."

Lee gave McClellan a withering glare. "Then you're a bigger fool than I thought, George."

McClellan jumped to his feet. "I won't be insulted." He banged his fist on the desk in support of his declaration.

Jackson's pistol flew from its holster. "Yes, you will." With the pistol, he gestured at the chair. "Now sit down."

McClellan did as he was told.

"We didn't break the surrender terms," Lee said. "This government did by arresting us, trying us, murdering General Stuart, burning Lexington and Staunton, by occupying our states and denying us the vote, by unleashing carpetbaggers, the Freedman Bureau, and the Union League upon our people to rob and devour us. If anyone has the right to be outraged, it is us. Not you."

"That was the work of the Radicals," McClellan said.

"No, that was the work of General Sherman, General Sheridan, the Radicals, and you," Lee snapped. "Even before you took office, you backed down like a dog cowering before its master and gave the Radicals what they demanded."

Sherman waited for McClellan to respond, but the truth of Lee's statement seemed to have stolen the words from the president. "What do you want?" McClellan finally spluttered.

"We want our freedom," Lee said. He pulled on his cuff again. "We want our states and votes. We want the money and land you have stolen from us returned. We want our elected senators and our congressman seated in the Capitol. We want the dogs and locusts you loosed on us rounded up and tried for their crimes."

"I'm sorry, but that is impossible," McClellan insisted.

"Find a way," Lee said coolly. "We've lived under your thumb long enough. Restore us as you promised, for if you are determined to reconstruct us back into this nation, I will call the men of the South to me."

"Then what?" McClellan tried to sound outraged. He just came across terrified. "You couldn't win the war the first time. So why should we give in to your threats now? It's just empty talk."

Lee shook his head. "I didn't come all this way to fill your office with empty talk. If you don't restore us to the Union as states and citizens with full rights and protection of the law, I'll unleash my wrath over Stuart's murder and make you pay a price you cannot bear."

Sherman stared at Lee. He had misjudged them. He honestly believed that when the autumn passed without an attack that the Rebs had accepted Stuart's death as just a casualty of war. But Lee stood before him, a god of war, angry because Stuart had been murdered and Lee had been denied justice. That same anger radiated from Jackson. In fact, it filled the room. The Rebs were exacting their revenge now, on their time.

McClellan laughed. "You can't hurt us."

Lee pulled on his cuff again. "I'll take my men, and I'll head into the mountains – out of your reach. I'll start a guerilla war that will shake your country's sense of safety to its foundation. You'll never know when and where I'll strike."

"No." McClellan folded his arms across his chest like a petulant child.

Lee stood. "Okay George, have it your way. But when the people find out that all you had to do was stand up to the Radicals and do the right thing, well – Lee gave a little shrug – I hope you weren't counting on a second term." He started toward the door.

Sherman thought Lee's response very clever for he had just hit McClellan right where he lived – his ego.

"Wait a minute! Wait a minute!" McClellan said, hurrying around the corner of the desk.

Sherman suppressed his laughter. McClellan hadn't even remained resolute for a minute.

The door opened and a Confederate soldier entered. McClellan used his entrance to retreat behind his desk. "General Jackson, this just came in at the secretary's office." The soldier handed over a telegram.

Jackson read it quickly. His eyebrows shot up in surprise. "It's from General Doubleday in Charleston. The city has been surrounded. General Kershaw is demanding the surrender of the garrison. Doubleday says he can't hold. He's waiting your instructions."

McClellan bolted from his chair. "Was all of this a stalling tactic while your men attacked Union garrisons throughout the South? How dare you stand there and declare you don't want to restart the war?"

Sherman had been watching Jackson closely. He was almost certain that Jackson had no knowledge of what was unfolding in Charleston, but he needed to make sure. "You didn't know about Charleston?"

Jackson shook his head. "Obviously General Lee's plea reached farther than we hoped."

"I can stop it," Lee said casually. "Give us what we ask for, and I'll tell the men to go home. Your General Doubleday will be quite safe."

McClellan laughed. "If you didn't send this General Kershaw to Charleston, then you've no control of the situation. What makes you confident you can order a retreat?"

"Because he can," Sherman said.

McClellan scoffed. "No man has that kind of authority."

"Sam did," Sherman said. "In fact, if he hadn't been killed, this tragedy would have never happened. He would have stopped Stanton from arresting anyone. He was the only one who could. I believe General Lee. If he says he can stop it, then he can." He faced McClellan. "You have the opportunity to right a terrible wrong. Not just to these men, but to the South. They surrendered and expected us to be honorable men and keep our word."

McClellan stood unyielding.

Sherman was stymied. Did he have to get an iron crow to pry McClellan from his fear of the Radicals? Lee had done it by hitting McClellan in his ego and ambition. Perhaps the strategy would work for him as well. "Mr. President, you're looking at the situation all wrong. This is no time for fear. If you stand up to the Radicals, the people will respect you." He shook his head. "Respect isn't the right word." He stroked his chin. "Do this, George, and the people will love you more than they do Lincoln."

McClellan wasn't convinced. "Even if I agree, the Radicals won't pass any law easing Reconstruction." He held up his hands. "I'm sorry. There's nothing I can do."

"You could sign an executive order," Sherman said.

"I don't know if…" McClellan hedged.

Sherman went all in. "You know the one thing I admired most about Lincoln was that he wasn't afraid of the Radicals. I guess I just don't understand why you are."

McClellan sat down, leaned back in his chair, and pondered Sherman's words. He sat up. "Okay, I'll do it." His words were wobbly, but at least he had said them.

Lee nodded. "Once I have the order, I will have my key operator wire the details to all the major newspapers in the North."

McClellan gasped in surprise. "That's coercion!"

Lee smiled. "Oh, you could look at it like that. But it'll be harder for you to go back on your word once the country knows about our deal."

McClellan huffed impatiently. "I suppose you want the order now."

"Yes, I would," Lee said.

Sherman smiled at how agreeable Lee could be while blackmailing the President of the United States.

With another huff, McClellan took up his pen and began to write.

"General Lee," Sherman said. "Would you rescind your order and allow Sheridan's men to return unmolested to Washington."

Lee was prepared to agree but Jackson interrupted. "No! Whatever happens to General Sheridan in his retreat, he deserves."

McClellan looked up from his paper. "General Sherman, should I stop writing?"

Sherman leaned back on the couch and shook his head. "Sheridan can take care of himself."

The room quieted. The only sound was McClellan's pen as it scratched out an executive order.

Church Hill
Richmond, Virginia
May 13, 1866
1:15 p.m.

Longstreet dismounted. The iron gate in front of the house was latched shut. It squeaked loudly when he pushed it open. He hurried up a walk overgrown with weeds. He was at the bottom of the front steps when the door opened. His oldest son, Garland, stood in the doorway.

"Father!" Garland whispered in surprise.

Longstreet took the steps two at a time. He stared at his son. "Can you really be my Garland? You were a teenager when I left. Now, you're a man." Garland stood rooted in place. "But not man enough that your father can't hug you." He wrapped his arms around his son and enveloped him in a bear hug.

"Are you home to stay?" Garland whispered in his ear.

"I'm home to stay."

Chapter Thirty Two

Johnston heard Mosby's scouts ride into camp and knew it would be only a few moments before Mosby would be beside his bedroll with news about the disposition of the enemy column. Johnston rolled onto his back, placed his hands under his head, and stared up into the sky now colored with the first streaks of dawn.

He smiled. Jackson's veterans were a marvel. They had marched three miles an hour yesterday through the broiling sun without complaint and easily gobbled up the miles separating them from the retreating Yankees. That was until they ran into a roadblock of Union stragglers, who didn't resist, but actually welcomed capture.

The prisoners impeded his pursuit. The Yankees were exhausted and slowed his column to a crawl. By sunset, he had over 300 Federals marching at the rear of the column. There was no way he could catch the Yankees if he had to drag 300 whining soldiers after him.

"Sir," Mosby whispered.

"I'm awake," Johnston said. He sat up. He raised his hand and allowed Mosby to help him to his feet. He groaned. He was far too old to be sleeping on the ground. He would be glad when this whole adventure was over. "Where are they, Colonel?"

"Two miles in front of us."

Johnston's mouth fell open in surprise. Two miles! He would catch them by midmorning.

"A courier came in last night. From Forrest. Washington has been taken."

272

Johnston raised his eyes to heaven in grateful prayer. It was finally over.

"Forrest says that he has 500 men..." Johnston stared at Mosby in shock. Did Forrest still plan to fight? "He's encamped about two miles east of Sheridan's picket line," Mosby continued.

Johnston shook his head. "We're not attacking. It's over. You ride back to Forrest and tell him so."

Mosby gulped. "Sir, the order to attack comes from General Jackson."

"General Jackson doesn't give me orders," Johnston said heatedly. "I'm not risking any more lives. Now go on and do as I say."

Mosby rallied. "Sir, Sheridan doesn't know it's over. We can stop him here..."

"Fine, Colonel," Johnston snapped. "Get me a map of the area and show me Forrest's exact location."

"I have a map at my camp." Mosby turned on his heel.

As soon as Mosby was out of sight, Johnston headed off toward the rear.

★ ★ ★

Johnston gave the trembling prisoner standing before him his most severe stare. It did its work quickly. Tears sprang into the young man's eyes. "How old are you?"

The young man flinched. "I turned nineteen in March," he warbled.

"Where are you from?" Johnston barked.

"Ohio," the soldier sobbed.

Johnston couldn't keep up his stern façade any longer. He put a friendly hand on the young man's soldier. "Go home."

The young man looked up at Johnston in shock. "What?"

"War's over. Go home!" The dusty, exhausted man continued to stare at him in disbelief. He pointed west. "Go!"

The soldier took off running. After a moment's pause so did the rest of the prisoners.

★ ★ ★

For Sheridan, the news was grim. There was a Confederate force entrenched two miles in front of him. A mixture of infantry and cavalry from what his scouts could tell. The Rebels had caught him from behind. For all intents and purposes he was surrounded and cut off from Washington. He sent a courier racing to Sherman for reinforcements. He arrayed his small force in a strong defensive perimeter, splitting his men to guard both the western and eastern approaches.

"White flag coming in!" He heard someone shout. "From the east!"

Sheridan raised his fieldglasses. A group of riders galloped out of the trees into the clearing. One carried a white flag. He scowled. One of the riders was Forrest. Another was Johnston. That didn't surprise Sheridan. He knew that Reb couriers were skirting his lines to the south. He just didn't have the manpower to keep the Rebs from communicating with each other.

Sheridan had Rienzi brought forward. He swung up in the saddle and rode off to meet the Rebs.

★ ★ ★

Forrest paced back and forth. Johnston stood nearby, leaning against a tree, his arms folded across his chest and his eyes closed. It was the sleep of the victorious. Forrest glared at the napping man. Johnston had gone and pulled rank, even over Jackson. Sheridan would be given a chance to surrender. Forrest agreed but he had done so too quickly. Johnston had narrowed his eyes and barked that Sheridan would be given a real opportunity to surrender. Forrest swallowed back his anger and disappointment. It was bad enough that

Lee had surrendered the country, but now Sheridan would escape retribution for what he had done in the Valley and to Stuart.

Sheridan rode up and dismounted. He gestured for his aides to remain where they were. Three quick strides brought him to the Confederate generals. "What do you want?"

It was Forrest who answered. "I have force sufficient to take your works by assault. I therefore demand an unconditional surrender of all your forces."

"Why should I surrender?"

Forrest stared at Sheridan in disbelief. The little man was begging to be attacked. He would gladly oblige. Johnston stepped forward. Forrest's hand twitched. He suppressed the urge to jerk Johnston back by his collar before he could offer Sheridan a deal the Union general would accept.

"General Lee has taken Washington. He has captured the Capitol and the Executive Mansion. It's over. There's no need for further bloodshed," Johnston said.

Sheridan paced for a moment. "I don't think it's come to surrender."

"Then I will take your works." Forrest earned a warning glare from Johnston. He ignored it. Sheridan wanted to fight it out, so Forrest was going to oblige him. "Let's go, General Johnston," he said before Sheridan could change his mind.

Johnston pointed at Forrest. "He wants to fight you."

Sheridan scoffed. "I'm not afraid of him."

"Well, you should be," Johnston said. "Because he'll win."

"Yes or no!" Forrest snapped, trying to goad Sheridan into a fight.

Sheridan paced again. "How do I know that you're not lying about what's going on in Washington?"

"We're not liars," Forrest said.

"No, you're just treasonous…"

Forrest didn't give him a chance to finish. He reared back and let his fist fly. Sheridan dropped hard to the ground. Forrest pointed an angry finger at the prostrate man. "You watch your mouth."

Sheridan came up spitting blood and curses. He clenched his fists.

Johnston stepped between the two. "General Forrest, as long as you're under my command, you will comport yourself as a gentleman." Forrest took a step back. "Now, prepare your men to move immediately upon General Sheridan's works." Johnston addressed Sheridan, who was still spitting blood from his mouth. "I collected your scraps yesterday. I know the quality of the soldiers that man your defenses. Are you insane enough to pit them against his seasoned troops?"

Sheridan spat on the ground. "What are your terms?"

"I gave you the terms," Forrest said. "Unconditional surrender. You served with Grant. You're familiar with the phrase."

"What do you suggest?" Johnston asked.

"You're not going to let him dictate terms, are you?" Forrest demanded.

Johnston glared at Forrest but addressed his words to Sheridan. "My offer expires in thirty seconds."

Sheridan exhaled. "My men and I go back to Washington."

"Unarmed and under my escort," Johnston said.

Sheridan paced as he pondered the offer. "I accept. For my men." He glared at Forrest. "From you, I demand an apology."

"General Forrest doesn't owe you anything," Johnston said lightly.

"Yes, I do," Forrest said. He reared back and struck the little man again. Sheridan crumpled to the ground.

"What was that for?" Johnston demanded.

"That was for Stuart," Forrest said. Sheridan struggled to his feet. "Oh, stay down."

Sheridan did as he was told.

Chapter Thirty Three

Washington was a ghost town. The streets were empty and the stores boarded up tight. It had been that way since the Confederates had seized the city. But the temporary occupation was being lifted today. McClellan's executive order had been printed and reprinted in the nation's newspapers. Sherman's office was sharing the telegrams flowing between Washington and the military administrators in the South with General Rodes. The garrisons were pulling out. The Freedman Bureaus were being shut down, and the carpetbaggers were being dispossessed of their ill-gotten gains before being run out of town on a rail. It was a beginning. Lee made it clear to Sherman that it was just a beginning.

Lee and Jackson debated if they should leave troops in the city but decided against it. Keeping troops in the capital wouldn't be enough to keep McClellan honest. If the president reneged on his executive order, then the South's response would have to be more ruinous than capturing a city. Jackson gave the order to Rodes and Early. The troops would depart the city at nine o'clock this morning.

Early vigorously protested. He wanted to hold the senators and congressmen prisoners until the South was fumigated of all Union stench. Lee had to intervene before Early prepared his troops for departure.

Jackson stepped out of the Kirkwood Hotel and glanced about. He was waiting for Lee and Johnston to finish their breakfast. Forrest rode up.

"General Forrest, I've a bone to pick with you," Jackson said severely.

"What?" Forrest. He slowly dismounted and crossed to Jackson.

"General Johnston tells me that you unleashed quite a punch on Sheridan on Stuart's behalf."

"Yeah." Forrest was defensive. "Do you have a problem with that?"

"I do, actually," Jackson said.

Forrest huffed. "Why?"

Jackson could barely contain his laughter. "Because you didn't hit for me." He smiled.

Forrest laughed. "I think Sheridan's at the War Department. I could go rectify my breech of etiquette right now. Just say the word."

Jackson held up his hand. "Maybe another day." He could tell Forrest was disappointed.

Lee appeared. "Good morning, gentlemen." He looked up in the sky. "Beautiful day." He put his hands on his back and stretched.

Jackson glanced skyward. It was a good day for traveling, and he was anxious to get underway. "When will General Johnston be down?"

"In a minute," Lee said.

Jackson hoped it would be just a minute.

"I've decided not to return to Clover Hill with you," Lee announced abruptly. "I'm going to travel on to Richmond with Joe instead."

"Well, I'm sorry to hear that," Forrest said.

Jackson walked away. He stopped when he reached the curb. He wasn't prepared to say goodbye to Lee. Not at this moment, at least. He heard Lee call his name, but he didn't reply.

Lee joined him at the curb. "I'll come to Lexington in the summer. I owe Jimmie a pony."

"We owe Jimmie a pony," Jackson laughed. The knot in his chest eased at Lee's words. The goodbye wasn't final. When Lee came to visit this summer, Jackson would employ all his power of persuasion to convince Lee to make Lexington his permanent home.

The door of the hotel opened. Jackson saw Johnston exit. "You need to get going. Richmond's a long way off. Will you need an escort?"

Lee shook his head. "There are enough men headed to the Richmond area. We'll be fine."

Jackson gave a small smile. "I'll miss our talks over coffee in the morning."

Lee smiled. "So will I."

Jackson extended his hand.

Lee shook his head. "A handshake won't do." Lee embraced him. Tears burned Jackson's eyes. He couldn't speak. Lee gave him another smile. "I'll see you this summer. General Forrest."

Forrest was with Johnston and both men walked to the curb.

Lee smiled at Forrest. "General Stuart was an excellent officer and the finest cavalryman General Jackson and I ever had the privilege of knowing. He was one of a kind. But, sir, I would have you lead my cavalry anytime. You've brought a level of skill and dedication to your duty that separates you from the rest. It has been an honor serving with you. I wish you the very best when you return to Tennessee. In the future, if you should need anything, please call on me."

Forrest swallowed deeply. "Thank you, General Lee. General Johnston this goes for you too. You have my admiration, sirs. And I'll never forget serving under your commands." He turned suddenly and walked away.

"Be careful," Jackson said to Lee. He shook Johnston's hand. "If you see General Longstreet, give him my thanks."

"I will," Johnston replied.

An orderly brought Traveller and Johnston's mare around. Lee swung up in the saddle. "Write me if you need me," he said to Jackson. He gave Traveller the signal and slowly walked down the street.

Jackson waved goodbye.

"General Lee's a real gentleman," Forrest said from behind him.

"Yes, he is," Jackson agreed. He turned and faced the cavalry leader. "Let's go home."

✯✯✯

The sun was rising behind the huge oaks when Jackson, Forrest, and Morrison rounded the final bend and the familiar farmhouse came into view. The porch was empty and the front door was shut. Jackson smiled. Everyone must still be asleep.

The three men pulled up and dismounted.

"Hello!" Jackson called. "Is anyone up?"

The door swung open and Rebel darted out. He jumped up and down in front of Jackson, demanding immediate attention. Jackson knelt down and gave the spaniel a proper petting. Rebel responded with a kiss on the cheek.

"You've come home!" Jackson stood and saw Anna standing on the top step. "Does that mean we've won?"

"It means we've won," Jackson said.

A stricken look appeared on Anna's face and tears filled her eyes. "Oh, no!" She moaned. "Where's General Lee. He isn't..."

"No, ma'am," Forrest said quickly. "By now, he's almost to Richmond with General Johnston and General Longstreet."

The front door banged open. Jackson saw Jimmie running across the porch. Without warning, the little boy jumped off the top step into Jackson's arms. Jackson staggered backward under his weight.

"I missed you, ole Stonewall." Jimmie threw his arms around Jackson's neck. "I prayed for you every night." He kissed Jackson's cheek.

Jackson wrapped his arms around the little boy and gave him a squeeze. "I missed you, too." Jackson set him down on the ground.

Jimmie looked about. He turned a fearful face to Jackson. "Where's Grandpa?"

"He went to see his family in Richmond," Jackson explained. Jimmie's lower lip quivered. "But when he comes to see you this summer, he's bringing you a pony."

The lip stopped quivering as a sunny smile broke out on the little boy's face. At the sight of it, Jackson's heart panged him. So much like his father. Jackson hugged the boy close again.

"Is there anything to eat?" Morrison asked. "I'm famished."

Anna laughed. "Why don't you let Jim know you're back? I'm sure he'll fix you a fitting breakfast."

Morrison didn't need to be told twice. He gathered up the laughing Jimmie and went into the house.

"Where are the girls?" Jackson asked.

"Still sleeping. As is Tom," Anna replied. A baby's cry suddenly pierced the quiet of the house. "I spoke too soon," she laughed. "Excuse me." She went into the house.

"What do you say, General Forrest. How about we sit down to a big breakfast?" Jackson climbed the steps. He stopped when he noticed Forrest hadn't followed.

"I think my men and me are just goin' to press on. We have the whole day ahead of us."

Jackson came back down the steps. "What's the hurry?"

"Well, we've been gone from our families for a long time. Now that it's safe, it's time we went home and rebuilt our lives."

Jackson found himself unprepared to say goodbye to Forrest either. "At least stay for breakfast."

Forrest shook his head. "No thank you. The men are waitin' on the road."

"Well, come in and say goodbye to everyone."

Forrest stared down at the ground. "I don't like good-byes. I ain't good at 'em."

There was finality in Forrest's voice. Jackson quit pushing. "Do you need anything?"

"No." Forrest gathered up King Philip's reins. He threw himself up in the saddle. He looked down at Jackson. "When I first heard the news that Richmond had sent General Longstreet to Tullahoma, I questioned that decision. In my complainin', I said to Colonel Kelley that if Richmond was goin' to go through all the trouble of sendin' us a new general, why didn't they send us that Stonewall fella 'cause he could fight. Now, after all we've been through, I still have to wonder if you had come, would we have won our independence. Sir, you're the greatest warrior I've had the privilege of knowin'. Thank you for allowin' me the honor of bein' your cavalry leader."

Jackson's throat tightened. "No, General Forrest, the honor has been mine."

Forrest drew his hand up in a salute. Jackson returned the salute. He held it until Forrest had cantered out of sight.

★ ★ ★

The river roared behind Lee. The James in a hurry to reach its final destination at Hampton Roads. The sun glinted off the water. Hollywood Cemetery was quiet, and Lee was alone. As he walked along the paths that cut through the bright green grass, he savored the silence. The cemetery was beautiful, built on a series of small hills. At the peak of each swell, the cemetery was framed by the James. A few feet down into a dale, and the James disappeared. He stopped at the top of a hill and looked at the map Custis had drawn for him marking the spot where Fitzhugh rested. Custis had volunteered to come along, but this was a journey Lee needed to make alone. He glanced around. Up ahead, he saw a large oak. He hurried to it.

There, at the base of the tree, stood a small stone marker. He knelt down and brushed leaves from the surface.

Major General
William Henry Fitzhugh Lee
May 31, 1837
May 22, 1864

Lee's fingers slowly followed the contours of each letter of his son's name. A tear splashed on the white stone, turning the spot gray. He pulled a handkerchief from his pocket and wiped his eyes. His fingers traced the word general. He knew Fitzhugh would have been pleased that his rank had been immortalized, but Lee was not. He wanted the line to read *beloved son of*. It was a father's fancy. Custis, who made the decision about the inscription, had made the correct one. Fitzhugh didn't just belong to his father. He had fought for Virginia and his country. The rank was a way for the son to finally escape his father's shadow.

Lee knew his shadow had cast a smothering presence over his family and had caused damage to his children. Custis had chafed under it all his life, and Mary, his oldest daughter, only came home to visit when forced. She usually left again when the first opportunity presented itself.

He heard a woman's voice, which was promptly joined by a man's. They were headed his way. It angered him that he couldn't even have this solemn moment to himself. Since his return from Washington, he had been under siege. The traffic to his door never ceased. Even in the middle of the night, he heard the constant rap of the doorknocker. Whether it was a veteran come to pay his respect to his commander, a widow with children in tow looking for a handout, or just a fan seeking an autograph, there was no peace in the house. And now, his fame was forcing him from his son's grave.

He gave the stone a final caress, rose, and turned the opposite of the way of the voices. He wasn't fast enough.

"General Lee! General Lee!" First the woman, then the man called after him. Lee pretended not to hear. He practically ran from the cemetery.

★ ★ ★

Clover Hill
June 2, 1866

The afternoon foretold of a hot, dry summer. Curtains in the open windows moved lazily in the breeze. The doors were jammed open in the hopes cooler air would invade the upstairs. The lunch dishes had been washed and dried. The girls were taking a nap, and Anna was upstairs giving Tom a bath. Now that Little Sorrel was back, Jimmie had begged Morrison to join him in a ride through the woods. Rebel lay on his back at the other end of porch.

Flora sat on the swing gazing out on the green carpet of clover that filled the lawn. This plantation had been properly named. She wished that she had the money to purchase the property. Since she had left Kansas, her family hadn't known the security of a home of their own. During the war, they had shuttled back and forth between Stuart relations and friends. It was a horrible way to live: afraid that you would wear out your welcome, or that you were never really welcomed at all.

Now that Jeb was dead, she didn't know what she was going to do. There were the proceeds of a life insurance policy to ease some of her worry. Her brother-in-law was working hard to liberate Jeb's bank account that had been confiscated at the beginning of the war. There was at least $5,000 in the account; the profits he received when he sold his saber attachment to the army.

Anna constantly hinted that she wanted Flora and the children to come and live with the Jacksons in Lexington. Flora knew that the hints were rooted in the promise Jackson made as Jeb lay dying. She also knew that a promise like that would fade over time, and she would feel like she had during the war – simply in the way.

It was ironic, but Clover Hill was the closet thing she had to a home in the last five years. It was a house filled with children and love and family. Of course, the family had broken up. Forrest left without saying goodbye. But then again, so had Lee. That had hurt. She realized she was being selfish. Lee just wanted to hug his family. But ever since Lee had adopted Jeb as a son, Flora had come to regard Lee as a father. So, to leave without saying goodbye. Yes, it had hurt.

Jackson came out of the front door. He didn't see her. He crossed to the porch rail and leaned out. A smile spread across the face. "I asked Mr. Waterman if he would sell this place to me."

He had seen her after all. "What did he say?"

"He declined. Upon his death, his oldest grandson will inherit Kilkenny Gardens and his youngest Clover Hill." Jackson crossed to the couch and sat down. "I always wanted to be a farmer."

"What will you do now?" Flora rocked the swing back and forth.

"I'll return to Lexington and rebuild the house and enlarge it so the children can have a nice, roomy nursery."

"That's nice."

"How large I make the nursery depends on you." Jackson smiled at her.

Flora stopped rocking. "That's very kind of you, but I won't hold you to the promise you made to Jeb. That wouldn't be fair."

"I didn't make that promise to Stuart because he was dying. I made it because he was my brother, and he asked me for one last favor." There was no anger in Jackson's voice.

Flora gazed out at the lawn for a long moment. She turned back to Jackson and smiled. "I won't hold you to that promise."

"Even if I want to be held to it."

Flora was stunned by the confession. She had given Jackson a way out, and he had refused to take it. She shook her head. "I can't be a guest in someone's house anymore. My children and I need a permanent home."

"I'm offering you one."

Flora avoided his gaze by staring out into the lawn again.

"Where will you go?" He asked.

"Stuart's brother said I can stay with his family in Saltville." She spoke to the clover.

"If that's your decision, I'll respect it." She heard kindness in his voice. "But I would like to have my say, if that's okay." She smiled and nodded. "I don't consider you Stuart's family. I consider you my family. Our two girls are inseparable. Tom reaches out for you as often as he reaches for Anna. And Jimmie..." Jackson laughed. "I love him as if he was my own son, and, Flora, if I can speak frankly..."

He paused and waited for permission. "Of course. Of course," she said.

"He's a rambunctious little boy, and he's going to need a strong hand. And Anna loves you like a sister. I'm telling you the truth. We want you to stay with us as long as you want."

She dropped her head. *As long as she wanted.* A cryptic message that meant you're expected to move on sooner rather than later. She raised her head and gazed out into the lawn again.

"Did I say something wrong?" Jackson questioned.

She shook her head. "No," she whispered.

"I think I did. Please tell me what it was."

"I've been invited to stay at homes as long as I wanted before, but I came to realize that phrase really meant you're welcome for a short visit, but you should be about making plans to find another place to live as soon as possible. I love Anna too much to know the awkwardness that comes when I've outstayed my welcome."

He sat down next to her on the swing and took her hand. "If that's what it means to you, then I'm sorry I said it because it's not what I meant."

His kindness was discomfiting. "What did you mean?"

"That you aren't our prisoner. That if you should decide for whatever reason to leave, I'll support you."

Her eyes sparkled with tears. "Why are you being so kind to me?"

"Because it's the last thing I can do for my dear Stuart." He let go of her hand. "I know if the situation was reversed, he would do the same for me. And Anna would be the one sitting here saying no because she didn't understand the bond that existed between Stuart and me. I can't force you to say yes. All I can do is tell you that you're very welcome and hope you believe me."

Flora burst into tears. "I will come with you to Lexington."

Jackson leaned over and kissed her cheek. "Thank you."

Chapter Thirty Four

Lexington, Virginia
October 17, 1866

Jackson stepped aside to allow the rest of the mourners to exit the church. Lee was the next one through the door. Johnston, Longstreet, Fitz and Custis Lee, and Henry McClellan spilled out and started down the steps to get ready for the procession to the cemetery.

It had been a year since Stuart had been murdered. The impromptu funeral in the living room of Clover Hill had always bothered Jackson. He believed Stuart deserved better. When he returned to Lexington, he began to arrange a memorial service for the fallen cavalry leader. Since Stuart had already been buried in Jackson's family plot, his original plans had not included a procession to the cemetery.

But Fitz Lee had other ideas. He went to Stuart's troopers and organized a subscription to buy Stuart a proper grave marker. Stuart's men had contributed a sizeable amount of money. Jackson had given and so had Lee. Forrest had even sent a hefty contribution from Tennessee.

A week ago, a twenty-five foot high limestone obelisk arrived from Richmond. Not prepared for such a grand monument, Jackson spent the afternoon searching for a new burial site. He found a clear section somewhat in the middle of the cemetery. He didn't like the fact that it was void of trees and shades. Silly thing to be worried about, but it troubled him. In the spring, he would plant oak saplings so in a few years, Stuart could rest in the shade.

Flora exited the church, holding Jimmie's and Ginny's hands. Anna walked behind. She handed a sleeping Julia to Morrison. Tom had been left behind with Jim, who was preparing a large dinner for the mourners after the ceremony. Jim had been invited to the service, but he declined to attend, which surprised Jackson. When Jackson pressed for a reason, Jim tearfully explained that he had already said goodbye to Stuart during the time he had prepared the cavalry leader for burial. He couldn't bear to say goodbye again.

Jimmie broke free and ran over to Jackson. "Hey ole Stonewall, can I go to Pa's burial place with you and Grandpa?" He pulled at his shirt's stiff collar. He was wearing a brand new suit and had squirmed and wriggled against the coarse material since Flora had put it on him.

"Is it okay with your Ma?" Jackson asked.

He pivoted sharply. "MA!"

"Jimmie," Jackson corrected immediately. "Go over and ask her."

Jimmie kicked at the ground with his new shoes, but did as he was told.

Longstreet joined him. "Beautiful service."

Jackson nodded at the compliment. "I hear rumors about you."

Longstreet smiled. "News reaches you all the way in the Valley?"

"Sometimes. So, it's true?" Jackson asked.

"I'm running for governor," Longstreet said.

"And he's going to win," Johnston said, coming up the stairs. "Beautiful service." This was directed to Jackson.

Down on the street, the band had assembled. Fitz was gathering the veterans into columns of six.

"It looks like we're about to begin," Johnston said. "We should get in place."

"Are you going to vote for me?" Longstreet pounded Jackson on his back.

"All depends. At dinner, you'll have to share with me your position on taxes. I'll warn you ahead of time. I'm against them."

Longstreet laughed and headed down the steps after Johnston.

Fitz was having trouble getting the chattering soldiers in place. His shouts began to rise above the crowd.

Jackson was on his way over to Anna when an arm reached out and stopped him. The arm belonged to Lee. "General, do you know Mr. Brockenbrough?"

"I do." Brockenbrough was the rector of Washington College. "How are you, John?"

"I'm fine," Brockenbrough said. "Beautiful service." Jackson smiled at the compliment. "I was just offering General Lee a position at the college." Jackson was stunned. Brockenbrough took his silence as a sign of interest. "As president."

"I don't know." Lee was self-effacing.

Jackson thought Lee a perfect fit for the job. But he also knew he was being selfish. He didn't like Lee living down on the Peninsula at Rooney's old plantation. "I think it's the right job for you, and you should say yes right now."

Brockenbrough beamed.

"It's tempting," Lee said.

"Be tempted," Jackson laughed. Voices rose from the street. Fitz was losing control of the soldiers. "But right now, go help Fitz. You know he has no authority with the infantry."

Lee went down the steps to order his men into position one last time.

"Try to convince him," Brockenbrough said to Jackson. "The college needs him."

"And he needs the college," Jackson thought. To Brockenbrough he said, "General Lee is his own man. I'll do what I can. Excuse me."

He continued on his way to Anna. He touched her arm and got her attention. He pointed to the column that was rapidly falling into order under Lee's command. "I'm going to go on ahead. I'll meet you at the cemetery."

Two steps down, he heard Jimmie calling him. "Can I go too, ole Stonewall?"

"Not this time, Jimmie." Folded arms and a pout was Jimmie's reply. "You go with Grandpa, and I'll see you at the cemetery." He continued down the steps.

Jackson hurried up Main Street. Through the iron fence he saw bystanders thronging the obelisk. Only the small parade stand remained empty. He kept his head down and wasn't spotted. He entered the gate and turned immediately to where a white stone cross marked a grave. He sighed. No matter how many times he came to visit, he would never get used to the idea of Sandie Pendleton lying beneath a green blanket of grass.

He heard the band draw near. He only had a few moments before the procession entered the cemetery and he would be missed. He removed his hat, bowed his head, and offered up a prayer. When he finished, he pulled his kepi down over his eyes.

He started toward the obelisk. As he walked, he looked straight ahead and saw the mountains which surrounded Lexington. The leaves had turned and the mountains were painted in reds, oranges, and yellows. He flung his hand into the air. *"I will lift up mine eyes unto the hills, from whence cometh my help,"* he quoted.

He lived his life in the belief that God works all things together for good. Even though he had just left the gravesite of the young man he had loved like a son and was headed toward the grave of the man he loved like a brother, these twin tragedies hadn't shaken that belief. Just the opposite. The war with all its victories, defeats, and losses had only strengthened his faith. He had turned to God every time he had suffered loss only to be reminded that God was good and merciful.

Everything in life was temporary except for the ever kind Providence who had created the mountains surrounding Lexington by the power of His word. One day, hopefully in the far distance, he would cross over the river and be laid to rest under the shades of the trees in this cemetery along side Pendleton and Stuart. But that was for another day.

Right now, he was happy. And for that happiness, he would continue to praise God, who had blessed him beyond his wildest imagination.

Epilogue

The President's House
Washington College
Lexington, Virginia
May 28, 1878

"Papa!"

Lee woke from his nap. He turned his head and saw a silhouette standing in a sunbeam by the window. He smiled. "Where have you been, Jeb?"

Stuart crossed to the bed. "Where's not important. I'm here now."

Lee scooted over to give Stuart room to sit down next to him. He reached over and took Stuart's hand. "You've been gone so long." Stuart smiled at the reprimand. "I've missed that sunny smile."

Stuart smiled again. "How are you feeling, Papa?"

A shadow passed over Lee's face. "The doctors aren't hopeful. Of course, they don't say anything directly to me. But I hear their whispers and see Custis' and Mildred's concern. I just drink my medicines like a good patient." He patted Stuart's hand. "But now that my darling boy is here, I shall be getting well in a hurry."

Lee took a long look at Stuart. He looked exactly the same as he did when he rode off with Jackson to meet John Reynolds that long ago day. He even had the same clothes on. A disturbing memory fought its way to the surface. Lee forced it back and grasped Stuart's hand tighter. But the memory surfaced and he knew the truth. "I'm dreaming."

"Does it matter?" Stuart asked.

It did matter, for dreams ended, and Stuart would be gone again. "No, it doesn't," he lied. "It's good to see you again, Jeb."

There was a knock on the door. The dream began to fade. "I don't want you to go."

"You'll see me again soon."

Another knock brought Lee fully awake. The door squeaked as it swung open. Lee observed Custis standing in the doorway. "Are you up to a visit from General Jackson?"

"Yes, of course." Lee heard his voice and was frightened by its weakness.

"Okay." Custis closed the door.

★ ★ ★

Jackson rang the bell and waited. The day was blistering hot and he had sweated through his shirt. The door opened and Mildred, Lee's Precious Life, stood before him. "I'm glad you've come," she said with a trembling voice.

"How is he?" Jackson questioned.

"He's fading. I just hope he lasts until Rob arrives tonight. I think we've called for him too late."

"I've cleared my schedule and told my adjutant I will be here." Jackson was no longer a professor of experimental and natural philosophy but the superintendent of VMI.

Mildred stepped aside and allowed Jackson to enter the cool hallway. "Jimmie's here, though. He sat with Father most of the morning."

Cadet James Ewell Brown Stuart, Jr. stood at attention when Jackson entered the living room. "General Jackson, sir."

"At ease, Jimmie."

Jimmie sat back down on the couch. Jackson sat next to him. Custis came from the kitchen. He had a cup of tea in his hands. "I'm sorry General Jackson, but I think Father's sleeping."

"Don't wake him on my account," Jackson said.

"Let me go check." He handed the tea to Mildred and disappeared down the hall.

"I got a letter today from Joe," Jackson said to Jimmie. "He was wondering if you would like to spend some of your summer vacation at Cottage Home."

"I don't think I'm going to have time." Jimmie produced an envelope from his pocket. "It's my appointment to West Point." He was a mixture of excitement and pride.

Jackson took the envelope and read the brief lines that announced Jimmie's appointment to the U.S. Military Academy. "Your Pa would be so proud of you." Jimmie smiled and, once more, Jackson saw the father in the son. "Have you told your mother?"

"I'm going to Staunton for my birthday. I'll tell her then."

Flora was now the headmistress of the Virginia Female Institute. Julia and Ginny were with her. It had been a difficult decision for Jackson to send away his only daughter, but the two girls, close as sisters, didn't want to be separated. They did spend their school holidays and summers in Lexington. A small balm for the wound in Jackson's heart. Tom, now twelve, James Ewell Brown Stuart Jackson, age eight, and Alexander Swift Pendleton Jackson, age seven, spent their school days at Reverend Pendleton's school. Tom had already voiced his intentions to follow his older brother, Jimmie, to the Institute.

"It's my eighteenth, you know," Jimmie said.

"I do know." Jackson had Jimmie's gift hidden away in General Paxton's stable: a grandson of Centurion.

"Ma promised me that I could have Pa's watch."

Custis came back down the hall. "General Jackson, he's wake and wants to see you."

Jackson handed the envelope to Jimmie. "Make sure you tell your Aunt Anna as soon as you get home. She'll want to plan a party to celebrate." He clasped Jimmie on the shoulder. "I'm proud of you, son."

"Thank you, Father," Jimmie said.

Jackson followed Custis down the hall and into a small bedroom. Lee lay on the bed. His brow was covered with sweat and his face was deathly pale. He looked small and shrunken.

Jackson sat in the chair next to the bed.

"Jeb came to visit me," Lee said with a smile.

Alarmed, Jackson glanced up at Custis.

"It's the medicine," Custis explained.

"It was a dream," Lee corrected.

"I'll leave you two alone." Custis shut the door behind him.

"How are you, Robert?" Jackson asked.

Lee smiled again. "I remember when I asked you to call me that. It was on the morning we were to hang."

"But we didn't," Jackson replied.

"Thanks to my darling boy."

"Don't forget Forrest," Jackson said with a laugh.

"He's quite unforgettable." Lee started to cough.

Jackson glanced about and saw a glass and vial of medicine on a nearby table. He stood and retrieved the glass.

"No, no," Lee said. "The medicine clouds my mind. I want to be conscience of my surroundings at the last."

Jackson's hand started to tremble. He set the glass back on the table and returned to the chair.

"I hear that you've been approached about running for governor," Lee said.

"I have, but I declined. I like where I am," Jackson said.

"Good." Lee closed his eyes. "I'm so tired."

"Do you want me to go?" Jackson asked.

"No." The bark of command rang out in Lee's voice.

"Then I won't." Jackson closed his eyes to keep back the tears threatening to consume him.

"My right arm," Lee said. "Remember at Chancellor's Crossing. You burst upon those people's flank and sent them running."

"Because you were fearless," Jackson said.

Lee turned his head and looked at Jackson. "Thank you."

"For what?" Jackson asked, stunned.

Lee didn't reply. Jackson waited, but Lee had fallen asleep. Softly, he began to creep from the room. The floorboard creaked. Lee woke up with a start. "Are you leaving?"

"I thought you were asleep," Jackson apologized.

"I drift in and out. And in my dreams, I see Fitzhugh and Annie. Agnes and my precious Molly. Then today, Jeb came."

Death was in the room, just like it had been at Manassas when he had held Stuart. Jackson shivered. "You thanked me."

Lee smiled. "People look to me as a symbol of our Cause and for the strength they needed to rebuild their lives. It was a responsibility I wasn't prepared for. So, I leaned on you. You weren't just my right arm at Chancellorsville. You've been my right arm for the past thirteen years."

Jackson could no longer hold back his tears.

"On that morning, when the guards came to take us to the gallows, I asked you where I fit into a family born of war. You said that I was the best of us. If that's true..."

"It is," Jackson assured him.

"Then it is because of you." Lee smiled faintly. "There stands Jackson like a stone wall. Rally behind the Virginian. Thank you for your faith in God and the example of your life. In the low points of my life, I have drawn upon it."

Jackson bowed his head unto his folded hands and sobbed.

"No tears for me," Lee admonished. "I have run my race. I have finished my course. It is time to strike the tent and head for home. I'm not sad." He held up his hand. Jackson grasped it. Lee's grip was weak.

Precious in the sight of the Lord was the death of his saints, Jackson thought as he felt Lee's grip weaken even more. "Let me get Custis and Mildred."

Lee nodded.

"Goodbye." Jackson bent over and kissed Lee on the forehead.

Lee smiled. "Until we meet again in Heaven."

A tear slipped down Jackson's cheek. "Until we meet again in Heaven."

Jackson hurried to the door and sprinted down the hall. Custis and Mildred were alone. Jimmie was gone. "It's time."

Mildred swayed violently. Custis took her elbow. She steadied.

"Thank you, General Jackson," Custis said.

They disappeared down the hall. The door shut. Jackson stood alone in the living room. From the bedroom, he heard Mildred's sobs. It was over.

He felt like an intruder in the family's grief. He stepped outside onto the verandah. The sloping lawn was filled with college students, VMI cadets, and townspeople. They hadn't been here when he arrived. Such a large crowd, standing so quiet, all waiting to hear.

"General Jackson?" One voice asked for them all.

"He is at peace for he is with the Savior."

Jackson walked down the steps. The crowd parted and let him pass. He continued on down the hill toward home.

Historical Notes
After Chancellorsville:

In 1864, **Jubal Early** led the Army of the Valley against Sheridan and was soundly defeated. After the surrender, he fled to Canada. He returned to Virginia five years later and resumed his law practice. Early died at the age of seventy-seven after falling down a flight of stairs.

After the Battle of Chickamauga, **Nathan Bedford Forrest** was given independent command in Mississippi. He captured Fort Pillow and won again at Brice's Crossroads before losing at Tupelo. He surrendered his forces on May 9, 1865. After the war, he settled in Memphis and found employment with the Marion and Memphis Railroad, eventually becoming the railroad's president. Forrest died in 1877 at the age of fifty-six.

Anna Morrison Jackson never remarried and wore mourning for the rest of her life. She lived out her life in her native North Carolina and raised her two grandchildren after Julia's premature death. Anna died in 1915 at the age of eighty-four.

Julia Jackson married William E. Christian in 1885 and had two children: a daughter, Julia Jackson Christian and a son, Thomas Jonathan Jackson Christian. Julia died of typhoid fever in 1889. She was twenty-six.

Thomas "Stonewall" Jackson was severely wounded at Chancellorsville. He developed pneumonia and died on May 10, 1863. Jackson's last words were, "let us cross over the river and rest under the shade of the trees."

After recovering from the wounds sustained during the Peninsula campaign, **Joseph Johnston** took command of the Department of Mississippi. He opposed Sherman during the long march through Georgia and was replaced by John Bell Hood during the Atlanta campaign. In the last days of the war, Lee requested Johnston be returned to command. Johnston died of pneumonia at the age of eighty-four.

After the war, **Fitzhugh Lee** took up farming. He served as Virginia's governor. In 1896, he was appointed as consul-general in Havana. When the Spanish-America war broke out, Fitz re-entered the army and was commissioned a major general of volunteers. He saw no action. Fitz died in 1905 at the age of sixty-nine.

On April 9, 1865, **Robert E. Lee** surrendered the Army of Northern Virginia at Appomattox Court House. After the war, he served as president of Washington College in Lexington. He died of heart failure in 1870. Lee was sixty-three years old.

The historical record is split on whether **Jim Lewis** was a slave. After Jackson's death, Lewis became Sandie Pendleton's servant. When Pendleton died at Fisher's Hill, Lewis was overcome with grief. Lexington's *Gazette and Banner* recorded his last words: "De dear ole General's gone and Marse Sandie too, it's Jim's time next."

After the war **James Longstreet** joined the Republican Party, endorsing his friend Grant for president, which caused his reputation to slip among many Southerns. He died of pneumonia at the age of eighty-two.

George B. McClellan lost the 1864 election to Lincoln. He used his biography, *McClellan's Own Story*, to justify his war record. It was published posthumously. McClellan died suddenly in 1885 at the age of fifty-nine.

Hunter Holmes McGuire had an exemplary post war career. He served as president of both the American Medical and American Surgical Associations. A monument in his honor was placed in Richmond's Capitol Square.

After Jackson's death, **Joseph Morrison** transferred to the 57th North Carolina and suffered a wound that resulted in the amputation of his foot. After the war, he spent four years in California before returning to his native North Carolina to run the Mariposa Cotton

Mill. Upon the death of his father, he inherited Cottage Home. Joe died in 1906 at the age of sixty-four.

Alexander Swift "Sandie" Pendleton continued to serve as assistant adjutant general for the Second Corps. He married Kate Corbin on December 28, 1863. He was wounded at the Battle of Fisher's Hill. Sandie died on September 23, 1864, five days shy of his twenty-fifth birthday.

After Chancellorsville, **John Fulton Reynolds** was offered command of the Army of the Potomac, which he turned down because of Lincoln's penchant for meddling. Reynolds commanded the First Corps during the Gettysburg campaign. He was killed on the first day of battle. Reynolds was forty-two.

Philip Sheridan was promoted to lieutenant general in 1869. Two months after sending his memoirs to his publisher, he suffered a massive heart attack. Sheridan is buried at Arlington in front of the Custis-Lee Mansion. Sheridan was fifty-seven.

After the war, **William T. Sherman** was promoted to lieutenant general. When Grant won the presidency, Sherman was appointed Commanding General of the United States Army. Sherman died in New York City in 1891. He was seventy-one years old.

After the war, **James Power Smith** returned to Union Seminary and was ordained as a Presbyterian minister. Smith died in 1923 at the age of eighty-six.

Flora Cooke Stuart survived her husband by sixty years. She served as the headmistress of the Virginia Female Institute in Staunton, which was renamed "Stuart Hall" in her honor. Flora never remarried.

James Ewell Brown Stuart was wounded at Yellow Tavern on May 11, 1864. He died the next day in Richmond. Stuart was thirty-one years old. Lee wept bitterly when he heard the news.

James Ewell Brown Stuart, Jr. married Josephine Phillips and fathered five children, including a son, James Ewell Brown Stuart III. Jimmie died in 1930 at the age of seventy.

Virginia Pelham Stuart married Robert Waller in 1887. She had three children. Ginny died in 1898, a month shy of her thirty-fifth birthday.

George Thomas participated in the Georgia Campaign and was the Union commanding general at both the Battle of Franklin and the Battle of Nashville. After the war, Thomas commanded the Department of the Cumberland and the Division of the Pacific. He suffered a stroke and died at the age of fifty-two

Army of Northern Virginia ✶ Army of Mississippi
Army of Tennessee ✶ Army of Trans-Mississippi

Lee, Jackson, Stuart, Longstreet, Forrest, Bragg,
Pemberton, Johnston, Cleburne, Hampton, Polk, Hood,
Kirby-Smith, and more...

Manassas, Dranesville, Perryville, Fredericksburg,
Chancellorsville, Chickamauga, Fort Stedman,
Franklin, Missionary Ridge, Fort Henry, Gettysburg,
and Appomattox Court House

THE STAINLESS BANNER
*an e-zine dedicated to the armies of
the Confederacy.*

Subscription is free.

www.thestainlessbanner.com